THE TWELVE JUDGES

By

Lt. Joe "Bill" Bradley

This book is a work of fiction. Places, events, and situations in this story are purely fictional. Any resemblance to actual persons, living or dead, is coincidental.

© 2003, 2004 by Lt. Joe "Bill" Bradley.
All rights reserved.

No part of this book may be reproduced, stored in a retrieval system, or transmitted by any means, electronic, mechanical, photocopying, recording, or otherwise, without written permission from the author.

First published by AuthorHouse 06/14/04

ISBN: 1-4184-6313-2 (e-book)
ISBN: 1-4184-4782-X (Paperback)

Library of Congress Control Number: 2003098992

This book is printed on acid free paper.

Printed in the United States of America
Bloomington, IN

DEDICATION

This book is dedicated to the few honest, efficient attorneys who represent their clients with integrity.

This book is also written to honor the honest, dedicated policemen, who spend years of frustration protecting the public and have thought many times of policing in the manner portrayed in the following stories.

The better part of this Dedication goes to my lovely wife, Mary, for her help, love and understanding.

ACKNOWLEDGMENTS

Clay Wood: My son and a computer graphic expert who thought of and designed my front cover and chapter illustrations.

Pat Matthews: My friend and typist. She can spell. I can't.

Cletus Brown: My friend and confidant. He allowed me to use his first name in the book as friend and confidant of the lieutenant.

Clyde and George Bradley: My brothers who gave up our frequent fishing trips so that I could complete this book.

Krystine Poston, Lauren Hobbs, Brandon Bradley, Carlie Porterfield, Sara Jo Porterfield, Brooks Bradley, Blake Bradley, Todd Bradley, Madison Wood and Audrie Albertelli: My precious grandchildren who are shielded by their parents from the elements of this book but who are always in my thoughts. I hope that the world we leave to them is a better, safer place.

THE TWELVE JUDGES

CHAPTERS **PAGES**

Chapter 1 An Idea 1

Chapter 2 The Chosen 17

Chapter 3 Loyalty To The Lieutenant 33

Chapter 4 Wholesales, Inc. 59

Chapter 5 Cub Reporter 85

Chapter 6 Choo Choo Train Vs Farm Tractor 91

Chapter 7 Justice For The Number One Pimp 147

Chapter 8 Sorry, Wrong Number 167

Chapter 9 Interrogation 197

Chapter 10 A Mexico Connection 203

Chapter 11 The Dunking Stool 275

Chapter 12 Fair Play At The Astrodome 295

Chapter 13 Organized Crime And Politicians ... 345

Chapter 14 The Making Of A New District Attorney 399

Chapter 15 The Heat Is On 421

Chapter 16 The Trial 481

CHAPTER I

AN IDEA

Summer 1985

Fred Till sat with his wife on the wooden bleachers watching their son play Little League baseball. He was glad the sun would soon be sinking in the West. His shirt stuck to his chest, soaked with sweat from the sweltering 98-degree heat. This time of year, Houston felt like a sauna and the only relief he could look for was a slight breeze that might brush by once the harsh sunlight disappeared.

The heat that summer had been unforgiving. There had been no measurable amount of rain for weeks. Even the lower leaves of the trees seemed to seek shelter from the oppressive heat by hiding under the higher branches. The baseball field was watered nightly and glistened like an emerald in the midst of sun baked brown grass and cracked, dried clay.

A fine dust filled the air each time a runner made a move on the bases. Till dropped his handkerchief to his feet, as it was full of the grit and sweat that he had wiped from his face.

Till was a uniform cop and worked the graveyard shift. Coming to his son's games gave him an escape from the brutal realities of his job. Because of his profession, he didn't spend as much time with his son as he would have liked. As often as possible Till would join his wife and daughter at the ballpark. Watching his son play baseball was the most delightful part of his week next to sharing those all too seldom quiet moments with his wife.

This particular afternoon had been pleasant in spite of the stifling heat. Fred and his wife were both proudly watching their son. Till had noticed that even his daughter seemed to swell with family pride as her brother took the mound for the final inning.

Suddenly, the baseball cheers were quieted by ear shattering screams. Fred Till stood and turned in the direction of the cries.

He saw two girls running toward the baseball stands waving their arms and screaming. They were coming from the direction of a clump of woods located next to the park. High school kids often used this area to sneak a cigarette smoke.

Till shoved aside the people in the rows in front of him and ran toward the two frantic girls. He reached the parking lot dodging parked cars as he ran. He could only see one of the girls. She was in hysterics, crying and screaming. As Till finally reached her, she could not talk. Till bent toward her to try to calm her.

"What happened? What is it?" he asked. She couldn't form any words. She only pointed in the direction of the woods.

Till had started to run again when he saw the second girl lying face down between two cars. He moved quickly to the girl and turned her over. There were no visible signs of injury.

"She's fainted," he thought. His mind was focused again on the woods, knowing that whatever awaited him would be hideous judging by the reaction of these two. As Till entered the dense trees he followed a footpath made by kids who came to the ballpark from the subdivision nearby. Down the path Till came upon a scene that made him nauseous. He stood for several seconds regaining his composure and clearing his mind.

Before him was the body of a young girl, maybe 15 years old, thrown naked under a sprawling oak tree. She had apparently been stripped of her clothes, which lay in a heap next to her motionless body. Her long blond hair was matted around her neck. Her body had been brutally violated. Her breasts had been gouged from her chest and between her legs were pools of blood.

Till didn't check for life, he knew the girl was dead.

He surveyed the scene and felt rage at the thought of this youngster's last terrorizing moments of life.

As he slowly regained his self-control, a poem he learned as a small child began to echo in his mind…

Lt. Joe "Bill" Bradley

"Now I lay me down to sleep, I pray to God my soul to keep, If I should die before I wake, I pray to God my soul to take."

While saying his own private prayer for this child, he became aware that other parents, having also heard the screams, were quickly approaching. Till instinctively knew he had to protect the crime scene for the homicide detectives.

"Pull yourself together, Till," he thought, "and get this area secured." He turned from the gruesome scene and stepped out of the woods toward the group.

"Call the police and tell them there's been a homicide," he shouted at no one in particular.

Till spread his large arms in front of the gathering crowd and kept them from going into the woods.

As he waited for the detectives to arrive Till's mind raced. He saw his wife standing in the group with her arm around their fifteen-year-old daughter. He couldn't keep his thoughts from the image of his own innocent daughter and the hideous scene that he had just left. He also tried in vain to visualize the kind of monster that could have done this.

The other parents were bombarding him with questions. He didn't answer anyone because he didn't know if the girl's parents were in the group. Till was relieved when he saw two police patrol cars and a detective car enter the park.

Fall 1985

Lieutenant Bill James had worked for the Houston Police Department so many years that few things ever surprised him any more. He was a tall, broad shouldered Texan. His face was etched with the lines of a man who had spent too many hours in the unrelenting Houston sun and his steel blue eyes peered out with an investigator instinct that could only be formed after years on the job. His vision took in every aspect of his surroundings but could still twinkle with the warmth that few seasoned cops possessed. His long legs always ended in a pair of freshly polished cowboy boots. His suits, while well tailored and fitted, had a distinctive Western appearance to them.

Every morning, he arrived early to his office to have some time to sort the day before the detectives came dragging in with all their commotion. He sat at his desk with a cup of steaming hot, black coffee and the morning newspaper.

His legs were stretched across the desk with his boots resting on the newspaper want ads. His secretary, Kathy, was always gripping about the marks his cowboy boots made on the desk so it was a small concession he made to her.

Kathy had been with him for so long and had put up with so much garbage from him and the other guys that James felt it was a small price to pay.

James glanced at the headlines.

"Accused Murder, Rapist-Turned Loose By Judge. Policeman Jailed For Hitting Defense Attorney."

Lt. Joe "Bill" Bradley

Lieutenant James set his coffee aside and read further.

"Judge Fred Boller ruled that accused killer-rapist Matthew Oliver's confession could not be read to the jury. Judge Boller stated that the detectives had ample time to take Matthew Oliver before a Judge to receive a warning of his rights.

"Detective Robert Luna testified that he had warned Matthew Oliver of his rights himself but this had made no difference to the ruling of Judge Boller. As Detective Luna was leaving the witness chair, Defense Attorney Mike George allegedly laughed at Detective Luna. The detective hit Attorney George, knocking him to the floor. Detective Luna was jailed and charged with Contempt of Court. It is not known if Attorney Mike George will file charges of assault. The District Attorney said he had no other choice but to ask for dismissal of charges against Matthew Oliver"

Bill James knew that Matthew Oliver had been charged with the murder of a Brookview High School student who had been found in the woods located next to a city baseball park.

Lieutenant James read further, "Matthew Oliver is a suspect in two out of state murders that fit Matthew Oliver's signature to this Houston crime. The out of state victims were also teenage girls.

"The out of state girls and the Houston girl had been at a school sporting event.

"They had been found with their breast and genitals cut from their bodies. The District Attorney stated, 'We do not have enough evidence at this time to charge Matthew Oliver with anything. There is

THE TWELVE JUDGES

insufficient evidence to charge Matthew Oliver in either of the out of state murders'."

Lieutenant James shoved his chair back from the desk and threw the newspaper down in disgust.

Standing, he thought to himself, "Shit! Another psychotic criminal set loose on the public!" Striding across his office, he threw open his door and headed for the coffee bar. "Oh Hell!" he reflected, "So what else is new! The criminal has more rights than the citizens! It used to be the exception rather than the norm."

By this time the room was beginning to buzz with the business of the day and James forgot about the article. He called the first detective into his office to give him the assignments on the pressing matters that needed attention.

At lunchtime James left his office for his favorite barbecue joint. Just outside the police department, James turned east and walked towards Buffalo Bayou. The bayou wove its way through the city in a curve and ran along side the police department. Parking at the department was on a first come, first serve basis for all the employees except for captains and the upper brass. James always parked under the bridge that crossed the bayou from the downtown area.

James eased his large frame into his unmarked police car and drove to the freeway that bordered the police department. Abruptly, he took an exit from the freeway onto a side street.

Here the pavement quickly turned from smooth concrete to little more than a dirt pathway filled with potholes and littered with garbage.

James grumbled to himself. He knew that the street was only a mile and a half from City Hall but hadn't been repaired in 20 years.

The neighborhood was a dilapidated area where rows of old houses lined the street. These homes were referred to as "Shotgun Houses" because if the front and back doors were opened you could shoot through the house without hitting anything. The bedrooms were on one side and the living room and kitchen were on the other side. Absentee landlords mainly owned the homes and the city of Houston treated the area like it was the forgotten stepchild.

The lieutenant's car looked as though he was maneuvering a minefield as he wheeled around the deep holes in the street.

Four young black boys played in a vacant lot covered with knee-high weeds. They momentarily stopped playing and glanced up as the lieutenant's car passed. The kids knew the car was a cop car; they didn't need it to be a blue and white to know the difference. They had seen these cars in their neighborhood before and wondered who was going downtown today. When it became apparent to them that the cop was not going to stop nearby, they resumed with their play.

James drove a couple of blocks down the street, stopping on the edge of the neighborhood. He pulled his car into a lot, parking among other police cars and a few luxury cars.

A large sign above the building read "Slim's Bar-B-Q". The building's sides revealed several layers of faded paint. The windows were darkened so you couldn't see inside. On the West side was a large

THE TWELVE JUDGES

fenced area with a looming brick smokestack that poured forth a pleasant aroma of mesquite and sauce.

Just as James exited his car, two detectives came from the restaurant. One of the men noticed the lieutenant and automatically glanced at his watch.

Trying to justify his presence at Slim's and for not serving the warrant James had given him that morning, the detective said, "We're goin' back to work now Lieutenant. We only took thirty minutes for lunch."

To get into Slim's you walked through a wide door in the middle of a black wall and were greeted with a large dining room. The walls were lined with cedar and there was a thin layer of sawdust on the floor. The tables were covered with plastic red checked tablecloths and each table was encircled with several folding metal chairs.

Slim was the owner, cook and in a pinch, the dishwasher. This nickname was given to him years ago in junior high school and had been used so often that few people even knew his given name. He was a tall slender black man; the only fat on him was his wallet from a small fortune made selling barbecue.

As James entered Slim's and walked to his table the smell of barbecue excited his taste buds. A waitress saw him coming and hurriedly changed the red and white checkered plastic on his table. James pulled out a chair and it stirred the sawdust on the floor.

Slim always claimed that every Sunday he put fresh sawdust on the floor. He said he fed the old sawdust to his cows because it was full of barbecue drippings and the cows loved it. And anyway, it made

Lt. Joe "Bill" Bradley

their meat tastier. Bill James knew this was bullshit but he also knew that Slim's story telling was legendary among his customers.

Slim saw James and came over to the table. Wiping his greasy hands on his apron he wore around his waist, Slim shook hands with James, spoke a few words and turned back to the register. On his way to the front, Slim hollered for a waitress to bring James a large plate of brisket and fixings.

James and Slim had known each other for years; no one questioned their friendship or how it began.

Slim had a shady past that caused some people to keep a respectful distance. James had helped Slim out years ago when he had been accused of murder. Slim hit a neighbor one day when the neighbor had been beating his wife with a golf club. The neighbor died when he fell, hitting his head on a fence post. James testified on Slim's behalf at the trial. Consequently, Slim was found guilty of a lesser charge and sentenced to probation. The two had been close friends since.

It was his relationship with people like Slim that gave Bill James the type of reputation that could swirl around him. He instilled either respect or fear, trust or suspicion, depending on which side of the law you found yourself. His reputation entered the room before he did.

James was known and respected as being fair and one of the few lieutenants who supported his men in times of trouble. He demanded the impossible from his Burglary and Theft detectives and received excellent police work in return although occasionally a

THE TWELVE JUDGES

little unorthodox methods were used. In return for this dedication to their work, James always went to bat for the detectives when the brass tried to squeeze them into one of the square pegs they thought a detective should fit into.

Seated alone at his favorite table, James could not help but hear Detective Hancock, an acquaintance of many years, who was seated at a table across the room.

"Damn sorry ass attorneys! They should never be allowed to be judges," Hancock was remarking. "Attorneys stick together like flies on shit. They just help each other make money!"

Talking in a loud abrasive voice, Hancock went on to tell the other detectives at his table how his case against a narcotic pusher had been thrown out of court that morning because of a technical error in his search warrant.

"Cops need to be sissy-ass English teachers in order to draw-up a damn search warrant that sticks," Hancock continued.

One of the detective listening to Jack Hancock spouting off looked at Lieutenant James across the room.

"Give it a rest, Hancock, the lieutenant is here."

"I don't give a rat's ass!" shouted Hancock.

Suddenly the room became quiet. Only the sounds of the diners' flatware on china could be heard. In a loud voice Lieutenant James said, "Hancock, if you ruin my lunch with your bitching, you're going to pick up everyone's tab."

The room broke into laughter and became noisy once more.

Lt. Joe "Bill" Bradley

After eating, Lieutenant James walked over to the cash register and paid his check. Slim slipped the lieutenant a brown sack already oozing grease along the bottom.

"Hey, Lu, don't forget your afternoon snack." Slim whispered.

"Thanks, Slim. Keep this up and you're going to make me as fat as our old Chief." James waved at Hancock as he went out the door.

Once again the lieutenant maneuvered his car around the holes in the street until he came to smooth concrete. In a few minutes he was back in his office at the main station.

James attacked the mounds of paperwork that is a necessity with policing. After trying for a while to complete the government forms, he tossed the documents aside as he remembered what Hancock had said at lunch.

"Crap! Hancock's right," Lieutenant James said out loud. "The courts are favoring the criminals and the damn police department's become nothing more than a damn public relations agency."

James rose from his desk. Taking two steps at a time he climbed the flight of stairs to the third floor where the police chief's office was located. James always used the stairs in the police building. The building had two old elevators, but one was out of order all the time and the other was slow and constantly full. James always thought that he would like to have the contract with the city to repair these elevators as it cost the city a fortune to have a repairman at the building every day.

THE TWELVE JUDGES

James ambled into Chief Ladd's reception room.

"I have an appointment with the chief," he said casually looking confidently into the secretary's eyes.

"Sure!" She laughed. "Lieutenant, you pulled that story on me once but not again. The chief is entertaining a civic group. You couldn't see him now even if you had an appointment."

"Why thank you, Ms. May. I won't bother him."

James then marched past the receptionist's desk into the chief's office with the secretary close on his heels.

"...And I want you to know that I am totally committed to the safety of our citizens," Chief Ladd was saying.

Hearing all the commotion, Ladd turned and saw Lieutenant James striding into the midst of his meeting.

"And here is Lieutenant James who solves hundreds of burglaries for you," Chief Ladd continued as he attempted to maintain his composure.

Bill James gave the civic group a quick hello.

"If you kind people would excuse us, I need to talk with Chief Ladd about an urgent problem," the lieutenant offered.

"It's now two o'clock, Bill. I'll see you at two-thirty," replied Ladd as he gave the lieutenant a firm go-to-hell look.

As James strolled from the office he glanced at the civic group, chuckled, and sarcastically remarked; "He's a fine Chief, for a fat man."

Lt. Joe "Bill" Bradley

The room filled with laughter as he left through the chief's door. Chief Ladd had been called "Fat Ladd" since the days at the police academy 20 years earlier. Chief Ladd had taken over the reigns of the department four years ago. His reorganization brought the Houston Police Department to near the top of police departments in the nation.

"You're really in for it now!" Ms. May warned as she closed the door behind them. "Sit down, and I'll get you a cup of coffee." James watched Ms. May as she walked to the coffee room.

She was trim, neat and attractive. Her shoulder length black hair was pinned to one side. She was in her forties with three children and a police patrolman for a husband. James knew why Chief Ladd's office ran so well, Ms. May was the reason.

Lieutenant James had finished two cups of coffee when he noticed that it was past 2:45 p.m. Minutes earlier the civic group had gone. At two-twenty-five the lieutenant saw them parade from Ladd's office and had heard the Chief lock his door. Ms. May would just look at James, shake her head and smile.

James was trying to be patient with Chief Ladd but enough was enough.

He slowly raised from his chair and stretched. He nonchalantly strode to the Chief's door and banged on it. The City of Houston emblem on the door swayed but did not fall.

"Come in," Chief Ladd hollered then James heard him roar with laughter.

When James hit the door the second time, Ms. May quietly retreated from the room.

THE TWELVE JUDGES

James heard the click of the lock and Chief Ladd opened the door. A man that could be a ready-made Santa Claus stood there grinning at the lieutenant. Ladd had a golf putter in his hand and had been hitting golf balls on the floor into a small plastic cup. All around the office were mementos of Chief Ladd's golf past. He even had a small bronze bust of Arnold Palmer.

"You know, Bill, I cut my golf score by several strokes just by practicing in my office each day."

The Chief took a seat at his desk, and motioned Bill James to a seat across the desk. James sat down picking a golden golf tee off the desk. Ladd suddenly jumped from his chair, leaned over his desk and grabbed the tee from James' hand and then sat back down.

"That tee was given to me by President Ford. Keep your filthy hands off it! What the hell do you want? No, wait, I know that look in your eyes. It's the same cock-eyed scheme you have every time you come in here. You want to be turned loose in this city with a bunch of crazed cops, as if I don't have enough worries? You want to create headaches for me?"

James propped his huge boots on top of the desk as Ladd frowned and gestured with his hands. Chief Ladd leaned back with a sigh of weariness as the lieutenant began.

"I've gone over this with you before. If you'd allow me to organize a select group of detectives, I'll make you a hero in this city, hell, maybe the whole damn country! Let me pick twelve men to work with me. Those twelve detectives, supervised by me, could investigate and put together ironclad cases against professional criminals. Every day shyster lawyers and liberal judges are setting these bastards free. My group would see to it that those S.O.B.'s would do hard time. I'll report directly to you."

Before James could be interrupted he continued, "I'll keep you informed. No one will know about this group except you. Just think of the publicity you'll receive when we bust these sleezebags and their attorneys can't get them off."

Lieutenant James baited the chief. He knew all too well that Ladd loved nothing more than to be in the spotlight with the television camera rolling.

The Chief smiled at Lieutenant James' last statement. He was annoyed with this argument and also worried that the lieutenant's plan was beginning to make sense. But, Ladd knew that the chief's job would be up for re-appointment soon and some good publicity wouldn't hurt.

"All right," the chief cautiously agreed. "I'll see that you get the men you want, plus the equipment and quarters you need," Ladd continued. Chief Ladd then pointed a finger at James and warned, "Screw it up and your ass is mine! I'll bury you in the Jail Division. Now get the hell out of my office and let me work on my golf game!"

Lieutenant James left Ladd's office with his mind searching for the names of twelve detectives. He needed the right men to make his idea work.

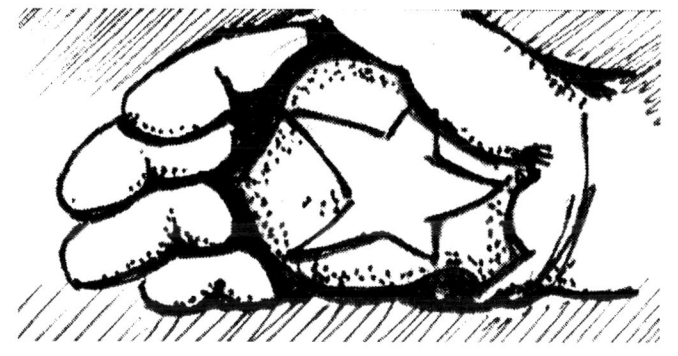

CHAPTER 2

THE CHOSEN

The following day, Lieutenant James worked with a new determination. Ladd had given him the tools to launch the battle against those forces that were daily corrupting his city. Bill James entered the Personnel Division and identified himself to the clerk.

"I'm Lieutenant James and I'm here to…"

"Yeah, I know. The Chief called me yesterday. Are you really looking for a spy?" the clerk asked.

James laughed and wondered what kind of crazy story Ladd told this clerk.

All the personnel records were made available to him. James decided that he would carry several boxes of possible candidate's home for an in-depth study.

James got help from one of the civilian employees in personnel to help carry the boxes to his car. The employee was glad to help. He had heard other police officers talk about Lieutenant James.

James drove out the Gulf Freeway from the downtown area of Houston. The five o'clock traffic was heavy so James got into the middle lane and turned on the radio to a country music station. There were no fast lanes on the freeway in Houston. James had found that the middle lane moved forty-five seconds faster on his thirty-five minute drive to the Clear Lake area.

After his divorce fifteen years earlier, James bought a small home that sat on Galveston Bay a few miles from the NASA Space Center. His love for the salt air and fishing drew him to this area.

His home was a small bungalow with two bedrooms. The property had a large back yard with a fishing pier that James had built.

He drove into the garage, got out of his car and walked over to a freezer removing a chicken potpie and a package of chicken necks.

James set the chicken necks out to thaw and went inside. After placing the chicken potpie in the oven, he spread a number of personnel files on the table and started reading. After reading for over an hour, James ate his dinner. He kept going over and over in his mind, the qualifications of the men in the files.

Following dinner, James fixed himself a good strong scotch and went into the garage. It was getting dark and he wanted to bait his crab traps. Picking up the chicken necks he walked to the pier. Lifting both traps out of the water, James inspected the contents. Both traps had crabs but they were too small. James

THE TWELVE JUDGES

shook the wire traps and the crabs tumbled into the darkening water. He then tied string around the chicken necks and tied them inside the traps.

After he lowered the traps into the bay water, James returned to his task of reading and studying personnel files.

James didn't realize that he had been studying the files so long. It was now 1 a.m.

Looking out over the bay, James could see two large oil tankers moving slowly for the Port of Houston. The Houston Ship Channel ran through the bay. On the other side of the bay was a large oil refinery. At night, all the lights at the refinery gave an impression of being a large city lit with holiday lights.

James spent several days working late into the night scrutinizing the records. Many officers were certainly honest but lacked the special attributes each member needed to bring to the new group. Each detective chosen had to have a special skill that complimented the strengths of the others.

Finally, over another meal of cold leftovers, he made his selection, and chose twelve policemen to form his group.

James contacted each man by telephone and informed him that each would soon receive transfer papers to a new unit.

The transfer papers contained no specifics about their new duties; they received only the order to report to Lieutenant James.

A dilapidated building sat on the outer edge of downtown Houston. At one time it had been a woman's clothing factory. It was one story and constructed of white Mexican brick. It had been built in the forties. Four seldom-used railroad tracks ran next to the building. James was surprised that many of the windows still had glass. If he had walked along these railroad tracks, as a kid, there would have been a strong temptation to throw rocks at the windows of this old, boarded-up building. The vacant lots behind and on each side of the building were over grown with weeds.

The City had purchased the land as the right-of-way for connections to the freeway loop around Houston. It was ideal for privacy because strange comings and goings would not arouse suspicion.

James worked the lock on the door with the key that the city real estate office clerk had given him. He pushed the door open. Years of dust fell on his clothes and in his hair.

"Damn it!" he thought. "I just got this suit from the cleaners yesterday."

He saw a small field mouse scurry quickly away and James wondered how the mouse lived in the stagnate air. His own lungs ached as he entered the building.

James walked quickly through the building opening any of the windows that were not stuck. The building had several small areas and one large room that could be used for meetings. This room also could easily accommodate twelve detectives with a desk for each.

One office had no windows and only one door. "This area will make a good interrogation room," James thought.

At the side of the large room was an office that stretched halfway across the width of the building with windows that overlooked a vacant lot. There were windows inside that surrounded the office. The office reminded him of a newspaper's office where an editor sat. James decided that this room would be his office, from here he could keep an eye on the inside and outside of the factory.

The building also had two showers and a large bathroom in the rear. The city had turned on the water at James' request. James turned on a faucet in one of the sinks. Brown rusty syrup looking water ran into the sink. James turned on the other sink faucet and both showers. He decided to run the water all day and night to get close to what would appear to be water. James made a mental note to get bottled water for drinking.

Chief Ladd gave permission for Lieutenant James to use the building provided the city would not be held liable should the roof cave in.

After his tour of the building, James left and drove to the police station to shower and change into a fresh suit. He always kept a change of clothes in his office and the police academy had good showers.

It took James an entire weekend to get the building in some type of disorderly order. He recruited some street people that he knew to help him. With the promise of some hot food and spending money, they pitched in with paint brushes and brooms. The lieutenant was accustomed to work but house cleaning was not one of his strong points.

James had desks, chairs, telephones, and outdated computers brought in and placed in the huge empty space. He had tried to get the best from the city storage department.

21

Lt. Joe "Bill" Bradley

He also got two of his volunteers to go with him to the police station. Earlier, James had seen six new four drawer file cabinets in a hallway at the police academy. James thought, "I'll just borrow them. They probably got too many anyway."

Borrowing a pickup from the police garage, James drove to the academy. After telling the two people with him that they were going to steal the file cabinets from the jail division, they loaded the cabinets in record time.

As they finished one of the men remarked, "The next time I go to jail for being drunk, I'll ask old desk Sarge Johnson if he's missing any cabinets".

The other one answered, "Yea, you do and you'll end up cleaning all the toilets in the police station by yourself."

They were so proud of their quick work that James stopped at a service station and bought them each a beer before they returned to the factory.

On Monday morning it still took some imagination to appreciate all the sweat and time spent cleaning the old factory.

Each detective had been contacted and told to meet James at the old factory at eight o'clock that morning. They were also told not to mention to anyone where they were going or whom they were to meet.

All of the men were there early, curious about their transfers. Rumors had been flying around the central station all week.

At exactly eight o'clock James stood before the group. They had all heard stories about Lieutenant Bill James, some knew him, but none had worked for him.

THE TWELVE JUDGES

"You were chosen for your ability to get a job done," the lieutenant began. "This unit will report to me and to no one else. You won't tell anyone about your activities and this includes your wife, your girlfriend, your chip or your priest. It definitely means no other cops. If you're asked, your answer will be that we're working on civil lawsuits filed against the City of Houston. You will depend only on each other; loyalty to me, to this group and each other along with results, will be your only guidelines.

"When you go after some crooked bastard, justice will prevail because you'll make only airtight cases. You'll get all the evidence needed to stand a bastard on his head and beat his damn lawyer in any court. You'll get it no matter what it takes. You all have informers; we'll make use of them.

"If you have any doubts about working with this unit, there's the door. I damn sure don't want to hear any old women bitching later!"

Feet shuffled and there was squirming in the chairs but no one said a word. There was not a single movement in the direction of the exit.

Lieutenant James concluded his instructions to his elite group, "We're going to put away some assholes that'd bragged they could never be touched!"

At this, Detective Bill Johnson hollered, "Amen!" Johnson then slid down in his chair and pointed in the direction of Detective Joe Kramer. It was usual for Bill Johnson to con his way out of situations.

Bill Johnson was average height and easily blended into any group. He had brown hair and eyes. James chose him because he was a master of disguise

23

and an accomplished actor. Johnson could pose as either a preacher or a pimp. He was considered a lady's man because of his convincing performances that landed him in some of the most exclusive bedrooms in town. What he lacked in looks he made up for with a sly charm. He also had an excellent record with the department.

Once Johnson posed as a bearded priest to stop the hijacking of an airplane. The story was told that Johnson was able to get on the airplane with the hijacker and a pilot. Once on the airplane he started foaming at the mouth and screaming at the hijacker, "You son-of-a-bitch, I'm hijacking this damn airplane, not you. If you want to go to Mexico with me, sit your ass down." The hijacker was so confused that he sat down and Johnson grabbed the hijacker's pistol while at the same time knocking the man out cold.

The only thing that Bill Johnson had in common with Joe Kramer was that they were both burglary and theft detectives.

Kramer was 29 and had recently married. A graduate of South Texas College of Law, Kramer was a classic clean cut nerd. He was short and stocky and wore thick eyeglasses that slipped down to the tip of his nose when he talked. He was the bookworm of the bunch, but he could write a search warrant that could withstand any legal scrutiny. He had been re-writing the Rules and Regulations of the police department and wanted out to do some real, pound the beat, police work. Kramer also had a knack with a camera. His eye could catch just the right photo that said more than any witness could testify to. James believed that the choice of Joe Kramer to his group was essential when

THE TWELVE JUDGES

it was a real possibility that they would go up against slick lawyers with fancy words and gimmicks.

Surveying the room, James was especially glad to see that no one had decided to leave the meeting.

The detectives fit his profile for this unit, even old Jack Hancock. Lieutenant James knew from the beginning that Hancock would be with him. Like himself, Hancock was in his fifties. His hair was still thick but was graying more than just around the edges. He was a large man, and as strong as a longhorn steer. Hancock was married with four grown sons. He was from the old school of policing, little public relations but lots of pounding the streets, protecting citizens, and getting the lawbreakers behind bars. Many considered Hancock a redneck and prejudiced; he wasn't. He just hated the crooked bastards of any color who broke the law. Hancock brought years of street smarts to the unit. He knew all of the informers and police characters that stray in and out of police hangouts with investigative leads for sale. He had worked in the Vice Division for a number of years where he met and learned the tricks of these information brokers. He also had one other talent to bring to this group; he could be trusted.

Once Hancock came to a scene where the S.W.A.T. Team had surrounded a house. The team had 20 men all wearing their black Schwarzenegger uniforms and flak jackets carrying high-powered rifles, pistols, and smoke grenades. The S.W.A.T. Team had already had the house surrounded for six hours. Hancock walked past the S.W.A.T. team's elaborate command station, down the walk and to the front door of the house. The captain of the S.W.A.T. team was screaming that he had information that there were five armed men in the house. Hancock kicked the door open and in just a few minutes dragged a scrawny little guy out. With 20 rifles pointing at the little man, Hancock laughed and said, "If ya'll would have had sense enough to check with me or the neighbors, you damned primadonnas would have found that Cedric has tape recordings that sometimes he plays real loud. They're of gunshots, bombs and explosions. Cedric is only helping his country and the neighborhood. He scares the aliens away that come from Mars."

Hancock received three days off without pay for that scene. He embarrassed and disobeyed the S.W.A.T. Captain.

Gary Edward brought the skill of firearms and explosives to this group. Detective Edward could spot danger approaching a mile away and would jump to the front lines to lead the charge. He was a Vietnam veteran and had been through his own private hell overseas. He was now in his thirties and spent most of his free time making parts for antique guns. He sported a well-groomed beard that looked one hundred percent better than the clothes he wore. His clothes always looked like he had just crawled out of a Viet Cong tunnel. Edward had brought a bride back from the war. He was quick to let everyone know that she was his greatest treasure.

A story had circulated throughout the department about Edwards when he was a marine in Vietnam. It was said that one day he blew the door, sides and top off the general's specially built outhouse, and left the general sitting on his toilet without a scratch. Edwards once had been the top man in the

THE TWELVE JUDGES

Houston Bomb Squad. He was removed from the squad when it was found that he was using the confiscated explosives from their raids to blow holes in the ground to be used by a rancher for water ponds for his cattle. Edwards tried to explain that he didn't charge for the holes, but the rancher did let him hunt on his property.

Larry Park and Thomas Murphy were a matched set. They met years earlier while conducting a long investigation. Both had placed illegal taps on the same telephone line without the other's knowledge. Park and Murphy had a suspect's business telephone line tapped. During a slow period of the day, Park used the line to call his girlfriend. While talking with her, a voice came over the line asking if that was Larry Park on the line. Park recognized Murphy's voice and they began a heated argument over who had priority on that investigation. Both tapes were illegal but that didn't stop them from hollering at each other. The friendship was born out of this dispute but to this day, they still argued about who had the first tap on the phone. Both were experts in the field of electronics, especially if it involved telephones.

They were the same age, thirty-five, had eventually married sisters, and were like brothers. They argued about everything. Park had a shock of screaming red hair, which contrasted with Murphy's coal black hair. Otherwise they had few differences. They were in excellent physical condition and they contributed this to climbing telephone poles. It was a rare sight if you saw one without the other.

Detective Charles Watson was a gifted forger. At forty, Watson had matured into a very distinguished gentleman. He stood six foot two with sandy blonde hair and a trim body. He excelled in appearing to be nonchalant and very composed while using fictitious credentials. He was called upon often for his expertise. Watson loved his work. He could duplicate a driver's license and the counterfeit would look better than the original. He had supplied many undercover narcotic cops with their fake identifications. The captain of the Narcotic Division said that Charles Watson could forge a title for the Queen Mary. When the Super Bowl was played in Houston, Watson forged and printed twenty-five tickets and took a boy's club to the game.

In the corner stood Roosevelt Washington. His large, muscular frame didn't look like that of a fifty-year-old man. He regularly worked out in the gym and could have owned the "Mr. America" title. He was a black officer who married late in his thirties and had three young children. Roosevelt won the title each year for the competition driving races held for Texas peace officers. He was dependable and loved his work. Once, the Intelligence Division had him drive an informer who was to testify against an organized crime figure. Roosevelt drove the witness from the Houston International Airport to downtown Houston's criminal courthouse. When Washington left the airport, there was a police car in the front and rear of him. On the way, Washington's car was allegedly shot at. When Washington heard on his police radio that a shot had been fired at his car, he used his race car ability to negotiate his way through the heavy Houston freeway traffic. Washington reached speeds over a hundred miles an hour. He delivered the witness unharmed to the courthouse but the witness testimony had to be postponed; the witness could not speak for three hours. The ride had frightened the man so drastically that he had peed in his pants. Later it was learned that the supposedly gunshot was a truck backfiring. Washington was also a jokester. James knew that Washington would fit well with his unit.

Albert King was known for his ability to obtain information. His informers liked him. He treated them well and even fixed their traffic tickets for them. King bragged about having cleared a juvenile prostitution ring as the result of fixing one speeding ticket. He knew most of the whores and every bookie in town. He had worked in the Vice Division for years. King had been married twice and blamed his divorces on his wives' failure to understand that he had to wine and dine beautiful prostitutes. All other divisions of the police department used King when they hit a dead end. If somebody wanted to know anything about a crook, they asked King. He knew their wives, their girlfriends, their methods, but most importantly King knew their hangouts and hiding places. King was of medium height with a full beard and impeccably dressed.

James hoped Frank Davis would not be a problem. At thirty-one, Davis was a handsome pretty boy, and women went out of their way to meet him. He had the classic good looks of an Italian movie star with dark eyes that could read into a woman's soul. His hair had just enough waves to it that women couldn't resist touching it. It was said by those who knew him, that if Davis was in the Army stationed with 10,000 other soldiers and the only woman on the base was the general's wife, Davis would lay her. He was once married to a beautiful model that spent a lot of time in New York. Davis had spent his time explaining to his wife why he was away from home working. He was an expert at picking locks and he would purchase the newest lock on the market to examine. He would work on the lock until he could open it with ease in as little time as possible.

Robert Luna was chosen because of his background in the homicide division. He also spoke fluent "Tex-Mex", Texas border Spanish. He had an olive complexion with coal dark hair and eyes. He would blend well with Joe Kramer. Luna was very meticulous when it came to details. His concise reports were seldom challenged. He was young but could work a case with the street-smart intelligence of a seasoned officer and the tenacity of a bulldog. Luna once worked a homicide case for three years, never passing up a lead and eventually solved the case and got a conviction. All these qualities were good but Luna was also an excellent cook. He was single and was always looking for the perfect woman for a wife. His fellow officers teased him for being so bashful with women. Once during testimony at a murder trial, Luna hit a defense attorney that had caused him a lot of problems with the brass in the police department. Those problems were behind him and now he just wanted to be a good detective.

Lynn Adams, young and intelligent, had the thinking of the new breed of policemen. He had a degree in psychology and had been a social worker before becoming a policeman. Adams blamed crime on social and economic conditions or, more precisely, the mother of a crook. James believed that if Adams

THE TWELVE JUDGES

had a few weeks of working with this group, he would realize that most professional criminals were just mean, sorry, no good bastards. Adams had a slight build with a delicate air about him. He reminded James of the little boy that never played in the mud. Adams was married to a psychologist and he attended weekly "Who Am I Meetings" with his wife. In spite of all of this, Adams had an excellent record of felony arrests.

Bill James chose these detectives to form his group. He believed the corrupt element in Houston would become aware of these men as ironclad arrests were made. Lieutenant James knew that the criminals and their attorney accomplices would come to fear the mention of his name. When this actually happened, James would know that he was close to winning some of the largest battles against the criminal element of Houston.

CHAPTER 3

LOYALTY TO THE LIEUTENANT

James assigned each of the detectives a vehicle. He had scrounged two vans, four pickup trucks, a wrecker and some vehicles that didn't resemble street worthy cars, let alone, police sedans.

It was important that their vehicles would not call attention to the men. Pickup trucks in Houston were like the packhorses of an earlier age. They were everywhere and hauled anything. Vans could adapt to any situation with the addition of just a magnet sign. Wreckers, referred to as vultures, were a common sight on Houston's congested streets.

Lieutenant James walked into the meeting room and began his second meeting. He looked over the group. It appeared that they might get along with each other seeing the number of bull sessions that were already in session.

Lt. Joe "Bill" Bradley

"Everyone grab a chair," he shouted, "and move over to the map." James had bought a large bulletin board, which he placed on a wall of their meeting room. He had filled the board with all kinds of posters, which James referred to as the "Do it my way crap" from the Federal, State, and City. He had been ordered by Chief Ladd to put these signs up. It was the Federal Law. A large Equal Opportunity poster fell from behind the map as James waited for his detectives to be seated. The Port of Houston area map showed the city wharves and docking areas for container ships.

"I've been working the last five months with an informer and several narcotic officers" James began. "We've been trying to pinpoint a connection for some of the cocaine coming into the Port. Last week the narcotic officers were assigned to another case with the D.E.A. so we can't count on their help. Besides, they don't know what I just learned yesterday. My snitch's information has always been reliable, and he gave me two names that are the drug connections we're seeking. We'll move on this tonight."

He then handed out two snapshots. One was of a guy who, by his clothes, looked to be a seaman from a foreign country. The second photograph stunned the detectives. It was of a well-known Houston attorney, Bob Thornton.

"These men are responsible for much of the cocaine coming into the Port of Houston and making its way into the arms and noses of our citizens. We're gonna' bust their asses tonight!"

The detectives were still astonished by the attorney's photo. That is except Detective Hancock,

THE TWELVE JUDGES

who declared, "I told you! Those damned attorneys are behind everything crooked!"

James expected these occasional outbursts from Hancock, which James ignored and continued with his briefing.

"The Adolpho, a Greek ship, will dock today at Wharf 9. Tonight, at eleven p.m., we'll set up a surveillance of the office building located on the same wharf. Adams, you, Kramer, Luna, Davis, and Edwards will be in one van. In the other van will be King, Washington, Watson, and Park. Murphy and Johnson will take one of the pickups. Hancock, you ride with me."

James continued, "I see that you're all familiar with Bob Thornton, the attorney in the photo. The second picture is Thornton's contact on The Adolpho. Thornton is expected to arrive at the docks around twelve-thirty. He should enter the office at Wharf 9 carrying cash, the payment for the drugs. He'll meet the seaman and the exchange will take place, cash for cocaine. When the money and the dope change hands, we'll be there. My informer will be on The Adolpho.

"When the seaman leaves the ship with the narcotics, my snitch will signal with a flashlight. When Thornton's contact arrives at the office, I'll inform everyone by radio. Just as the seaman from the Adolpho enters the office, Hancock and I'll move in. The Adams group will move into place behind us. King, you and your group will make sure no one from the ship, or anyone else enters after us. After the bust, we'll have a long talk with Bob Thornton and that bastard seaman. I'm sure Thornton will want to tell us all about it, especially since he'll be holding the evidence," James concluded with undisguised optimism.

"Be here tonight at ten o'clock sharp!" barked James, "ready to go!"

James left for the remainder of the day. As he drove onto NASA Road 1, he picked up his mobile telephone and dialed. A male voice answered after the first ring and simply asked, "Everything's set?" James answered, "Yes" and pressed the clear button on the telephone.

James was anxious that everything for tonight was set and went well.

He continued driving down NASA Road 1 pass the imposing fences of the Johnson Space Center to the Kemah Bridge. The bridge spans the ship channel, which connects Clear Lake with Galveston Bay. Marinas dot the shoreline here and each slip is filled with sailboats and power -boats. At times the bay resembled a sea of masts. James thought, "If all of these boats were ever on the bay at the same time, a person could walk boat to boat across the bay".

Wedged in among the marinas are seafood restaurants that cater to patrons arriving either by boat or auto.

James loved to eat at the restaurants on the water. The seafood was fresh and the view was spectacular, beautiful women sunning in small bikinis on the decks of their rich friend's yachts.

Sometimes it was downright comical watching some of the idiots try to dock their boats. Most of them were weekend captains who had trouble even parking their cars. At least once a week, one of these weekend sailors ran into the docks along side of a

THE TWELVE JUDGES

restaurant. The owners of the eateries had partially solved this problem by placing double rows of huge truck tires along the side of the dock.

James parked at the Shark Inn Restaurant and went inside. He ordered a fried flounder dinner. This was a heavier meal than he usually had at lunch but he knew that he had a difficult assignment ahead of him that night. He wanted his mind clear and well rested so after eating he drove home for a quick nap.

James slipped his shoes off and lay down on his unmade bed. His mind raced as he thought of the bust that might go down that night. He was able to doze for only a short time when the alarm on his watch went off. James showered, dressed and headed for his office.

When James arrived at the factory, the detectives were checking their weapons, radios and vehicles to make sure they were in working order. Park inspected the night scopes and determined that they were functioning properly. There was an air of excitement among the men.

All except Joe Kramer. He was mad as hell at Jack Hancock, who was still spouting off about attorneys.

"All attorneys are not corrupt! I'm an attorney and I'm not dishonest!" Kramer said very firmly.

Taking his thick glasses off, Kramer pressed his nose into Hancock's face.

"We'll probably find that you're crooked after we've worked with you for awhile," was Hancock's only reply.

Hancock stood his ground waiting for the next remark or move from Kramer.

Lt. Joe "Bill" Bradley

"Come on guys. Save the fight for the real bastards. We've got enough to do before tonight," said Gary Edwards.

At that, Kramer and Hancock broke the stare contest and continued their preparations for the bust. Occasionally they'd shoot a glance at each other.

James noticed that some of his men were teasing Detective Adams.

The majority had returned to work in slacks and sport shirts. Lynn Adams was dressed in a three-piece suit and looked as if he was going to church. He sat by himself busy polishing his shoes.

"Hey, Adams! When's the choir practice?" someone yelled.

"Oh, don't ya' remember it's on Tuesday night. Tonight's the night Little Lynn helps the old ladies in their quiltin' bee," Davis answered.

James listened to the harassment directed at Adams and wondered why he sat there taking it without tossing in a few jabs. It seemed that this new breed of police not only had new ways of going about their jobs but also failed to enjoy the camaraderie with brother officers.

James again studied the map and the places where he wanted the two vans and pickup truck to park. He briefed the detectives again and gave his final order. "Let's go, and keep in constant radio contact."

As Hancock drove out Canal Street from the downtown area he remarked, "Boy, if this brick street could talk, it could really tell you some stories. Look at that old house there! In the 50's when you and me were rookies that was one hell of a whorehouse.

THE TWELVE JUDGES

Houston was wide open then. Now the whores are street walkers or call girls."

James replied, "Captain Birt of the Vice Squad told me that he didn't need to police some intersections out here, all that was needed was a traffic cop because of the number of johns circling the block looking to pick up a whore".

Hancock was still laughing as they turned towards the ship channel.

James and his detectives arrived at Wharf 9 at precisely 11 p.m. The men moved their vehicles into the assigned places.

The office that they were to watch was at the end of a large warehouse, longer than five football fields. The Adolpho was moored at the docks just where James had been told it would be. It was a large dirty black cargo ship with containers waiting to be unloaded. Lights were on all over the ship but it appeared that all the seamen were either in bed or had gone to town for the night.

As radio communications were checked the dullest part of police work began, the wait.

The waterfront air was damp and stagnant. A fog bank was slowly creeping across the channel. The sound of a horn pierced the quiet of the night as a tugboat appeared and then disappeared in a white, misty cloud down the ship channel.

Houston, the oil capital of the Western world, had the smelliest dirtiest ship channel in the U.S. Ships from all around the globe came to the port. They brought their cargo but also dumped their garbage alongside the docks. On hot summer nights the stench could turn the strongest man's stomach.

Lt. Joe "Bill" Bradley

At midnight, radio silence was broken by Detective Bill Johnson's voice crackling over the radio. "Hey Adams, I need one of your dry pockets in that pretty suit you're wearing. I gotta pee."

Laughter poured from the vans.

James grabbed his radio mike shouting into it, "Knock it off! We don't need to advertise that we're here!"

At twelve forty-five a gray Lincoln Continental rolled into the parking area of Wharf 9. Its lights were turned off. It was several seconds before anyone stepped from the vehicle. The interior lights did not come on when the driver's door was opened. As the shape moved into the lights of the dock, James recognized the figure as Bob Thornton.

Thornton entered the office at the end of the warehouse. James saw that lights were turned on because a sliver of light shone along the edge of heavy curtains.

From the radio came the whispered voice of Albert King.

"Can you believe this. It really is that son-of-a-bitch!"

"I guess King didn't hear me, stay off the damn radio!" snarled Lieutenant James.

About fifteen minutes later, the walkway from the Adolpho was lit. Before anyone emerged on the ramp, Hancock announced that he had to piss and started to get out of the car.

"Hold it," James said. "Someone's coming down the ship's walkway, carrying a large suitcase."

Another dark figure appeared at the top of the walkway and a small light flashed on and then off.

THE TWELVE JUDGES

Lieutenant James picked up the radio mike and ordered, "Get ready! This is it!"

The man from the ship carried the suitcase on his shoulder and hurriedly walked toward the same office door that Bob Thornton had entered.

"Let's take 'em!" Lieutenant James commanded as the seaman entered the office.

James was the first to the office door but the door was locked.

"Knock that damn thing down!" shouted Bill James.

Washington, who was supposed to stay outside, ran up to volunteer, "Let me show you girls how it's done."

With one solid kick, Washington knocked the door from its hinges. As the door fell through the opening everyone tried to enter the room at once.

Bob Thornton stood alone in the room. The seaman was no where in sight. In two long strides Bill James was across the room and face to face with Thornton. James barked orders to find the seaman.

"Thornton, you really screwed up this time!" declared James. "Last time I saw you in court you got a bastard off scot-free, but no one's gonna walk from this. Where's the damn narcotics and that filthy money?"

"What in the hell are you talking about?" asked Thornton, trying his best to look innocent. "I'm here to meet an injured seaman about a lawsuit I just filed for him. You've got no business breaking down that door and coming in here like a bunch of common thugs. I'm a respectable man and you just stepped into a situation you're gonna regret!"

41

"Crap on you, Thornton! I've got a warrant to search this whole damn ship channel," James said as he poked the paper in Thornton's face.

The detectives saw that the lieutenant was becoming highly agitated.

Hancock knew what was coming next because he knew James. He had seen James in action before when James planted his feet and his fist slowly closed. He knew that Thornton had better duck because James was closing his fists.

James hit Bob Thornton, knocking him to the floor. He then straddled Thornton's body and shouted down at him, "Where are the drugs, you bastard, and who delivered them to you?"

Bob Thornton appeared to be bleeding from the mouth and nose. He looked at up at Bill James. "To hell with you! I'm gonna get your damn job for this!" coughed Thornton.

James pulled his 45-caliber pistol from his waistband and stuck it into Bob Thornton's mouth. "One more chance, Bastard, who brought you the narcotics?" James threatened.

The detectives watched their lieutenant in silence. James jacked the slide back on his 45. There was a loud explosion! The bullet splintered a hole inches from Thornton's head. Bob Thornton's eyes were as big as silver dollars and you could see his face turn from red to snow white.

"Shit!" was all James said.

He kicked Bob Thornton in the ribs. Thornton groaned and it appeared as if he was going to cry.

"Get up, you son-of-a-bitch!" James growled.

The attorney continued to lie on the floor.

As James stepped away from Bob Thornton, Gary Edwards hollered, "Look what I found!"

Edwards was holding a suitcase. He opened it. The suitcase was filled with bags and bags of what appeared to be pure cocaine. Edwards placed the open suitcase on top of a desk as the detectives crowded around.

James turned back to look at Bob Thornton on the floor and coldly said, "Now! We've got your ass up tight! You better talk, you bastard?"

Jack Hancock walked over to Bob Thornton's limp body lying on the floor.

"Thornton, you can get your lazy ass up now," Hancock told him. "The lieutenant has his evidence."

When Bob Thornton didn't move, Hancock checked for his pulse. Hancock slowly rasped, "I think this bastard's dead." Hancock continued to try and find some signs of life pushing back Thornton's eye lids to check his eyes. A stony silence fell on the room as James walked over to Thornton. He knelt and felt for a pulse.

"Damn! I think you're right. Thornton must have had a heart attack."

Suddenly the room seemed to erupt into heated discussions. Lynn Adams looked as if he was going to cry and mumbled, "The F.B.I. is lookin' for something like this. We're all going to jail. Bob Thornton is too well known and no one will believe he was involved in drugs."

"Shut up. Shut up!" James hollered. "Let me think!"

Lt. Joe "Bill" Bradley

Silence engulfed the room while James paced the office. Suddenly, James turned on his heels and said, "I've got a story I think will fly."

Washington broke in, "Fly hell, I'm not going to be a party to this. I've got too many years invested with this department and I'm not gonna' blow my pension."

Some of the other detectives nodded their heads in agreement.

Hancock grabbed Washington by the shoulder and spun him around glaring at him and shouted, "Don't you think James has a lot of time with this department. You know his reputation; he takes care of his men. What in the hell do you think we were organized for, to go by pantywaist rules and regulations? You think Lu knew this sorry bastard had a weak heart."

The room became very quiet once more.

Washington surveyed the room looking at each detective and finally said, "For once Hancock, You're right."

Turning to James, Washington said, "I'm with you, Lu, and I know the rest of the guys are too."

"Thank you, Washington. What I suggest is that the story will be that Bob Thornton came down here on business; he was robbed, shot and killed. Sweet and simple. It happens every day in this damn city, so who the hell's gonna know?"

At this Bill James walked over to Bob Thornton's body and shot him in the chest with his 45. The pistol had been so close to the body that you could see the powder burns on Thornton's coat.

THE TWELVE JUDGES

Detective King and the other detectives had entered the room just before Lieutenant James shot Bob Thornton. Everyone stood staring in disbelief.

Suddenly, Detective Robert Luna burst into the room. "Hey, Lieutenant, come look at this. Here's where the seaman escaped."

Lieutenant James walked to the rear of the large office where Luna was standing. Behind a partition was a staircase leading downward away from the room.

"I've been down," Luna said. "It leads to some catwalks under the docks. Part of the damn ship channel is under this office."

James walked down the stairs and looked around. The office was built on pilings over the water. A catwalk ran from the office and disappeared in the dark, probably going to other parts of the warehouse.

Lieutenant James climbed the stairs back to the office. All twelve detectives stood in silence as he spoke.

"I told all of you when I formed this group that we wouldn't work like ordinary cops. This bust went wrong so now we'll make it right. We recovered a hell of a lot of narcotics, and put a sorry bastard out of business."

"Hancock," James ordered. "Take Thornton's Rolex watch and his wallet and then help me move him to the catwalk below. Thornton will be found in a few days after his body floats up and starts to stink. It'll look like a robbery. While Hancock and I are getting rid of Thornton, the rest of you wipe fingerprints from any area you might have touched.

Edwards, dig my bullet from the floor, throw it into the ship channel and fill the hole with something."

At that, Bill James and Detective Hancock carried Thornton down the stairs. They were out of sight of the other detectives but not so far removed that the detectives couldn't hear a loud splash of water.

When Lieutenant James and Hancock returned to the room, James issued orders, "Get back to the factory. I had planned a small party for you and I iced down some beer to celebrate this bust! We might as well go back and have a cold one. We need to settle our nerves and make sure that everyone damn sure leaves what happened here in this room. Just remember we were not here tonight! King, check outside and make sure we can get to our cars without being seen."

"Lu, it's clear," said King as he returned to the office.

"Let's go. I'll see all of you back at the factory," James ordered. "No one is excused!"

Everyone took off for the vehicles, some even running.

The detectives arrived at the factory before James. Some were already drinking beer. There was not much talk. The usual joking and teasing was missing.

Lieutenant James popped a beer open and went into his office. The detectives watched as he made a phone call.

After the telephone call, James came back and told his men to leave. "Go home and keep your mouths shut. What happened tonight, well, it was just one of those things. I'll dispose of the narcotics we

THE TWELVE JUDGES

recovered. I'll see all of you in this office at eight sharp tomorrow morning!"

The detectives filed out of the offices without a sound. James left feeling that he had not heard the last of tonight's episode.

James decided to stay in town for the night. He drove to the Allen Park Inn, which sits near the downtown area on Buffalo Bayou to get a room for the night.

James had become a close friend with the owner twenty years ago. When the owner bought the motel it was full of whores and a haven for dope heads. He had remodeled the motel and it was now a first rate motel. Movie producers and stars stayed at his motel when they came to Houston.

James had met the owner when he made an arrest at the motel years ago. James had kicked a motel door to pieces getting into the room to make the arrest. After the arrest, the owner came to James and gave him a passkey to the motel saying, "Next time use this pass key. Those doors cost me money."

The next morning Bill James got up and went to the Nashville Room at the motel for breakfast. The breakfast consisted of eggs, Tennessee ham, red-eye gravy, grits and large buttermilk biscuits.

Lieutenant James drove to the factory and as he got out of his car, he saw Detective Frank Davis at the door.

"Chief Ladd has personally called five times and his secretary, even more times," a very nervous Davis said. "Shit Lu, call the Chief, I think he's pissed."

Lt. Joe "Bill" Bradley

Bill James casually walked to his office. As he closed the door, he noticed that not all of the detectives had arrived. He picked up his phone and called the Chief's office.

"Chief's office," answered Ms. May.

"Is the fat chief in?" James asked.

"What did you do this time, Bill? The Chief is mad as hell. He hasn't even had breakfast so you know he's really upset. He has the First Assistant District Attorney in his office and every other phrase I hear is, `damn Lieutenant James'. You better get over here fast!" warned Ms. May.

"Well, tell the fat man to putt some golf balls, I'm on my way," replied James.

As the lieutenant drove to the main police department, he stopped for a dozen fresh donuts, and thought to himself, "Maybe I can bribe the Chief, but I had better eat one now. When the Chief sees these, he'll eat `em all."

When James arrived at the Chief's office, Ms. May was visibly shaken. She motioned him to hurry.

Lieutenant James sauntered into the office. He offered the donuts to Chief Ladd.

If Bill James thought the donuts would make a peace offering he was dead wrong. Chief Ladd slammed the box on his desk without even giving the contents a glance.

Ladd could scarcely contain his anger.

"Sit your ass down, James!" hollered Ladd. "You're going to tell me what the hell took place last night and I don't care if the D.A hangs your ass out for buzzard bait!"

THE TWELVE JUDGES

Lieutenant James glanced at the assistant district attorney sitting next to the chief's desk. James never cared for Jamie Owens. The Lieutenant thought Owens was a spoiled, rich boy whose family bought his law degree and influenced the D.A. to give Owens the position of First Assistant District Attorney. Jamie Owens wore a foot long split goatee and his head was shaped like a basketball. James felt that Owens also thought like a lot of other stuck-up D.A.'s, that he was the number one cop in Houston. Jamie Owens had a shit-eating grin on his face that indicated, "Now I've got you, you son-of-a-bitch."

As James pulled a chair up to the chief's desk, Ladd's voice came at him like a shot from a cannon.

"I should have never listened to you! You're going to tell me what happened last night and you're going to tell me the truth! I've explained to Jamie Owens that I'm not involved in what went on last night! You're going to confirm that I was not involved! You will also tell him in no uncertain terms that I did not know nor authorize what went down last night."

Bill James shot a quick glimpse at the obnoxious Jamie Owens and then back at the Chief.

Casually James asked, "How's your golf game, Chief?"

Chief Ladd was so dumb struck that he could barely breathe and his face looked as though it had been staked out in the hot, South Texas sun.

Before Ladd could reply, Jamie Owens spoke. "I've heard stories about you, Lieutenant. Some not very good, and some downright frightening. I can help you but you must confide in me about the incident with Bob Thornton."

Jamie Owens continued, "There is no need to involve the Chief or your men. I know you're man enough to take all the blame. I've taken the initiative and drew up resignation papers for you to sign."

Owens handed the papers to James.

The lieutenant looked at both men with disgust.

"Shit, Ladd! Just sit there and let him walk all over me! Owens, you know what you can do with your damn resignation papers. Or maybe, since you wouldn't know your ass from the chief's, I need to draw you a map."

As Lieutenant James started toward Owens with the resignation papers crumpled in his hand, Chief Ladd stepped between them.

"Hold on! You think we don't know what took place last night? How stupid do I look? Sit down, you bastard, I've got news for you. I'm smarter than you ever gave me credit for," the chief shouted.

James looked at Chief Ladd and wondered why he was putting on such a show in front of Owens.

Owens stomped out of the office and into the adjoining room. James heard Owens tell someone, "Don't be scared, James' ass is mine now. Come into the office and let Lieutenant James see you!"

When Owens returned to Chief Ladd's office Detective Lynn Adams, one of the Chosen, followed him.

"Hello, Lieutenant, Sir," he cautiously whispered.

Chief Ladd turned to James; "Detective Adams went to Jamie Owens last night after he left your

THE TWELVE JUDGES

office. Adams told him everything that took place last night. It looks like you're on your own on this one, Bill. I've helped you through some tight spots but this is capital murder. It was your detective that spilled his guts to Owens."

The Assistant D.A. began to speak, "I wanted you to see your detective. He was present last night. Detective Adams has done his duty and I know the whole story. You can holler for an attorney, but it won't do you any good. I want a detailed confession from you, James. You're going to say that you acted on your own and that the chief was not involved. Do you know how it's going to read in the newspapers? Bob Thornton, well-known defense attorney, shot by police."

Jamie Owens looked pleased. All he could think about was that he was going to burn a cop. That would be a jump up the ladder. Only this was not just any old cop. This was a smart-ass lieutenant who dared to believe that he could out-think an attorney. Owens believed this bust would be his ticket to becoming the D.A.

Lieutenant James stood up. As he did, Detective Adams face turned white and Adams nearly fell from a standing position as the tall lieutenant reached full height.

"Chief, let me make one phone call. I wouldn't call an attorney if you held a gun to my head. But with one call I can clear this matter up. I can only guess at what Detective Adams must have told you. I admit I made a mistake but the only damn mistake I made was allowing Adams on my squad. He's a lying son-of-a-

Lt. Joe "Bill" Bradley

bitch who makes up stories in an attempt to glorify himself. Just give me a lousy fifteen minutes."

"Okay," Chief Ladd replied. "But no attorney had better show up in my office. You got that James?"

Lieutenant James picked up the receiver from the Chief's telephone and called his office.

"Hancock, bring everyone, and I mean everyone, to the Chief's office, now!"

James hung up the telephone and sat down. He crossed his lanky legs and casually asked, "Well Chief, how's your golf game."

"Shit! Shit! Shit!" was all that Ladd could mutter.

Jamie Owens rose from his chair. "Chief, you, me and Detective Adams need to talk in the next room."

As they left, Lieutenant James moved behind the Chief's desk to munch on a donut.

A few minutes passed before Chief Ladd, Jamie Owens and Detective Adams returned.

"Well, James, what do you have to say about last night?" asked Owens.

Before Lieutenant James could respond, Ms. May interrupted the conversation by paging Chief Ladd over the intercom.

"Chief, Lieutenant James' detectives are here and they want to see you."

"Tell them to come in", growled Chief Ladd. "They probably want to tell the truth like Detective Adams has done."

All eyes turned to the Chief's door as it opened. In marched Detective Jack Hancock, Detective Robert Luna, Detective Frank Davis, Detective Gary Edwards,

THE TWELVE JUDGES

Detective Albert King, Detective Roosevelt Washington, Detective Charles Watson, Detective Larry Parks, Detective Thomas Murphy, Detective Bill Johnson, Detective Joe Kramer, and last and most amazingly, Attorney Bob Thornton.

When Chief Ladd saw Bob Thornton, he was speechless. The Chief leaped at Bob Thornton and hugged him, saying, "I was told you were dead."

Ladd then looked from Lieutenant James to Detective Adams and then looked to where First Assistant Jamie Owens had been sitting.

Jamie Owens was gone. When Bob Thornton entered the room, Jamie Owens had slipped quietly out.

Ladd then realized that he had been the butt of some kind of vicious scheme.

"Lieutenant James, you're going to tell me what the hell is going on," the Chief bellowed.

While the Chief had been ranting, eleven detectives had not taken their eyes from Lynn Adams.

Detective Adams turned white and left the room without permission.

"The rest of you get back to work!" Lieutenant James told his detectives. "I won't be here long."

Thornton and James settled into some chairs with the donuts and some coffee from Ms. May.

After the detectives left the Chief's office, Lieutenant James began, "Chief, Bob Thornton and I have been friends for years. Don't be so dumbstruck that there's an attorney that I could confide in. We pulled this stunt, so I could be certain of who I could trust. We're going after some sorry bastards and some of these slimeballs will be prominent citizens. There can be no leaks in my organization. It had to be done this way, Chief, if the work at the factory is going to be successful."

As Bill James continued his account of the night's activities, Chief Ladd roared with laughter. His belly would shake with each new revelation.

"Did they really throw you into that filthy ship channel?" Ladd asked Thornton.

Bob Thornton grinned and replied, "No, they threw an oil drum instead. The fake blood capsule I bit down on really tasted bad. By the way James, that blank bullet you shot me with burned like hell through the vest you gave me. You owe me a new suit."

James answered, "Bob, I knew you'd find some way to charge me a fee."

Lieutenant James was relieved to have Bob Thornton with him; otherwise, the Chief would have really been chewing on his ass.

As James finished the story of what took place, he announced that he was going back to work.

"Lieutenant, you had better keep your nose clean," Chief Ladd warned. "I don't want any bad publicity from you, do you hear me? Play it by the book! Owens will be out to prove you wrong and to get me along with you!"

James didn't say a word. He shook Bob Thornton's hand, excused himself and gave Ms. May a wink. As he strolled from the office he could hear Ladd.

"Bob, aren't you a member of the Shadow Way Country Club. I hear they have a great golf course. I'm free this afternoon, why don't we get a foursome."

THE TWELVE JUDGES

James returned to the factory and entered his office. There was a loud applause from all the detectives.

"Get to work, you flunkies," barked the Lieutenant.

He was very pleased but knew better than to show it.

"Get in here, Hancock," he shouted and slammed his office door.

Detective Hancock had known the Lieutenant since their early days on the force. They had worked many difficult cases together and trusted each other. Hancock had been in the know on the scam from the start.

"Jack, I'm worried about Lynn Adams, he could really run his mouth about this group. I think maybe you and I need to have a talk with him."

"Lu, I'm, way ahead of you." Hancock answered. "I had some of the guys pick up Lynn Adams and I had a long talk with him. He's not going to open his mouth about anything. You know he was so scared he pissed in his three-piece suit! The worst of it, he was sitting in the back seat of my car. Washington is the one who caused Adams to piss so I'm trying to make Washington trade cars with me. I could use your help, Lu"

This time, Lieutenant James laughed out loud. "Hancock, get your butt out of here and find me some crooks!"

When Detective Hancock left, Lieutenant James leaned back in his chair to relax. His telephone rang.

"Lieutenant James. May I help you?"

Lt. Joe "Bill" Bradley

"Lieutenant, this is Judge Claude Edwards in San Antonio."

"Yes, Sir, what can I do for you?"

"Your personnel department advised me that my son, Gary, is working for you."

"Yes, Sir. He is."

"I'm a Federal Judge in the Southern District of Texas. You know, I had my heart set on my son becoming a lawyer and someday becoming a judge like me, but I guess the cop blood over-ruled that dream. Gary's uncle was a cop here in San Antonio until he was killed. I guess that's where Gary got his background, but enough about my family. I've been trying to get in touch with Gary. His wife is out of town and I guess that he still works all hours. Gary's mother is having her sixty-fifth birthday and I need to tell him where the party in her honor will be held. Would you have him call me, please?"

"I will, Sir. You have a fine son and I'm proud to have him working for me. And call me Bill."

"Okay, if you call me Claude, unless you're in my court and I'm sure you know the procedures there. Thank you for your help, Bill."

As James hung up the receiver, he again leaned back in his chair to relax. He thought of Gary Edwards and his father.

"So, Gary's father wanted him to be a lawyer. What a difference in father and son," thought James. Then his mind wandered back to his chosen detectives. "I've still got eleven good detectives and myself. That's twelve. An even dozen should raise some hell in this town. I've got a feeling that the criminal element is going to regret this group was organized.

The Chief will be pissed because I chose some rouges, but the degenerates in Houston will be even more pissed when these rogues bust their crooked asses."

CHAPTER 4

WHOLESALES, INC.

Thirty minutes into the morning meeting, Bill James was interrupted by the sound of the front door bursting open. In walked Detectives Larry Park and Thomas Murphy.

"Hey Lu, yawl come see our van." Park yelled.

"You're late," Lieutenant James growled, "but if the van passes inspection, you'll be excused."

James had ordered the two detectives to outfit one of the vans to be the main surveillance vehicle.

As everyone filed outside, the lieutenant seemed to stop in mid-stride. He was amazed at the conversion. The van looked as if it had just rolled off an assembly line; it gleamed with a fresh blue coat of paint with red and white stripes down the sides. The interior had been gutted and replaced with plush blue carpeting and wood paneling. The control panel resembled an aircraft's panel with multiple switches and dials.

Detective Murphy began to serve as tour guide, "A captain's chair for the driver and also a captain's chair for the co-pilot. The van has carpet throughout and cabinets down one side."

"We've also got every type of radio you can think of," Detective Park interrupted. "We can talk to our dispatcher, the Sheriff dispatcher, oh hell, we can talk to any damn cop, anywhere! We can even listen in on the F.B.I.! For you, Washington, we have a T.V. and a mean sounding stereo system. That's O.K., isn't it Lieutenant?"

Before James could respond, Park continued with his narrative, "The cabinets are lined with sponge rubber so that our camera equipment won't be destroyed if we have to take off after someone."

Everyone was examining the interior when Charles Watson climbed into the van and pointed to a funnel that was attached to a hose, which ran through the floor.

"What's this for?" Watson asked.

Detective Murphy spoke up, "Will someone tell stupid what the funnel's for."

Detective Edwards was laughing, "If you're on surveillance and you have to piss and you can't leave to find a restroom, you piss in the funnel and your pee forms a puddle under the van."

Bill James was pleased with the work; it was a bit luxurious but still very functional.

"Murphy, Park," Lieutenant James asked, "How much did this set the city back?"

THE TWELVE JUDGES

Murphy spoke up, "Not a dime, a van company owed me a favor. Communications owed me a favor. I bought the funnel. Don't ask where we got the refrigerator, sink and T.V."

James knew better than to push the subject. He told Murphy and Park that it had been a job well done.

"Lu, me and Murphy also have a matter to discuss with the group," Detective Park said. "I met with one of my informers and I've got something good."

Lieutenant James turned and said, "Let's go inside and hear what these two scavengers have to say."

"Come on Washington, get out of the van. Everyone back inside."

Once inside, Lieutenant James told Murphy, "You and Park have the floor."

Murphy started. "There's a man named John Peters. He owns a second hand appliance store on 19th Street in the Heights section of the city. He's buying stolen appliances, T.V.'s and music equipment from burglars and thieves. He's also buying stolen guns off the street. He's one hell of a fence. My snitch doesn't know where the fence sells his stuff, but you can bet we'll find out. The informer does know that Peters has some mini-warehouses rented somewhere. When the fence gets a load large enough for a tractor-trailer he moves the stolen property. My informer also thinks that Peters moves the property out of town to sell it. Peters has been busted before for having stolen property in his store. His cases are always dismissed because Peters produces receipts showing he bought

Lt. Joe "Bill" Bradley

the property from thieves off the street and he always claims he didn't know the property was stolen."

"This sounds like it's tailor made for us," Lieutenant James said. "Kramer, start a background investigation on John Peters, find out where he lives, dig up everything you can about him. Also you might as well get started on the paperwork for a search warrant so we'll be ready when we find out where the warehouses are located. We will also need some Houston Telephone Company signs for the old van."

At this time Murphy hollered, "Wait a minute Lieutenant! I didn't remodel that beautiful van to let it just sit while I have to work in the other van. That other one's a piece of shit."

Lieutenant James ignored his complaint and continued his orders.

"The old van is gray and is perfect for this assignment. Detective Watson has some magnetic Houston Telephone Company signs that you can stick on the doors. Now do you get the picture, Murphy?"

"Sorry Lu, I still don't like it, but I do get the picture," Murphy answered.

Bill James then instructed detectives King and Davis to use the "good time" van, and set up surveillance on John Peters and his business.

James wanted detailed records of the comings and goings of all customers.

"King, when you and Davis see a customer carry something into John Peters' second hand store," continued James, "call by radio back here to the factory. The rest of you guys will be here for now. I want a check on license plate numbers to get owner's

THE TWELVE JUDGES

names and then, I want a rundown to see if they have a criminal record."

Detective Johnson spoke up, "Lieutenant why can't I get a T.V. from the police property room, mark it inside with my name and then sell it to John Peters? I'll tell him that I just stole it and that I could get him more."

Lieutenant James considered the suggestion and then said, "That's good. You can get the layout of the store when you go in. Get Murphy to put a body mike on you, so we can record your conversation."

James turned and walked outside with Detectives Larry Park and Thomas Murphy.

"Do you have all the necessary equipment for your assignment," asked Lieutenant James.

Tom Murphy said, "Not only do we have the necessary equipment, we have such sophisticated electronic devices that the F.B.I. would like to get their grubby hands on it."

"Just keep me informed," responded Bill James.

Murphy and Park left in the gray van with a Houston Telephone sign on each side. Watson had a supply of all types of magnetic signs. Murphy and Park were even wearing Houston Telephone Company shirts. They looked like two repairmen going to their job.

All the way out to the Heights Subdivision where 19th Street is located, Murphy bitched about the van they were in.

Finally Park shouted, "Shut your damn mouth and quit crying. You know the Houston Telephone

Lt. Joe "Bill" Bradley

Company doesn't have many nice vans. They work in beat-up pieces of shit like we're in".

The Heights area of Houston is one of the oldest subdivisions and sits close to downtown. Real estate prices went through the roof when a few wealthy owners bought old three story wooden homes and remodeled them. The homes on Heights Boulevard have become show places serving as Bed & Breakfast homes with the restored Victorian façade and beautiful antique furnishings inside.

Murphy drove the van down Heights Boulevard to 19th Street in the direction of John Peters' second hand store. Turning onto 19th Street, they passed the second hand store.

"Boy, are we in luck!" Murphy said, "There's an alley at the rear of the store. Drive down the alley and let me spot the telephone line coming from the store. We can follow it to the lug box on a telephone pole."

"O.K.," Murphy agreed, "But you're climbing the telephone pole this time, I climbed the last four."

As the van passed the rear entrance to John Peters' store, Park hung his head out the window.

"I see the telephone line, keep driving. Damn it, slow down. I gotta have time to look."

Park spotted the lug box on the telephone pole that supplied the phone line to the store at the end of the alley.

"Did you call the telephone company man?" Park asked.

"Yes," Murphy replied. "He's meeting us at Jimmy's, the café down the street. Man, this is a good location to tap into the telephone line. We'll be four stores from our target and in the rear."

Rex was a Houston Telephone Company employee who had helped Murphy and Park in the past. He would pinpoint the right connections to be made in the lug boxes on the telephone poles to tap a certain telephone. He worked well with the detectives. Rex also enjoyed being a part-time cop and helping catch the burglars and thieves that the cops went after.

The two detectives drove to the café and parked next to an old beat up Houston Phone Company truck just like theirs. They went inside. Rex was sitting alone in a booth. Murphy and Park slid into the booth and ordered a Lone Star long neck beer.

"What is it this time?" Rex Asked, "A bookie or Park's chip that you want to listen in on."

Murphy said, "Don't call Park's girlfriend a chip, she's a whore."

Murphy and Park told Rex the telephone number of John Peters' second hand store and where the telephone pole and lug box were situated.

"I'm running late today," Rex said. "I'll go mark the lugs for you; pay for my beer. Where did you get that piece of shit you're driving? You misspelled Houston on your sign."

Murphy got up and hurried outside to look at the sign on his truck. He came back in and slapped Rex on the back "Houston's spelled right, you just can't read."

With that, Rex smiled and left leaving Murphy to pay for his beer.

Lt. Joe "Bill" Bradley

Murphy and Park gave Rex enough time to drive to the location, climb the pole and mark the lugs before they left the café.

When they arrived at the pole where the telephone tap was to be placed, Rex was gone. Detective Park strapped his climbing spikes onto his boots and went up the pole like a squirrel. Park opened the lug box and hollered.

"Shit!"

Murphy, looking up asked, "What's wrong?"

Park hollered down. "That damn Rex marked the lugs with dog shit! I hope Rex got dog shit all over him when he climbed the pole".

After attaching the green and red wires to the lugs, Park threw down the spools of wire. Murphy retrieved the spools and put them into the van.

When Park came down off the pole, he said, "I'll fix Rex one of these days, but for now, I gotta wash my hands."

Park spotted a water hose behind a business in the alley and went over to wash his hands.

When Park returned to the van, Murphy had already hooked up the open telephone extension. Now they could listen to every telephone call made to or from John Peters' store.

Murphy and Park listened on the phone until John Peters closed his store. All they heard were orders being taken and customer's asking prices.

Park said, "You think we should have set up on his home telephone?"

"Hell no! The Lieutenant said the store," replied Murphy. "I'm not gonna go against his orders. He'll have our ass if something were to go wrong."

THE TWELVE JUDGES

Murphy unhooked the telephone extension and stapled the extension telephone wires to the base of the telephone pole. After securing the scene for the night they called Lieutenant James and reported in.

By the end of the next day the telephone tap had still produced nothing, but the surveillance on the comings and goings of all the customers had paid off. Lieutenant James had been given a list of names of those customers who had gone into the store and sold merchandise. Nine were discovered to be convicted thieves.

Lieutenant James laughed when he saw Detective Johnson's name on the list. Detective Kramer had used a camcorder and taken a movie of Johnson for future evidence in court but mostly it was for the entertainment of the group. Detective Johnson looked more like a thief than a thief did. Johnson would stop; look around like he was checking to see if he was being followed.

On the fourth day of surveillance, Lieutenant James' telephone rang. It was Detective King with Detective Hancock at the phone tap.

"We scored! Peters' mini-warehouses are on Harwin Street. A truck will pick up a load of stolen goods in two days. The truck is coming from Dallas."

"That's the best news I've heard in days," James said. "Is Hancock with you?"

"No, he's gone to tell the guys in the "Good Time" van what we heard."

"Tell Hancock to give me a call."

A few minutes later, Detective Hancock called Lieutenant James.

Lt. Joe "Bill" Bradley

"Lu, this is Hancock. You heard about the warehouses?"

"Yes", replied James. "I need you to locate and check out Peter's warehouses. Locate the merchandise. Get the makes, models and serial numbers. We'll need them when we draw up a search warrant. Take Davis and a couple of guys with you. When you get the information we need, contact Kramer and give him all the pertinent information for the search warrant. Tell the others, not to let Kramer know how you got the serial numbers of the stolen property. Right now he's too new to this. I'll tell Kramer myself."

Later that night, Detectives Hancock, Davis, Johnson and Washington met at the factory and left in the "Good Time" van for the warehouses. Washington was driving and noticed that the others were drinking a beer. He also noticed that Hancock was holding two beers.

Hancock said, "Washington, you being colored or black or an Afro American, or Negro, can you drink with us?"

Washington replied, "Give me a damn beer; I can drink with Davis and Johnson but not you."

Hancock smiled and handed Washington a beer.

Washington headed for Harwin Street and to the location of the mini-warehouses. It was obvious that Washington had won many honors in competition driving.

As Washington wove through the traffic on the Southwest Freeway, at excessive speeds Jack Hancock

THE TWELVE JUDGES

observed, "Washington, if a cop sees you in this pretty van, he's going to think your black ass stole it."

Washington looked back at Hancock and sneered; "If it's a black cop, I'll tell him you're a white Miss Freddy and the van belongs to you."

Hancock fell out of the seat laughing. Miss Freddy was a well-known woman impersonator and one of Washington's informers.

The van pulled up to the warehouse just after sunset so that the detectives would have the cover of darkness to work. There were no renters present and the business office had closed for the day.

Washington wheeled the van into the driveway of the warehouses. There were four rows of mini-warehouses each warehouse being like a garage.

Detective Davis got out of the van and walked to the gate at the entrance. The gate had a padlock on it. Davis took out his lock picking set and began to work. Within minutes, Detective Davis had the lock open. As Davis slid the gate open, Washington drove through and Davis locked the gate behind them.

When Davis rejoined the group in the van, King said, "I timed you and you're slipping; it took 3 ½ minutes for you to pick the lock."

"Try and stay up with me when I open the locks on the warehouse doors", challenged Davis. "Just be sure and lock the doors of the warehouses after you've inspected the contents so no one will know we've been here. And put everything back like you found it."

Davis started on the first lock and in a few minutes, five mini-warehouse locks were on the ground.

Lt. Joe "Bill" Bradley

The other detectives scrambled into the storage rooms to begin inspecting the contents. There was a large assortment stashed in the mini-warehouses, everything from boats to household items and even a stuffed six-foot brown bear.

As Davis neared the end of the first line of warehouses, he hollered to the others, "Come down here! I've hit pay dirt!"

The next eight warehouses contained boxes of the new TVs, guns and stereo equipment. Working as quickly as possible the detectives recorded serial numbers to many of the firearms and electronic equipment.

In the meantime, Detective Davis had been closing and locking the first stalls and hollered to the others, "I told you bastards to lock up and leave things like we found them. Now I have to do it."

"I believe these eight stalls are all that Peters has. Hurry up! Let's get the hell out of here", Davis commanded.

After getting serial numbers, all of the detectives got back into the van and Washington drove to the exit gate.

As Davis got out to open the lock on the gate, King stuck his head out of the van and started counting, "1, 2, 3, 4..."

King had counted to 20 when Davis opened the lock to the gate, bowed and waved the van through.

Washington waited as Davis locked the gate.

The next morning at the factory, everyone began checking the serial numbers on the computers. The police department had a computerized stolen property file where suspected stolen items could be

THE TWELVE JUDGES

checked. They could also check the computers of Texas Department of Public Safety which is known as, TCIC and the F.B.I. computers which is known as NCIC for stolen property. Detective Joe Kramer was also running serial numbers on his computer.

"How in the hell did you guys get so many serial numbers?" Kramer asked. "I'm getting stolen reports on most of the guns and some of the TVs. There's enough here for a ten page search warrant."

Park stepped forward and said, "I have a confidential informer who knows John Peters. This informer has been getting serial numbers for me without Peters knowing it."

Kramer turned to Park, "You know, unless you have used this informer before, we can't use his information to obtain a search warrant."

"Kramer, believe me, I've used this snitch a number of times and he's always reliable."

"That's great," responded Kramer. "That means I won't have to name the informer in the search warrant."

Detective Washington gave a loud, "Thank God!"

Joe Kramer had his head buried in the paperwork for the next couple of hours. When he finished the search warrant for the warehouses, Kramer took the finished product into Lieutenant James.

"Lieutenant, you want to read the search warrant?"

"Sure Kramer. Sit down."

Bill James took the papers from Kramer and read each word and studied each paragraph. After he had scrutinized the search warrant, he looked at

Lt. Joe "Bill" Bradley

Kramer and said, "This is a fine piece of work, Kramer, now about the affidavit where Hancock said he received serial numbers from a reliable confidential informant. I want to apologize to you. I didn't get a chance to talk with you earlier. You remember, I told you and the others that we were going to be a different sort of cop, we were going to get the job done and put some sorry bastards away, no matter what? I'm going to tell you outright about the confidential informer. If you have any problem with what I'm going to tell you, I'll understand. You worked hard for your law degree but Kramer; this group really needs you. None of the other detectives will blame you if you decide to transfer from this group."

Kramer looked bewildered, "What are you trying to tell me, Lieutenant?"

Bill James studied his thoughts before he answered.

"Hancock, Park and some of the others are the confidential informants and believe me, they're reliable. They burglarized Peters' mini-warehouses last night and got all the serial numbers you have in the search warrant."

Kramer looked at Lieutenant James and started laughing.

"Boy, Lieutenant, they're good! I have no problem with what they did and it'll be a pleasure to be the attorney for all those rogues. I've been studying cases that judges have overturned, that let criminals back on the street. Most of those cases have to do with technical matters and slick attorneys. No, I don't have a problem putting career criminals away, even if the

THE TWELVE JUDGES

guys bend the law a little. I'm here to stay Lieutenant."

As Kramer and James shook hands, Bill James said, "I better get the guys to sit surveillance on the warehouses and wait for that truck from Dallas."

Lieutenant James walked out to the other detectives who were lounging about and ordered, "Park, you and Murphy can use the "Good Time" van now. Let's start now. It's early, but I don't want to miss the bastard. Kramer will set up a schedule for relief."

As he turned and started back to his office, James stopped abruptly in front of Detective Davis. "Davis, I don't want any chips, whores, or girlfriends in that new van! Do you understand? None!"

Detective Davis gave Lieutenant James a disappointed look.

Later that evening, Lieutenant James finally left his office for the day. Since he was divorced now, he sometimes stopped at his favorite watering hole, the Rotary Table, for a little attitude adjustment before going home to his empty house.

The Rotary Table was the favorite hangout for oil patch people. Executives and salesmen of the oil industry used this bar for business and pleasure. In the past some multimillion-dollar oil deals had been made in the bar. Once the bar and restaurant were an old tin barn. It's tin roof and walls had been replaced many times during the years by Juan, the owner. It was the last piece of land owned by Juan's father. At one time Juan's father owned fifty acres of farmland around this location. Because of the construction of the Galleria Shopping Mall, the farmland became valuable and

Lt. Joe "Bill" Bradley

taxes were too high so Juan and his father sold the land and the money was split among eight kids. Juan kept the two acres with the barn.

Tacked on every wall and the ceiling were hundreds of businessmen's cards. Among the business cards was every type of paper money from every country in the world. The oilmen would come back from overseas with foreign money and Juan would staple the money on the walls. Bets were made all the time that Juan did not have a certain currency from a certain country. After bets were placed, Juan would point out the money and someone had to buy drinks for everyone.

Juan was the best informer Bill James ever had. He was also a friend. Juan did book a few football bets on the side each year, but James overlooked this. It was easy to turn his eyes the other way because Juan gave him accurate information. Besides, James left the arresting of bookies to the Vice Squad and knew if all Houston football betters were arrested at the same time, they would fill the Rice University stadium.

James parked at the front door of the Rotary Table and went inside. He walked to the bar but before he could even sit down and order, Juan had placed a J & B scotch and water in front of him.

"Hi, Cap", Juan said. "You're late today."

Juan always called Lieutenant James by the name Cap, the ex-con's term for those in authority. Juan had spent three years in the Texas Department of Correction for bookmaking.

"Juan, have your cook fix me some shrimp to take home in about 30 minutes."

THE TWELVE JUDGES

"Cap, you know no one can cook for you 'cept me," Juan stated as he headed towards the kitchen.

Several businessmen spoke to Lieutenant James while he sat at the bar. They all had a story to tell about how the cost of doing business was rising because of thieves and burglars and the EPA.

Shortly, Juan returned from the kitchen.

"Cap, your food is ready."

"Give me a double scotch this time," James told Juan. "Then cut me off."

Bill James finished his drink and made a move to leave. Juan carried the lieutenant's food and walked him to his car.

"I'm going fishing Saturday, how about comin' along? You work too much, Cap."

"Thanks, Juan. I'll call you if I can break loose."

James drove off headed home with a great shrimp dinner.

The next morning when he arrived at the factory, James learned that there had been activity at the mini-warehouses during the night. John Peters had unloaded boxes of stereo equipment and some rifles.

"Who's on surveillance this morning?" asked James.

Kramer said, "King, Watson and Johnson. I've been taking video film of the goings on."

"Everyone is on standby today", James told Kramer. "Tell the guys at the mini-warehouses to call as soon as the tractor trailer from Dallas pulls in."

Lieutenant James then went into his office and had his morning coffee. After he made a few phone calls, he thought to himself, "I've got to get me a good

Lt. Joe "Bill" Bradley

secretary; no one in this bunch knows how to make good coffee."

James called Chief Ladd, "Chief, stay loose today. It looks like we're going to get you on T.V. We got something good going down."

Chief Ladd talked fast, "Don't make a bust today, I've got a golf game with three oil men and I always pick up some good cash when I play these rich suckers."

James responded, "Well if you can't make it, I'll call the D.A.'s office. Maybe Jamie Owens will want to be on T.V. today".

The Chief exploded, "Damn you, this better be a good bust! Call me as soon as it goes down." Ladd slammed the phone down.

Lieutenant James came out of his office and called the detectives together.

"When we roll on this bust, the entrance and exit gates will probably be open, if not, Davis will unlock any gate that needs to be open. The place has an office opened during the day. When the tractor-trailer arrives, let the bastards load the stolen property, unless you want to load it later and I seriously doubt that you do. Washington, you take a pickup truck with Hancock."

"Why do I have to ride with Washington?" Hancock complained.

Washington complained, "Why do I have to ride with Hancock?"

Lieutenant James didn't bother to answer either one of them.

"Luna, you and Edwards take the other pickup truck. Park and Murphy will take the gray van."

THE TWELVE JUDGES

Murphy spoke up, "Lieutenant, you mad at us or something? Since the "Good Time" van's not here, can't I at least use a good car?"

Lieutenant James replied, "No, since the "Good Time" van is already at the mini-warehouse location, I want you to block the tractor trailer if it tries to leave. I don't want to use a good vehicle in case they decide to run."

"Oh Great!" said Murphy. "I get this damn case started, I get the damn "Good Time" van fixed up and now you want to get me run over by a damn eighteen wheeler! I guess this is payment for a job well done!"

Lieutenant James continued as if he hadn't heard the complaints from Murphy, "Kramer and Davis will be with me."

As Lieutenant James walked back into his office, he could still hear Murphy and Park bitching about having to use the old van.

At 11:00 a.m. Kramer, who had returned from surveillance, came into the lieutenant's office. "Lu, King just called on the radio. The tractor-trailer has arrived and is parked on the street by the warehouses."

James bolted to his feet, "Great! Tell the guys to get ready. It's time to move."

It looked like a flushed bunch of quails as the detectives headed for their vehicles.

When the caravan left the factory, Bill James called Detective King on the police radio, "Number 12 to 105."

"Number 105 to 12. Go ahead, Lu."

"Any activity?"

Lt. Joe "Bill" Bradley

"Yeah, Boss. Peters has arrived. He has three Mexicans loading the truck. The truck driver's just sittin' around."

"Good, we'll be there shortly. I'll contact you when we get a block away."

James set his mike down.

A block from the mini-warehouses, Lieutenant James picked up his police radio mike, "Number 12 to 105."

"Go ahead, Boss," answered King.

"Have they finished loading yet?"

"Getting close, Boss. I'll let you know."

"Number 12 to the rest of the units. Stay back until 105 tells us to move in. Follow me in."

The Lieutenant and his detectives parked in a shopping center parking lot two blocks away. There they sat waiting for King to give the go ahead.

"Number 105 to Boss, I mean 12," crackled the radio.

"Go ahead," answered James.

"They're closing the back of the truck; Peters is headed for his car."

"Take 'em!" announced Lieutenant James.

Screeching tires filled the air as the cars sped from the shopping center parking lot.

Lieutenant James was to be the first car in when they arrived at the mini-warehouses, but he was the last car.

As he pulled into the warehouses and got out of his car, he saw that John Peters had already been handcuffed.

Bill James headed towards Peters.

THE TWELVE JUDGES

"Mr. Peters, I do believe you are under arrest. We have a search warrant for your mini-warehouses and the tractor-trailer. Have any of my detectives told you of your rights."

"Yeah, I have, Lu," Hancock said. "I told him, he had the right to go to jail."

John Peters was very nervous as he spoke, "Lieutenant, I heard that the police will make deals, can we make a deal? I know a lot of policemen and people in the D.A.'s office."

Lieutenant James replied, "Sure! When you tell me how many stolen loads you shipped, and to whom, I'll give you the number of years you'll get in the joint. Kramer, put Peters in my car and read him his rights."

Detective Park came over to Lieutenant James, "Lu, the three Mexican boys aren't involved; they were hired only to load the trailer."

James told Park to call a uniform police patrol car and have the three Mexicans taken to the factory for statements, then they could be released.

"Be sure that Peters pays them," added James.

"I'll let the truck driver drive the tractor-trailer to the police compound with me," King offered. "The driver said this is his fifth trip and I know he wants to tell me more."

It appeared to Bill James that King had successfully convinced the truck driver to confess with dates and places. King was good at that type of persuasion.

After Kramer had placed John Peters in the Lieutenant's car, he took video pictures of the entire

Lt. Joe "Bill" Bradley

scene. By that time everyone was ready to head for the factory.

Once at the office, Detective Kramer got busy telling everyone what he needed for his report. When Kramer mentioned that the tractor-trailer would have to be unloaded and the contents inventoried, everyone turned from Kramer and became busy with their own paperwork.

"We'll inventory the contents!" James announced. "Everyone!"

As they groaned and headed for the police compound where the tractor-trailer was parked, Lieutenant James said, "The sooner you complete the inventory, the sooner I'll spring for drinks at the Rotary Table."

"Quit you're moaning," Hancock yelled. "I need a drink!"

John Peters was confessing so fast to Kramer that he had to slow Peters' talking. He could type fast but not fast enough to keep up with this canary. Along with his confessing, Peters kept asking for a deal, repeating, "Just let me pay everyone back. I'll return everything."

Lieutenant James returned to his office and called Chief Ladd.

"Chief, we made a hell of a bust. I have a tractor trailer full of stolen televisions, guns, and stereo equipment. If you get moving you can be on the ten o'clock news."

Chief Ladd was thrilled, "Great, I'll be right over."

Fifteen minutes later Ladd was banging on the door of the factory.

THE TWELVE JUDGES

Detective Edwards went to the door but did not unlock it, he only hollered. "Lu, you better come here."

James went to the door and looked out. There stood Chief Ladd and with him were T.V. reporters and cameras.

James thought, "Nice of the Chief to keep my group secret. I guess it's my fault. I should have told him to go to the police compound. Let me out, Edwards, but lock the door behind me and don't let anyone in!"

As Lieutenant James stepped outside, he said, "Chief, I told you I wanted no one to know about this group."

"Lieutenant, I told the reporters that one of your men accidentally stumbled onto a tractor trailer full of stolen T.V.'s and guns. I'll do the interview on T.V. Damn it! You know I need the publicity! I won't even mention your name or your group. O.K.?"

"Chief, take the reporters to the police compound. Some of my guys are unloading the truck. You be sure to tell my men to stay out of the T.V. pictures."

Ladd's face lit up as he waved his hand for the T.V. reporters and camera crews to follow him.

Lieutenant James went back inside and spoke with Kramer, "As soon as the inventory is complete, take the case to the District Attorney's office and file charges on John Peters. After you file charges, take a copy of the case to the Burglary and Theft Division. I'll make arrangements for them to do the follow-up work in Dallas. Tell all the guys to meet me at the

Lt. Joe "Bill" Bradley

Rotary Table when they're finished inventorying the truck contents. Tell them to bathe!"

Kramer laughed and went back to work.

At 9:45 p.m. Lieutenant James arrived at the Rotary Table. When he walked in, Juan met him at the door.

"Lieutenant, your detectives have been here since 8. They're really putting the drinks away, and on your tab!"

"That's O.K., Juan. Just make sure they also get something to eat before they pull out of here tonight."

Lieutenant James then joined his men. During the next couple of hours, everyone had a war story to tell that could top the previous one told. Hancock had brought his guitar so the singing followed, being led by Washington.

After another hour, James slipped away from the group and motioned to Juan, who walked the lieutenant to his car.

"Juan take care of the guys, I'll see you tomorrow."

James headed home thinking about his men. It was a job well done and this group was just getting started.

The next morning, when Lieutenant James arrived at his office at 8:00 a.m. Detective Kramer was the only person present.

"Get me a cup of coffee and come to my office, Kramer. I don't believe the rest of the troops will be here until noon. No telling what time they left the Rotary Table last night."

THE TWELVE JUDGES

When Joe Kramer had them both a cup of coffee, Bill James motioned him to a chair.

"Kramer, you really did a fantastic job on the paperwork. You know you're going to be swamped in paperwork working with these guys. The other detectives can do the legwork, but they just can't put it down in black and white for the D.A.'s office. I remember one time when Hancock busted a fence. His whole report including all the stolen items but the serial numbers were written on three matchbook covers. The D.A.'s office never got a report from Hancock and the fence pled guilty for ten years. I hope you don't mind helping guys with their paperwork?"

"No, Sir. I'll do anything for those guys. I'm really enjoying this assignment."

At that the phone rang, and when James answered he immediately recognized the caller. It was First Assistant District Attorney Jamie Owens. Without any pleasant conversation Owens cut to the chase.

"Kramer brought me the case on John Peters but something is wrong. I've never seen such a complete and airtight case come from a bunch of cops."

"Because Owens, you don't know how to police, we do."

Owens hesitated and then reluctantly said, "I only wanted to congratulate you on a fine job."

"Sure, thanks," countered Lieutenant James.

Owens then asked, "Who was the informer?"

Lieutenant James calmly replied, "That's confidential and you know it."

Lt. Joe "Bill" Bradley

Owens said, "I doubt if this case ever comes to trial! It's such a pat case. But, if it does, you'll have to reveal your informer to me. See you."

With that the phone line went dead. James turned to Detective Kramer, "Remind me to tell the guys never to trust Jamie Owens at the D.A.'s office. He'll take you in his trust and then stab you in the back!"

Lieutenant James leaned back in his chair and thought, "What a group. I wonder what crook is next. His ass will be sucking air when he finds out this bunch is on his case."

CHAPTER 5

CUB REPORTER

Evelyn Mixon slowed her new red sports Mazda almost to a stop as she drove over more than four pair of railroad tracks that crossed the street.

Dust settled on her car's freshly polished exterior as Evelyn parked on the side of the road. She needed to read the directions she had written on a pad to Lieutenant Bill James' Office. She brushed her long blond hair out of her eyes studying her hand drawn map.

Mixon was a police reporter for the Houston Post. Evelyn had graduated from the University of Houston with a degree in Journalism. She was young and inexperienced in her field.

The seasoned reporters at the paper teased her saying she was too cute and innocent to handle the police beat. She had taken a lot of harassment since she had gone to work for the Post.

Lt. Joe "Bill" Bradley

One day when she came to work, pictures of her when she was the Homecoming Queen at the University were pasted all over her office. Everyone watched as she took each picture down, autographed each picture, and handed them out, even giving one to the editor. She knew by this game she had been accepted.

Evelyn had received a tip that the Houston Police Department had a secret group. A lieutenant, who was creating headaches for the criminals in Houston, led the group.

Her source had been an officer in Public Relations for Chief Ladd.

Evelyn saw an old, dilapidated, one-story brick building across the street.

Most of the buildings in this area were boarded up or were old warehouses that were being used by companies to store their merchandise. Many were not in use and soon were to be torn down.

Down the street stood the old Union Railroad Station that was a beehive of activity during the Second World War. Now it stood empty as a monument to the glorious days of the train, waiting for some entrepreneur to revitalize it.

The building where she believed that Lieutenant James' office must be, looked like the city wasn't doing their job of condemning buildings and tearing them down.

The new buildings of Houston's skyline created a contrast from this vantage point.

Parked in the lot of this old building were several cars, but only one she recognized as an unmarked police sedan. The other cars were a mixture of cars including a wrecker and not one resembled a police car.

There was one new van parked at the building but the rest looked like they were ready for the junkyard.

Evelyn parked and walked toward the entrance of the building.

The door opened as she approached. A bearded man dressed in slacks and a white muscle shirt stepped out. His voice and message were to the point.

"What do you want? Are you lost, madam?"

"No, I am here to see Lieutenant James and it is to his advantage to see me," quipped Evelyn. Evelyn was nervous making such a comment. She had been with the newspaper such a short time and seen the old timers throw their weight around when they were looking for a story.

A tall man, in his fifties, stepped in front of the young man. He was in a gray business suit with a gray conservative tie. Evelyn noticed he was wearing black cowboy boots.

"Cop" was written all over his face and Evelyn knew that he must be Lieutenant James.

She had done her homework researching James before she decided to interview him.

Evelyn Mixon had learned from police personnel files that James had been with the department more than twenty years. He had been born in a small oil refinery town on the Texas Coast. He was the youngest of the clan.

A Christian father and mother, giving him insight into the values of life and the fair treatment of

Lt. Joe "Bill" Bradley

individuals, had raised him. There were no complaints from citizens about excessive force in his file.

Bill James had been a football hero in his hometown, which led to a sports scholarship at a university. He had earned a degree in Police Science.

Upon graduation from college, he entered the Houston Police Academy. This had been a life-long dream for James. He rose to the rank of lieutenant in a short time.

Evelyn Mixon had also gathered opinions about James from his fellow officers.

He was regarded as a "Policeman's Policeman."

Bill James had elected not to advance in rank, as he knew the higher ranked officers were administrators. James wanted to be a working, street cop.

James invited Evelyn Mixon into the building.

As she followed him to his office, she noticed that he walked with a slight limp in his left leg. Her research showed that two robbers at a convenience store shootout had wounded him. Evelyn moved to one side to look at his left ear. In the same encounter, the lower lobe of one ear had also been shot off, but his black and silver hair obstructed her view. James had killed both robbers.

James invited Evelyn Mixon into his office. In James' office, he pulled a chair up to the front of his desk for her. Evelyn felt dwarfed by his six foot three frame.

Bill James held the back of the chair as she sat down, and Evelyn Mixon realized that gracious Southern chivalry was obvious by his actions. Evelyn

THE TWELVE JUDGES

liked that; very few men nowadays even opened a door for her. She guessed the woman's movement did have some bad points.

Evelyn glanced around the room. None of the walls had the usual certificates and awards that most men displayed in their office. There was one picture on the wall. It was of a fisherman on a beach.

As Lieutenant James leaned forward, his face revealed a sturdy, authoritative look.

In his mind, James knew this young reporter wasn't here for a story about lawsuits against the City of Houston. He knew someone had leaked information about him and his group.

James knew a story would hurt what his group was trying to accomplish. He began the conversation by coming straight to the point.

"If it's an interview about me and what my group are doing, I'm going to give you an exclusive, but you will not use it until I say you can use it! You understand!"

James continued, "Write down a telephone number where you can be contacted at a moment's notice. You will get a story if you keep this meeting confidential."

Evelyn circled her pager number on her business card and handed the card to Lieutenant James.

James slipped the card into his police identification holder and said again, "Do you understand?"

Looking straight into Lieutenant James piercing blue eyes Evelyn found herself saying, "Yes, Sir." without any hesitation.

Lt. Joe "Bill" Bradley

She also found herself responding to the tone and manner of his authority as she once answered to her father. She knew she would not write a story until Lieutenant James told her she could.

James walked Evelyn Mixon to the door and returned to his office. He dialed Chief Ladd's private straight-line number.

Chief Ladd answered, "Randy, is that you? I can't play golf today. I've got a meeting with the surrounding chiefs. It's about why U.S. Immigration won't take all the illegals we arrest."

James said, "And you're surprised at what the Federal government won't do?

"James, what in the hell do you want? I guess you want some of the new police cars that just came in!"

"No, Chief, I want you to stop a leak in your Public Relations Office about my group. If you don't, I will."

James told the chief about the meeting with Evelyn Mixon, the Houston Post reporter.

Chief Ladd said, "Damn. I'll get on it right now. I've got some new people in that office and I guess I had better tell them the rules."

"Thanks, Chief. I'll send four guys over for four new cars."

Chief Ladd replied as he hung up his telephone, "You got all the cars you are going to get."

James leaned back in his chair and thought. "Damn! I'm glad that my two lover boy detectives were not in the office when the cute reporter came in."

CHAPTER 6

CHOO CHOO TRAIN VS FARM TRACTOR

Lieutenant James was looking over expensive jewelry that Detectives Bill Johnson and Frank Davis were signing into the evidence room at the factory.

The detectives had arrested a pawn shop owner for fencing stolen jewelry. They had ten Rolex watches and several diamond rings. They were completing their paperwork when Detective Albert King walked in wearing a full-length mink coat. It was 90 degrees outside.

"If you girls had a body like mine, you too could wear mink!" King bragged.

Everyone turned to look at him. Washington let go with a long "Hi ya, babe" whistle that really got everyone's attention.

Lt. Joe "Bill" Bradley

King pranced around opening and closing the mink coat like a seasoned flasher.

James couldn't keep the smile off his face and asked, "Where in the hell did you get that fur coat?"

King replied, "Lu, I have three more of these in the car. By the way Boss, do you remember Uncle Stevens? He's the bookie the Vice-Squad's been after for a long time?"

"Yeah, I know Uncle," answered James. "Does he still own a titty bar?"

"Yeah, the Golden Bar."

King removed the mink coat. His shirt was soiled with sweat and it ran down his nose making a trail on the floor as he approached James. "Well, I really got old Uncle uptight this time." King continued. "I did a favor for one of his dancers, an informer of mine. She called me and said Uncle had bought some stolen furs and he had them in his office."

Washington laughed with sarcasm said, "I bet you did the dancer a favor." Everyone agreed and the catcalls started.

King continued his story making gestures with his arms, "I walked right in on Uncle while he was makin' plans to sell the minks over the telephone. Strangest thing! After Uncle saw me, he decided since I was in his presence, he didn't want the furs. He got down on his knees and begged me not to arrest him. I thought he was going to kiss my ass! I didn't arrest Uncle, but I told Uncle that Burglary and Theft detectives would probably be in touch with him for a statement. If it's O.K. with you, I'm gonna' give this case to them, and tell 'em not to arrest Uncle.

THE TWELVE JUDGES

Something bigger came up involving that pimping, fencing bookmaker."

Still sweating profusely, King said, "The titty dancer met me later, away from the Golden Bar so I could pay her for her information."

As King continued, the catcalls started again and King, turning in a circle, indicated to all he was number one.

"She said that Uncle is fencing farm tractors and heavy equipment. There's a young guy from Richmond, Texas, who comes in twice a week to the bar. He spends a lot of money on the dancers and is always in a head huddle with Uncle in his office. She said that this guy's first name is Sonny; she's seen Uncle pay Sonny as much as $10,000.00 cash at one time."

Lieutenant James interrupted, "I've got a bulletin from the State Auto Theft Bureau; there's been a lot of heavy equipment stolen in the last few months and they don't have a lead on who's doing it. King, sounds like you might have the key to where the equipment is going."

King noticed that the other detectives had ceased teasing him and were interested in his story.

King asked, "Can't Park and Murphy work with me on this? You know we get more information from the telephones than anywhere else."

"They can," offered Detective Washington, "if you can keep them out of the titty joint."

"Park, you and Murphy get with King and come up with a plan," ordered Lieutenant James. "Then we'll all get together and finalize a plan. King

Lt. Joe "Bill" Bradley

take those furs to Burglary and Theft and tell them to stay away from Uncle until they hear from me."

As James turned toward his office, he overheard Frank Davis tell King, "Tell Lu, you need to send me into the titty bar to do some undercover work."

Bill Johnson spoke up, "If anybody goes undercover, it's gonna be me; I'm really good under covers or under sheets."

King shrugged his shoulders as he, Murphy and Park left the factory. They headed for the Golden Bar to find a location to tap Uncle's telephone. This was the "plan" the lieutenant ordered. As they were going out the door, Murphy looked at King and held his nose and said, "Man you really stink from all that sweat, I'll get you some deodorant from the van."

King, Murphy, and Park returned to the factory after looking over Uncle's club.

Bill James was telling the rest of the detectives to call it a day. When he saw King, Murphy and Park come in, he called to them.

"Let's hear from our totem pole climbers before we leave."

"Lieutenant," Murphy said. "We need $300.00. There's an old apartment complex directly behind Uncle's Golden Bar. The telephone pole that supplies the Golden Bar phone service is next to the apartments. We checked and there's an apartment we can rent that overlooks the rear of the Golden Bar."

"Sounds good to me," Lieutenant James said. "Come in the office and I'll give you $300.00 out of our expense money."

THE TWELVE JUDGES

Park spoke up, "Lieutenant, Murphy has already rented the apartment and it was only $200.00. He's trying to get to you."

"Is that right Murphy?" Bill James asked.

"Lu, Park is lying his ass off. He just wants to cause me trouble cause our mother-in-law loves me and hates his guts."

Lieutenant James knew this old game. It was played over and over again with the same detectives. This time Bill James was not going to play. He gave Murphy $400.00 and said, "Buy some cold drinks and snacks so the guys won't need to go out for food while they're doing surveillance. No liquor! Do you understand?"

"Sure, Lieutenant." replied Murphy.

Murphy was disappointed that he couldn't anger the lieutenant over the expense money.

James turned back to the group and said, "King, Murphy and Park will start the surveillance at the apartment. Kramer will make a schedule so everyone gets some time on the stakeout. Stay in touch; I'm going home."

Murphy drove out Memorial Drive that parallels Buffalo Bayou from the downtown area. He turned on South Shepherd passing River Oaks where the fat cats of Houston lived.

King remarked, "You think people living there worry about a pension?"

Not far from River Oaks lies a stretch of nightclubs and titty bars. Murphy pulled the van into the apartments. It was now dark. The apartments were two story apartments and were some of the first apartments built in Houston. They looked as if they were in their last days. The apartment complex was square with a swimming pool in the courtyard. Every apartment faced the swimming pool.

The three detectives got the necessary equipment from the van and went into the apartment, which was on the second floor.

An alley was between the apartment they had rented and the back door of the Golden Bar. All of the rear of the bar could be seen from the apartment window.

In the apartment Murphy said, "The lieutenant is gonna be pissed when he learns we didn't take the old van."

King asked, "Don't you need the Houston Telephone Company van to climb the telephone pole so no one will get suspicious?"

"Hell no!" said Murphy, "the telephone pole is just out side of the window. Park can climb the pole with his eyes closed."

An argument started between Murphy and Park to see who would climb the telephone pole. Park finally said, "O.K., call our telephone man and tell him the wires will be ready for him to hook up tonight."

Park grabbed a roll of telephone wire and headed out the door after putting his boot spikes on.

Murphy and King watched Park out the apartment window as he climbed the pole.

Murphy turned to King and said, "You know, its pitch black out there but I could swear Park shot us the bird."

"I really don't believe that Park is the kind to give us the finger," King responded sarcastically.

They both laughed.

THE TWELVE JUDGES

Murphy opened the window as Park came down from the telephone pole. He took the screen off the window and Park threw the roll of telephone wire over to Murphy.

"Did you call the telephone man?" asked Park.

Murphy replied, "Yes, madam, I followed your orders."

After Park returned to the apartment, the three sat drinking beer and watching T.V. They waited on the telephone man. A couple of hours later, there was a knock on the door. King opened the door and there stood an angry Rex, the telephone man.

When he spotted Murphy and Park, Rex grumbled, "The President's life had better be in danger. That's the only reason for me to come out at night."

"Come in Rex", said Murphy as he offered him a beer.

"Come to the window. See those two little wires going to that pole? All you have to do is hook 'em to the two little lugs going to the Golden Bar and I'll cover your tab in the titty bar for the rest of the night."

"Oh, no you don't!" Rex hissed. "Cover my tab now!"

Park said, "Pay the man. By the way Rex, I really thought I could find the right lugs without calling you tonight, but every business in the shopping center is in that box. You gonna' have to teach me better than you have."

Rex replied, "You're too dumb to learn how to find the right lugs. You're calling in life is to just to climb the poles, I'll do the rest."

Lt. Joe "Bill" Bradley

Murphy knew why the lieutenant had really given him the extra money. Murphy slipped Rex a $100 bill. When he finished his beer, Rex left the apartment. The detectives watched through the window as Rex climbed up the pole and climbed back down in a matter of just a few minutes.

"Did you see that?" remarked King. "He gave you the finger!"

Murphy hooked up a speakerphone to the wires, and they settled in for the night, drinking beer and watching the 10 o'clock news. There had been no activity from the tap except some of the dancers calling their clients.

One customer even told a dancer, "I told you not to call me at home!"

To which the dancer replied, "Oh hell, darling, I thought you were working late and this was your office number."

At 10:30 p.m. the Golden Bar's phone rang.

"This is Uncle, can I help you?"

"Uncle, this is Sonny."

"Sonny! Where is that video machine? You were supposed to deliver it yesterday!"

"You won't believe what happened," Sonny said. "Raymond had the video machine on a trailer and was delivering it. He ran a red light in Houston; a damn cop stopped him and put the bastard in jail for D.W.I. I didn't know he was drinking when he left me, believe me. I just got back from springing him out of jail. The cops didn't check the truck with the video machine on it. They left it on a side street and I had to send a wrecker for it. It'll be delivered tomorrow night for sure."

THE TWELVE JUDGES

"It better be delivered tomorrow night or your fee will be cut!" Uncle threatened.

"It will," Sonny promised. "Tell Cheri and Princess to keep their bodies hot, I'll be in soon to watch them dance."

The phone conversation ended and King said, "Damn! Who is Sonny? Who is Raymond? Is Uncle in the video game business?"

Park said, "Kramer can find the D.W.I. arrest tomorrow and that'll tell us who Raymond is."

Murphy, Park and King listened to the Golden Bar's phone until 2 a.m. All they heard were men calling to make dates with the strippers after closing time. When the three detectives left, they wrote Johnson, Luna, and Watson a note summarizing the night's happenings. The second team was to take up surveillance at 10:00 a.m.

As the alarm clock shattered the quiet at 8:00 a.m., King sleepily dialed the factory. He knew Kramer would be there early.

"City of Houston Complaint Department," answered Kramer.

"Shit, Kramer! You don't have to be that formal, it's me, King."

"How come you're not at work?" taunted Kramer.

"Kramer, listen to me. Two days ago there was an arrest of a subject by the name of Raymond for D.W.I. I don't know if Raymond is a first or last name. The police left his truck and trailer on the street. Kramer, find that case and then call me at home. I think I know the bastard that was arrested."

Lt. Joe "Bill" Bradley

King crawled back under the covers and had just fallen asleep when his phone rang.

"King, I found your case. Robert Raymond was arrested for D.W.I. The arresting officer called Games, Inc. about the truck Raymond was driving. Raymond was pulling a trailer with a farm tractor. Games, Inc. told the officer that Raymond worked for them and they came and picked up the truck, trailer and farm tractor. Raymond is an ex-con."

"Kramer, you're a sweetheart! I'll be down as soon as I shower. Would you start a background on Games, Inc.? Get everything you can on them."

When Detective King arrived at the factory, Lieutenant James, Kramer, and the other guys were in a head huddle.

When Murphy saw King he said, "Uncle and Sonny weren't talking about video machines last night. They were using video machines as their code words. They were talking about a tractor."

"I realize that now," said King. "I know Raymond; he's a heavy equipment thief. I thought he was still in the joint. I put him there four years ago."

Kramer had all the information on Games, Inc. and Robert Raymond.

Lieutenant James said, "King, here's the address on Games, Inc. The business is in Richmond. Take some of the men and go see if you can locate the truck with the farm tractor. If you can, get the make, model and serial number of the tractor, set up surveillance so we can follow it to where it's being sold."

THE TWELVE JUDGES

An argument began as to which detectives were going to the field and who had to stay at the factory, leaving James to make the assignments.

"Kramer, you and Watson stay here in the office. Luna, you and Johnson go to the apartment and keep me informed about Uncle. King, you, Murphy and Park take a van. Davis, you and Edwards take a pickup truck. Hancock and Washington also take a pickup."

Hancock looked at Washington and mumbled, "Shit!"

"Hancock will run the show until the truck with the tractor moves," continued James. "If the truck and tractor move, call me and I'll join you. This will give us enough vehicles to follow them."

The detectives left the factory on their way. Richmond, Texas was located just outside Houston. Hancock and his group located the address of Games, Inc. There among the other trucks of the business, was a Games, Inc. truck with a trailer loaded with a farm tractor.

Hancock picked up the mike to his police radio and announced to the other vehicles, "This is 101, we scored! The farm tractor is on the back parking lot. We're going to find a spot to park and hide. Do the same with the van. The rest of you stay away from this location until you hear from me."

Trucks from Games, Inc. came and went all day carrying pinball and video machines. No one approached the truck with the tractor.

At 6:30 p.m. an employee locked the back gate where the truck and tractor were stored and all the employees seemed to be leaving for the night. There

Lt. Joe "Bill" Bradley

was only a new white Oldsmobile left in the parking lot.

At 7:45 p.m. a young, white male came out and went to the Oldsmobile.

Hancock called, "101 to 109. Murphy, get a picture of that guy. I bet he's Charles Stockton. He's supposed to be the owner of Games Inc."

Murphy snapped a few pictures using a night scope before the Oldsmobile left.

Hancock once again spoke over his police radio. "Park, now it's your turn, see if you can get inside the truck yard and get the serial number of that tractor."

"O.K., I'm gone," answered Park.

Park got out of the van and ran across a vacant field to the truck yard. Park then went over the fence.

Murphy remarked, "Park went over that fence like some husband was after him."

Hancock could see Park's pin light turn on and off. He watched Park climb the fence again and run back to the van.

When he got in the van, Hancock called over the radio. "109, did you get the serial number?"

"Hell no! I couldn't find it," answered Park.

Murphy started to laugh but Park hit him in the stomach.

"Call Kramer at the factory and see if anyone knows where the damn serial number is located on a John Deer tractor!"

Just as Hancock picked up the radio mike Park shouted, "Hold it! A pickup just pulled in at the gate to the truck yard."

THE TWELVE JUDGES

The detectives peered through the dark night trying to see. Murphy got the night scope and started taking pictures. Over the radio, King said, "That looks like Robert Raymond. It is that son-of-a-bitch!"

Robert Raymond unlocked the gate and drove his pickup into the yard. He walked straight to the tractor. After making sure that the tractor was secure, Raymond climbed into the cab and started the truck.

As he drove toward the gate a white Oldsmobile pulled into the truck lot and Charles Stockton stepped from the driver's side. He and Robert Raymond talked for a few minutes.

Raymond then returned to the truck with the tractor and drove outside the lot onto the street.

Charles Stockton got into his Oldsmobile and stopped behind Raymond's truck.

Raymond then locked the gate, got into the truck and drove off. Stockton followed in his Oldsmobile.

Hancock turned to Washington and said, "It looks like Stockton is going to make sure of the delivery tonight. That's great! We'll bust him right along with Raymond."

Hancock picked up the police radio mike, "101 to all units, they're moving. I'll let you know what route they take."

Then Hancock called the factory, "101 to Base 12."

Kramer answered. "Base 12 to 101, go ahead."

"101 to Base 12, they're moving. They're headed North toward Houston on old Highway 90."

"Base 12 to 101, clear. I'll tell the lieutenant and we'll join you."

Lt. Joe "Bill" Bradley

"101 to all units. Did you hear where they're headed?"

"Clear."

Hancock hearing the two clear responses said, "Can't you use your damn radio numbers?"

Washington spoke up, "Shit, Hancock! Why should they, we're the only ones on this radio frequency."

Robert Raymond drove out of Richmond over the Brazos River headed for Houston.

Hancock said, "Now, there's one bad river! It starts in central Texas at Waco and by the time it gets here, it's really churning. Several people drown in that river every year."

A few miles out of Richmond, the truck with the tractor turned to Highway 59 headed north. Highway 59 runs through Houston as a freeway.

Just before the downtown area, Lieutenant James' voice crackled over the radio.

"12 to 101."

"101 to 12, go ahead."

"101, what is your location?"

"Lu, we're on 59 headed north at the downtown exit."

"Good 101. I'll be with you in a minute."

"Lu, one crook is driving the truck pulling the trailer with the tractor and the other crook is following him in a white Oldsmobile; license number X-Xray, N-Nora, S-Sam, 531."

"Number 12, Clear."

Murphy waved to Lieutenant James when he caught up with the caravan.

THE TWELVE JUDGES

Over his radio, Lieutenant James said, "I see the truck up ahead Washington, it looks like they're taking 59 north out of Houston, pass them and stay in front. If they turn off, we'll let you and Hancock know."

"106 to number 12, clear, and that license plate I gave you registers to a Charles Stockton."

"And don't use our radio numbers anymore," James said over the police radio.

Kramer was riding with the lieutenant and spoke up, "What about Federal communication rules, you're supposed to use your radio numbers at all times."

"Screw the Feds!" Lieutenant James growled. "Do you see any Feds around?"

Kramer sank into his seat and became very quiet.

Bill James and his detective followed Charles Stockton and Robert Raymond for the next hour. Fifty miles from Houston, in a small East Texas town, Washington broke in over the police radio.

"Lieutenant, they have their turn signals on to take a left, I'm going on through the town and turn around."

James responded, "Clear, we're going to drop back. Edwards, since you look natural in a pickup, take a left with the bastards but stay far enough behind them so you won't get burned. Keep us informed."

"Clear, Lieutenant. We're on them. Boss, they're headed out Farm Road 1091. They're slowing down for some railroad tracks. Hey boss, they stopped on the railroad tracks for some reason. I guess they have to piss. We're gonna pull over with our lights out

Lt. Joe "Bill" Bradley

and wait a few minutes to just watch. Shit! Boss! Both are out looking under the trailer with flashlights. Oh crap! I believe the stupid bastards have stuck the damn lowboy trailer on the railroad tracks!"

Hancock broke in, "Just our luck, the idiots don't know how to drive a lowboy over railroad tracks."

Edwards broke in over the radio very excited.

"Lu, they've unhooked the trailer from the truck and are runnin' around like two chickens with their heads cut off! Shit, Lieutenant! I know why they are so excited. Look north. There's a light swinging back and forth coming down the railroad tracks. There's a damn train coming!"

Detective Edwards watched as Stockton and Raymond jumped into the white Oldsmobile and the Games, Inc. truck. They drove off at a high rate of speed leaving the trailer and tractor on the railroad tracks.

"Oh Shit! I can see the light on the train!" Edwards hollered. "Lu, the son-of-bitches have left the trailer on the railroad tracks!"

Lieutenant James and the others heard a train whistle break the silence of the night.

Detective Edwards held his police mike out the window and pushed the button to open it to the police airwaves. The damnedest crash you have ever heard came over the police radio.

Edwards was to say later that when the train hit the trailer and tractor, the train didn't budge one inch. The train threw the trailer and tractor off into a creek bed. He also said that it took the train over a mile to stop.

THE TWELVE JUDGES

No one had been hurt on the train but it definitely interfered with justice that night.

Lieutenant James made an anonymous telephone call to Texas Highway Patrol about the accident and then over the police radio said, "There will be another time. These thieves aren't going to stop. Everyone report to the factory tomorrow afternoon at one."

All the way back to Houston, Washington made sounds like a train whistle over the police radio ending with a distress whistle and the sound of a crash.

James stopped for lunch at the Rotary Table the next afternoon before going to work.

"Juan, before I leave, I need to talk with you."

"O.K. Cap, as soon as I get the oil field brass squared away, I'll have a drink with you."

Juan returned in a few minutes and pulled up a chair.

"What do you need, Cap?"

"It's about Uncle. I'm into his business, not his bookie business, but—."

"Into his clothes buying," Juan broke it. "Cap, I've told you before, Uncle buys a lot of stolen suits, furs and expensive woman's clothes. Bust that sorry old pimp and my bookie business will pick up."

Lieutenant James laughed and then asked. "What is Uncle's connection with Charles Stockton? Do you know Charles Stockton?"

"Yeah, I know the little squirt. I have two of his video machines in my place. I didn't know he was connected with Uncle. He comes in here sometimes. He can't keep his hands off of my waitresses. Charles is from a very political family that has strong ties in

Lt. Joe "Bill" Bradley

Austin. His father puts pressure on the club owners through the liquor board to use his son's machines. I get good service on my machines, but I would sure like to whip the creep's ass. Why do you ask? I'm sorry Cap, you've told me before, you ask the questions, I answer questions."

"Thanks for the lunch Juan, I'll see you later."

When Lieutenant James returned to his office, he made a few phone calls while waiting for his men to arrive.

Detective Kramer was the first one to report to work.

"Lieutenant, the lowboy trailer and farm tractor were reported stolen from Galveston County. The Highway Patrol asked why I wanted to know about the tractor and I told them I had heard about the train wreck. Luna and Johnson are still at the apartment. They said they would stay there awhile. I think they're enjoying listening to the girls talk to their dates. They've got a lot of information on stolen clothes to give to the Burglary and Theft Division when this thing is over."

"O.K. but let 'em stay on Uncle's line. Tell the other guys to go about their regular business. Tell them also to keep in close contact with you in case we hear from Luna and Johnson."

Lieutenant James spent most of the afternoon filling out a questionnaire from the police Planning and Research Division. They wanted to know how much stress was involved in making an arrest and how it affected the officers in their home life. More bullshit.

THE TWELVE JUDGES

At about 4:00 p.m., Detective Washington, followed by Hancock, came into the factory. Both were shouting at each other.

Kramer came running into the Lieutenant's office and said, "You better come out here. Hancock called Washington a dumb ass nigger and Washington told Hancock that he was lower than white trash cheating in a dice game at the welfare office."

Bill James got up from his desk and walked out where Washington and Hancock were shouting at each other.

"Settle down, both of you. I have enough trouble with Chief Ladd! Do I have to listen to you two? What the hell is wrong with you?"

Washington spoke first, "I made a mistake and let Hancock drive. Lu, you know, I've been after Ivory, the numbers con man, for a long time. I had him today, and Hancock blew it."

Ivory was a black man who knew numbers better than the math professors at the University of Houston. Ivory ran a numbers game. His customers were mostly blacks who played the wheel, a lottery game, spending nickels, dimes and quarters. Every day Ivory went around picking up the day's plays and money. At the end of the day, Ivory gave out the winning numbers. Ivory cleared ten thousand dollars every week. His clients said he was an honest gambler. The only honest thing about Ivory was that he let a few win each day.

Calmly Lieutenant James said, "Washington, tell me what happened."

"I let Hancock drive today," Washington began. "He kept bugging me that he was a better

Lt. Joe "Bill" Bradley

driver than me. He's not! We followed Ivory to ten different stops where he picked up money and bets from his runners. Ivory was in his pickup. He keeps two washtubs in the bed of his truck that he puts the day's coins and bets in. The tubs were full of coins. When Ivory drove to his last stop over in the Third Ward you know, the black area, Hancock got too close. I told Hancock a white guy, driving a pickup in the Ward would stand out like me at a KKK meeting. He wouldn't listen. Ivory spotted us. Do you know what the bastard Ivory did?"

"How do you think the lieutenant would know? The lieutenant wasn't there, ass-hole," Hancock smirked.

Lieutenant James said, "Go on, Washington."

Trying his best not to cuss, Washington continued his account. "The sidewalks were full of black brothers and sisters. When Ivory spotted us, he took a washtub of coins and dumped 'em in the middle of the street. Coins went everywhere! Brothers and sisters came from everywhere! They blocked the street picking up coins. Fights broke out. We were blocked off! I told Hancock to run over the bastards, but he just sat there!"

"Lieutenant," Hancock said, "There were 200 people in the middle of the street! I wasn't gonna drive through them, they would have probably hung my white ass."

"Both of you settle down. There'll be another time for Ivory," James concluded. "From now on, Washington will do the driving when you're in the Ward. If he drives through a crowd of people and even

THE TWELVE JUDGES

bumps one person, Hancock, I'll personally give you the rope the courts will need to hang both of you."

Lieutenant James went back into his office followed by Kramer. "Lieutenant, don't you think you should separate Washington and Hancock?"

Lieutenant James turned to Kramer and said, "Kramer, you can't see it, but those two worship each other. I would hate to be the person who messed over one of them. The other one would take that person for a ride, a one way ride to the bottom of the ship channel."

Kramer left the office shaking his head.

Another day passed and there was still no word from Luna and Johnson about stolen heavy equipment. The surveillance at the apartment on the phone hookup was getting long and boring.

At 4:00 p.m. Luna called Kramer from the apartment. "We missed one delivery. Charles Stockton called Uncle and told him about the tractor being hit by a train. Charles really got a kick out of telling Uncle the story. Also, they must have picked up another farm tractor and delivered it. That's not all, Stockton told Uncle that he had a large video machine already loaded and was going to delivery it tonight. He didn't say what time."

After Kramer spoke with Luna, he told Lieutenant James what Luna had said.

"Call all the guys," ordered James. "Tell them to set up surveillance on Games, Inc. If they move something tonight and Charles Stockton is with the load, we're going to take them down."

Kramer left the lieutenant's office and informed the detectives who were present. He then contacted the others by radio and informed them of the same orders.

King, Murphy and Park were in the van when they received Kramer's radio transmission, and they headed immediately for Richmond.

When they arrived at their surveillance location, Park said, "Look at that, will you?"

King picked up the police mike and said, "105 to Base 12."

Kramer answered, "Base 12 to 105. Go ahead."

"Tell the lieutenant that a bulldozer is loaded on a lowboy and is parked in the Games Inc. yard."

"105, we copy. Lu said to stay with the bulldozer! We're checking with the State Police to see if we can find a recent stolen report."

"This is 105. Can you also find out where the serial number is located for a D-9 Cat bulldozer?"

"Base 12, clear."

"King, you think Park can find the serial number this time?" Murphy asked.

"If you think you're so damn good," Park snapped back, "tonight you can get the damned serial number yourself."

"I'm just kidding, Park. I could never make it over the fence."

Thirty minutes slowly passed as King, Murphy and Park played Mexican dominoes in the rear of the van.

"Base 12 to 105."

"105 to Base 12, go ahead Kramer."

"Don't use my name on the air! Can you copy a serial number?"

THE TWELVE JUDGES

"Yes, Creamer."

"Base 12, It's 7 B-Boy, C-Charles, 1-4-8-9."

"105 clear, I got it."

"Base 12 to 105. Please repeat the number so I will know you have it right. This is a serial number of a bulldozer that has been reported stolen from Brazoria County."

"105 to Base 12. The number is 7 B-Bastard, C-Crap, 1-4-8-9."

"Base 12 clear, the serial number is located on the right side of the engine next to the dip stick."

"105 clear, Ms. Creamer."

As the other detectives arrived on the scene, they contacted the guys in the surveillance van. By sunset everyone was at their assigned positions.

Games, Inc. closed their operation at 5:30 p.m. and Charles Stockton left in his white Oldsmobile. As soon as it was dark, Park got out of the van and climbed the fence. He was in the yard checking the bulldozer for just a few minutes when he ran back to the fence climbed over running at full speed to the van.

"That's the stolen bulldozer," Park announced. "The serial number Kramer gave us matched! We're going to bust their asses tonight!"

Just like a rerun of the previous surveillance, Robert Raymond pulled up to the Games Inc. yard, got out, opened the gate and parked his pickup truck.

Robert Raymond started the truck that was hitched to the lowboy with the stolen bulldozer on it and drove out the gate and parked on the street. Raymond then got out of the truck and locked the gate. Once back in the truck, he drove through Richmond and started out Highway 90 toward Houston.

Lt. Joe "Bill" Bradley

King said over the police radio, "105 to all units, he's moving, but the white Oldsmobile is not with him. He's headed north on Highway 90 by himself."

As the truck and lowboy drove over the Brazos River, Robert Raymond pulled the truck over onto the side of the highway. White clouds of steam rose from under the hood of his truck.

King moaned, "What the hell is going to happen this time! The last time it was a damn train, this time it looks like his radiator or water hose blew up."

King got on the police radio and said, "105 to Base 12. The truck with the bulldozer has broken down. Advise, Lu."

Lieutenant James responded, "12 to 105. Since you know Robert Raymond, take him down. Maybe being an ex-con, and the fact that you know him, he might talk with you. After you bust him, bring him to the office. Have the truck and bulldozer picked up by a wrecker. Just you three bust him. There's no use in him seeing the other guys at this time."

"105 to 12, clear. 105 to all, did you read the lieutenant?"

"Clear."

"Clear."

As King drove up behind the lowboy, he said, "I'll stay here in the van. Ya'll walk up like you want to help Raymond. If Raymond sees me, he'll run like a rabbit."

Murphy and Park got out of the van and walked up to Raymond where he was standing in front of the truck.

THE TWELVE JUDGES

As Raymond saw them approach he grumbled, "I don't need your help. Get your ass out of here!"

Murphy replied, "Gee, Mister, you sure sound bad."

Before Robert Raymond knew what happened, he was on the ground and handcuffed.

Raymond screamed, "What the hell's going on? Are you cops? I'm just delivering this bulldozer for someone. The papers are in the truck."

Raymond was face down on the ground. As Park rolled him over, Raymond looked up into the face of King.

"Oh shit! I have nothing to say to you, King. You're not going to pin this one on me. Not this time!"

King reached down and picked Raymond up by his collar and placed him on his feet.

"Pin what on you, you thieving bastard? Let's me and you go to the van and talk quietly for awhile."

King turned to Murphy and Park.

"I'll call for a wrecker from the van. Let me talk to this bastard alone for a few minutes."

King took Raymond and put him in the van. Murphy and Park could hear King questioning over the noise of the passing traffic.

"Raymond, you thieving son-of-a-bitch. You're going to tell me how many pieces of heavy equipment you've stolen, where you delivered the equipment and who's involved with you."

"Screw you, King! The last time I talked with you, I went to jail!"

Lt. Joe "Bill" Bradley

King stuck his head out the van window and hollered to Murphy and Park, "I called for a wrecker for the truck and lowboy. I'll be right back."

King drove off leaving Murphy and Park standing beside the highway.

He drove down the highway to a crossover and made a U-turn. He headed back toward Richmond and turned off just before the Brazos River Bridge. This was a turn-a-round for the highway that went under the bridge and next to the river. At this point the river was 40 feet deep with steep banks that suddenly dropped to the river.

King parked the van by the river and got out and opened the back door of the van. Searching through a drawer in the cabinets of the van he pulled out a long rope.

"I knew Murphy and Park outfitted this van with everything," he mumbled to himself.

Raymond was watching King silently but when he saw the rope he cautiously asked, "What are you going to do?"

"Shut up!" King growled. "I should hang you. Too bad you're not a horse thief or I would hang you. Believe me; I'm not going to lay a hand on you."

King went around to the side of the van and pulled Raymond out. He was still handcuffed. King took Raymond down to the bank of the Brazos River.

The Brazos River is one of the longest, fastest moving, rivers in Texas and the water is the color of melted chocolate ice cream. At this point the river waters surged and swirled as they hit the pilings of the highway bridge. The pilings also created huge whirlpools.

THE TWELVE JUDGES

Raymond was still handcuffed when King took him down to the bank of the Brazos River. The only noise was the river's water hitting the piers that supported the highway bridge. With no moon it was deathly dark under the bridge.

King took a small pencil like flashlight from his pocket and turned it on placing it into his mouth. Now he could use both hands with what he was going to do.

King found a huge oak tree next to the riverbank. He tied one end of the rope around the trunk of the tree and then walked over to Raymond and tied the other end around Raymond's waist. King then took the handcuffs off Raymond.

Taking the pen light from his mouth King asked, "Raymond, are you going to talk with me about the stolen equipment?"

"Shit on you!" Raymond replied. "I know better than to talk to you. I'm not going to the joint again. I'm smarter now."

King spun Raymond around so that Raymond faced the river with King in back of him. King raised his right foot placing it on Raymond's butt. King gave Raymond a hefty push with his foot and Raymond slid down the muddy river bank. The rope gave a twang as Raymond hit the water. As the swirling water took Raymond under, King pulled on the rope and Raymond surfaced gasping for breath.

King called down, "Now you want to talk? Ass-hole?"

Raymond shook his head and cussed King as his arms splashed the water trying to get back to the bank. Raymond finally made it back to the bank and he tried to climb the muddy slope. King kept the rope tight as Raymond clawed his way up the bank. Just as Raymond was clawing for the top of the river bank, King let go of the rope and Raymond slid down the mud bank back into the muddy water. Raymond tried to scream as a giant whirlpool took him under.

King really had to tug on the rope to get Raymond to the surface. Raymond came up spitting water and let out a scream that King thought could be heard in Houston. King let go of the rope again and Raymond was pulled under by the swirling waters.

After the fourth time under the waters, Raymond surfaced coughing and begging, "Pull me up, please pull me up. I'll talk to you."

King had to use the tree for support as he pulled Raymond up the muddy bank. King let Raymond sit down for a few minutes to catch his breath.

"See there, I didn't lay a hand on you," King said. "You're going to tell everything you know on the trip back to Houston or you're going swimming again. The next time the rope might break and you won't come up until you have floated down the river to the Gulf of Mexico and the crabs are eating on you."

King remarked, "Damn you stink, did you shit in your pants."

Raymond's only reply was "No, Sir!"

After placing handcuffs back on Raymond, King put him in the van.

King then pulled onto Highway 90. A mile up the road he saw Murphy and Park at the truck and lowboy. A large wrecker was hooking onto the front of the truck.

THE TWELVE JUDGES

King turned to Raymond and said, "Just remember, you slipped and fell into a ditch."

"Yes, Sir" Raymond replied.

As King pulled along side of the detectives, Park screamed, "Where in the hell have you been?"

"Been fishing," King calmly answered. "Get in and get your pad out. Raymond wants to talk to you."

As Park slid back the van door, he saw a muddy, dripping wet Robert Raymond. Raymond hadn't even bothered to wipe the wet hair from his face. Park screamed, "My van, my pretty van! What have you done? You can't put that filthy son-of-a-bitch in my van, he stinks!"

"Get your ass in and start writing," snapped King. "I want all Raymond knows before we get back to the factory."

Murphy and Park climbed into the van and both began to holler at King about the mud.

"King, you're gonna' clean my van when we get back. If you ruined the carpet it's gonna' cost you. The seat that Raymond is on will have to be thrown away."

"Oh crap", King replied, "you made this van too pretty for working cops anyway, now get with it, Raymond wants to talk to you."

Park looked at Robert Raymond and said, "How many tractors have you stolen."

Raymond started talking. While he talked, every so often he would glance at King who was driving. Raymond told how he and Charles Stockton had been stealing all types of heavy equipment on orders from Uncle. He said it all started over a year ago when Stockton got in trouble with Uncle betting

Lt. Joe "Bill" Bradley

on football games. Stockton owed Uncle $50,000.00. Stockton paid Uncle off the first three months stealing and selling heavy equipment. Uncle found buyers for them.

Murphy asked, "You've told us about 40 pieces of equipment, now where did you deliver them?"

Raymond said, "I can tell you where every piece was sold, except 5 pieces."

"Why can't you tell us about the 5 pieces?"

Raymond became very nervous and again glanced at King. He hesitantly answered, "A county commissioner's buddy is a Sheriff. He has the five pieces. If I tell you, I'm dead! They have connections. They'll have me killed."

King came to a crossover on Highway 90 and made a sharp U-turn. "I guess its back to the river."

"I'll tell you! I'll tell you. Just keep that crazy King away from me!" Raymond pleaded.

Murphy put his hand on Raymond's muddy shoulder and softly said, "Raymond, I don't know what King did to you and I don't condone how the asshole works, but I don't think I can stop him. I not only think, but I know the bastard is crazy!" Murphy lit a cigarette and handed it to Raymond.

Murphy reached over and put his hand on King's shoulder and said, "King, stay off Raymond's back! He wants to talk with me. Raymond, let's move to the back of the van, away from these two bastards."

As Raymond and Murphy moved to the rear of the van, the only thing Park could utter was, "Shit, shit, shit! Look at that mud. You're ruining my van seats!"

King smiled and came to a crossover, made a U-turn and headed for Houston.

THE TWELVE JUDGES

King and Park could not hear Raymond and Murphy talking but they knew Murphy was getting a lot of information.

When they arrived in Houston, they parked the van in front of the factory and went inside. Lieutenant James and several detectives were waiting for them.

James saw Robert Raymond and his muddy wet clothes. "What in the hell happened to you?"

King spoke up, "He fell into the ditch along the side of the highway, tell the Lu, Raymond."

"That's what happened, Sir."

King said, "I'll let him take a shower and put on some of my coveralls. Lu, he's cooperating with us. He's going to give us one hell of a written statement. Aren't you Raymond?"

Raymond simply nodded his head and remained silent.

Lieutenant James didn't ask anymore questions about Raymond's appearance. Instead he turned and said, "King, give me a run down of what took place. Kramer, call the other guys and tell them to come in."

As the other detectives crowded around to listen, King related what had taken place and the information that Raymond had given them. That is, King told everything but he accidentally forgot about Raymond's swim in the Brazos River.

Bill James turned to Kramer, "Take a detailed written statement from Robert Raymond. Don't let him use a phone at this time. Murphy set up a phone so we can make some tape recordings. These will be legal so I want the best recordings possible. After Raymond gives his statement, we'll get him to call Charles Stockton and set up a meeting with him so we

Lt. Joe "Bill" Bradley

can bust him. It appears that there are several different locations where the stolen heavy equipment has been sold. We're going to need more manpower. I want to hit all the locations we can at one time without any warnings. I'll call Captain Sims of the Texas Rangers. His credentials read, "The State of Texas." They can team up with us and then we can go anywhere."

Murphy returned with a freshly washed Robert Raymond.

Kramer held out his hand and said to Raymond, "Sir, I'm Detective Kramer. I'll be the one taking your statement."

Raymond just nodded his head yes and followed Kramer into an office. As Kramer closed the door to his office, everyone heard, "Mr. Raymond, have you been given your rights?"

Park had been taking a drink of coffee when he heard Kramer's question to Raymond, and choked on his coffee spitting it on three detectives sitting nearby. As the whole room erupted in laughter, Lieutenant James retreated to his office.

After an hour, Kramer came into the lieutenant's office with a twenty page typed statement.

Bill James read the statement. "Very good! It's already 3:00 a.m. so take Raymond over to District Judge Andrews' home so he can officially be given his rights. This is too good of a case not to wake the judge up. Have Raymond sign his statement in front of the judge. Better yet, take King, Murphy, and Park with you in case Raymond balks. I'll call ahead and wake the judge. Give a copy of Raymond's statement to Luna. He can determine the locations where the stolen heavy equipment is located. Since we've made our

THE TWELVE JUDGES

move on this case, we should just as well stay up and finish it."

As Kramer left the lieutenant's office with his orders, James walked out of his office and announced to the remainder of his detectives, "Go home and kiss your wives. You'll be busy for a few days. We're going to run with this case until we finish it! Be back here at the factory by 10 a.m. for a meeting. Get some rest if you can."

The detectives left the factory and Lieutenant James went back into his office to wait for Kramer and the others.

Kramer, King, Murphy, and Park came back to the office after taking Robert Raymond to the judge. They stopped by the police booking office on their way to the factory and placed Raymond in jail. Orders were given to the jail not to let Raymond make any calls at this time.

Lieutenant James said, "You three can run home and clean up. I've called a meeting for 10:00 this morning."

Kramer said, "Lieutenant, I've already called my wife and I've got more paper work to do. I'm going to stay here."

Murphy and Park both said they were going home to change clothes. After they left, Lieutenant James told Kramer, "I'm going to stretch out on the couch for awhile, wake me a 9."

James turned on his radio to some 50's music and quickly fell into a deep sleep.

At nine o'clock, Kramer came in with a cup of coffee, "Lieutenant, some of the men are here and there are two Texas Rangers here also."

Lt. Joe "Bill" Bradley

Lieutenant James took a fresh shirt from the closet in his office and went back to shower and shave. When he finished, he walked out and saw Captain Bert Sims of the Rangers sitting comfortably in James' chair.

Sims was a tall, lanky Texan who wore a western cut suit. His white western hat bore no feathers. You didn't wear feathers in your hat if you worked for Captain Sims. In fact, if you worked for Captain Sims, your clothes had better be neat and your boots shinned and your belt better have an emblem of the Texas Rangers.

"Bill, you didn't tell me much on the phone. I do hope you have a lead on the stolen heavy equipment. What are you into this time?"

"Good morning Bert. I want you to read a statement from a crook we arrested last night."

Sims moved to the couch as James handed him the written statement given by Robert Raymond.

As Captain Sims read the statement, Bill James busied himself with his own paperwork.

When Sims finished reading he said, "Son-of-a-bitch! Robert Raymond mentions a commissioner in Monty County. I bet I know which one."

"I thought you would like to go on this bust with me." James baited.

"You bet I want to go, you couldn't stop me! What about the other locations? It's going to take more than one day to round up all the stolen equipment."

"If it meets with your approval," suggested Lieutenant James, "I'll team your men up with mine and they can handle the different locations where the stolen equipment is located. Can you and your men get started this morning?"

"I'd insist on it!" Sims said.

Lieutenant James and Captain Sims walked to the large room where the detectives and Rangers were talking, and called for silence.

"After we give you your assignments, report back by radio or telephone to Kramer with descriptions of the pieces of equipment you have recovered. I'm sure the buyers of the stolen equipment will return it when they understand that they could go to jail. If they won't release the equipment and you have any problems, bring the S.O.B.'s to jail. Kramer will then draw up a search warrant to seize the property."

After the men were given their assignments they left, except Murphy, Park, King, Hancock, and Washington. They remained behind to go with Lieutenant James, Captain Sims and two of his rangers.

"Let's go to Monty County!" announced Bill James.

Captain Sims rode with Lieutenant James. It would be an hour and a half drive to the location in Monty County.

While the Lieutenant had been asleep on his couch, Detective Luna had taken Robert Raymond's statement and had located every address where the stolen heavy equipment would be.

Kramer found that a County Commissioner in Monty County had a construction company that he owned with his brother. They were building a subdivision on Lake Connors. This Commissioner had bought some of the stolen heavy equipment.

Lt. Joe "Bill" Bradley

Captain Sims told Bill James, "It really fits now; I had a Ranger check some rumors that a County Commissioner was using county equipment to build a road to the lake in Monty County. The Ranger couldn't find any Monty County equipment being used. Now, I know why. The bastard was using stolen equipment. Bill, even if the commissioner cooperates, I'm going to put his ass in jail."

When they arrived in Monty County, Lieutenant James turned off the main highway and drove to the construction site on Lake Connors.

James, followed by the other men, drove to a motor home parked at the site. The sign out front indicated that this was the office of Monty County Construction Company.

As Lieutenant James and Captain Sims started for the motor home, the door to the motor home opened.

Fred Jacobs, the brother of Monty County Commissioner Bob Jacobs, stepped forward and asked, "May I help you gentleman."

Lieutenant James identified himself and said, "We're here to inspect your equipment."

"Is there a problem?" asked Jacobs.

Captain Sims answered, "We wouldn't be here if there wasn't a problem. I hope you're not part of the problem."

Fred Jacobs looked at Lieutenant James and then at Captain Sims and then announced, "This is private property, you can't..."

Fred Jacobs didn't get to finish, Captain Sims shoved a Texas Ranger badge in his face and said,

THE TWELVE JUDGES

"You know what this badge means. It means the "State of Texas". Isn't this damn place in Texas?"

"O.K." answered Jacobs. "But I'm going to call my brother. He's a county commissioner. You're going to be in real trouble. You city boys sometimes forget how things work in the country."

Captain Sims said, "No. I think you country boys have forgotten how the Rangers work. First, you're going to sign this."

Fred Jacobs looked at the piece of paper Captain Sims handed to him. He hesitated to sign the paper, but then he noticed that Captain Sims was showing serious signs of agitation. Jacobs reluctantly signed a "Consent to Search" form.

Lieutenant James turned to the detectives and rangers who had been watching the confrontation and said, "Get busy! Check everything!"

James walked with Fred Jacobs into the motor home. Jacobs called his brother on the telephone, "Bob, you better get down here, the Texas Rangers and the Houston Police are here. What should I do? O.K. but hurry!"

Fred Jacobs turned to James and Sims, "My brother will straighten you out! He's bringing the Sheriff with him!"

"Good!" Sims replied, "It's been a long time since I've walked all over a Sheriff! Let's go outside Bill, and see how the work is progressing"

Outside, Park was trying to drive a bulldozer.

James hollered at Park, "What in the hell do you think you're doing?" James hollered but Parks was busy trying to steer the bulldozer and it was making so much noise James couldn't be heard.

Lt. Joe "Bill" Bradley

Black smoke belched from the bulldozers' upright exhaust. The engine was racing out of control. Park was pulling levers back and forth trying to drive the bulldozer forward. The huge machine jerked forward, stalled and then jerked forward again. Park gunned the motor and the bulldozer lunged forward. Park pulled a lever back and the dozer spun 180 degrees, spun again and then took off jerking every few feet. Park drove the dozer straight into a tin storage shed and flattened it. Park finally stopped the dozer just before it hit Lieutenant James' car.

Fred Jacobs ran to the bulldozer and jumped on it and turned the key off. "Look what you did, you idiot! That's going to cost you. That damn building cost a thousand bucks."

Park being in a near panic and pissed off, grabbed Jacobs by the throat and shouted, "It's not gonna cost me a single cent! It's gonna cost you, you son-of-a-bitch! This bulldozer is stolen."

As Park let go of Fred Jacobs' throat, he gave him a not so gentle shove. Jacobs fell from the bulldozer, his bottom hitting the ground with his arms out stretched. Jacobs got up, brushed his pants off and then ran in the direction of James and Captain Sims.

"I didn't know it was stolen! Believe me. I've got papers where I bought that dozer!"

Hancock came over to where the Lieutenant and Captain were standing. He had found two backhoes, which were stolen, also a stolen road grader and welding machine.

"We can't find the last piece. There's suppose to be five stolen pieces here according to Raymond," Hancock said. "It's gotta be here somewhere."

THE TWELVE JUDGES

"Hancock," Lieutenant James ordered. "Go in the office with Fred Jacobs. He claims he bought all this equipment and says he has paperwork to prove it. Get what paperwork he has!"

"O.K., Boss."

Captain Sims turned to Lieutenant James and motioned in the direction of a cloud of dust coming toward them, "Look what's coming!"

There was a Monty County Sheriff car coming down the road stirring up dust from the East Texas red clay. When the car got to the motor home, it slid to a halt. Out stepped Sheriff Evers and County Commissioner Jacobs.

Sheriff Evers stomped over to Captain Sims and announced, "I'm Sheriff Evers. What in the hell is going on here?"

Captain Sims calmly shook the Sheriff's hand. "This is Lieutenant James. He has some serious business here in Monty County."

Sheriff Evers said, "This is my county! No city cop is going to come into my county unless they're first cleared through me!"

"Sheriff, I know I don't have to show you my badge and explain to you that, as a Texas Ranger, I have jurisdiction in your county. So, if you're not involved in this shit, get your ass back to your car and wait for me! If you are involved in this shit, you better get in your car and get the hell out of here! I would also strongly urge you to find yourself a good lawyer."

The Sheriff looked at the Texas Ranger's stern face and turned and walked to his car.

Lieutenant James then informed Bob Jacobs, "I believe you are involved in this shit, Commissioner.

Lt. Joe "Bill" Bradley

The bulldozer, the two backhoes and the grader are stolen. Since you're the owner of the company, I guess that means you have some explaining to do."

The commissioner's face turned white with anger. "I don't know a thing about any stolen equipment. My brother bought all this equipment through legitimate business deals."

"You're really a nice guy," smirked James. "You're going to let your brother take all the blame."

Bob Jacobs was so nervous, his voice began to quiver, "My attorney will set you straight. I want to call him now!"

The Commissioner turned to the Sheriff who was sitting in his squad car and hollered. "Sheriff, call my attorney, Marvin Tate. Tell him to get his butt here fast!"

Lieutenant James told Bob Jacobs, "Go tell the Sheriff to have your attorney meet us at the Monty County Courthouse. We have to take you and your brother to see a judge before we take you back to Houston. Then we're gonna put your ass in jail!"

"Yeah, damn it! You've got to go before a Judge so he can tell you your rights, that's the screwed up law!" agreed Sims.

Hancock stuck his head out of the motor home and shouted, "Lieutenant, I found all the sales contracts for the four pieces of heavy equipment and guess what? I checked this damn motor home out. It's stolen! I called Kramer and gave him the serial number and he confirmed it."

Lieutenant James glanced at a very weak looking Commissioner Jacobs. James called Captain

THE TWELVE JUDGES

Sims over to one side so that Bob Jacobs could not hear their conversation.

"Sims, keep Bob Jacobs outside. I'm going in and have a talk with his brother."

"O.K.," agreed Sims. "I'm going to call Sheriff Evers out of his car and talk to him in front of Bob Jacobs."

When Lieutenant James entered the motor home, he found Fred Jacobs sitting in a chair. "Hancock, we don't need the paperwork. Fred's brother is telling the Ranger Captain the whole truth. Bob said his brother Fred handled all the equipment for his company and if the equipment is stolen that Fred must have known it and Fred also must have forged the sales contracts because Fred handled the paperwork too."

Hancock immediately sensed what direction the lieutenant was going and played along. "Forgery! Fred you know that's a federal offense when it comes to heavy equipment. It looks like you could go to both Texas and Federal joints for a long time. Boy, you're ass is really going to be in trouble if the F.B.I. gets involved."

Fred Jacobs jumped from his chair. "Bob is the one who got the papers for the stolen equipment! He knew where all the equipment came from. It's his deal. He's a friend of a guy named Stockton. My brother knows everything. I just followed his orders and he treats me like shit. I'm not gonna let that S.O.B. pin all this on me!"

Lieutenant James said, "Hancock, let's give Fred a break. Write out a statement and get him to

Lt. Joe "Bill" Bradley

sign it. If he'll give you a written statement, we can keep the federal charges off him."

Hancock knew when to play it straight, "Awe Boss, why should we give him a break? We should give his brother the break. He's important, he's a county commissioner."

"Do what I said!" ordered James.

Lieutenant James reached out and patted Fred Jacobs on the shoulder. "Sit down with Hancock. Your brother is giving a statement to the Ranger and so you better get your recollections straight."

James went outside and walked over to the Sheriff's car where Captain Sims was talking with Bob Jacobs and the Sheriff. Captain Sims motioned to James. "Bill, come over here and let's talk."

The two men walked a distance from the Sheriff and Bob Jacobs.

"Bill, while you were inside, Judge Mathews of Monty County called on the Sheriff's radio. He ordered me to bring Bob Jacobs to his court now!"

"Sims, can you stall for awhile? Hancock is taking a confession from Fred Jacobs."

"No shit? We won't leave until he finishes.

Captain Sims returned to Bob Jacobs and the Sheriff. "Sheriff, we'll head for the courthouse as soon as Lieutenant James makes arrangements for the equipment to be picked up."

Commissioner Bob Jacobs spoke up. "You're not taking my equipment anywhere!"

Captain Sims called one of his Rangers over and said, "Put this bastard in handcuffs and put him in Lieutenant James' car."

THE TWELVE JUDGES

"Captain, that's not necessary," Sheriff Evers pleaded. "I'll drive Bob to the courthouse with me."

"Do what I said," ordered Sims to the Ranger. "I shouldn't have to repeat myself."

Bob Jacobs started threatening legal action and cussed Lieutenant James and Captain Sims all the way to the car. Sheriff Evers, knowing that his badge had shrunk in size, got into his car and sped away.

Detective Hancock came out of the motor home waving a handwritten confession.

Lieutenant James went in the motor home and telephoned Kramer at the factory. "Kramer, get some of the men and Rangers to the office as soon as you can. Get Robert Raymond out of jail and have him call Charles Stockton on the phone. Tell Raymond not to use the code word, video machines, but to say there's trouble with the bulldozer. You know what questions need to be answered by Stockton so we can use the tape as evidence. Get Raymond to set up a meeting with Stockton and have the men bust Stockton. Have them bring him to the factory. We'll be back in a few hours."

"Yes, Sir," replied Kramer.

As James hung up the receiver he turned to Hancock, "You can ride with me and the Captain. I'll have the rest of the men get this equipment picked up and stored."

"Lieutenant, can I drive the motor home to the factory?" Washington asked.

"Have at it, Washington. Just don't use Interstate 45 as a race track."

Hancock handcuffed Fred Jacobs and took him to the Lieutenant's car.

Lt. Joe "Bill" Bradley

On the drive to the Monty County Courthouse, Fred Jacobs asked his brother, "What did you say in your statement?"

Startled, Bob Jacobs looked at his brother and said, "You stupid son-of-a-bitch, you didn't give them a statement did you?"

As they drove further up the road, James had to pull over and let Fred Jacobs out of the car. He threw up.

At the Monty County Courthouse, Lieutenant James parked in Commissioner Bob Jacobs' parking place. "I guess I won't get a ticket here."

The Monty County Courthouse was built 70 years ago. It resembled a castle with towers at each end of the building. As they climbed the stone stairs to the courthouse James noticed the steps were worn from years of people entering the courthouse.

Bob and Fred Jacobs were brought through the front door of the courthouse in handcuffs. Some county employees saw them. The word of their arrest had spread like wildfire through the small community. James asked a young deputy standing in the hall what court was in session. The deputy was so dumb struck seeing the commissioner and his brother in handcuffs he could only point. James, the Captain and their prisoners walked into Judge Matthew's Court.

As they entered the courtroom, Marvin Tate, the commissioner's attorney, came rushing up to them. "Are you all right, Bob?"

Turning to the judge, the attorney screamed, "Order them to take the handcuffs off my clients immediately!" Attorney Tate kept repeating this over and over to the judge.

THE TWELVE JUDGES

Tate finally lowered his voice and said, "These two men are not dangerous criminals," and pointing said, "This is our county commissioner."

Judge Mathews said, "Ranger! This is my courtroom and what I say is the law. Mr. Bob Jacobs and Mr. Fred Jacobs, just relax a few minutes."

Judge Mathews then informed Commissioner Jacobs and his brother of their rights.

When Judge Mathews finished all the formalities he said, "Mr. Jacob, you and your brother's bond is set at $100.00 each. You can make bond with me now."

Marvin Tate turned to Lieutenant James gleefully and said, "Go home, city cop. We run things here in Monty County."

Lieutenant James moved in the direction of the attorney threatening through clenched teeth, "I'm going to whip your ass."

Captain Sims quickly stepped between James and the attorney just in time for James fist to miss its mark. "Bill, play it cool for now." whispered Captain Sims.

Sims turned to Judge Mathews and said, "Thank you, your honor for your time."

Captain Sims then turned to Commissioner Jacobs saying in a loud stern voice, "Keep your bags packed, I'll be back soon."

As James and Sims were leaving the courtroom, Marvin Tate tried one more maneuver, as he hollered, "Judge, tell them to leave Fred Jacobs' statement with the court."

Lt. Joe "Bill" Bradley

Lieutenant James turned and gave the attorney the finger and slammed the courtroom door behind him.

"Did you see that Judge? Hold him in contempt!"

By then Captain Sims and Lieutenant James had already left the building only to find themselves surrounded by reporters.

"Boy, word really got out fast. Captain, tell the reporters everything about the commissioner, but leave me and my detectives out of the story. Understand?" Bill James requested.

"I understand, Bill. Cool Down."

Captain Sims went with the reporters.

Lieutenant James and Hancock went to the car to wait. There was a parking ticket on Lieutenant James' car. Hancock could see the blood rush to James' face and his temper flaring.

James snatched the parking ticket off of the windshield and tore it into small pieces throwing them all over a small sign which read, 'Do Not Litter'.

James then pulled Commissioner Jacobs parking sign out of the ground and threw the parking sign on the courthouse lawn. James got into his car and slammed the door.

When Hancock got in the car with James, he turned, his eyes meeting James eyes and Hancock said, "I do believe you're pissed, Lieutenant."

They both broke into uncontrollable laughter.

Captain Sims joined them after talking with the reporters. "I gave the reporters everything and more. Can you believe that those reporters got here this fast from Houston? I bet the Sheriff called them. I can't

THE TWELVE JUDGES

wait to get the Texas Attorney General involved in this."

Lieutenant James drove off headed for Houston.

"You know that all of the T.V. reporters will be waiting for us when we get back to Houston," Sims said. "Bill, you want me to handle the news media?"

"Hell yes," James replied, "I'll drop you off at your office. You can have a news conference there. Don't mention me or my group. Tell the news media anything you want but we need to be anonymous to be successful."

Captain Sims said, "Bill, don't worry about the news media. I'll put a good story on them. I understand what you do and why. I only wish we could work like you. We're so visible and the news media looks for only the negative in us. You have my support."

Captain Sims picked up Lieutenant James mobile phone and called his office. "Susie, if any reporters call, tell them I'll be there in an hour."

After Sims hung up, he said, "Shit, they're already there."

James and Sims planned their strategy on the way back to Houston. It was decided that Captain Bert Sims would call the Texas Attorney General and tell him how Judge Mathews had acted and that the judge said, "The Attorney General of Texas is not big enough to come into my county and put one of my commissioners in jail."

Lieutenant James knew the Attorney General; he came up the ranks the hard way. He had been an honest prosecutor. James knew that when the Attorney

General got through, the Jacob brothers would be going to jail and no deals would be cut for them.

James drove to the rear parking lot of the Department of Public Safety in Houston to discreetly leave Sims at the back entrance to his office.

"Bill, I've enjoyed this. You really have a good thing going with your men," Sims complimented. "I'll be over as soon as I get rid of the reporters."

James said, "Don't mention my name or my bunch, Bert."

"There you go again. You don't have to tell me that, Bill."

Lieutenant James and Hancock headed for the factory. When they arrived and walked to the door, Kramer met them.

"Lu, things have gone great." Kramer's face was beaming. "I called Johnson, Davis and two Rangers back to the office. Over the telephone, Robert Raymond had Charles Stockton agree to meet him. They busted Stockton and he's in the back room. Stockton is spilling his guts! And, guess what? He told them about a gun store he and Raymond burglarized and Uncle shipped the guns to Mexico. A Ranger is taking a written statement from Stockton. Boy! King is gonna be hot when he finds out Raymond didn't tell him about the guns."

"Kramer, get in touch with the rest of the guys. Tell them to knock off for the time being. We'll get started again in the a.m. That is, all except for busting Uncle. I think he needs to see the inside of our jail tonight."

Kramer went to the base police radio and started calling the men in the field.

THE TWELVE JUDGES

It wasn't long until all the detectives and Rangers were back at the factory along with Captain Sims. As Sims told everyone about his television interview, there was a tremendous amount of teasing. Washington was offering to tape the 10 o'clock news for Captain Sims for a price.

Sims took all the harassment in stride as he casually made his way to Lieutenant James' office.

"It's been a good day," Bill James said. "You know, Bert, the public sometimes wonders why we work so hard on heavy equipment and auto thefts. Well, there's always a link between stolen vehicles and crooks of all kind. Sometimes it's just another piece of a bigger puzzle."

"You're right, Bill. Over half of the cars stolen are used in committing crimes such as bank holdups and burglaries. I really get upset when I hear the D.A.'s office and the new media say, Auto Theft is just joy riders."

"Bert, Detective King started this case. I'm going to let him bust Uncle tonight."

Lieutenant James walked with Bert Sims to the back of the factory where the men were gathered around a T.V. watching the late news.

Washington shouted, "Be quiet, our hero is on."

On T.V., Captain Sims was saying, "The Texas Rangers have been working on this case for a long time. We received information from an informer about Commissioner Jacobs and his brother in Monty County. The Rangers recovered a million dollars in stolen heavy equipment from Commissioner Jacob's construction company."

139

Lt. Joe "Bill" Bradley

Lieutenant James' detectives and the Rangers all hollered at the same time, "Shit-t-t-t-t-!"

The news interview continued, "Since we received no cooperation from Monty County officials, this case and evidence will be turned over to the Texas Attorney General for investigation and hopefully eventual prosecution."

After the T.V. broadcast, the teasing of Captain Sims started again, but Sims knew it was all part of police work.

Kramer walked over to Lieutenant James, "Lieutenant, Assistant District Attorney Owens is on the telephone."

James went to his office, "This is Lieutenant James. What can I do for you, Owens?"

"James, damn you, I know you're the one that busted the Jacob brothers. I got a call from a rancher where your men picked up a tractor. I want this case! This publicity could make me the District Attorney some day."

"You're wrong, Owens. This is a Texas Ranger's case, we just assisted them."

Lieutenant James slammed the phone down and walked out of his office. He told Captain Sims about the phone call.

"Don't worry, Bill. I don't like that son-of-a-bitch either. The Attorney General can handle him."

James got everyone's attention. "King is the one who started this case so he gets the prize tonight. King, pick two men and go get Uncle."

Davis and Johnson fell all over King saying, "We'll go."

THE TWELVE JUDGES

King answered, "Hell, come on! I know you two just want to look at the stripper's titties."

Lieutenant James said, "After you arrest Uncle and put him in jail, we'll be at the Rotary Table. These high paid Rangers might buy you a drink."

A Ranger in the group spoke up saying, "High paid! The guys you see picking up trash on the highway make more than we do. But, since I had so much fun today, I'll buy King his first drink."

King left the factory and drove to the Golden Bar. The three detectives walked into the bar and took a seat at a table next to the runway where the girls dance. Three strippers came over and sat on their laps.

"Is Uncle here?" King asked.

"Yes, and he know you're here. He knows it when any cop walks through the door."

Drinks were brought over without being ordered.

"Go Tell Uncle that I need to talk with him."

One of the girls left and went to Uncle's office.

Davis and Johnson began telling the other two girls. "There is going to be a great party at the Rotary Table about 2:00 a.m. Get some of the other girls and be there."

One of the girls said, "Ask Uncle and if he says O.K., we'll be there."

Johnson said, "Old Uncle won't mind, will he, King?"

King started to answer when he saw Uncle come out of his office towards where they were sitting. The girls left.

"Want to see me, King?" Uncle asked.

Lt. Joe "Bill" Bradley

"Yeah, we want you to do a table dance for us, O.K.?"

Uncle managed a fake laugh. He knew these three cops were not here on pleasure. He had heard about the 10 o'clock newscast.

King ordered, "Let's go outside, Uncle."

Davis and Johnson started to protest because they were enjoying the scenery. They followed King and Uncle outside.

"Uncle, you're in a heap of trouble! We've got Charles Stockton, Robert Raymond and Commissioner Jacobs and his brother."

Uncle's face dropped as he said, "I need to go back inside and make arrangements for someone to close my club later and call my attorney."

King said, "Get your ass in the car! You're going with us. Now!"

Davis and Johnson got into the back seat putting Uncle in the middle.

Davis reached over and grabbed Uncle's chin turning his face towards his and said, "If you want to confess, go ahead and start. We really don't want you to talk. We have your ass up tight and if you talk, it will just mean more paper work for us."

It was pretty quiet on the way back to the factory. Uncle had been to the joint twice and King knew he wouldn't talk unless he could make a deal. King didn't want to talk to him anyway; they had Uncle by the ass. King spent the time telling Uncle how many years he was going to spend in the penitentiary.

King also told Uncle he was going to make sure he didn't get out on bond.

THE TWELVE JUDGES

When they walked into the factory, Uncle saw Robert Raymond and Charles Stockton.

Uncle turned to King and said, "Let's make a deal, I'll talk to you, if you will let me plead out in court for only 5 years in the joint."

"No deal! You're not only a fence, you are a sorry ass pimp!"

King took Uncle into the Lieutenant's office and James made the introductions. "Captain Sims this is Uncle. I don't believe you two have met."

Uncle stuck out his hand.

Captain Sims said, "Lieutenant, put this piece of shit in jail! I don't want to talk with him and I know you don't."

Bill James laughed and said, "King, book him! When you get through with your paperwork, you know where we'll be."

Lieutenant James walked out where the other detectives and Rangers were waiting. "Captain, why don't we go to the Rotary Table. These guys are going to work all night."

The detectives and the Rangers were out the factory door before Lieutenant James finished his statement.

On the way to their cars, Captain Sims said, "Bill thanks for calling me in on this. I'll meet with the Attorney General and take the case from here. Let's go and have some drinks tonight and celebrate being good cops."

When Lieutenant James and Captain Sims walked into the Rotary Table, Juan met them at the door. "Come in, I've got the perfect table for you."

Lt. Joe "Bill" Bradley

Juan called to one of his waiters, "Get these two gentlemen whatever they want."

As the two lawmen sat down, Juan brought over a bottle of J&B scotch.

Captain Sims asked, "How did the boys get here before us, I didn't see them pass us?"

Lieutenant James called to Juan. "Juan, don't let anymore customers in tonight. Try and ease the ones that are here out. I believe the guys are going to raise hell tonight."

"Sure, Cap. When the last customer leaves, I'll lock the door."

Two hours passed. All of the regular customers were gone. War stories and lies filled the club.

All of a sudden the noise in the club ceased, as there was a heavy loud knock on the front door. Someone was really beating the door like they were trying to tear it down. A loud recognizable voice shouted, "Open the damn door, you better open up the door if you want some goodies."

Lieutenant James recognized Detective Johnson's voice. Juan looked at the lieutenant. James nodded his head. Juan opened the door and in walked five strippers from the Golden Bar, followed by Johnson, Davis, and King.

The guys let out yells that could be heard downtown. The party was taking shape in more ways than one.

After an hour of talking and watching the girls dance, Lieutenant James turned to Bert Sims. "I believe it's time for us to hit the road."

THE TWELVE JUDGES

"Bill, I think you're right. Let's slip out and don't even tell them bye. If we do, we'll be here all night."

Juan let the Lieutenant and Captain out through the kitchen.

"Juan, take care of the guys, you have my home phone number if these rogues get out of hand."

"No trouble Cap, they just letting off some steam. See you later, Cap."

Lieutenant James climbed into his car waved to Captain Sims as he drove off. All of a sudden he realized just how very tired he was as he headed for home.

At home James slipped out of his clothes and sleep caught him fast.

Lieutenant James' telephone rang breaking his sound sleep. He looked at his clock. It was 5:00 a.m.

"Hello."

"Lieutenant James? This is Captain Horwick of the Vice Squad."

"Yes, Captain. What can I do for you?"

"It's your damn detectives," Captain Horwick hollered. "I got a phone call earlier waking me up. My night shift Vice Squad men got a call to the Rotary Table about drinking after hours. They slipped in through the kitchen to get inside."

"Well, what's the problem, Captain?"

"Your damn drunk detectives threw my men out of the Rotary Table. One of my men has a black eye, another broke a finger and another had a tooth knocked out. What are you going to do about it?"

"I'll give them all three days off with pay."

Lt. Joe "Bill" Bradley

Captain Horwick said, "Don't be a smart ass, I'll have your ass for this! I'm going to talk to the Chief about your rouges."

"You can't, he's playing golf today," Lieutenant James said. He then hung up on Captain Horwick.

Lieutenant James thought, "Damn! I hope the Chief has a good golf game so he won't chew me out too bad." James was still tired. He rolled over and went back to sleep.

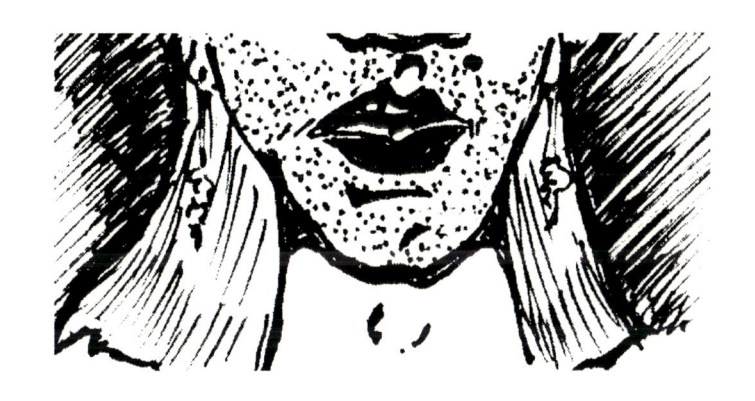

CHAPTER 7

<u>JUSTICE FOR THE NUMBER ONE PIMP</u>

The next few days were spent with everyone including the Rangers taking care of the loose ends of the heavy equipment case; paperwork was the unavoidable drudgery of police work.

Commissioner Jacobs, his brother, Robert Raymond, Uncle and Charles Stockton had all been indicted by a Special Grand Jury led by the Attorney General of Texas. Captain Sims of the Texas Rangers had been given the personal pleasure of putting Fred and Bob Jacobs in jail.

Lieutenant Bill James felt a sense of pride from a job well done but he also knew that it was a never-ending war against the criminal element.

James was conducting a meeting at the factory regarding a group of hold-up men who were robbing Savings & Loan businesses.

Lt. Joe "Bill" Bradley

Everyone was present except Detective Gary Edwards. Halfway through the meeting, Edwards stormed in, cussing and breaking up the meeting. His eyes were blood-shot and it looked as if he had slept in his clothes. Edwards' beard, which was always well groomed, was a mess.

"Edwards," Lieutenant James asked, "What's wrong? Do you need to talk with me in the office? Did you have an accident or something?"

"No, Lieutenant. I need help from all of you." Edwards looked emotionally and physically drained.

"Just tell us what's wrong and how can we help."

"Yeah," Murphy offered, "You really look like hell."

Through clenched teeth, holding back the tears, Edwards began his story…

"I've been looking for a son-of-a-bitch all night. I was going to kill him. My sister called me this morning at one. Her daughter, my niece, is in the hospital. My niece, Diane, is a beautiful girl, homecoming queen in high school, just beautiful. I'm very close to her. She's been attending college at the local university. I hurried to the hospital. My sister couldn't tell me what was wrong because she was crying too much. When I got to the hospital and took one look at my niece lying there in the hospital bed, I knew what had happened. Lu, she didn't have a spot on her body that didn't have a bruise mark. She had been beaten with a coat-hanger and kicked all over. Even one of her eyes was swollen closed. You know that's the trademark of a pimp, whipping their girls

THE TWELVE JUDGES

with coat-hangers; that's how pimps keep their girls who are whoring for them in line."

Edwards wiped the tears from his eyes and continued…"Somehow, she got involved in a high class prostitution ring. How, is not important to me at this time. She was getting $500 a trick. Diane was able to talk a little and tell me that her pimp was Mark Dillon."

Wiping the tears from his eyes Edwards continued, "I went to the Vice Squad and got a picture of Dillon. The Vice Squad told me that they knew of him, but it was nearly impossible to make a felony case stick on him. They told me that every time they've made good felony on Dillon, the District Attorney's office always reduces the case to a misdemeanor. Dillon always got out of the charge by paying a small fine. He never does jail time. The Vice boys really want his ass. They say that Dillon is a pimp for the wealthy class. That's how he gets the cases reduced to a misdemeanor, the rich bastards who are his clients pull strings."

Washington handed Edwards a handkerchief as he spoke. "Dillon supplies prostitutes for wealthy businessmen, and they use their influence at the D.A.'s office."

Edward's mood changed to hate as he continued. "Lieutenant, it's the same old story, cops saying they can't do anything because they have too much work and the courts have tied their hands. Businessmen are using their wealth and influence with the D.A. to cover their ass. That's bullshit! I'm not going to stand by and let this sorry ass pimp get away with what he's done to my niece. I'm going to do something!"

Edwards blew his nose and said, "Dr. Phil Abbott, Diane's physician, told me that he met Diane months ago and they had fallen in love. They met in Hermann Park. Boss, here's an educated doctor who knows that Diane's a whore and he still loves her and wants to marry her. Dr. Abbott said she only had a 50-50 chance of making it. Dr. Abbott told me the story of how he met Diane."

Detective Edwards gave the detectives the following account of Diane's and Dr. Phil Abbott's relationship.

> Hermann Park is a beautiful park located next to the Medical Center.
>
> The Medical Center is the largest of its kind in the world. Dr. Phil Abbott jogged each day in the park. On his daily run he would see this beautiful girl sitting on a park bench reading. One day, he stopped next to the girl.
>
> "Hi, I'm Dr. Phil Abbott. Each day, I've wanted to stop to meet you, but never had the courage. I finally got up enough nerve. May I sit down?"
>
> When Diane looked up, Phil could hardly believe his eyes. She was even more beautiful up close.
>
> "Sit down, Doctor. I'm Diane Smith. I feel flattered."

"Everyday I see you sitting in the sun reading. What is so interesting?"

"<u>East of Eden</u> by John Steinbeck, I just love his writing," Diane replied.

"I may as well ask you," Phil Abbot cautiously said. "Are you married? I'm not."

"No, I am not married and I don't plan to be married any time soon."

"I'm sorry for asking that, I just wanted to meet you. But, now that I've met you, I don't know what to say."

"Tell me about yourself, Doctor Abbott."

He told Diane how he had worked his way through medical school and was now doing his internship at the Hermann Hospital.

Diane told the doctor that she was attending the University of Houston majoring in English.

"I need to go back to work now," Dr. Abbott said as he looked at his watch. "May I see you again?"

"Doctor Abbott, if you're running in the park again, you can stop here and rest."

"Call me Phil."

"O.K., Phil. Have a nice day."

Lt. Joe "Bill" Bradley

Doctor Abbott started jogging towards Hermann Hospital. He felt as if his feet were not touching the ground.

"Wow!" he cried out loud.

During the next two weeks, Diane was only in the park four times. Each time, Phil Abbott stopped to visit with her. He planned to ask Diane for a dinner date.

On their next visit Abbott asked Diane, "What kind of food do you like?"

Diane smiled broadly. "Phil, if you would ask me to dinner some evening, you could find out."

"Great! When and where do I pick you up? I'm off tonight."

Diane gave Phil her address. "I'll be ready at 6, but I'll have to be home by 10. I have some studying to do."

The next few weeks were filled with joy for Phil Abbott. He and Diane spent as much time as they could together. But one thing in his relationship with Diane puzzled Abbott. When they were out together at night, Diane always insisted on being back home before 10.

They made love, but always at his apartment and always with attention on the clock. Doctor Abbott knew he could no longer go on this way, he had

THE TWELVE JUDGES

fallen in love with Diane and he felt certain that she was in love with him. He bought a ring and planned to propose, where he had first met her, in the park.

The following day after buying the ring, Phil Abbott jogged to the bench in the park where Diane was sitting.

"Hi beautiful. Waiting for someone?"

"Yes, you."

Doctor Abbott suddenly dropped down on one knee and said, "I love you Diane. Will you marry me?"

As he placed the ring on her finger, Diane broke into tears and began sobbing uncontrollably. Finally she wiped her face with Abbott's T-shirt and said, "I love you very much Phil, but you don't want me. I'm a whore, a damn slut!"

"What do you mean a whore? I don't understand."

"Phil sit down, it's time for the truth. Last year, I met a man at a society function. After dating him for a short time, he owned me. Don't ask me how, but he did. I became one of his girls, sleeping with wealthy men, one or two times a week. I've tried to get away from him, Phil but I was scared. You should see what he does to girls that tried to quit working for him. One of the girls he beat up, died. Phil, I'm so sorry. I had no right to let you fall in love with me. Phil, I do love you."

Phil was stunned; he could not believe his ears. Immediately, as in a trance, Phil stood and started walking down the jogging path toward the hospital. He could still hear Diane sobbing.

Phil had walked a short distance when he said, "To hell with it!"

He ran back to Diane taking her into his arms, brushing away her tears, and assured her, "I don't give a damn about your past! I'm in love with you!"

Diane's sobbing became louder. Phil placed her on the park bench and looked straight into her eyes. "I'm going to marry you and that's that! Where can I find this creep?"

"No Phil, he'll hurt you."

"Go home now! Pack a suitcase," Phil instructed. "I'm going to the hospital and change clothes. I'll pick you up as soon as I can. You're going to move in with me today."

"Phil?"

"What?"

"I love you."

Doctor Abbott took off running in the direction of the hospital. Diane drove back to her apartment. She took her suitcase out of the bedroom closet. As she was packing, Diane heard the front door of her apartment being unlocked. She knew that Phil didn't have a key. Suddenly, in walked Mark Dillon, her pimp.

"It looks like I got here just in time. I've been calling you all day. The other girls were right, you are trying to leave Old Daddy."

Dillon hit Diane in the mouth splitting her lip knocking her to the floor. She tried to get up, but he started kicking her. He reached down, grabbed her blouse, and ripped it off. He tore Diane's skirt and undergarments from her body stripping her naked.

"You bitch! You're not going to leave me! Nobody leaves me! You are going to keep making me money."

Dillon staggered over to the patio drapes and jerked them down. He took out a knife and cut the cord from the drapery rod. He turned to Diane where she laid in pain and naked. He tied each end of the cord to both wrists.

Pulling her to her feet, he placed the cord over the bedroom door and pulled the cord until Diane was on her tiptoes with her hands over her head. Dillon then tied the cord to the doorknob. Each time that Diane tried to scream, Dillon hit her in the stomach.

Diane hung there naked. Fear overtook her body.

Dillon then went to Diane's closet and got a wire coat hanger. He straightened out the hanger and came back to where Diane was hanging.

"You bitch! How much money did you hold out on me? A good beating is what you need. When I get finished with you, you're going to make me a lot of money and remember who owns you."

Dillon began to beat Diane with the coat hanger. Every time Dillon hit her beautiful body, a bloody stripe appeared. She tried to scream, but no sound came from her mouth. The pain was unbearable.

Diane eventually passed out. Dillon went to her closet and with his knife cut her clothes to shreds. He then left, locking the apartment door behind him.

Phil Abbott arrived at Diane's apartment located on the first floor of the building. He rang the door bell but there was no answer. Abbott knocked on the door, and still there was no answer. He continued to beat on Diane's door. A neighbor from across the hall opened her door.

"She's there, I saw her come in. Maybe she's on the patio."

THE TWELVE JUDGES

Doctor Abbott went outside and around to the apartment patio. As Phil opened the wooden gate, he saw that the patio sliding glass door was closed. He tried to slide the glass door but it was locked. Phil noticed that the drapes for the sliding glass door were on the floor. His eyes turned to horror as he saw Diane hanging naked from a door. A wave of nausea came over him.

"Oh my God, oh my God!" he cried.

Phil tried with all of his strength to open the patio door but he could not.

Phil picked up a flowerpot sitting on the patio and threw it through the glass door and stepped over the broken glass into the apartment.

He carefully took Diane down from where she had been hanging and carried her to the bedroom and placed her on the bed. He checked her pulse. She was alive, but she didn't look it.

Doctor Abbott grabbed the telephone and dialed 911. He shouted into the telephone, "Get an ambulance here immediately." Phil knew Diane was in shock. Doctor Abbott then ran to his car and got his medical bag.

When he returned, the neighbor had entered through the broken patio door. She was in hysterics. Doctor Abbott told the neighbor to shut up and

Lt. Joe "Bill" Bradley

to get some clean sheets. Phil Abbott did the best he could for Diane.

While the ambulance attendants were putting Diane on a stretcher, Phil Abbott called Hermann Hospital emergency room.

"This is Doctor Abbott! Alert Doctor Walters and his staff! Have them meet me in the E.R.! I'm on my way with a trauma patient!"

Doctor Abbott rode in the ambulance with Diane to the hospital.

When Detective Gary Edwards had finished his story, he turned to Lieutenant James, "Lu, I'll have to transfer from your group. I'm going to find that sorry pimp, and kill that son-of-a-bitch!"

Detective Washington stood up. The look on his face was serious and one of hate. He was emotional as he began to talk.

"Gary, we're all together in this group. If a bastard messes over one of us, he messes with all of us. Your problem's our problem. You can't kill that sorry bastard. Sorry as he is, the courts will hang you, especially since you're a cop. While you were talking, I was thinking. We were organized so assholes like Mark Dillon will get what they deserve. What would serve justice best? All I could think of is Miss Freddy. Let's give Dillon to Miss Freddy. When Miss Freddy gets through with him, he'll never beat another girl."

Lieutenant James was surprised at Washington, but he allowed Washington to continue.

THE TWELVE JUDGES

As the idea was beginning to sink in with everyone, Kramer broke in. "Washington. Who is Miss Freddy?"

The other detectives laughed at Kramer.

"Miss Freddy is a six foot four black homosexual. He lifts weights and is stronger than a pink dinosaur. Miss Freddy owns six gay bars. He's an informer of mine who I've used more times than I can count. He trusts me, but knows what will happen to him if he every crosses me. Miss Freddy is envied throughout the gay community, many of his peers wish they were as powerful and as well hung as he. It's said, he would make a mule jealous," Washington explained. "Another story about Freddy is that he can crack a walnut with his dick. Freddy also likes to torture his lovers before he mounts them. I think we should locate Mark Dillon and give him to Miss Freddy with instructions that he can do anything he wants with the bastard."

"Washington," Hancock said, "You finally came up with something good!"

Everyone turned and looked at the lieutenant. James spoke, "Gary, if you promise to stay out of this, I'll turn these rogues loose on Dillon. You can stay here in the office with Kramer."

"Come on Lieutenant. It's my niece; let me go on this one!"

"No! You stay here with Kramer. I don't want to end up with a dead pimp and the D.A. trying to connect this group or you with his death!"

"O.K., Lieutenant, but just like in the movies, if you don't find Dillon in 24 hours, his ass is mine."

159

Lt. Joe "Bill" Bradley

Edwards gave out pictures of Dillon that he had gotten from the Vice Squad and a description of the car he was driving to the other detectives.

Detective Washington got Miss Freddy on the telephone. The others could hear Washington's conversation.

"I'm not lying, Miss Freddy, you can have him as long as you want and do anything. Just remind him every once in awhile, what he did to a cop's niece. When you're through with him, tell him, it would be good for his health if he left Houston."

Lieutenant James divided the detectives in pairs and said, "Let's go find that bastard!"

Bill James took Washington with him and they checked a few clubs up and down Westhiemer Street and Richmond Avenue. Westheimer and Richmond were known to the cops as "Coke Alley" and a lot of pimps hung out in the clubs. Mark Dillon was known to frequent these clubs looking for young girls.

It was still early in the day. Dillon was not found in any of the clubs. All afternoon the group searched for Dillon.

Just as the five o'clock traffic started to get heavy, James and Washington heard Detective Luna's voice come over the police radio.

"We've found our man!"

Lieutenant James picked up his police mike and said, "Clear, Call me over my mobile phone."

The lieutenant's mobile phone rang. Without any formalities James answered his telephone, "Where is he?"

THE TWELVE JUDGES

"Boss, Dillon's at the new Country Club in Sugarland, playing cards. His Cadillac is parked in the lot."

Sugarland, Texas borders Houston and has very wealthy subdivisions, just the atmosphere for Dillon to find his clients. Now stood expensive homes where once were bald black gumbo clay prairies.

"O.K., stay with him, we'll join you."

"Too late, Lu! He's getting in his car now."

"Keep me informed, Luna."

In a few minutes, Luna's voice came over the police radio again, "He's headed toward downtown Houston on the Southwest Freeway."

Lieutenant James' car phone rang, "Where is he, Luna?"

"He is taking the Louisiana Street exit off the freeway to the downtown area."

"Good, we're close to that location now. We'll pick him up if he passes us. Who's with you?"

"Hancock," replied Luna.

"Good. Stay on the car phone, Luna, and stick close to him," responded James.

Washington hollered, "There he is, Lieutenant!"

"Luna, we see him," James announced on the phone. "We're right behind you. Slow down Luna, so we can get in front."

Dillon drove to the heart of downtown Houston and his turn light on his Cadillac indicated he was going to make a right turn.

Lieutenant James made the turn behind the Cadillac and followed Dillon to a hotel parking garage.

Lt. Joe "Bill" Bradley

"We're right behind him, Luna. He's going into the parking garage of the Main-Ritz Hotel. When he parks, we'll take him. Follow us in and back us up."

"O.K., Boss."

James turned quickly into the parking garage and snatched a parking ticket from the entrance meter. As the wooden arm rose so they could enter, he gunned the motor and sped up the ramp.

As they came to the third parking level they saw Mark Dillon parking his Cadillac.

"Washington, don't let the bastard see your face when you put him down!"

Mark Dillon was getting out of his car and had his back turned from them. Dillon was short and skinny. He was wearing a $800 suit and $200 alligator shoes. In one sweeping motion Washington slid out of the car and hit Dillon upside his head. Washington threw him into the back seat of the Lieutenant's car.

Washington got into the back seat and handcuffed Dillon and placed a blindfold over his eyes.

Lieutenant James picked up the police radio mike and called Luna and Hancock.

"We have Freddy's gift! Follow us."

The garage-parking attendant looked puzzled as James handed him a ten-dollar bill and told him it was also for the car behind him and to keep the change. The two cars sped from the parking garage.

Washington had made arrangements to leave Miss Freddy's van parked in a secluded alley behind the Commerce Bank in the downtown area. As Bill James drove to the bank Luna and Hancock followed.

THE TWELVE JUDGES

On the way Dillon regained consciousness. He was moaning and started screaming. Washington placed a gag in him mouth.

At the bank parking lot, Dillon was thrown into Miss Freddy's van by Washington and Hancock.

"Washington," Hancock baited, "it's a good thing you had the van parked in a white area, otherwise it would have been stripped."

James shook his head and turned to Washington.

"Washington, you drive the van over to Miss Freddy. I'll see you back at the factory. Be careful, Washington. You sure you don't want Hancock to go with you in the van?"

"Lu," teased Washington, "Hancock would probably want to stay with Miss Freddy."

Hancock started to say something but changed his mind.

Washington left with Mark Dillon. When Washington got to Miss Freddy's home, the garage door was open. The garage was dark.

Washington pulled slowly into Freddy's garage. As he stepped from the van, he could smell Miss Freddy's sweet perfume that he always wore. The door going into the house opened. Washington could see the outline of what appeared to be a large woman standing in the doorway. It was Miss Freddy dressed in a long red velvet dress wearing a blond wig and red high heel shoes. Miss Freddy handed Washington a pair of handcuffs. Washington quickly replaced Miss Freddy's cuffs on Dillon's wrist for his.

Miss Freddy giggled and said, "Oh my, oh me, isn't this my lucky day?"

Lt. Joe "Bill" Bradley

Washington didn't say a word. He handed the keys to the van to Miss Freddy and walked out of the garage hoping he didn't have the cheap smell of Miss Freddy's perfume on his clothes.

Washington heard Freddy saying, "Come on, you sweet thing. Oh! Mercy me, mercy, mercy me! You didn't tell me he was white!"

Washington walked as fast as he could toward his police car parked around the corner. He had left his car there earlier in the day when he had picked up Miss Freddy's van.

As Washington walked down the street he thought to himself, "This pimp is going to get what he's been giving to his girls but in a bigger way."

Washington laughed when his thoughts sunk to a most basal pornographic level, and he envisioned Miss Freddy's mule dick screwing the pimp in the ass.

Washington was abruptly returned to reality when he saw his car, "Oh shit!"

All four tires and wheels had been stolen from his car. At the telephone booth on the corner, Washington called the factory.

Hancock answered the telephone.

"I've had car trouble, send me a wrecker and someone to get me."

Hancock laughed and said, "I'll come get you, where are you?"

Washington said, "No, I would rather ride with someone else." He told Hancock his location and hung up.

Washington thought, "I hope the wrecker gets here before anyone arrives to get me. I can hear

THE TWELVE JUDGES

Hancock now. You stupid bastard, you should have known not to park your car in a black neighborhood."

A few minutes passed and Hancock pulled up in his car.

Hancock stuck his head out of the window and said, "You stupid bastard, you should have known not to park your car in a black neighborhood."

Washington thought, "Someday, I'm going to squeeze Hancock's neck until it turns black."

All the way back to the factory, Hancock bugged Washington. "Tell me, what did Freddy do when you gave him Dillon?"

Washington expanded on the story of turning Dillon over to Miss Freddy.

Every few minutes Hancock would say, "All right! No shit!"

When they arrived back at the factory and walked in, everyone shouted, "Hip, hip, hooray! Washington! Washington!"

When the guys settled down, Hancock said, "Hip hooray, bullshit! Washington let his brothers steal the tires off his car."

Detective Washington then took center stage. Everyone wanted to know what Miss Freddy did. Washington did an impression of Miss Freddy's walk. The whole room rocked with laughter. Everyone but Edwards shook Washington's hand after his performance. Edwards was the last one to congratulate Washington for his job. Edwards reached up around Washington's neck and hugged him, his eyes filled with tears of pride for this group.

One by one the detectives left for home following another more than ordinary day.

Lt. Joe "Bill" Bradley

    Rumors in the gay community a week later were strong about the pimp Mark Dillon and Miss Freddy. It was being said that Miss Freddy had told Mark Dillon that he was going to keep him so he could be his regular lover. Dillon escaped after two weeks of Freddy's love making. Dillon refused medical treatment at a local hospital. He was taken to a hospital in another city where a team of doctors spent twelve hours in the operating room trying to make him a new ass-hole.

    After his operation, Mark Dillon also had to have sessions with a head doctor as each time he heard the words, "Twelve Judges" he began to scream uncontrollably. Mark Dillon wanted no part of Houston ever again.

CHAPTER 8

SORRY, WRONG NUMBER

Bill James was in his office and as usual he was drowning in paperwork, when his telephone rang.

"This is Lieutenant James," he answered.

"James, I'm getting heat from the Houston Phone Company!" complained Chief Ladd.

"There are some crazy idiots running around town shooting pay telephones. Some thug is shooting the locks off the damn telephones and taking the money boxes. Last night they shot fifteen telephones! I want it stopped, get on it. Now!"

"O.K., O.K. By the way, Chief, I need a secretary. This paperwork's eating me up."

"You can pick any secretary in this Police Department, but first you stop the damn telephone shooters."

Lt. Joe "Bill" Bradley

James knew the Chief played a lot of golf with the high-ranking telephone company officials. They always picked up the Chief's tabs so James knew he had better get on this case to keep the Chief off his back.

"Bye, Fats." James didn't give Ladd any time to respond to his last statement as he hung up the telephone.

Lieutenant James rose from his chair and walked to the main room where a few of his detectives had gathered doing their own endless paperwork.

"Kramer, get everyone together. We've got an assignment straight from the Chief."

It didn't take Kramer long to round up the detectives. Most were in the back room playing Mexican dominoes as an escape from their paperwork.

When they were all present, Lieutenant James began.

"There are some crooks going around the city shooting telephone booths. Can you believe that? The Chief is so upset about it that I think the Houston Phone Company must be buying him a new set of golf clubs. Anyway, contact your informers and—."

"Lu," Detective Murphy broke in, "I've got some information on some phone shooters."

"Well, Murphy, let's hear it."

"Lieutenant, I had this info when I got caught up in the Miss Freddy case. I was going to give it the Burglary and Theft Division today."

"Sure you were," Park sarcastically quipped.

"Murphy, stop with the excuses and get up here and tell us what you know."

THE TWELVE JUDGES

Murphy started digging through a stack of papers on his desk. "It's here somewhere, Lu." After a few minutes Murphy shouted, "Here it is!"

Park sarcastically said again, "Bout time you found it. If you kept your paperwork straight like mine, you wouldn't have trouble."

Murphy responded with, "At least I have some cases. I've been carrying you for weeks."

James broke up the argument, "Both of you shut up."

Lieutenant James sat down and Murphy took the floor.

Murphy began, "My informer gave me the names of two crooks he had been in prison with. He ran into 'em at a motel bar one night and they tried to recruit him. They claimed they were making a lot of money shooting pay telephones. I checked them out and both are ex-cons for burglary. My snitch says they live in Tyler, a small East Texas town. They're also hitting Fort Worth and Dallas. Here's the way they work; they find a pay phone booth that's used a lot by the public. In the early morning hours, they stick a 30-30 rifle barrel into the lock of the telephone and shoot it out. They take the change box full of coins and split. Lieutenant, I didn't think they were getting much money! Besides, the telephone company has their own security people."

"Murphy, they're stealing $1500 or more a night in quarters, besides the damage they're doing to the telephones!" answered James."

"Boy, that's a lot of quarters!" King remarked.

Murphy went on. "According to my snitch, they really like Houston. He says there are two motels

Lt. Joe "Bill" Bradley

where they usually stay, the Stardust Motel and the Cowboy Inn."

"Why didn't you act on this information before now?" asked Park.

"Shut up, ass-hole!" snapped Murphy. "You also knew about this information. You're just trying to get me in trouble with the boss."

James and his detectives had a lively discussion regarding how to best handle this investigation.

After listening to his detectives, James said, "Edwards, you and Watson get ready and take off for Tyler. Locate the two crooks and find out all you can on them. Get some expense money from Kramer. When you locate the crooks, call me. I doubt that they're still in Houston, but to be on the safe side, Murphy, you and Park, check the Stardust Motel. Luna and King check the Cowboy Inn. The rest of you help Kramer. Also, call the Fort Worth and Dallas Police Departments to get all the dates the crooks hit there. Let's chart those dates against Houston's incidents. Also, tell them if any telephone booths are shot in the next few days, let us know."

Watson and Edwards left to go home and get a change of clothes for their trip to Tyler.

Lieutenant James went back into his office to tackle his never ending paperwork. An hour later, Kramer came into the office.

"King and Luna are on their way back to the office. The crooks left the Cowboy Inn a couple of days ago. The men checked the motel records but didn't find any home addresses. Murphy also called. The crooks were at the Stardust Motel two months ago. Murphy went through the motel records and found the

THE TWELVE JUDGES

crooks names. They listed their business as The Auto Shoppe, with an address in Tyler, Texas."

"Great!" replied James.

"When Edwards and Watson call in, I'll pass on this information."

Much later in the day Kramer came in with a list of pay telephone booth cases that had occurred in Houston, Fort Worth and Dallas.

"Boss, look at this list. These crooks are really making some money. Davis placed a city map on the wall and the other guys are placing pins on every location that's been shot here in Houston."

"Kramer, when I leave for the day, let the guys go. We'll start fresh in the morning."

Wearily James looked at the papers on his desk and shook his head.

After three hours of paperwork, James shoved the work aside and said to Kramer, "Edwards and Watson have been on the road for over four hours. If you hear from them, call me at home or page me on my beeper."

"Yes Sir, Lieutenant."

After leaving the factory for the day, James drove to the Rotary Table for a quiet dinner. Just as he was starting to eat, his pager began to beep. Calling Juan over to his table, James said, "I need to use the private phone in your office."

James followed Juan to his office. There was a waitress on the telephone.

Juan motioned to the waitress, "Tell them bye, Honey. I need the telephone."

Lt. Joe "Bill" Bradley

After the waitress hung up the telephone, Juan walked out locking the door. He knew that Lieutenant James would want privacy.

James telephoned his office. "Kramer, are you still working?"

"Yes, Sir. Watson called. They checked into a motel in Tyler. They'll drive by the Auto Shoppe tonight and will call if anything develops."

"Good, Kramer. When they call back, tell them not to be seen. It would probably be a good idea for them not to contact the local police. The locals might not know the crooks but no telling who the crooks know in that small town. Close the office and go home. I'll see you tomorrow."

"I'm on my way, Lieutenant."

Late that night Detectives Watson and Edwards drove by the Auto Shoppe in Tyler.

Tyler was a neat small East Texas Town known all over the world for their roses. The best known rose is Earl Campbell, who played football for Texas University and the Houston Oilers.

The shop was dark so Watson and Edwards headed back to the motel for some sleep.

At 8 the next morning the telephone rang. Edwards grabbed the telephone.

"Good morning, this is your 8:00 a.m. wake up call."

Still half asleep Edwards said, "Screw you!"

A female voice on the other end said, "I beg your pardon."

"Oh! I'm sorry! I thought this call was one of those damn recordings."

THE TWELVE JUDGES

"That's O.K., it's really not a bad thought this time of the morning." She giggled and hung up.

After Edwards and Watson showered, dressed, and ate breakfast, they drove by the Auto Shoppe. No one was there and the shop looked as it was not open for business. They decided to watch the place until ten before they tried to find where the crooks lived.

At 9:30, a new Ford pickup drove into the parking lot of the Auto Shoppe.

Watson said, "It's one of the crooks."

Edwards was looking at the mug pictures of the crooks that Kramer got from the Texas Department of Corrections, when he noticed another arrival.

"Yea, and here comes another new Ford pickup. Man they must have really stolen some quarters. Both are driving new pickups."

The second Ford pickup parked and the men went inside. The two men began to carry bags that appeared to be bank bags from the shop. They placed the bags into the bed of one of the pickup trucks.

Edwards exclaimed, "Damn, we should have gone in their shop last night! Those are all coin bags. We should have stolen all their quarters and then they would have gone out shooting phone booths again."

Both men got into one of the pickups with the moneybags and drove off. They drove four blocks and pulled into a bank. They removed the money bags from the pickup and went inside.

"I'm going inside," Edwards announced.

Once inside the bank, Edwards located the two men. Edwards went to a table and pretended to write a check so he could watch the two. They were talking with a pretty blond bank teller. Edwards thought, "I

Lt. Joe "Bill" Bradley

bet they use her every time they come into the bank. I bet she gets plenty of candy and flowers."

The teller poured the bags of quarters into a coin counter. After the money had been counted, the teller gave the suspects a deposit slip; they then returned to their truck.

Edwards ran to where Watson was parked.

"Man, you ought to see the gal they use to count their quarters. She's a 10 plus. I bet they take care of her in more ways than one."

Edwards and Watson followed the two men back to the Auto Shoppe. The two detectives watched the Auto Shoppe until noon, but there was no further activity.

Edwards turned to Watson, "I wonder why the local police haven't discovered these two bastards never work on cars."

A short time later, both men came out of the shop and got into their pickups and left. Edwards and Watson followed them as they drove to an apartment complex located just off the main highway. Both men went inside an apartment.

The crooks stayed in their apartment the rest of the day and into the night.

"Hell!" Watson said. "They're not going anywhere tonight. I'm sure getting' hungry."

"Me too. Lets go find a good chicken fried steak."

The detectives found a small mom and pop type café.

After eating, Watson remarked, "These East Texas people really know how to cook a chicken fried steak. I'm going to order another one. Want to split it with me?"

"Sounds good to me, but Kramer will catch it on our expense account. I've tried to pad my expenses before. Kramer thinks if he saves some money on our budget, the city will give us more. I've tried to tell him that's bullshit."

"Come on, the price for the dinner is $4.50. In Houston, they'd charge you fifteen dollars for this dinner."

"O.K., order me another beer. I'm going to the bathroom."

When the detectives finished eating, they drove back to the crook's apartment. The pickups were still there.

Watson let out a big yawn, "Think we ought to watch the crooks all night? I'm really tired."

"Hell no! But if we lose them, you are in charge. Lu would transfer us both."

They decided to start early in the morning so they headed back to the motel.

On the way, Watson said, "We should look in their shop."

"Man, we can't do that," exclaimed Edwards. "This is a small town. The cops might knock us off."

"No they won't. You don't realize how good a burglar I am. Drop me off at the shop and then come back for me in twenty minutes. Just stay away from the local cops if you see any."

"O.K., but if you're busted by the local cops, I'm not going to make your bond. Oh shit, let's don't even think about screwing up."

Lt. Joe "Bill" Bradley

Edwards pulled over on the side of the road and stopped.

"What're you doing?"

As Edwards opened the driver's door, he said, "I'm putting a toothpick in the door button so that the dome light won't come on when you get out. Do the same for your door. See how smart I am."

Edwards headed for the Auto Shoppe. There was no traffic on the street. Watson slipped out of the car and headed for the back of the shop. Edwards drove off.

Watson tried two windows before he found one unlocked.

"I hope these bastards don't have a burglar alarm."

Watson raised the window and waited a few seconds. There was no alarm. Watson climbed through the window into the shop closing the window behind him. Inside he used his penlight.

"Look at this," he said out loud. There were a number of pay telephones on a table. They had all been taken apart."

"I guess the bastards wanted to know how they worked and what angle to shoot out the lock." Watson quickly copied the telephone numbers.

He then spotted a stack of automobile license plates. Watson went through the stack writing down each license plate number. The license plates were mostly Texas, but there were two from Louisiana and one from Arkansas.

Watson then went through a desk but there was no information of importance.

THE TWELVE JUDGES

Edwards drove through the downtown area for the third time. Twenty minutes had passed and there was no sign of Watson.

Edwards spotted a police patrol car in the next block as he drove past the Auto Shoppe. He waved at the officer when he passed him. Edwards drove for another five minutes and seeing there was no traffic around, headed back to the Auto Shoppe.

As he approached the shop, Watson ran from behind the building and jumped in.

"You know Watson, you're a nut! There are only two cars on the streets tonight, me and the police!"

"Yeah, I know, the patrol car came by the shop once. I thought he saw my pen light, but he went on. Let's go get some sleep."

"Sleep hell! Let's get a drink!"

After a few drinks in the motel bar, the detectives went to their rooms for the night.

At 7 the next morning, the telephone rang. Edwards thinking it was the sexy voice with a wake up call said, "Good morning darling. Thank you for waking me. Are you going to give me room service this morning?"

Lieutenant James snarled, "I'm not your darling, but if you don't get your ass out of bed, you're going to need a darling."

Edwards nearly dropped the telephone. "Lieutenant! Here, talk with Watson." Edwards threw the phone to the bed Watson was in, hitting him in the chest.

Lt. Joe "Bill" Bradley

Watson got on the telephone with Lieutenant James and told him what they had found in the Auto Shoppe.

"Stay with them, Watson. If they leave let me know where they're headed. If they go to another city, I'll contact the police there to assist you. Kramer is on the telephone with me. Give him the license numbers you have. Watson, tell Edwards, I know he's horny, but I'm not his darling. Here's Kramer."

When Kramer had been given all the information, he said, "Tell Edwards that Lu is really pissed because Edwards called him darling. He's really not, but make Edwards think he is. Edwards stole my lunch the other day and I'd like to see him squirm."

Playing his part, Watson said, "Thanks Kramer, I'll warn Edwards."

Edwards raised up in bed. "Warn me about what?"

"Edwards, I could hear the Lieutenant screaming in the background. Kramer said the Lieutenant was really pissed at you for calling him darling and was going to ship you to the Juvenile Division."

"Oh, shit! Maybe I should call the him back."

"You better just keep your mouth shut." Watson was enjoying seeing Edwards squirm.

"Let's get some breakfast and locate the crooks."

"I'm not hungry now. All I can think about is Lu sending me to the Juvenile Division."

"Come on Edwards, let's get packed. The crooks might make a move today. I'll pay our motel bill on the way out so we won't have to come back if they make a move today. There's a café close to the Auto Shoppe where we can have breakfast and watch for them."

"What if they have already left town and don't come back to the shop?"

"Then Edwards, we'll just have to screw up the motor in our truck and say our truck broke down. It would be hell to pay with the Lu if we lost them. I think they'll be back. They need license plates for their pickups. I bet they change license plates every time they make a trip."

Edwards and Watson drove to the café. Watson had bought a local newspaper and had read it twice while watching for the crooks.

"There they are!" whispered Edwards.

Watson and Edwards watched as the two men parked at the shop and went inside. A few minutes later they came out.

Edwards said, "Can you believe this? They're changing the license plates on their pickups in broad daylight. Pay the bill! Let's go!"

Both detectives went to their truck. After the crooks changed the plates on their pickups they went back inside the shop.

After 30 minutes the two crooks came out and got into their pickups. They drove south on the highway that led out of Tyler. A mile up the road, both pickups pulled into a truck stop. They had stopped to get gas.

"There's a phone booth, Edwards. Call the Lieutenant and tell him the crooks are moving.

Lt. Joe "Bill" Bradley

"You call him. I don't want to talk to him just yet. I bet he's still pissed at me."

Watson parked next to the phone booth. Kramer answered the phone back at the factory.

"Let me talk to the Lu, fast."

Lieutenant James got on the phone. "What do you have, Watson?"

"Lieutenant, they're on the move. My bet is that they're headed for Houston. That's the highway they're on now."

"Stay with them, Watson. I'm going to get airborne. I'll follow the highway out of Houston towards Tyler. I should be in your area in a couple of hours. I'll contact you by radio."

James called the small airfield where he kept his personal Piper Cub. The airplane was old but a good one. He used it most of the time for fishing. He flew to South Padre Island a lot, landing on the beach to fish in the surf.

"Jake, this is Lieutenant James. Get my piper ready. I'll be there as soon as I can."

Lieutenant James went into the large gathering room and spoke to the other detectives, "The crooks are on the move. Two of you will be at the Stardust Motel and two at the Cowboy Inn. The rest of you will station yourself along the Eastex Freeway. I'll contact you when the crooks get close to Houston. Hancock, you go with me."

James and Detective Hancock drove to the private airfield in the north part of Houston.

Jake was a mechanic for the airfield and always kept the Lieutenant's Piper in top condition. It was ready to go when they arrived.

THE TWELVE JUDGES

"Jake, I won't be filing a flight schedule, but tell Houston International to keep me on radar."

"O.K., Boss."

As the small Piper rolled onto the runway, James increased power. The small plane was like a kite, it didn't take but a short distance and the airplane lifted from the runway. They were headed for East Texas. The cub was ideal for following cars on the highway as it flew at slow speeds. James knew it would not be a problem staying close when he found the crooks.

As they flew over Conroe, Texas just outside of Houston, James said to Hancock. "See if you can contact Edwards and Murphy."

"101 to 104"

"104 to 101, go ahead. Boy! Hancock, you're really coming in clear."

"We should come in clear. It's over 5000 feet to the ground. I usually don't talk to other cars from this height and I'm not too happy about it now. By the size of this airplane, I think Lu bought it from Toys R Us."

"104 to 101, we're on Highway 59. We just left Lufkin."

Hancock turned to James and asked. "Where are we, Lu?"

"We're coming to the Sam Houston National Park outside of Huntsville. Tell them, I'll move over to Highway 59 and head their way. When they see us, tell them to give us a call."

"O.K., Lu. 101 to 104, we're headed your way. When you see us, let us know."

"104, Clear."

181

Lt. Joe "Bill" Bradley

Edwards pointed out the window. "Look Watson, there they are. Boy, that's sure a small airplane. I don't think I'd like to ride in that toy."

"104 to number 101. You're passing over us right-t-t-t now."

James banked the airplane sliding into a turn. After lining up with Highway 59, he powered the Piper Cub.

"104 to number 101, you're nearly on top of us."

Lieutenant James slowed the airplane down.

"101 to 104. We see you. That must be the two black pickups just ahead of you."

"104 Clear, that's the crooks."

"Hancock, tell Edwards and Watson to back off a couple of miles. We'll climb a little higher and stay with them until Humble, Texas. Kramer is going to have some of the detectives waiting in Humble and they can follow the crooks to whatever motel they're going."

Hancock called 104 and repeated what James had said.

For another two hours, Lieutenant James kept the Piper behind the crooks.

During the flight, Hancock noticed at times that the engine of the small plane would seem to cough and sputter.

Hancock looked at James and hollered, "Are we running out of gas?"

"No, Hancock, We're flying too slow. The engine is trying to stall."

"Oh shit! I wish you wouldn't have told me that, Lu."

THE TWELVE JUDGES

As they approached Humble, James told Hancock to contact the units on the ground.

"101 to any unit in Humble."

"108 to 101, go ahead."

"101 to 108, the crooks are just entering Humble. They are both driving black pickups. 104 will give you their license plate numbers."

"108 to 101, we're set up along side the freeway in the middle of town. There are a couple of units outside of town. We see them now. We'll take them from here."

"101 to 108. Clear."

Lieutenant James turned the plane southwest and headed for the airport. James contacted the tower and received permission to land. The airport only had one runway which was next to a golf course.

As you landed, the plane came in low over hole number nine. James often wished someday that Chief Ladd would be putting on hole nine when he landed. He would scare 50 pounds off of him. Lieutenant James landed and taxied to his hanger where he kept his plane.

As the Piper came to a stop, James turned to Hancock and said, "The men could have handled the surveillance all the way from Tyler but I thought you would enjoy a ride."

Hancock's only reply was, "I guess you brought me along to rewind the rubber band on this damn plane."

"Come on, Hancock. You know you enjoyed the ride. Now you can go fishing with me in Brownsville."

Lt. Joe "Bill" Bradley

"No thank you! I'll go fishing with you but we are going to drive and stay on the ground."

Jake met them at the hanger.

"Gas it up and check it out real good Jake and thanks."

"Anytime, Boss."

Bill James and Hancock headed for the factory. They could hear the other detectives talking over the police radio. The crooks had gone to the Stardust Motel.

When James and Hancock arrived at the factory and walked in, only Kramer was present. "Everyone in place Kramer?"

"They're all at the Stardust Motel. Murphy and Park have all of their electronic gadgets with them. They're going to put a transmitter on the crook's pickups so they can be located if they lose them."

James heard a familiar female's voice. "Do you still drink your coffee black, Bill."

James turned and there stood Kathy Moss.

"Kathy!" Lieutenant James gave her a hug nearly spilling the coffee.

"I'm now your secretary. Your office was a mess! You haven't even filed one hour of overtime for the men or yourself. Chief Ladd called me. He knew I had been your secretary when you were in the Burglary and Theft Division."

Kathy Moss was a great secretary. Lieutenant James had a great deal of respect for her. She knew her job and he knew she would be an asset to the group. She was loyal and could be trusted. She was excellent at typing search warrants and statements. Kathy only had one fault, if it was really a fault. James

THE TWELVE JUDGES

knew anytime he was upset with one of his detectives, she would go out of her way to defend the detective and cover for them.

"Kathy, watch these detectives, they're all rogues."

"Lieutenant, I know most of them, they're sweet guys."

The telephone rang and Kramer handed James the telephone, "Lu, it's Watson."

"What does it look like, Watson?"

"Lieutenant, we've rented the room next to the crooks. Me and Edwards are going to stay in the motel room. We've got four vehicles ready to follow 'em tonight. Murphy and Park will be in separate vans with their receivers, to monitor the bugs on the their pickup."

"Watson, don't say bugs over the phone."

"Sorry, Lieutenant."

"Rent another room away from the crooks. Ya'll can hang out there until they move. Make sure the room you rent is where you can watch the pickups. And, tell them no drinking!"

"Sure Lu, they'll really believe me when I tell them that."

"Call me when the crooks start to move."

"Yes, Sir."

"Kathy, can you work overtime tonight?"

"Of course, I know these guys need my help."

Handing Kathy some money, James said, "Better go get some drinks and hamburgers. It's going to be a long night."

Kramer said, "I'll drive you, Kathy."

185

Lt. Joe "Bill" Bradley

When they returned with the hamburgers, Kathy cleaned a table where they could eat.

James told Kathy about each detective and what the group was trying to accomplish.

After James had finished telling Kathy about all of the detectives, she said, "Thank you, Bill, for trusting me."

She followed James to his office. They talked for a long time. Lieutenant James had her make a list of all the supplies that she would need.

At 11:30 p.m. Edwards called, "Lu, the crooks are stirring. Each carried a blanket to their pickup. It looked like their rifles were wrapped in the blankets. I called the other guys and they're in their cars standing by."

"You and Watson stay at the motel. Check the suspects' room when they leave. We're on our way. Come on Hancock things are starting to move!"

Kathy called to James as he left the factory. "Tell the boys to be careful."

On the way to meet his detectives, Lieutenant James could hear Murphy and Park talking over the radio.

James broke in. "Number 12 to all units. Let them shoot two telephone booths before you bust 'em. On the third shooting, bust 'em as soon as they shoot."

All of the detectives acknowledged the Lieutenant's transmission.

Park broke in over the radio. "Murphy, did you check the transmitter on my crooks truck before you put it on."

"No, you were suppose to."

"The hell I was!"

THE TWELVE JUDGES

Lieutenant James broke in. "Number 12, what's wrong?"

"108 to number 12. The transmitter on the truck I'm trailing is not working. We lost him in heavy traffic."

James replied "Damn it! Check the shopping centers and all the telephone booths in the area. I'll get back to you later. 109, do you still have a reading on your crook."

"109 to 12. Yeah Lu, I always check my equipment. Some people don't."

A loud fart came over the airways.

Murphy said, "I hope you shit in your pants, 108"

"Lu, my man is pulling into a Lucky's Food Store. The store is closed. There are two telephone booths. We're going to pass by and let 106 watch him."

The detectives following Murphy pulled over to the curb with their lights out.

In less than 20 seconds the crook had jumped from his pickup truck, shot the telephone locks out, grabbed the money boxes and drove off.

"106 to 12. Lu, he shot both telephones. Boy is he fast. Do you want us to take him on the next one?"

"Number 12 to 106. Yes, take him down. I wanted to see him shoot one, but take him down and be careful."

"106 to 12. Clear."

James pulled into a service station parking lot to wait.

187

Lt. Joe "Bill" Bradley

"This should be good. Turn the radio up so we can hear."

Murphy's voice came over the police radio. "109 to all units, he's taking a right onto North Shepherd headed south. It looks like he's going to the grocery store in this next block. He is! 106, turn your damn lights out!"

A few minutes passed and Murphy got on the police radio.

"109 to 12. Lieutenant, we have him. Can you believe that he shot three telephone booths in that short of a time?"

"Number 12 to 109, take him to the office. I'm going to the motel and check with Edwards and Watson."

Lieutenant James and Hancock drove over to the Stardust Motel.

On the way, Detective Park was contacted. "12 to 108, any luck on the second truck?"

"108 to 12. Lu, we can't find the bastard."

"12 to 108. Park, you know about the federal rules, no cussing over the air."

"Sorry, Lieutenant."

"Well, keep looking for the bastard."

Park could hardly talk from laughing. The Lieutenant did hear a "O.K."

James and Hancock knocked on the door where Edwards and Watson were on surveillance. James heard feet shuffling and as the door was opened Edwards was trying to hide empty beer bottles.

Edwards face was bright red as he said, "Lu, I didn't drink any of the beer. I don't know whose beer it is, but I didn't drink one beer. Lu, I don't want to go to the Juvenile Division."

Lieutenant James said, "What in the hell are you talking about Edwards?"

Watson doubled over laughing.

James asked, "What about the suspects, room, anything there."

"Just their clothes and some boxes of 30-30 shells," answered Edwards.

James sat down on the bed and said, "Let's think this out. If we arrest the crook that we lost when he gets back to the motel, all we'll have is a rifle and some quarters unless he talks. I'm sure he has thrown the coin boxes away. Being an ex-con, I doubt if he'll talk. They're using soft lead bullets. There hasn't been a bullet recovered that has been intact, so we can't match the rifle with the bullets. We know that he's not going to stop shooting phone booths just because his partner was caught. Let him slide this time. We know who he is now. The next time, we'll get him right. We'll give his name and truck descriptions to the other police departments. Edwards, you and Watson stay here until he returns. Get the broken transmitter off his truck. Hancock stay here with them. He may think his partner is still out shooting phone booths. I'm afraid, when he returns and his partner doesn't, he's going to hit the road for East Texas."

James left for the factory.

At 4:00 a.m. King, who was at the motel window said, "Isn't that the other crook that just pulled into the motel?"

Lt. Joe "Bill" Bradley

Watson peered out the window, "That's him. He's going to his room. He's not carrying anything."

Park said, "I'm going to get the transmitter from his truck, hold the door open and holler real loud if you see him coming my way."

Hancock held the door open and Park ran to the truck and crawled under. The transmitter had a magnetic base and was attached to the frame of the truck. Park pulled the transmitter off and crawled out. He ran back to the motel room. When Park entered the motel room he asked, "Where's Watson?"

Edwards said, "The crook came out of his room and went to the front desk. Watson followed him."

Detectives then heard a sound of a key in the door and Watson came busting in.

"The son-of-a-bitch is checking out."

Edwards said, "Good! That'll give me time."

Edwards grabbed an Army looking bag and flew out the door.

Hancock and Watson stuck their heads out the door just in time to see Edwards using a "slim jim" to open the crook's truck door. They could hear Edwards talking to himself.

"What a pretty 30-30 rifle you are. Here is something for you. Now let me powder you a little. Now for the finishing touch."

Hancock said, "The bastard's gone crazy. I always knew he spent too much time in those tunnels as a rat when he was in Nam. What do you think he's doing?"

"He's probably getting the serial number off the rifle," answered Watson.

THE TWELVE JUDGES

Edwards placed the 30-30-rifle back into the truck and locked it.

Just as Edwards got back to the room, the crook came out of his motel room in a dead run to his truck.

The three detectives didn't have time to get to their cars to follow.

"Edwards, I'm going to tell Lu that you screwed things up."

"Come on, Watson. Don't do that. Let's tell the Lieutenant that we followed him until he left town and he was headed for East Texas."

"I guess we better or you'll be in the Juvenile Division for sure! Let's go to the office."

When they returned to the factory, the first suspect had already given a statement to Kramer. The crook would not tell who his partner was or where he lived. He bragged that he had shot over 2000 pay telephone booths in Houston, Dallas, Fort Worth and a few small towns.

Hancock told the Lieutenant that the other suspect had headed back to East Texas. James gave instructions to book the first suspect and file charges on him.

Kramer said, "Lieutenant, one crook out of two isn't bad. At least you did what the Chief wanted."

"Just wait a few days," Edwards said. "We might get two out of two crooks."

"What do you mean by that?" Lieutenant James asked.

"Oh, nothing, Lu! Nothing!"

"It's late. Kramer take Kathy home." Lieutenant James ordered. "You men did a fine job. Chief Ladd will be happy. Now, maybe he'll get off of

Lt. Joe "Bill" Bradley

my back for awhile. The office will be closed tomorrow, I'm going fishing. Want to go with me Hancock."

"Not if you are flying," Hancock answered.

Everyone gave a yell and headed home.

A week later, in his office, Lieutenant James was dictating a letter to Kathy. The phone rang. Kathy answered it.

"Yes sir, just a moment please. Bill, it's Captain Adams from the Beaumont Police Department."

"This is Lieutenant James, what can I do for you?"

"Lieutenant, Captain Sims of the Texas Rangers said I should call you. He said you would know if anyone would know about the man I have in custody. I've been trying to find out information on crooks shooting pay phones. The strangest thing happened here last night. An ex-con was found in a pay phone booth with one of his hands and half of his face blown off. He's still alive but he can't talk right now. We figure he was trying to shoot the lock out of a pay telephone and his 30-30 rifle blew up. Lieutenant, I've never in all my years seen a rifle blow apart like this one. Half of the gun barrel is gone."

"How bad is the guy, Captain?"

"Like I said, he's in the hospital but he'll live. He'll never shoot another rifle again if he was right-handed. You won't believe where we found one of his ears. We found a whole ear that had been blown off. When his rifle barrel exploded it blew the whole right ear off, intact. The crook's ear was stuck on the glass wall of the phone booth."

THE TWELVE JUDGES

"You're kidding. Sounds like the rifle shell he used was overloaded with too much gun powder or something was in the rifle's barrel."

"I'll send you a picture of the ear. It's quite a sight. Captain Sims didn't come right out and say your men were involved, but he couldn't stop laughing when I told him the crook kept mumbling, `those damn twelve judges in Houston.' What did he mean by that?"

"Captain, we know your crook. He got away from us a few weeks ago. We've got his partner in custody and charged with shooting phone booths here. Send me your report and I'll send you mine. How far is your investigation going to proceed?"

"It's completed now since I've talked with you and Captain Sims. I'm going to carry the report as, `Accidental Injury, Due to Faulty Firearm' and I'm going to charge our man with `Malicious Mischief of a Public Communications Device."

Both men started laughing and it was a few minutes before James heard, "Thanks, Lieutenant. Captain Sims said you would know this crook. Boy, justice really was served this time. See ya."

"Kathy, stay here in the office. I don't want you to hear the ass chewing I'm about to give."

James closed his office door as he walked out and yelled. "Edwards!"

All the detectives took notice at the sound of the lieutenant's voice.

"He is in the back, Lieutenant."

"Get him and the rest of the guys!"

When Edwards and the other detectives had gathered, James said, "Edwards, I don't know who started the rumor that you were going to the Juvenile Division, but you are if I don't hear the truth coming out of your mouth."

James then related Captain Adams' story.

When he had finished, Edwards said, "Lu, do I have to tell you in front of the guys?"

"Damn right you do!"

Edwards, trying to look serious, said, "In the interest of justice and as my duty as a law officer..."

Lieutenant James broke in, "Cut the bullshit, Edwards."

Edwards hastily continued, "Before the other crook left the motel, I got his rifle out of his truck. I took a little bit of liquid solder and gun powder and put it in the barrel of his 30-30 rifle."

Washington jumped to his feet and started singing and doing the "Hokey Pokey", "You take a little bit here, you take a little bit there, that's the way you lose an ear."

Edwards was the only one who didn't laugh, he was thinking of the Juvenile Division. He continued his story. "All I hoped for was to split the gun barrel when he fired the rifle. I guess I used too much plastic explosive with the gun powder."

Lieutenant James and the other detectives couldn't hold back their laughter any longer. James had tears running down his cheeks and managed to say, "I guess you did Edwards, I guess you did."

Detective Washington started to clap his hands and everyone joined in.

James told everyone to be quiet. "Edwards, I had you tell your story for two reasons. One, we're not going to kill anyone unless we have too. Number two, this story stays with this group. I'd better not hear anything about it outside of this group or there'll be a lot of transfers to the Juvenile Division!"

"Lu, am I going to the Juvenile Division?"

"Hell no, Edwards! I'm going to keep you here to blow up this damn factory so we can get better quarters."

Detective Johnson spoke up. "Lu, make Edwards leave his Army bag in his car. He's got enough shit in his bag to blow us all to hell!"

Lieutenant James looked toward Edwards.

"O.K., I'll put my bomb bag in my car, but none of you bastards can borrow my car."

Washington said, "Who wants to!"

James returned to his office. "Kathy, look out there? There will never be another group like this in the history of this police department. There is talk on the street, don't let Lieutenant James' detectives get on your case. If they do, you've had it! They will arrest you, judge you and sentence you."

James learned the next day that Detective Edwards was taken out by the other detectives that night. They drank a toast to Edwards until the wee hours of the morning.

As the celebration continued the men teased Edwards into making a firecracker. The firecracker had blown a three foot hole in the street and set off burglar alarms in all of the stores in the area. Calls came into the police dispatcher's office about the explosion causing their telephones to light up like a Christmas tree.

Kramer said there was a mad scramble to leave the scene before the uniform officers arrived.

CHAPTER 9

INTERROGATION

Lieutenant James, working late one night, stood and stretched his tired body.

"Kathy, I'm tired of working on this damn budget report and I know you are too. Can't we be late sending the report in?"

"No, Bill, It's got to be in the Financial Office at 8 a.m. in the morning."

The phone rang. Thinking it was one of the men, Kathy answered, "James Accounting Department. Oh, Hi Carolyn. Yes, he's here but be nice to him. He's trying to get his budget ready and he's not in a good mood."

"Bill, it's for you. It's Detective Carolyn Moat from the Sex Crimes Division."

Lt. Joe "Bill" Bradley

James picked up the telephone receiver and said, "Hello Carolyn, how's the prettiest red- head in police work?"

"Not too well, Lieutenant. I tried to get you at home. Why are you working so late?"

"Damn budget, Carolyn. What can I do for you?"

"I have a suspect in custody and I know he's the son-of-a-bitch who's been molesting young boys as they leave the school grounds in the Oak Forest area. We have a little boy missing from a school where this suspect was seen at the close of school. I can't get him to talk. I've tried everything. I even tried some of the tactics that you taught me when I worked for you. We're going to have to release him soon. His attorney has called three times. I'm so concerned he has killed the little boy. Do you have time to come over and interrogate the bastard? Sorry about my cussing Lu, but this pervert can't be turned loose."

"Damn right I have time! I'll be right over."

Lieutenant James was happy to leave the office and the budget to his secretary.

James kissed Kathy on the cheek and said, "I'll be at the Sex Crimes Unit for awhile. Please! Get this damn budget finished before I return."

Kathy smiled and said, "It's going to cost you dinner tonight."

Going out the door, James said, "If you finish that damn budget, just name the restaurant. I'll spring for dinner."

James headed for the Sex Crimes Division at the main police station. Detective Moat was waiting for him when he entered.

"The suspect is in the next room, Lieutenant. His attorney is waking up a Judge now and filing a Writ of Habeas Corpus to get him out of jail."

"Let me talk with him alone, Carolyn. You can watch and listen through the one-way mirrored window."

Detective Moat handed James a file on the suspect.

Lieutenant James walked into the interrogation room and closed the door.

"Marion Claude Reynolds. I'm Lieutenant Bill James. Pull your chair over next to the desk. We're going to talk."

"I'm not going to talk to you without my attorney being present. I told the other detectives, I didn't hurt that little boy and I don't know where he is. I need a drink of water. Can I have a drink of water?"

"Marion, you can have a drink of water when I need one and right now, I don't need one. What kind of name is Marion? Did your parents want a girl?"

"Don't call me Marion, I hate that name. My name is Claude and I've nothing else to say. I want my attorney."

James took his Colt 45 automatic pistol with stag handle grips from his belt and laid it on the table between himself and Reynolds.

"O.K. Marion, I mean Claude. I need your present address and next of kin. I can see for myself how you look and what you're wearing."

Reynolds watching James couldn't keep still in his chair. The pistol lying in front of him on the table made him nervous. As Reynolds watched James, he swayed from side to side looking at the ceiling and then down at the pistol.

James began to type faster. James looked up from the typewriter and said, "Calm down Marion! Be patient with me. I need to type this report before we're swamped with reporters and television cameras."

"What kind of report? What are you typing? Why are the T.V. people coming here? I haven't been charged with anything, have I?"

"No, Claude, you haven't, but you know news reporters. They cover all homicide scenes. They couldn't exist if their lead story on the evening news didn't show blood and guts."

"If you hurt me, I'll get my attorney to sue you. I've sued cops before."

"Sit back down Marion, I mean Claude. I'm not going to touch you. Let me finish typing this report. What is your date of birth and social security number?"

"I've already given my date of birth and social security number to the other detective. Quit calling me Marion! You've typed two pages already and I haven't told you anything. What are you saying in that report?"

"Don't interrupt, Marion. I'm nearly finished with this report."

"If that's a confession, I'm not going to sign it. Sure, I admit I saw that little boy leaving school, but I was there to apply for a janitorial job."

"Didn't you just get out of prison for raping a young boy?"

"I did my time in prison for that. You can't hold that against me."

"Well Marion, what about the other two boys you raped."

"How did you know about the other two boys. I haven't told anyone about them and I didn't rape them. What are you saying about me in that report?"

"Shut up Marion! I'm nearly finished. There, it's finished."

Leaning across the table looking straight into Reynolds eyes, in a harsh voice James said, "You son-of-a-bitch. Read the entire report before you say anything else to me. You understand?"

James slid the report across the table to Reynolds.

Marion Reynolds picked up the report and started to read. After reading the report, Reynolds started to shake. Reynolds stood up waving the report back and forth screaming at Lieutenant James.

"I committed suicide? What is this, some kind of sick joke? I want my attorney. That female cop told me she was going to call a guy in to talk with me that was crazy and mean. I believe you are crazy. Your damn report says, `while under interrogation, Marion Reynolds overpowered Lieutenant James and took his pistol'. It also says that I screamed, 'Forgive me.' I then shot myself. I can tell by your eyes you're crazy and serious."

"I'm very serious, Marion Claude Reynolds. Sit your ass back down in that chair."

"O.K! O.K., Lieutenant. I don't want to die. I didn't mean to kill that little boy. He kept hollering, `Mama, Mama'. I just tried to keep him quiet, but he wouldn't shut up. I didn't want to hurt him."

Lt. Joe "Bill" Bradley

"I know you didn't mean to hurt the boy, Claude. I'm going to help you all I can, trust me. Where is the boy, Claude?"

"He's in a culvert next to the tennis courts at the school. Get that female in here, I'll show her but I don't want to be around you. You gonna' charge me, Lieutenant?"

"You bet your ass I am."

CHAPTER 10

A MEXICO CONNECTION

Lieutenant James was busy at his desk signing all types of forms. "Kathy, what in the hell am I signing today?"

"Bill, just sign the papers, I'll do the rest. Where are all the men?"

"It's qualifying day at the pistol range. I have to qualify also. Crap, on these papers! I've never seen so many damn required forms! No wonder cops can't police anymore; they're all inside filling out forms!"

Kathy entered James' office gathering the paperwork that James had signed.

Kathy looked at James and said, "Quit your bitching! Think of all the people this paperwork gives jobs to."

James picked up his telephone and called Sergeant Peters at the pistol range. Peters had been in

Lt. Joe "Bill" Bradley

charge of the pistol range forever. Sergeant Peters knew every type of firearm and ammunition manufactured. He also coached the department's pistol team, which was one of the best in the nation. When on the range, a shooter went by his safety rules and if you horse-played or broke the rules you would find yourself going to a night class on firearm safety. No one got by with anything when it came to operating the firing range except, maybe, Lieutenant James.

"Sergeant, this is Lieutenant James."

"I figured I'd hear from you. Your detectives are here now. O.K., Lieutenant. What score do you want this year?"

"Make me an expert this year, Sergeant."

"Lu, the brass is watching pretty close this year. It's gonna cost you two fifths of Jack Daniels."

"You got it, Sergeant. I hope all my men are qualifying. Tell them I came in earlier and shot expert. Be sure and ride Hancock, he can't take it if he knows I out shot him."

"O.K. Lu, but if Hancock gets pissed at me, it's gonna' cost you another fifth."

As James hung up his telephone, his straight-line telephone rang. Lieutenant James recognized the voice immediately when it sweetly asked, "What are you doing for lunch?"

"I'm probably going to take the most beautiful girl in Houston to lunch."

"With a statement like that, I'll buy lunch. Meet me at the Steak House in the Village at noon. I'll be at the bar."

"You have a date. By the way, how's your son?"

THE TWELVE JUDGES

"He's doing just fine, Bill. He completed college and has a great job with an oil company. See you at noon."

Lieutenant James had known Barbara for years. At one time she was an expensive, high-class prostitute. She had a day job now with an insurance company. When she had been a prostitute she worked two nights a week. Her clients were the money elite of Houston or their distinguished out of town visitors. Barbara had put her son through college whoring. She was a rare breed of prostitute; she hadn't gotten into the dope scene. She was in her early forties and seemed to be more attractive than when she was in her twenties. Now she only worked at her day job. Her son was her treasure.

James had helped her through the years when she was busted by the Vice Squad, but that was rare. He met Barbara when he had been a detective in the Vice Squad. She had never had a pimp. Once, a pimp tried to take her over but James had convinced the pimp it was better for his health to leave her alone.

Barbara was also one of the best informers that Lieutenant James had. She called him at times to give him information. Sometimes she called just to have lunch or dinner; they enjoyed each other's company.

At 11:30 a.m., James left his office for the Steak House.

James drove down Main Street past Rice University turning onto University Boulevard. James always admired this drive. Large oak trees lined both sides of the boulevard and the entrance to Rice University. Hermann Park and the Medical Center were on the South side.

Lt. Joe "Bill" Bradley

As James made his turn he wondered how Doctor Abbott and Diane were doing. She had gotten out of the hospital and she and the doctor were planning their wedding.

James pulled up to the Steak House, parked and went inside, he walked to the bar.

Barbara saw the Lieutenant in the bar mirror as he approached. She smiled and spun around on her stool, her shoulder length brown hair shinning from the neon signs over the bar. She brushed her hair out of her eyes as James kissed her on the cheek and sat down beside her.

There were two drinks in front of Barbara. One would be his, scotch and water, and the other would be her drink, vodka and tonic with a lime. It was always this way when they met. First one there ordered the drinks.

James looked around. He noted the disappointment on the faces of the men seated at the bar; it was evident that they had hoped she was at the bar alone. It wasn't too long before the bartender told them a table was ready.

James could not help noticing her slim figure as they walked into the dining room.

"Barbara, you look great. Being a day time worker has sure agreed with you."

"Why thank you, Bill. You look pretty good yourself. Being single must agree with you."

Bill didn't answer. He knew if he told the truth, it would be that he missed having a woman around.

They talked awhile about Barbara's son before she said, "Bill, let's not order now. I have some information for you. I've been dating a man for about six months. Boy is he wealthy! He owns a chain of pawnshops here in Houston and some in San Antonio. Twenty, I believe. His name is Douglas Napier. They call him Doug."

"I know the man. His pawn shops call my office when they think they bought something stolen. Pawnshops do that to make it appear that they cooperate with the police. Go on with your story."

"Doug gives parties at his home for a select group of friends every so often. He always has the same group. The others bring their girl friends. I've never gone to bed with Napier. He always invites me to the parties, but I think he just has me there for show and to wait on him. In the group there is an attorney by the name Steve Minter. I don't think he practices law, he just works for Napier. There is also a Captain Sam Links and a Sergeant George Epps from your department. A wealthy Mexican National has been to some of the parties but not often."

James interrupted, "I know Links and Epps. The Sergeant is the Captain's hey boy. Hey boy do this. Hey boy do that. He's been with the Captain a long time."

Barbara went on, "They party about once a month. I've been picking up bits and pieces of what this group is doing. There is always cocaine at the parties for the girls they invite, but never a huge amount. Last Wednesday night; Doug and Captain Links went into the library. Doug asked me to get him another drink. I mixed him a drink and walked into the library. Doug was handing Captain Links a stack of money. Bill, the money wasn't even wrapped! It was

Lt. Joe "Bill" Bradley

all $100 bills. Doug told the Captain 'Here's $20,000.00. On the next trip, we both get more.' The Captain got really bent out of shape and mad when he saw me. Doug took two one hundred-dollar bills from the Captain and handed them to me. He then told Links, 'She's all right, forget it.' I stayed away from the Captain the rest of the night."

Barbara's face gave an irked look as she said, "Sergeant Epps gets drunk a lot and I've heard him brag about selling guns in Mexico and getting high prices for them. He said that some of the guns wouldn't even shoot, but they sold them to the Mexicans anyway. Doug owns a Winnebago motor home and Sergeant Epps said they drive it to Mexico for hunting and fishing. A Mexican National meets them somewhere on the border. I know this because Sergeant Epps brags about everything. He bragged how they could drive the Winnebago across the border into Mexico, without being checked, because this Mexican was really important and had connections. They go fishing on some lake in Mexico, I forget the name."

Lieutenant James exploded, "Fishing, hell! All Douglas Napier's pawn shops take in stolen property. He's a known fence. He's been busted before but there's never been a good case made on him. He also comes up with pawn tickets where he had bought property and says he didn't know the property was stolen. I bet those bastards are selling guns in Mexico and bringing back narcotics."

"Bill, keep your voice down. Everyone is staring at you."

THE TWELVE JUDGES

"Barbara, there is only one thing that I hate worst than a thief, it's a crooked cop! If Captain Links is dirty, I'm gonna burn his ass! Let's order now before I really lose my cool."

"Bill, how are you doing since your divorce?"

"Well, I'm fishing more, but I sure miss having a woman around." James didn't mean to admit to that.

They finished lunch and walked outside together. At Barbara's car Bill asked, "What are you doing the rest of the day? I don't feel much like going back to the damn office."

"Let's go to the zoo," Barbara suggested. "I haven't been there in ages. It's just down the street across from the Medical Center. I've heard that the city has really improved it."

"Sounds great! You drive. It'll be the start of a lazy afternoon."

Bill James and Barbara spent the rest of the day buying bags of popcorn to feed the birds and animals. It was wonderful for James to be away from the factory and just relax with Barbara's conversation.

At the end of the day, Barbara drove Bill back to his car.

"Thanks for a nice day, Bill. I'll call you when Doug has his next party. Even better, come over some evening and I'll cook you a good dinner."

Barbara gave James a kiss on the mouth and a hug at the same time. They both stepped back, gave the other a look of approval and then got into their cars and left.

As James drove home he thought of the kiss Barbara had given him. It had aroused and excited him.

Lt. Joe "Bill" Bradley

The next morning, Lieutenant James called Kathy at his office. "Kathy, I'm going to be a little late. I want to deliver some baseball equipment to a church."

"Are you still buying equipment every year for Father Gomez?"

"Yeah, I just know they're going to win the pennant this year. He has his whole team back this year. They've lost every year since I became their sponsor. I bought them new uniforms this year. I can't wait to see their faces. Call a meeting with the detectives for eleven."

James drove to the Eastside of Houston. A few years ago at a fund raising event at the Rotary Table, Juan had introduced Father Gomez to him. Lieutenant James had made the mistake of asking Father Gomez, "What can I do for you?"

Father Gomez took pride in squeezing every nickel he could out of anyone for his kids and his church.

Every year since that day, James had bought the baseball equipment for Father Gomez' kids.

Lieutenant James drove to the front of the church and parked. The old Catholic church had been built soon after the first Mexicans came to Houston from across the border. A group of young Mexican boys spotted him right away. He knew by the smiles on their faces that they knew he had something for them. They all crowded around his car.

"One of you go tell Father Gomez I'm here," James said.

"He's coming now, Mr. Lieutenant. If he doesn't trip over his skirt."

THE TWELVE JUDGES

James shot back quick, "You want me to tell Father Gomez what you said, that he wears a skirt."

"Oh no, Sir, Mr. Lieutenant, Father would make me play right field or sit on the bench. I'm the pitcher this year."

Father Gomez had insisted that the boys call James, Mr. Lieutenant. James had informed the boys not to, but it hadn't done any good. They respected Father Gomez too much.

Father Gomez, with his usual large smile, holding his robe up with both hands hurried down the steps of the church. Looking through the back window of James' car he said, "Are all those boxes for my kids?"

James nodded his head.

Father Gomez gave orders for his boys to take the boxes to his office. The kids opened the car door and grabbed the boxes. Temptation was too much. One of the boxes of baseball shirts was opened. The kids saw the new shirts and hollered. Arguments started about who was to get what number.

Father Gomez just smiled, shrugged his shoulders and let the boys continue.

"Come in awhile, Bill. Help me hand out the uniforms."

"I can't Father. I'm overdue at the office."

"Thanks and God bless you, Bill. Are you coming to the first game?"

"I'll be there, Father."

James opened the door to his car to leave but he knew Father Gomez and he knew it wouldn't be that easy. Bill knew what was coming next.

211

Lt. Joe "Bill" Bradley

"Bill, I know you're not Catholic, but I also know cops have problems too. A good confession helps. You need to come for a longer visit."

"Still trying, aren't you, Father."

Giving Bill a hug, he said, "That's my job, Bill, that's my job."

"See you, Father."

Lieutenant James left and drove to the factory. When he arrived, everyone was present.

"Murphy and Park, get your equipment and sweep the factory for any electronic bugs."

James didn't trust anyone except his detectives. He had heard that Jamie Owens at the District Attorney's office was working on rumors that some policemen were tapping phones. He wouldn't put it pass Owens to have his investigators bug his office. James knew that Owens wouldn't have the guts, but he could suggest it to his investigators.

After Murphy and Park told Lieutenant James the factory was clean, he began with the story Barbara had told him. The room was filled with tension when the Lieutenant finished.

"I know it's distasteful to investigate another officer but you have to look on him as just another crook if this information pans out. Do any of you have any objections to working a case on another cop? Would you rather me give this to Internal Affairs?"

Detective Watson spoke up, "Lu, Captain Links is in charge of all the high school sporting events on his off duty hours. If you work a moonlighting job for him, you gotta kickback part of your pay to him. He's a rotten bastard! And besides, all those suck-asses in

THE TWELVE JUDGES

Internal Affairs only know how to play with themselves."

"Lu," Hancock spoke up. "I believe I can speak for all the men. We do things I know the courts would frown on, but we have been getting results and we're not thieves! This is a dope deal. If there are cops involved, I'd rather we bust them than have the Feds bust them!"

James backed what Hancock had just said. "I think we owe it to Chief Ladd and our department. Let's look into this matter and I won't tell the Chief until I need to. The Chief did let me create this group."

Everyone agreed.

James continued, "Kramer, here are the names of the people involved. Gather all the information you can on them. Murphy, you and Park find out what kind of Winnebago Douglas Napier has. Go to Joe's Winnebago dealership. He is a friend of mine. Inspect the same year and model from top to bottom that Napier owns. I want listening transmitters put throughout Doug Napier's Winnebago. When they leave for Mexico, I want a transmitter also on the Winnebago's frame so we can follow at a safe distance. Tell Joe, that I'll need a motor home on a moment's notice for a long trip. Also look over Napier's home. He's bound to have several telephones and you two know what to do there."

Murphy said, "Got your meaning Lu."

James turned to Washington, "You and Hancock also check the area of Napier's home. Find his Winnebago."

Lt. Joe "Bill" Bradley

Hancock said, "Do I have to ride with Washington again?"

"You heard me. We need to set up surveillance. There's no use putting surveillance on all the pawnshops, they'll probably take the guns to wherever the Winnebago is located. Stay with the Winnebago. Wherever it goes, I want you to go. Kramer will make a surveillance schedule. The rest of you men assist Kramer while Murphy, Park, Washington, and Hancock are gone. All of you pack a bag in case I decide we all need to go to Mexico."

Kathy followed James into his office. "Bill, don't you think you should call Chief Ladd about Captain Links?"

"No Kathy, it's best to keep this thing among us right now. If it works out that Captain Links is dirty, I'll tell the Chief just before the bust."

James thought for a minute, "If this information is true, it's going to stir up some shit that the news media will love."

Later in the afternoon, Hancock and Washington came in.

"Lieutenant, Napier lives in an expensive neighborhood. All the homes there are in the $400,000.00 price range. His Winnebago is not at his home. We found it at a junkyard that Napier also owns. The junkyard is next to one of Napier's pawnshops. He has an office located there also."

Lieutenant James growled, "Why aren't you watching the Winnebago? I told you to stay with it when you found it!"

Pointing at Washington, Hancock said, "Cause two thieves going into the pawnshop spotted

THE TWELVE JUDGES

Washington. They know Washington. They got back in their car and took off. We had to leave. We didn't want to blow the deal."

"What vehicle were you in?" asked James.

"One of our pickups."

"Then use the Good Time van. You can't be seen through the dark windows. Get back to the junkyard and stay out of sight!"

"Boy are Murphy and Park gonna bitch again because they won't get to use the good van," remarked Washington.

"Let them bitch," James said. "They'll need the old telephone van anyway so they can blend in."

Washington and Hancock left for their assignment at the junkyard.

Murphy and Park returned to the factory.

Park said, "Everything's taken care of at the Winnebago dealership. Napier's home sits on a couple of acres. Things will work just fine for surveillance. Lu, where is my Good Time van? We need it. Guess what? We won't have to climb a pole. All the utilities out there are underground."

"Hancock and Washington needed the Good Time van more than you, "answered James.

"Lu, it really did me a lot of good to fix up that van. You never let me use it."

Murphy kidded Park, "Now don't cry, I found you a nice mattress that will fit in the telephone van so you can rest your little head."

Park kept bitching. "Lu, you know how hot it is out there. It'll be 150 degrees in that old van."

Murphy kept kidding. "Wear your bathing suit like you did once before."

Lt. Joe "Bill" Bradley

Park left the lieutenant's office still bitching as Kramer came in. "I have the schedule worked out for both vans, Lieutenant."

"Good, cut down the hours in the old van at Napier's home, it's hot as hell out there."

Everyone left for the day except detectives Murphy, Park, and Davis. Washington and Hancock had been pulled off their surveillance on the junkyard and pawnshop.

Davis was pleading, "Come on guys, let me go with you tonight. I can be your lookout."

Murphy and Park finally gave in to Davis' begging.

"All right, but only one of us is going into the motor home. Keep your ass out of our way."

They waited until after dark and then Murphy and Park left with Davis driving. They parked next to the junkyard where Napier's Winnebago was parked. A fence, with ribbon wire on top of it that could cut a hand off surrounded the area. Murphy got out of the van and walked up to the fence. A large Doberman Pincer jumped at the fence trying to get to Murphy.

The Doberman's lips curled upward showing his large teeth. Murphy got down on his knees teasing the dog. The dog charged the fence hitting it and biting the chain link fence. Murphy shot the dog with a tranquilizer gun he had borrowed from a city dogcatcher. In a few minutes, the Doberman began trying to run in circles. The dog dropped to the ground next to the fence.

Murphy took a stick and poked the dog. He was out.

THE TWELVE JUDGES

"Come on Davis, pick the lock on the gate. I can't climb the fence because of the sharp ribbon wire at the top. I'll cut my pretty ass to pieces."

Davis proudly said, "See, you did need me!"

Davis walked up to the gate and in a few minutes had picked the lock. Davis didn't return to the van. He opened the gate and walked into the junkyard and headed for the Winnebago.

"That Bastard! I told him he couldn't go in. Park, you better stay out here and be our lookout."

Murphy hurried after Davis. Just as Davis reached the Winnebago, Davis heard a low growl. A second large Doberman charged Davis, sinking its teeth into Davis' leg.

Murphy ran back to the van grabbed the tranquilizer gun and took off running back to where the dog and Davis were. The dog still had Davis by the leg and wasn't about to let go. Davis was pounding the dogs' head with his fist, which only made the dog mad. Murphy shot the dog. The dog let out a deep growl, let go of Davis and started for Murphy. The dog jumped at Murphy and landed in a heap at Murphy's feet. Murphy knew the dog was finished for at least an hour.

Davis' right calf was torn open and bleeding. The dog had been chained to the bumper of the Winnebago and had not made a sound until Davis had walked into his range.

Murphy remarked, "That must be some bad ass dog to have him chained up inside a fenced yard." Murphy continued, "I better get you to a hospital."

Davis in a hurting voice replied, "Hell no, Just rip my pants and tie it around the wound so I won't bleed to death while you're in the Winnebago. If you help me stand, I'll get out of here."

Murphy disappeared into the darkness of the Winnebago. While he was inside, Davis limped back to the van. Park helped him inside.

"Where in the hell did the second dog come from?"

"The son-of-a-bitch was chained to the bumper. As Murphy said, he must be a bad ass dog to be chained inside of a fence. The bastard didn't even bark before he bit me. Shit! I hurt! Murphy's sure taking his sweet time. My leg hurts like hell!"

Once inside, Murphy hid four voice transmitters at different locations in the Winnebago. He was able to wire them into the power supply. Each transmitter also had it's own battery for back-up power when the Winnebago's power supply was turned off. When Murphy finished, he went outside and slid under the Winnebago. On the frame Murphy placed a magnetic transmitter that would emit a radio signal so the motor home could be followed at a safe distance. Finding an electrical connection, he also wired the transmitter into the Winnebago power supply.

Murphy crawled out and started toward the gate. He turned and went back and found the blood spots where Davis had bled. Using his shoe he covered the spots with gravel and then ran to the gate. As Murphy locked the gate, Park started the van.

"Get in, we're taking this guy to an emergency room." Park drove fast as he could in and out of the traffic to Ben Taub County Hospital.

If you were shot, cut, beaten, or run over, this was the hospital a cop wanted to go to first. The doctors here knew from experience how to treat any trauma. They had saved many lives of shooting victims, cutting victims and victims of car accidents.

The doctor who treated Davis at the County Hospital was really upset when Davis told him the dog could not be found. Twelve stitches were needed to close the wound on his leg.

"You better go see your personal doctor about getting rabies shots." The doctor had advised Davis.

When the three had left the hospital and were in the van, Murphy and Park started in.

"Rabies shots. You know they use a big needle that's a foot long and the shots are in the stomach."

"Shut up, both of you! Stop and get me a beer!"

"You can't drink on top of all the pain pills the doctor gave you."

Davis kept insisting. "Stop bastards, get me a beer. You owe me that much. Both of you idiots should have known there were two dogs. It's all your fault, so get me a beer!"

"O.K., asshole! But if you die, we're just going to dump you at the dog pound."

Park pulled into a convenience store and bought a six pack. Davis finished his first beer before Murphy had time to even open his.

"Damn! You did need a beer. Just think Davis, if the dog had bit the head of your dick off, I could have all your chips."

"You couldn't handle all my chips," remarked Davis.

Park and Murphy took Davis to his apartment and put him to bed. Murphy then telephoned

Lieutenant James at home and told him about Davis' encounter with the dog.

James then called Davis and told him he was not to come back to work until his doctor gave him an O.K.

The next morning all the detectives arrived on time.

James started his morning meeting with Murphy and Park going over last night's episode involving the Winnebago and Davis being bitten by a dog. When they had finished there were a lot of questions about Davis' condition.

Washington remarked, "Good thing the dog didn't bite the Davis family jewels. A lot of women would be really sad this morning."

James continued the meeting. "Park, you and Murphy get the telephone van and tap into Douglas Napier's home telephones today. Kramer, after Park and Murphy complete their job, set up surveillance schedules at both locations."

"I've been thinking about this case. We need some help. I'm going to contact Jeff Barton. He's in charge of U.S. Customs here in Houston. He's an honest man and has contacts in Mexico. Barton will keep his mouth shut. His men won't be involved directly with us but his undercover men can give some protection and information while we're in Mexico. They know more than the F.B.I. and D.E.A. about what's going on at the Texas-Mexico border. Also, they can handle the Mexican part of the investigation with all their contacts that they have."

Bill James stopped at this point and considered his next statement. Slowly he continued, "I know what

THE TWELVE JUDGES

I'm fixing to say will piss some of you, but it has to be this way. Captain Links and Sergeant Epps know me by sight. I can't be seen in Mexico by him. I'll run the operation from here and from whatever border town they cross. How many of you know Captain Links and Sergeant Epps?"

There were some moans and groans as hands were raised.

Lieutenant James went on. "Davis said they don't know him. If he gets better, Davis will make the trip with Park, Murphy, Johnson, Luna, and Hancock. Hancock will call the shots when I can't. Lets go to work."

Hancock spoke up, "Washington, you can ride with King while I'm gone. He'll take care of you."

Washington's only response was to give Hancock the bird.

James went to his office and told Kathy, "Get Jeff Barton with Customs on the telephone." Kathy made the call and handed the telephone to James.

"Jeff, this is Lieutenant James. Can you break away and come over to my office? I have something you'll really be interested in. Kathy, my secretary, will give you directions to the office. See ya in a little while."

Park and Murphy left for Doug Napier's home. Round the clock surveillance was begun on the Winnebago.

"Kathy, get us some coffee, please."

Lieutenant James met Barton at his office door. "Come in, Jeff."

"Boy, Bill, you must have really pissed Chief Ladd off to be quartered here. From the outside it looks like this building is past being on the list to be demolished."

"Believe it or not, the fat chief likes me."

Looking around at the old building, Jeff said, "Yeah, I can really tell he likes you."

"Jeff, we think we're going to get into a rather large narcotic and gun running operation. What I'm going to tell you must stay with you and your men for the present."

"You've got my word, Bill."

"That's good enough for me, Jeff."

Lieutenant James told Jeff Barton the story of the involvement of Captain Links, attorney Steve Minter and the pawnbroker. James did not mention the transmitters or the telephone taps. James knew Jeff Barton would not accept any illegal telephone taps or bugging devices without a court order.

When James finished, Jeff Barton said, "Bill, knowing you, I know you want to bust the Captain but I can take the heat off you and handle this matter myself."

"Hell no, Jeff! My detectives can get information you can't and besides, if they're dirty cops we need to be the ones who bust them. Jeff, you've got contacts in Mexico that I don't."

"Just tell me, Bill, what you need."

"Your men need to cover my guys while they're in Mexico. When we find out who the Mexican National is, you can handle the Mexico investigation. I'd like you and your men present when we bust the bastards back here in Houston. I believe we can get better results in Federal Court than we can in a State Court."

THE TWELVE JUDGES

"You are right, Bill. But I sure would like to be in on this all the way."

"Jeff, I'll keep you informed all the way."

"Bill, tell your men that they'll be covered. They won't know who my men are, but if any problems develop, they'll be there if needed."

After discussing their operation further, Jeff Barton left and Kramer came into the office.

"Lieutenant, the men watching the Winnebago said that a two wheel covered trailer was brought in and hitched to the bumper. I bet that's where they carry the guns."

"You're probably right, Kramer. Have you heard from Park and Murphy?"

"No, Sir."

"If you do, tell them about the action at the Winnebago. Sounds like our suspects are getting ready to make a trip. The men that aren't going to make the trip, put them on surveillance. Tell Luna and Johnson to go to Joe's and pick up a motor home for the trip. Tell them to get it ready and put everyone's gear in it. Also, tell them to hook up a tow bar so they can take a pickup truck with them. They might need it."

"Right, Lieutenant."

After a few minutes, Kramer returned to the office. "I was right Lieutenant, they are loading the trailer with guns."

"Damn, Kramer! They're going to make a move before we find where they're going to cross the border. We should have a tap on Napier's office too. Call Park and Murphy and see if they've heard anything."

Lt. Joe "Bill" Bradley

Kramer went to the police radio. Lieutenant James could see Kramer shaking his head no. The day ended with no information regarding the trip to Mexico. Lieutenant James went home.

James was watching a late western movie and having his usual scotch and water when the phone rang.

"Lieutenant, this is Edwards. A Mexican just called Doug Napier. I didn't get the Mexican's name but Napier told him they were coming down Friday. Napier said he was bringing everyone on this trip. He said the load was a large one and wanted the Mexican to have his end ready. Lu, they talked openly about it over the phone. The Mexican asked Napier if he had the cash that was to go with the guns. Napier said that Steve Minter was bringing the money. The Mexican told Napier to call him at 9-8734 in Villa Acuna, Mexico when he got to Del Rio, Texas. Napier told the Mexican to have party girls ready and he would see him Friday night. Napier has gone to bed for the night."

"You got what we needed, Edwards. Knock off the surveillance and take the telephone truck back to the factory. I'll see you in the morning."

"Lu, King is with me. Neither one of us know how to unhook the telephone wires. We're afraid that we will screw up if we try it. Should I call Murphy or Park."

"No, cut the two wires at the box and tape each end of each wire. We might have to hook up again. Park or Murphy can tidy things up tomorrow."

"O.K., Lu."

THE TWELVE JUDGES

At the morning meeting, Lieutenant James told the detectives what Edwards had heard while on surveillance.

"We've got two days to get ready for the trip to Mexico. We'll keep surveillance on the Winnebago. Murphy and Park will be in the Good Time van with all the communication equipment on the trip to Del Rio. Murphy, here's an address in Del Rio. Once you get to Del Rio, a U.S. Customs agent will meet you at that address and help you get the van into Mexico without any hassles."

Murphy raised both hands over his head, "Thank you God, we get to use the good van!"

Davis walked in as Lieutenant James was talking. Everyone started teasing.

"Where's your dog?"

"Have you started your shots?"

Washington began to bark like a dog.

Davis tried not to limp. He was waving a piece of paper, which he handed to Lieutenant James. "Lu, here is a doctor release, I'm ready to go."

Watson kidded, "Better let me check that doctor's report, Lieutenant. It's probably a forgery."

James said, "Sit down, Davis. If you think you're well enough, you can make the trip. As I was saying, Davis, Johnson, Luna, and Hancock will be in Joe's motor home. Kramer and I will fly to Del Rio and set up in a motel. King, I will contact you back here as soon as I get settled. I'll call you on my straight-line telephone in my office. Edwards, you, Washington, and Watson will assist King. While we're gone, get pictures and the legal description of Doug Napier's home, office, junk yard and all of his

Lt. Joe "Bill" Bradley

pawnshops. We'll need that later for a Federal search warrant. Hancock, keep a few miles to the rear of Napier's motor home. Murphy and Park will stay in radio contact with you all the way and keep you informed where Napier is located. I want everyone to be ready to move by Thursday night. Let's get ready!"

The next day everyone was ready. James called U.S. Customs.

"Jeff, they're going to make a move Friday. Kramer has taken an affidavit from me to be used so you can get a Federal search warrant when needed. I'll also have pictures and information on Doug Napier's home and pawn shops."

"That's great, Bill. I've already spoken with the U.S. Attorney and he O.K.'d the warrants based on your information from your informer. Why can't I go with you?"

"Jeff, don't ask."

"Bill, can you keep a secret."

"Depends on the secret."

"I checked the name of the crooks through D.E.A.'s computer. You know those bastards won't share information, but I was able to use a sneaky source."

"Go on, Jeff."

"Doug Napier's name came up on their computer. The D.E.A. suspects him of big time activity but they don't have any information like you do. The D.E.A. is going to shit when we bust him. You know their favorite saying, `You should have stayed out of our business. You messed up an investigation of a major drug ring'."

THE TWELVE JUDGES

"Screw the D.E.A.! They're overrated anyway. If they were doing their job, Houston streets wouldn't be full of narcotics. I'll keep in contact, Jeff."

"Good luck, Bill."

Thursday night, the Napier's Winnebago was moved to his home by Sergeant Epps.

Early the next morning everyone who was to ride in the motor home was present at the factory.

Detective Kramer informed Lieutenant James that Detectives Washington and Watson were on surveillance at Napier's home.

"Tell them to follow the Winnebago out of Houston until Murphy and Park can catch up. You guys in the motor home can start out now. Wait in Brookshire, on I-10 at the truck stop. Murphy will contact you when the suspects pass you on I-10. If there are any problems, contact King here at the factory. He'll know how to contact me. Good luck!"

As the detectives left to get started on the long seven-hour trip to Del Rio, Texas, Kathy gave the Lieutenant his briefcase. "Everything is in there that you might need. I've already called Jake and your airplane is ready."

James looked at his watch.

"9:30, I guess the crooks are waiting for the morning traffic to clear before they start."

As James was walking back to his office, he heard over the police radio.

"106 to base 12."

Kramer picked up the base police radio mike.

"Base 12 to 106. Go ahead."

"They're loaded and on the move, headed for I-10."

Lt. Joe "Bill" Bradley

"Base 12 to 106, clear."

"Lieutenant, did you hear?"

"Yes, notify Murphy and the guys in the motor home."

"Base 12 to 109, they're moving."

"109 to Base 12. We heard 106. We're on our way."

"101 to Base 12, we heard 106 too. I guess we can play catch up when we get on I-10."

"Base 12 clear."

"Kramer, let's give them a few hours on the road and then we'll take off for Del Rio."

Two hours later, Lieutenant James decided to leave for Del Rio. He informed Kathy that he would call her from Del Rio when he arrived. James and Kramer then left for the airport.

Murphy adjusted the monitors in the Good Time van. The only conversation heard from Napier's Winnebago during the first part of the trip was talk about fishing and women.

It was an uneventful long drive on I-10 for the first few hours.

Just before the Winnebago got to San Antonio it stopped at a truck stop. The suspects filled their Winnebago with gas. Murphy notified Hancock and the others in the motor home and they pulled to the side of I-10 to wait.

Hancock said they would fill up with gas when Napier left. Murphy didn't need any gas for the Good Time van, there were two large gas tanks installed on it by Park when they had first remodeled the van.

After the suspects had gassed up, they drove out of the truck stop.

THE TWELVE JUDGES

"109 to 101."

"This is tour bus 101. Go on ahead you sweet thing."

"109 to 101. They didn't get back on I-10. We're following them. Why don't you head out Highway 90 and wait?"

"Tour bus 101 to 109, okey dokey. When we get gas we will."

Murphy and Park followed the Winnebago toward downtown San Antonio.

Murphy said to Park, "Look, they're parking at a pawn shop in that strip shopping center. I bet they are picking up more guns at one of Napier's shops."

The Winnebago pulled into the shopping center and stopped in front of the AZ Pawn Shop. Napier got out and went inside. Three men came out with him, carrying guns of all kinds. The men made four trips back into the pawnshop to get more guns. The guns were put inside the Winnebago. After loading the guns, they left and drove out to I-10.

Outside of San Antonio the Winnebago turned on to Highway 90 and headed for Del Rio. Park got on the radio and told the guys in the motor home what had taken place. He turned on the transmitter monitors so they could hear the conversation in the Winnebago.

Over the monitors they heard, "Sergeant, stay on the speed limit. I would hate to get stopped buy a Texas Highway Patrolman with all these guns. I don't believe he would buy the story we're gonna use all these guns for bird hunting."

Park then heard Captain Sims say, "It's your deal."

Lt. Joe "Bill" Bradley

"Sounds like they're playing cards and having the Hey Boy Sergeant chauffeur them," Park said.

Park and Murphy followed the Winnebago out Highway 90 for the next hour. All the conversation coming from them was that of card playing.

Park then notified Hancock that the Winnebago had stopped at a truck-stop and they had all gone into a restaurant and that he and Murphy were going to stop also and get a bite to eat.

"101 to 109. We'll pull into the next roadside park and wait also."

A few miles up the highway, Hancock saw a roadside park.

"Davis, since you're not worth a damn with your poor little dog bitten leg, make us all a sandwich."

"I guess you want a beer too."

"Yeah, I need one. I'm driving."

Forty-five minutes later, the detectives in the motor home heard, "They're moving again."

Hancock started up the motor home.

"101 to 109, clear. Do you guys want a sandwich? Davis is a hell of a waitress."

"No, we did better than that. We stopped at a barbecue stand. Sorry you have to eat those cold sandwiches."

The Winnebago was followed through Bracketville on toward Del Rio.

"109 to 101. Have you ever seen so many pick-em-up trucks filled with white wing dove hunters? Mexico is gonna be full of Gringos."

THE TWELVE JUDGES

"101 to 109. Yeah, drunk Gringos in their pretty pick-em-up trucks. They think they own the highway."

As Hancock wheeled the motor home through Bracketville he picked up the radio mike and said, "This is tour bus 101. On my right is Alamo Village where John Wayne made the movie "The Alamo". On my left is the fort where General Patton trained. You guys didn't know I knew so much history, did you?"

Murphy snapped back over the radio, "We still don't."

Hancock replied, "O.K. smart ass! Did you know at one time the U.S. Army tried using elephants at this old Army base?"

Murphy snapped back again, "Did the elephants use duffel bags or trunks."

Hancock replied, "You want to bet me on that little piece of history?"

Murphy laughing into the radio mike said, "Hell no, old as you are, you were probably there."

Hancock didn't reply. He just increased the speed of the motor home.

The caravan sped on to Del Rio on Highway 90.

"109 to Tour Bus 101."

"Go ahead, 109."

"Before we reach Del Rio, we're going to pass Napier. We have to meet an U.S. Customs agent and get the necessary papers, so we can cross the border unchecked into Mexico. We'll meet you at the entrance to the International Bridge."

"101 to 109, clear."

Lt. Joe "Bill" Bradley

Twenty miles out of Del Rio, Murphy and Park passed the suspects in their Winnebago.

Park said, "They're only doing around 50 miles per hour, so kick it in the ass and we'll have time to meet the Customs agent and get to the bridge before they cross."

Murphy gunned the van as they sped down the highway.

Looking at a map of Del Rio, Park gave Murphy directions.

Murphy pulled into the parking lot of a bank in Del Rio, the location where they were to meet the custom agent. They sat there for a few minutes.

There were only a few cars at the bank. An old pickup occupied by a Mexican was also parked on the lot. It appeared the Mexican was asleep.

A few more minutes passed.

Murphy said, "Where in the hell is that customs man. We need to get to the bridge."

Murphy and Park saw the Mexican get out of the old pickup truck and head for their van.

Murphy and Park both reached for their pistols. The Mexican walked up to the van and said, "Open the window."

Murphy opened the driver's window to the van. The Mexican handed Murphy a small brief case through the window. The Mexican gave them a "hi" sign and said, "Good fishing," and turned and went back to his pickup truck and drove off.

After the Mexican had gone, Park opened the brief case. All the necessary papers to cross the border were inside.

"Damn, we even have insurance papers! Let's get to the International Bridge."

On the way to the bridge, Murphy and Park could hear a lot of talking going on in the Winnebago. They heard Napier make a telephone call to a Spanish speaking person when they arrived in Del Rio. Napier told the Mexican that they would pick him up.

"Senor Reynaldo Melendez. Glad to have you aboard."

"Senor Napier, you have the guns exposed too much. Put the guns on the floor in the shower stall and lock the door. The border guards will not come inside, but they will look through the windows. Open all the curtains so they can see in. Did you bring the money?"

"Yes, Senor Melendez."

"Give me five 20 dollar bills. That's all I will need for the border guards. I have already paid their bosses."

Murphy drove to the American side of the bridge. He saw Hancock and the other detectives parked by the entrance to the International Bridge. Park jumped out of the van and ran to the motor home.

Hancock opened the driver's window.

"Hancock, here are your papers to get across the border. Napier is going across now."

Park ran back to the van and jumped in. He pulled into the line to go across the Rio Grande River into Mexico. The American guards waved them through.

Murphy was waved to a stop at the Mexican guard post across the river. He paid the toll. When one of the Mexican guards peered inside the van, Park

Lt. Joe "Bill" Bradley

handed him a 5-dollar bill. The border guard waved them on.

"Park, did you see which way Napier went?"

"They're straight ahead about two blocks up."

"Can you see if Hancock got through O.K.?"

"They're stopped at the Mexican checkpoint. Here they come now."

The streets of Villa Acuna, Mexico were full of people. Small kids ran along the van trying to get Park, who had his window down, to buy their boxes of gum. By the time they cleared the downtown area, Park had bought ten cartons of gum.

"It's going to be tough following from here on."

"No it won't. There are too many American white wing hunters and fishermen around. Just look at the pickups and motor homes. Napier won't suspect a thing."

Outside of Villa Acuna the Winnebago turned west following a dirt road that was parallel to the Rio Grande River. The road was fine gravel and dirt with large holes every few feet.

Parks bouncing up and down from the bumps in the road said, "I hope the guys can get the motor home down this road. Mexico should hire Brown & Root to fix their roads."

"Hell, Park, it would take Brown & Root twenty years to fix just the roads around the border towns."

Murphy and Park had driven five miles when over the radio came, "Where in the hell are you going! This motor home has bottomed out a number of times. I think we lost part of one muffler. Stupid ass Davis

THE TWELVE JUDGES

didn't secure everything and we've got food and dishes all over the floor."

"109 to 101, hang in there, Hancock. We just passed a sign, Rio Grande-Amistead Fishing Marina, 7 miles."

Park and Murphy heard conversation coming from inside Napier's Winnebago. Reynaldo Melendez was talking.

"The last two cabins on the right are ours. I rented two of them for you. One cabin is full of liquor and pretty girls. Leave the guns where they are for right now. Tomorrow night when we go to Villa Acuna, my people will transfer the guns you brought. Your goods will be put in the Winnebago's shower. You can store the narcotics in another place later or just leave it in the shower. No one will bother us here. We will take the money you brought into Villa Acuna tomorrow night."

The detectives heard Captain Links say, "Sergeant, you stay with the money in the R.V. tonight."

"But Captain, what about the girls?"

"Sergeant, I said, stay with the money, you can have all the girls you want later."

"Yes, Sir."

After they had arrived at the marina, Murphy and Park went into the office. There were several young Mexican boys inside. One of the young boys ran to meet them.

"You need a fishing guide, I am the best," bragged a young boy.

The fat attendant told the boys to shut up and get out of the way.

Park said to the man behind the counter. "We need two hookups, one for a van and one for a motor home."

The man replied. "Senior, there is only one spot left and it is rented. The fishermen are coming in tonight."

Park took out a hundred dollar bill and said, "Senior we really need a hookup now."

The attendant took the hundred dollar bill and said, "Too bad the people are late. You can park both vehicles at number twenty. That will be thirty-five dollars please."

"What is the thirty-five dollars for?"

"Senior, it is a parking fee."

Knowing he would not get the hookup unless he paid, Park handed the attendant the money.

The attendant kept talking, "A guide will be another one hundred dollars please. Our rules are, you must have a guide."

Park said, "We will get a guide later."

"No, I'm sorry. Rules say, you must pay now."

Park gave the attendant another one hundred-dollar bill.

Walking outside, Murphy commented, "I would hate to ask what the cost of a damn fishing pole would be."

Hancock and the others had arrived in the motor home.

Park waved to them and said, "Follow us, we have hookup number twenty. Let's go find it."

After the detectives found their site and hooked up the electricity, Park said, "Has anybody seen the water hook up?"

THE TWELVE JUDGES

Johnson said, "They don't have water hookups. I saw some outside showers as we were coming in, but don't drink the water unless you want to get the trots."

Hancock and Luna were standing at the rear of the motor home.

"Hancock, can you believe we are parked right across the road from those assholes?"

Davis joined them. "Listen to that, those bastards are having a party."

"Davis, tell Johnson to set up a VCR camera in the rear of the motor home. We're going to take home movies of their every move."

"O.K., Mr. Boss Man."

"And tell everyone that we'll have a meeting in ten minutes."

"Yes, Sir, Mr. Boss Man. Anything else, Mr. Boss Man?"

"Yeah," Hancock replied. "Screw you and don't call me Boss Man!"

The six detectives went into the motor home. Hancock picked up the radio mike. "101 to number 12."

There was no answer.

Hancock then told the others, "I don't think they will do anything tonight or during the daylight hours tomorrow. We can take turns on the video camera. Film every move they make. They're going into Villa Acuna tomorrow night. They're taking the money to pay the narcotic connection. The narcotics are going to be delivered to the Winnebago while they're gone. Park and Murphy, will use the night scope tomorrow night to film the transfer of the guns and narcotics. The rest of us will go into town and try to follow them. We have the name of the Mexican National, but we need to identify the narcotic connection. I only hope we can contact an U.S. Customs undercover man when we go into town. They can follow them better than we can here in Mexico. We better take turns tonight watching the Winnebago in case they change their plans."

As Hancock finished talking, Lieutenant James' voice came over the police radio.

"12 to 101."

"There's the Lu. Hancock answer him."

"101 to number 12."

"Where are you located?"

"101 to 12. Lu, we're in Mexico."

"Hell, I know you are in Mexico, Hancock, but where?"

"We're at the Rio Grande-Amistead Fishing Marina. It's about 15 miles from Villa Acuna. Everything's in fine shape. The transfer will be made tomorrow night on the guns and narcotics. The payment of money to the connection will take place in Villa Acuna. We've no idea what type of vehicle they'll use to drive to Villa Acuna or where they'll be going or who they will meet."

"12 Clear. U.S. Customs couldn't stay away. Jeff is here with me. Jeff's men will cover the meeting in Villa Acuna with the dope connection. You would get burned if you tried to follow them. You stay with the Winnebago."

When Hancock pressed the police radio mike to acknowledge Lieutenant James' transmission, Davis hollered, "There goes our good time in Villa Acuna."

THE TWELVE JUDGES

"Number 12 to 101. Tell Davis that I heard him! Go ahead and let some of the guys go into Villa Acuna but their ass had better be back before 4 a.m. I believe Napier will leave in the a.m. Tell Davis and all if they are not back, their ass will be left Mexico."

"101 to 12. Clear Lu."

After talking with the Lieutenant, Hancock said, "I'll watch the Winnebago the first two hours. The rest of you better get some sleep."

The next morning, Hancock woke up to the smell of frying bacon. Luna was outside at a portable stove fixing breakfast for everyone. His breakfast burritos and tacos smelled great. Park was at the rear of the motor home reading a book.

"Any activity, Park?"

"Napier and the rest went fishing early this morning. Except the Sergeant. He's still here. I guess he's still sitting on the money."

Luna had even set a table for breakfast. He stepped into the motor home and hollered, "Get up you clowns, if you want breakfast. When you finish, one of you wash the dishes; I'm going fishing. There's a fishing pier at the marina. I'm going to catch us lunch."

Hancock headed for the breakfast Luna had cooked. He wasn't going to miss out on a good meal. As he took a bite of a breakfast burrito, Hancock remarked, "Where did you get these jalapeno's from, a burning volcano?"

After all the detectives finished breakfast, Luna got his fishing rod and tackle box and headed for the fishing pier. He was proud of his new rod and reel. It

Lt. Joe "Bill" Bradley

had cost him $200. He bought the rod and reel especially for this trip.

Luna walked to the end of the fishing pier. The water was so clear that you could see the bottom 10 feet down. Luna saw a number of small perch darting in and out under the pier. They ran for their lives even when a small bass came by.

Luna was excited, "Boy I'm fixing to tear those bass up with my new gear."

Luna tied a new artificial lure on to his line. He started casting. After about twenty more casts, Luna changed to a different colored lure.

Out loud Luna said, "I didn't spend all this money for nothin'. Come on big bass, I know you want this pretty lure."

He kept casting, and finally, caught a small one pound bass. As he let the bass go, Luna remarked, "Go tell your big brothers and sisters that the best fisherman in Texas is here."

Luna started casting again, but just as before he had no luck. Back down the fishing pier Luna heard a noise. He glanced down the pier and saw a young boy pulling a string out of the water with his hands. On the other end of the string was what had to be a five pound bass. The boy unhooked the fish and put it in a bucket.

What happened next, Luna could not believe! The boy wound the string around a Coca-Cola can. A chicken feather was tied on the other end with a hook and a small rock for a sinker. He took the Coca-Cola can in one hand waving it in circles over his head. All of a sudden, the boy extended his arm out towards the lake with the coke can in his hand in a heil salute. The hook with the feather and rock shot out over the water.

THE TWELVE JUDGES

As the homemade lure hit the water, the boy sat the soda can on the pier and grabbed the string. He pulled the string toward him, with jerking motions. A bass grabbed the chicken feather with the hook and the boy fought the fish using his arm as a rod. The boy lifted another five pound bass onto the pier.

"Here I stand with $200 of the best fishing gear a man can buy and he's catching fish with a damn chicken feather and coke can."

Luna walked over to the boy and sat on the pier to watch. The boy had caught nine bass that weighed three to six pounds.

Luna was amazed! He thought for a moment, "If I go back and tell the guys about this boy and I haven't caught a keeper, I'll never hear the end of it."

Luna spoke to the boy in Spanish. He then took out his billfold. He offered the boy a five-dollar bill and asked in his best Tex-Mex, "Que mas dinero?" as he pointed at the fish in the bucket.

The boy's face grew to a large snaggled-tooth smile and he said, "Gracias, Senor."

The boy grabbed the five-dollar bill and took off running. Luna thought, "At least he could've left me his Coca-Cola rod and reel."

Luna took his fish stringer from his tackle box and put the nine bass on it and walked to where the motor home was parked.

When Luna stepped into the motor home, Hancock hollered, "Holy owl shit! Luna really is a damn good fisherman! I didn't believe him when he said he was one hell of a fisherman. Come see what this son-of-a-gun has caught!"

Lt. Joe "Bill" Bradley

Everyone gathered around to see the fish. Luna began to tell them of the big ones that got away. As Robert Luna went outside to clean the fish, the others stood around admiring his catch. They were looking forward to fried fish for lunch. As Luna cleaned the last fish, he saw the young boy that he had bought fish from, walking toward him. He had two other boys with him. Each was carrying their own homemade 'Coke' rod and reels.

Luna, looking back at the other detectives, reached in his pocket and gave each boy a five-dollar bill.

In a low voice so the other detectives could not hear he said, "I don't need any more fish. Don't come back. Vamos!"

The three boys looking puzzled walked away. Luna heard one say, "Loco Mexican gringo."

Luna returned to finish cleaning the fish.

Davis asked, "What was that all about?"

"I told them earlier that I would pay them to clean my fish. They came too late but I gave them each a dollar anyway."

The detectives ate fried fish, french fries, pork and beans and white onions for lunch while they listened again to Luna brag about his fishing abilities.

After lunch, Luna and Hancock walked down to the marina to watch the fishermen come in with their day's catch.

Doug Napier and Reynaldo Melendez had already come in from fishing. Luna said, "Here comes Captain Links and Steve Minter. Look at the string of fish they've got. We should bust them. They're over the limit."

THE TWELVE JUDGES

Hancock said, "You're in Mexico, there's no limit on fish here."

The detectives watched as the guide docked their boat. Minter instructed the guide to clean their fish and bring them to their cabin. Hancock and Luna watched them until they entered their cabin and then they returned to the motor home.

At six o'clock, Johnson said, "Look, two taxis just pulled up to Napier's cabin. Hancock you better call Lu."

"101 to number 12."

"Base 12 to 101. Go ahead, this is Kramer."

"101 to Base 12. Where's the Lieutenant?"

"Base 12 to 101. He's in the other room with Jeff."

"101 to Base 12. Tell Lu, Napier and his bunch are fixin' to leave, they're loading now."

"Stand by 101. I'll get Lu."

"Go ahead 101, the lieutenant's here."

"101 to 12. Napier and Melendez are leaving in the first taxi. Captain Links, Sergeant Epps and Steve Minter are in the second taxi. Both cars are from the White Wing Taxi Company."

James' voice came over the radio. "12 to 101. What are the license numbers of the cabs?"

Hancock relayed the license numbers. "Lu, the first taxi has license number 5-0-4-3-9-2. The second taxi has license number 3-2-5-7-0-1."

"12 to 101, clear. Jeff will assign his men to cover them while in town. Tell Davis and Johnson not to get in trouble with the women tonight in Villa Acuna."

"101 to 12. You've got to be kidding, Lu."

Lt. Joe "Bill" Bradley

The detectives watched as the two taxis left.

Hancock said, "You guys get ready if you're going to town with me. I'm going to the office and call us a cab. I know you won't be in shape to drive back here tonight."

A cab arrived an hour later and Hancock, Luna, Johnson, and Davis headed for Villa Acuna.

The first thing Johnson told the cab driver was, "Senor, take us to Boys Town where the whores are."

Hancock said, "If you want to go to Boy's Town this early, you can drop us in town. Luna and I are going to Ma Crosby's and get a good Mexican dinner first."

"I don't want any Mexican food," replied Johnson. "I want a good drink and a good woman."

"Johnson, you and Davis can go on to Boy's Town, but I'm warning you, you better be back at the camp at four."

When the cab arrived at Ma Crosby's, Johnson and Davis stayed in the taxi. Hancock and Luna went to eat.

"Boy, it's sure crowded with all the dove hunters in town. I bet the whores are making money tonight," Luna remarked.

The two detectives found a table and sat down.

After a good dinner, Luna said, "Let's walk the streets and shop. It's a lot of fun, horse trading with the shop owners."

"Sounds good to me. I'd like to find some silver pistol grips for my 45."

As they left Ma Crosby's, Hancock remarked, "Can you believe that, four beers and two dinners cost only five dollars?"

THE TWELVE JUDGES

"Hancock, here's a shop that has pistol grips."

The two detectives walked in. Hancock spotted a pair of silver 45 pistol grips. The owner came over.

Hancock turned and said within earshot of the owner, "Can you believe this Luna? These pistol grips are $75. Down the street they're $60. Let's go back."

"Wait a minute, Senor. I'll give you a good deal. The silver market is low now. I haven't changed my prices. For you, I will. You can have them for $55."

Hancock dug into his pocket and pulled out two twenties and a five.

"Crap! This is all I have. Loan me ten dollars, Luna."

"I can't, Hancock, I'm broke. I don't have a dime."

Luna turned his pockets out like he was searching for money.

Hancock made a move to walk off and the shop owner said, "I am losing money, but you can have the grips for $45."

Hancock gave the shop owner two twenties and a five.

When they were outside, Hancock said, "You played your part great. Let's go to Boy's Town and see if we can find the two lover boys."

Boy's Town is on the outskirts of Villa Acuna. It consists of five whorehouses. Each has a club and a sex floor show. During deer and dove hunting seasons, there are more hunters in Boy's Town than are in the hills hunting.

Lt. Joe "Bill" Bradley

Hancock paid the taxi when they got there. He and Luna walked the main street. None of the streets were paved and dust hung in the air.

Barkers' were on the street offering the first drink free if you would come into their club. At the second club, Hancock and Luna went inside. As soon as they took a table, two women joined them.

"You are bird hunters? You want good time? Buy me drink, we talk dinero."

Luna said, "That's the only English they know."

After the whores saw that they were not going to get a drink they left to hustle other customers.

"Look! There's Johnson."

"Where?"

"At the table by the stage. He's got three whores with him."

Hancock called a waitress over. "See the guy in the black shirt next to the stage with the three girls?"

"Si, Senor."

"Go tell him that his wife wants him on the telephone."

Hancock gave the waitress a couple of dollars. They watched as the waitress bent over to talk to Johnson.

Suddenly Johnson stood straight up looking around the club. When he spotted Hancock and Luna, Hancock waved them over.

Johnson walked over to their table and sat down, bringing the three whores with him.

"I knew you couldn't stay away. Meet my three wives."

"Where's Davis?" Hancock asked.

THE TWELVE JUDGES

"He's gone back to town. Said he was tired of the whores. Hell I'm not. These girls really go for you as long as you have money."

Hancock said, "We've got about two hours. Then we need to head back. Is the floor show any good?"

"Yeah, it's good if you like to watch an orgy on the stage. I don't see how they do it or the males get it up with people watching."

Luna relied, "Money man, money!"

The three detectives drank with the girls and watched the floor show. Five naked girls, all dancing around one well hung male.

Detective Davis walked the streets of Villa Acuna. He came upon a small taco shop. Looking through the window, Davis saw one of the prettiest girls he had ever seen. "I've got to meet that gal," he said to himself.

Davis went inside.

There were no customers. He ordered two tacos from the girl. She appeared to be about 18 years of age. When she brought Davis his tacos, he asked her to sit down. She looked at the fat Mexican man behind the counter and he nodded his head.

She did not speak English. Davis tried to tell her she was beautiful. She just giggled. He was able to determine that the fat man behind the counter was her uncle. The girl acted like she was scared of her uncle by the way she kept glancing at him.

He asked her, "Can you leave for awhile?"

Her uncle overheard Davis and came over to the table. "Senor, it will cost you $100 if she leaves with you."

Davis thought, "You fat son-of-a-bitch, I guess you want me to rent a room from you too."

Davis showed the uncle a $50 bill.

"This is all I have."

The uncle took the bill and waved his hand and walked off. Davis took this as a sign the girl could leave with him.

Davis took the girl by the hand and walked out. They walked hand in hand for a couple of blocks. Davis tried to talk with the girl.

"I'm from Houston, Texas. I'm at a fishing camp. Do you want to go there and cook for me and some other guys?"

Davis was finally able to get the girl to understand that he wanted her to go with him. She hugged his neck.

"I don't mean to Houston," Davis warned her. But she kept repeating, Houston, Houston in her broken English.

Davis hailed a taxi and he and the girl left Villa Acuna. All the way back to Rio Grande, Amistead Marina, Davis told the girl how beautiful she was. He was finally able to make her understand that he was going to call her Angel.

When Davis and the girl arrived at the motor home, Murphy stepped out. "What in the hell are you doing? How stupid are you? You can't bring that girl here! We've work to do and we're leaving soon."

"Come on Murphy, she's just going to spend a couple of hours with me. I'll use the van and then send her back in a cab."

"Get a blanket and use the ground. I don't want you messing up my van."

THE TWELVE JUDGES

Davis said, "It's not your damn van and I'm going to use it."

Davis and the girl disappeared into the Good Time van. Murphy went back into the R.V. shaking his head.

"Park, you won't believe what Davis brought back from town."

"I saw her, Murphy. She sure doesn't look like a whore. She's gorgeous. I wonder where he picked her up. Not in a whorehouse. She's too fine looking for that."

At 3:30 Hancock, Luna, and Johnson arrived back at the marina. Johnson had to be carried in and put to bed. The beer had taken its toll on him.

"Has Davis returned?" Hancock asked.

"He's shacked up in the van. He brought some young girl back with him. Man, she's beautiful! She doesn't look like a whore. I have no idea where he picked her up."

Hancock said, "We better try to get some sleep. We're gonna be on the road a long time tomorrow. Was the dope delivered?"

"Yeah, and the guns are gone. We got pictures of everything. I called Lu and told him. Lu said Customs identified the dope connection. Park and I'll stay up and watch the Winnebago. We've been catnapping all night. You won't believe what that damn Park did. After they delivered the cocaine and took the guns, Park found the driver's window open on the Winnebago. He climbed in and not only took pictures of the packages of narcotics, but he put a bug in one of the packages."

"Well the Lieutenant wanted to know when the dope went into Napier's home," Park protested. "Now we'll know."

"Hancock, they've probably got five million dollars in cocaine stacked in the shower!"

The detectives decided to call it a night.

The next morning, Murphy woke everyone; it was already 10.

"They're moving around next door. Get ready to move."

Murphy and Luna stepped out of the motor home to get it ready to roll. There sat Davis with the girl.

Luna stumbled and nearly fell looking at the girl. He thought, "This is the kind of girl that you see only in your dreams."

"You like her, don't you, Luna? Isn't she pretty."

"Yeah, she's fantastic! Where'd she come from? Where did you meet her? What's her name? Man, she's beautiful."

When Hancock walked away Davis said to Luna, "She's going back to Houston with me. She wants to go and I'm going to take her."

"You're crazy, Davis! How are you going to get her across the border? You're plain nuts!"

"I've got a plan, but don't tell the others. No one will know a thing."

When the motor home was ready to travel, Hancock said to Murphy and Park, "Since we know Napier is going back to Houston, we'll leave and stay ahead of them. Customs has some agents around here somewhere. They will follow them to the border from here. If you have any problems, call us."

Davis grabbed Hancock by the shoulder, "I need to talk with you."

"What do you want, Davis?"

Davis lied. "The girl I picked up last night is being held by her uncle and made to work. She's been with him for over a year now. The uncle beats her and makes her work day and night. Can we take her as far as Bracketville? She has a sister there."

"Davis, I'm not taking a chance screwing up this dope case, smuggling a Mexican girl across the border. The lieutenant would have my ass!"

"Let me use the pickup that the motor home is towing. We don't have a need for it and we haven't used it since it was hooked on. I'll do this on my own."

"Go ahead, dumb-ass, but if you get caught, you're on your own! Have you ever seen the inside of the jails they have in Mexico? The Mexican police don't give a damn if you are a gringo cop."

Davis tried to fake being serious, "I owe it to society to free this young girl. Haven't you heard of individual world rights?"

Hancock replied, "Davis, you are full of shit. Don't tell the border guards you are with us."

Hancock walked away with his head bowed shaking his head.

Davis hurried to unhitch the truck from the motor home.

Hancock and the detectives left in the motor home followed by Davis and the girl in the pickup.

Lt. Joe "Bill" Bradley

Murphy and Park got into the van to wait for the departure of Napier. The two detectives had to sit in the van for another hour. They saw the suspects load their personal gear into their motor home.

"They're leaving. Call Lu."

"109 to number 12."

"Number 12, go ahead."

"The Winnebago is leaving. Hancock and the others have already left. They've got about an hour head start."

"Clear 109. We'll see you in Houston."

When Hancock drove the motor home onto the International Bridge, the Mexican border guards waved him on. He saw in his mirror that Davis was right behind him in the pickup truck.

Hancock hollered, "Where are the papers for the motor home? I need them to get through the American check point."

Hancock looked in his rear mirror again as he drove across the bridge. Davis was waving papers out of the pickup window.

"Damn him! That son-of-a-bitch stole our papers!"

Hancock stopped at the American checkpoint. The border guard asked, "Do you have anything to declare?"

"No, Sir. We gave all our fish away and didn't buy a thing. The gentleman in the pickup behind me has all our papers."

All the detectives rushed to the rear of the motor home and watched as the American Border Guard walked back to Davis in the pickup. Angel could not be seen. Davis jumped out of the pickup to meet the border guard.

"Hi. We sure had a great fishing trip. I'm Detective Davis with the Houston Police Department. Don't I know you? Weren't you a policeman in Houston? You sure do a great job here."

The border guard, looking in the bed of the pickup truck, said, "No, I was a cop in Corpus Christi before I took this job."

Davis went on, "Boy, you sure look familiar. Here are all the papers. How do you keep up with so much paperwork? Looks like you're getting eat up with paperwork just like us. It's hard to put somebody in jail now with all this damn paperwork."

The border guard didn't even look at the papers. He just said, "Do you have anything to declare?"

"The only thing I have to declare is that those guys in the motor home beat me fishing."

"O.K. then, you better move on. You're holding up traffic."

The guard waved the motor home and the pickup through. The detectives in the motor home broke out in laughter.

Johnson hollered at Hancock, "Step on the gas before they change their minds and search Davis' pickup. Can you believe Davis? He's got her in a sleeping bag in the bed of the pickup."

A few miles out of Del Rio, Davis pulled to the side of the highway. He unzipped the sleeping bag Angel was in. She was completely wet with sweat.

Lt. Joe "Bill" Bradley

He put her in the cab next to him and gave her an ice-cold coke. Davis sped along the highway until he caught up with Hancock and the rest.

Later as Hancock drove the motor home through Bracketville, he glanced into the rear view mirror, "Damn! Davis didn't drop that girl off! He's still behind us. That bastard is taking the girl to Houston!"

"He better not be taking her to Houston," Luna said. "If he does, we'd better keep this from the boss or everyone's ass will be in trouble."

Hancock headed the motor home for Houston.

Murphy and Park in the Good Time van, cleared Customs at the International Bridge. They watched as Senor Reynaldo Melendez again helped Napier's crew clear Customs.

Park said, "Look at that. A motor home full of dope crossing the border with ease. Just think of how much comes into the states and the different ways they bring the dope in."

Napier dropped Melendez off at an office building in downtown Del Rio. They all got out to say their good byes.

When the Winnebago pulled out, Murphy let the suspects get ahead of them a few miles as they left Del Rio.

"They're sure not talking much. All of 'em must have partied too much last night. They've sacked out leaving the driving to Sergeant Epps. He's such a pussy! I can't wait to put handcuffs on him."

The Winnebago pulled into a truck stop as they arrived in San Antonio. Murphy and Park passed them not noticing that the Winnebago had taken an exit.

THE TWELVE JUDGES

"Murphy, you must've passed them. The needle on the meter is pointing behind us. Better do a U-turn and park at the truck stop."

"I'm going inside and get us a hamburger," Park announced. "What do you want on yours?"

"Everything, Park. Just hurry!"

When Park returned; Napier's Winnebago was leaving.

"I think we'd better keep them in sight from here on."

For the next two hours, the only conversation coming from the Winnebago was that of another card game.

As the suspects neared Houston and were passing through Katy, Texas, Murphy and Park heard over the monitor, "George, I am going to call Aguirre. I want to get rid of the cocaine as soon as I can."

The detectives listened as Doug Napier used his mobile telephone, "Aguirre, we're about forty-five minutes from my home. We have the amount we discussed. Can you meet at my home? Say in about two hours? Bring the money, the full amount! You know nothing can be released unless you bring the money. That's good. I'll see you in two hours.

Napier was heard again, saying, "Captain, have you ever seen a million dollars in cash. You're about to. Let's all have a drink."

After Napier's phone call, Murphy said, "Park, you better call Lu."

"What do you think I'm doing?"

"109 to number 12."

"12 to 109. It's about time you answered your radio."

Lt. Joe "Bill" Bradley

"We didn't hear you calling, Boss."

"12 to 109. Where are you?"

"109 to 12. We just passed Katy on I-10."

Park then told Lieutenant James what he had heard over the monitor.

"12 to 109. We're on surveillance at Napier's home. You better not follow him to his home. You might be spotted and besides, I'm sure they are a little antsy hauling that much dope. We're going to wait until the money arrives before we execute the search warrant. Stop a block away from Napier's home. I'll let you know when we hit the house. You can join us then. I only hope they take the narcotics into Napier's house. Jeff says under Federal Law, Napier's home can be seized if we recover the cocaine inside."

"109 to number 12. Boss, we'll know if they move the dope."

"Number 12 to 109. How can you know that? Oh shit! Forget what I asked. I should have known Park would bug the dope."

Over the air waves came a disguised voice, "Don't use the word bug on the radio, Lu."

James pressed the mike button, "Sorry, that's my line isn't it."

With the police mike still open, Lieutenant James said, "Jeff, Chief Ladd, you didn't hear that."

Chief Ladd said, "I didn't hear a thing, did you Jeff?"

"Not a thing, Chief."

Murphy said, "He's got Chief Ladd with him, holy shit!"

"Number 12 to 109, call me when they start into the subdivision."

THE TWELVE JUDGES

"109 Clear."

"103 to 101."

"What do you want 103?"

"103 to 101. I'm having car trouble. Pull into the Memorial Shopping Center so I can ride with you."

"101 to 103. No, you're on your own."

"Come on Hancock! I don't want to miss the action."

"All right, lover boy, but make it fast."

Hancock took the exit to the Memorial Shopping Center. Davis parked his pickup and ran to the motor home. "Let's go," he shouted.

"You bastard! You're just going to leave her here?" asked Luna.

"I gave her $10 and told her to go into the mall. I told her that I would be back for her. Let's go, we don't want to miss the bust."

Hancock drove onto the freeway and headed for Napier's subdivision off Memorial Drive.

Murphy and Park were still monitoring the conversation in the Winnebago.

"Kick it in the ass Park, the beeper signal in the dope indicates they've stopped. They should be at Napier's home now. We better tell the Lu."

"We can't tell the Lieutenant! He's got Chief Ladd and the Customs Chief with him. If we tell him on the air, they'll know for sure that we bugged the crook's motor home. You know how the Feds are on buggin' without a warrant."

"Murphy, they already know about the bugs, stupid. Be quiet Captain Links is talking."

"Sergeant, get my bags and put them in my car. After you do that, bring the bags of cocaine into

Lt. Joe "Bill" Bradley

Doug's library. We're going in and have some drinks."

"Yes Sir, Captain."

Park laughed, "Epps is not only a hey boy, he's the captain's porter."

"Park, look at the meter. The Sergeant is moving the cocaine. Better call Lu. We don't want to blow this one."

"109 to number 12. They're moving the drugs."

"Number 12 Clear."

Murphy and Park spotted the motor home with Hancock and the others. They were parked a block from Napier's home. Murphy and Park joined them inside the motor home.

Murphy said, "I hope Lu let's us lead the charge into Napier's home, instead of the Federal men."

"He should," Davis bragged, "I've got a key to the front door."

"What do you mean you have a key to the front door?" asked Luna.

"One day when I was on surveillance, no one was at home at Napier's house. I made a key to the front door. I know it works, cause I tried it. I couldn't go in because the house has one hell of an alarm system."

Hancock said, "Do you think it'll open the front door?"

"Didn't I just tell you the key worked? The keys I make always work."

THE TWELVE JUDGES

Johnson said, "Tell the lieutenant about the key, Hancock. Having a key to the front door will put us up ahead of the Feds."

"101 to number 12. Call me on the mobile phone, Lu."

"12 clear."

The mobile telephone in the motor home rang. "Lu, Davis has a front door key to Napier's home."

Hancock held the telephone out from his ear. Everyone heard the Lieutenant shout, "What?"

"He does, Lu, he has a key! Can we go in first?"

Hancock placed the mobile telephone back on its receiver, and hollered, "We're first!"

There was a yell from the other detectives. The next hour was spent waiting. Luna saw Hancock take a sawed-off double barrel ten-gauge shotgun from a case.

"Damn Hancock, you don't need that! There's only four of them."

"If Davis' key doesn't work on the door, this baby will."

"Hell, Hancock, it'll blow the whole damn door off! That damn shotgun is so big it need wheels."

"12 to all units. We have a male subject parking in front of Napier's home in a black Mercedes. He's a Mexican male with black hair. Standby. He went inside. He was carrying a black suitcase."

"Number 12 to 101! Move out! We'll be right behind you!"

Hancock didn't even acknowledge Lieutenant James' transmission. He gunned the engine on the motor home. The other detectives had to reach for

Lt. Joe "Bill" Bradley

support as the motor home lurched forward. The tires squealed as Hancock wheeled it around a corner. Davis was pressed against the door so he could be first out. Hancock drove into the circle driveway and slammed on the brakes nearly hitting the parked Mercedes.

Davis bolted from the motor home followed by the other detectives. He ran to the front door and put his key in the lock. The key worked. He quickly opened the door. Johnson, Park, Murphy, and Luna ran past him. Hancock could see other cars coming into the driveway from both ends.

As Hancock got out of the motor home, a group of Federal men ran past him to cover the rear of the home.

Kramer and the detectives who had not made the trip to Mexico ran into the house.

Hancock saw Lieutenant James, Chief Ladd and the Customs Chief coming toward him. Ladd was puffing and straining trying to stay in stride with the others.

James was joking with the Customs Chief, "I guess my detectives found the door unlocked."

Hancock greeted them, "Yeah, Lu, the door was open. I didn't even need my shotgun."

"We better get inside before Captain Links and Sergeant Epps are lynched."

As they walked into Doug Napier's home, Davis hollered, "We're in the dining room, Lieutenant."

When Lieutenant James entered the dining room, he saw that Captain Links, Sergeant Epps and Doug Napier were handcuffed facing the wall. The

THE TWELVE JUDGES

lawyer, Steve Minter was sitting in a chair, his face buried in his hands. The cocaine was stacked on the dining room table along with an empty black suitcase. A million dollars in cash was on the table.

Lieutenant James announced, "Gentlemen, I do believe you are under arrest. Would you all turn around so we can see who you are?"

When they turned around, Captain Links saw Chief Ladd. His face turned white and his knee's buckled.

"Chief Ladd, I can explain this."

"You're not going to explain anything to me, you sorry son-of-a-bitch! This is a Federal case but they're going to put you in my jail first. Lieutenant James, get the Captain's and the Sergeant's badges and identification."

James walked over to Captain Links. After removing his identification and badge, Lieutenant James walked over to Sergeant Epps. Blood was pouring from the Sergeant's nose.

"What happened to you?"

Nodding his head toward Murphy, the sergeant said in a broken voice, "That one, right there, hit me."

Murphy threw his hands up. "He was trying to escape."

"I was not! He called me a pussy and then he hit me."

Lieutenant James walked back over to Captain Links. Links was crying.

Bill James whispered in Captain Links' ear, "You're a sorry piece of shit. Too bad the Feds have you and I won't get to question you. If there's ever a next time, the Feds won't be here and I'll blow your ass away. You're a sorry ass crooked cop that's going down."

Captain Links continued to cry.

Watson grabbed Lieutenant James' arm. "Lu, the T.V. reporters are here! Me and Edwards can't hold them out much longer."

"All right, Watson. Tell Chief Ladd the reporters are here. He can handle them. Tell all our men to slip out the back door. I'll turn everything over to Customs."

"Jeff, can I see you a minute?"

"Sure, Bill."

"Jeff, we are going to leave things with you. The T.V. reporters are outside. Chief Ladd needs the publicity and so do you. Call me when you finish here."

"Bill, you bastard! Don't leave me here with the chief and these reporters."

"I have to, Jeff. My bunch shouldn't be seen on T.V."

"Bill, look at that!"

Both men watched as Park ripped a piece of tape off one of the cocaine packages.

"Bugs are expensive, Jeff. You didn't see that did you?"

"See What, Bill?"

"Jeff, I'm out of here."

As Lieutenant James left the dining room, Watson and Edwards let the reporters into the house.

Attorney Steve Minter started hollering that his rights were being violated by letting the T.V. reporters take his picture. He was protesting even louder for his attorney.

THE TWELVE JUDGES

Chief Ladd spread the money out on the dining room table along with the seized cocaine. He made Captain Links and the others stand behind the table so that the T.V. cameras could take pictures.

As James walked down the hall of Napier's home to the back door he heard Washington's voice in another room.

"King, I can't carry any more. The other guys have already taken enough."

Lieutenant James looked into the room from where Washington's voice was coming. Washington had an arm full of expensive bottles of liquor. So did King.

King peered through the bottles he was carrying and said, "Well you said the Feds were going to seize this house. We're just helping them."

James saw the large liquor cabinet was nearly empty. He shook his head and kept walking toward the door, "Get your ass out of here! Let's go to the factory. Did Park and Murphy get all their equipment off Napier's motor home?"

Washington answered, "Yeah Lu. They got it all."

King and Washington followed James out the back door. Both had an armload of liquor.

It was late when Lieutenant James and the detectives arrived back at the factory.

"Everyone go straight home, reintroduce yourself to your wives and take tomorrow off. I would like to say you all did a great job. It's a pleasure to have each and every one of you on my team. There is one less Captain now. Maybe fat Ladd will promote me. By the way, where's Davis?"

Lt. Joe "Bill" Bradley

Hancock spoke up, "His leg was hurting, so he went on home."

Washington said, "Yeah, his middle leg."

James left the factory leaving Johnson telling stories to the detectives who had not made the trip about Boy's Town.

Luna was telling about how great of a fisherman he was and how he had caught enough fish to feed everyone.

The next morning Lieutenant James stepped outside and got the morning paper, the lead story read…

"…Chief Ladd, working with U.S. Customs, busted one of the largest drug rings ever in the Houston area…"

James put the newspaper aside and started his breakfast. As he sat down to eat, the telephone rang.

"Lieutenant, you did it again! I know it was you. You better start working with me. Someday I am going to be District Attorney and you're going to need me."

It was Assistant District Attorney Jamie Owens.

"My breakfast is getting cold," was Bill James' only response as he hung up the telephone.

After breakfast, James dressed, got his fishing gear and drove to Galveston.

He loved the beach. He drove down to the San Luis Pass bridge. He spent the day fishing in the surf and walking the beach. When James returned to his home that night, he was very tired but it was a good tired. There was a call from Barbara on his answering machine. He called her.

"Sorry, I didn't call you sooner."

"That's all right. I see by the newspaper it went well with you," Barbara said.

"It sure did, thanks to you. Barbara, what are you doing next Saturday night? I'm giving my detectives and their wives a dinner party at the Rotary Table. I want you to go as my date."

"There you go again. I hate the word date. Sounds like I'm going to work like I use to in the past."

"O.K. then, come and be my trick."

"You're something else, Bill! What if I'm recognized?"

"You won't be. If you are, so what? I'm the boss. All my detectives have friends that are in low places. You're high class."

James started to sing, "Waltz across Texas with you in my arms…"

"O.K. I'll be your trick if you promise not to sing."

Saturday night James arrived at the Rotary Table with Barbara. The restaurant was closed to customers and was full of Custom officers and James' detectives.

Juan met the lieutenant at the door, "Mr. Jeff, the Federal boss, is already here. I have a table set up for you and him."

"This is Barbara, Juan."

"Hi, Barbara. I am finally glad to see Cap with a woman and a pretty one. Cap, before you go in, I have a problem. Hancock and Washington brought me six boxes of liquor. It is expensive stuff. I told them I couldn't use it. My bottles of liquor have to have state and federal tax stamps on them. Bottles without state and federal stamps can't even be brought into the club. Washington ran me out from behind my own bar and told me to stay out of the way. He and Hancock went behind the bar and filled all of my bottles that were half full. I now have all full bottles. I must say, they did match brands."

"Let them go, Juan. I'll tell Hancock to put the empty bottles in the trunk of his car."

When James walked into the main room of the Rotary Table, he and Barbara were spotted by his detectives. The whistling and catcalls started.

Barbara laughed and said, "Why Bill, you're turning red."

Bill James and Barbara stopped at each table meeting the detective's wives and working their way over to the table where Jeff sat. Jeff stood up to greet them.

"Lieutenant, this is Sandy, my wife."

James introduced Barbara and they joined Jeff and Sandy.

Jeff began to tell what had taken place since the bust. "I'm a hero in Washington, thanks to you. Even the big boss called me."

Jeff leaned over and spoke with James so no one could hear, "You told me that you had an informer, but you didn't tell me who he was. My boss in Wahsington, D.C. authorized me to give this to you for your informer."

Jeff handed the Lieutenant a large envelope that contained cash.

THE TWELVE JUDGES

"Thanks Jeff. You Federal people have all the money. Jeff, let's forget about the bust for right now and have some fun."

The party really got into full swing. Juan's waitresses were kept busy bringing drinks and food.

James asked Barbara to dance. When they got on the dance floor everyone formed a ring around them. Lieutenant James tried to shout above the music. "I'll get you for this, Hancock."

He and Barbara danced to the song's end. Everyone applauded. When Barbara and Bill returned to their table, Barbara asked, "Bill, do you see that young Mexican girl sitting over there? Isn't she beautiful? I would kill to have beautiful black hair like she does. Her hair covers her shoulders."

"Which girl are you talking about? Oh, I see her. I don't know who she is. I think she's with Davis, one of my detectives."

Davis was sitting with Kramer, Luna, and Johnson. Davis leaned over to Luna and said, "You've been staring at my girl all night and I'm tired of it."

"I'm sorry Davis, Angel is just so damn good lookin'. I'd do anything she wanted if she were mine."

"Shit, Luna! I think you're in love with her. You want her, you can have her. I'm tired of her."

"Don't kid me, Davis. I've got feelings, you know. I've never been able to approach women like you do. I just envy the hell out of you."

"I'm not kidding. I have her in an apartment that I'm renting by the month. Give me three hundred bucks for the apartment I'm renting and she's yours."

"Are you serious?" Looking in his wallet, Luna said, "I don't have but about a hundred on me."

Lt. Joe "Bill" Bradley

"Well, you really missed out. I'm going to sell her tonight."

"Wait, Davis. I'll be right back!" Luna said almost in a panic.

Davis turned to Kramer and said, "Watch me make three hundred dollars real fast. A friend of mine who own some apartments let me have a free apartment for her. Can you believe I brought her all the way from Mexico and I haven't slept with her yet? She won't let me near her. She is a good cook and cleans my apartment but I hate to admit it, I haven't laid her yet. She won't let me get in her pants. I wouldn't mind unloading her."

Kramer was feeling no pain from the liquor he had consumed and only mumbled, "She's smart not to sleep with your sorry ass."

Luna returned to the table. "Davis, I borrowed the money." Luna handed Davis three hundred dollars.

"That's not enough, Luna."

"But you said three hundred dollars! Didn't he, Kramer?"

"Don't get me involved in this garbage. Both of you are wrong and have no feelings," Kramer responded.

Davis went on, "Luna, I want that watch you're wearing."

Luna visibly shaken said, "Davis, I won this watch for being Rookie of the Year. It's the watch that the 100 Club gave me."

"Do you want the girl or not?"

"Damn right I want her! I'll take care of her."

"Well, give me your watch."

THE TWELVE JUDGES

Luna slowly took his watch off and carefully studied it before he handed it to Davis.

"It's got my name on it. You can't use it."

Davis laughed and said, "I'll have it buffed off."

"Davis, explain to the girl who I am and that I'm going to take care of her. Also, give me the keys and address to the apartment."

Davis talked to the girl a few minutes. She seemed confused but then got up and went and sat in Luna's lap. She had noticed Luna watching her since she had left Mexico.

Luna's face lit up as he began to talk to her in his broken Tex-Mex.

Detective Kramer got up and walked over to the Lieutenant's table. Kramer wasn't a drinker and it showed. He took short steps to steady himself.

"Lu, I need to talk with you."

"Something wrong, Kramer?"

"Let's go where it's quiet."

James followed Kramer into Juan's office.

Lieutenant James noticed that Kramer had too much to drink. He knew Kramer was not accustomed to drinking and what little he did drink got to him.

"Lieutenant, do you promise not to tell the others I snitched? Do you promise not to fire anyone?"

"What are you trying to tell me Kramer?"

Kramer was having trouble putting his words together. Kramer then raised his voice, "Do you promise, damn it?"

James started to laugh but realized Kramer was serious, said, "O.K., I promise."

"Did you see the Mexican girl with Davis?"
"Yes, I saw her."
"She's such a nice girl," Kramer sighed. "I don't believe that Davis should have smuggled her out of Mexico."

Lieutenant James was stunned.

"Davis did what?" growled James.

"Davis smuggled her out of Mexico."

"I heard you, Kramer, the first time. Keep your voice down."

With a thick tongue, Kramer said, "Davis is an asshole. Can you believe he just sold her! For three hundred dollars and a 100 Club watch. Can you believe Luna gave up his Rookie of the Year watch for that girl?"

The liquor was really taking its toll on Kramer and he became sad, "Lu, she's such a nice girl. She doesn't know what's going on. I hate to see her hurt. What are you going to do? She probably doesn't know anyone in Houston."

"I'm going to have Davis' ass."

"But Lu, you promised, you promised."

"Kramer, go back to your table. I'll wait a few minutes before I do anything. Tell Juan, I want to see him."

Kramer stumbled out of the office. A few minutes later Juan came in. James told Juan about the girl.

"Juan can't you put her to work?"

"Cap, I've noticed her too. She's not the type to work in a joint like mine. She's young, beautiful, and some fast-talking dude will sweep her off her feet and make a whore out of her. Let me place her with a friend who'll help her. He and his wife help a lot of illegals get their green cards and a job."

"Can you call your friend tonight?"

"I'll call him now."

Juan made a telephone call. When he hung up he said, "They're coming to get her now."

Lieutenant James returned to the party and to his table. "Barbara, I'll be tied up for awhile. Jeff look after her."

James walked over to the table where Luna, Angel, Davis, and Kramer were sitting. Kramer's wife was telling him that it was time to go home. James took Angel by the hand and said, "Davis, you and Luna come with me."

Lieutenant James led the girl to Juan's office.

Hancock, seeing what had taken place, turned to Washington and said, "The party's about to get good! The shit's fixing to hit the fan!"

Lieutenant James slammed the door to Juan's office.

Pointing a finger, James started in on them. "A waitress talked to this girl in the restroom. Davis, you brought her back from Mexico didn't you?"

"But Lu, she wanted to come," Davis said. But as he noticed James' eyes began to narrow, he confessed. "Yeah Lu, I did."

James turned to Luna, "You knew about it, didn't you?"

"Yes, Sir."

"What do you two think I should do?"

Luna and Davis spoke at the same time. "We'll take her back! We'll do anything you want, Lu!"

Lt. Joe "Bill" Bradley

As Lieutenant James continued to rant and holler there was a knock on the door.

"Come in!" shouted James.

"Cap, here's the couple I was telling you about."

"Good, Juan. Tell the girl that she's leaving with them."

Turning to Luna and Davis, James barked, "You were just saved by Juan."

Juan spoke to the girl in Spanish. She didn't say a word but got up and started to leave with Juan.

Lieutenant James said, "Wait a minute! Davis, don't you have three hundred dollars of Luna's money?"

"Yes, Sir."

"Give it to the girl."

Davis looking at his Lieutenant's stern face handed the money to the girl.

"Davis, the three hundred dollars was Luna's money. How much money do you have?"

"About two hundred, Sir."

"Give it to the girl."

Davis reluctantly handed the girl his two hundred dollars.

The girl kissed Davis and Luna. As she kissed Luna, he reached and held her hand. Luna whispered softly in Angel's ear, "I'll see you soon, I promise."

The girl answered in Spanish, "I hope so."

Angel smiled and left with the couple.

Juan left the two detectives with James.

"You two are going to catch every shit detail that comes up for the next month," ordered Bill James. "If either of you screw up again, the Juvenile Division will have two new detectives! Now let's go back to the party."

As they were leaving James heard Luna ask Davis, "Can I have my watch back? It sure means a lot to me."

"You can, if you get me my two hundred dollars back."

James joined Barbara and said, "Pour me a double, I need one after talking with those two."

Lieutenant James and Jeff said their good byes to their men and left the party an hour later.

After walking Jeff and his wife to their car he and Barbara left. On the way to Barbara's apartment, James pulled an envelope from his pocket and handed it to Barbara.

"What's this?"

"That's your fee for being my trick tonight."

Barbara threw the envelope back at Bill.

"Pick up the envelope, Barbara."

Barbara picked up the envelope and opened it.

"Bill, where did all of this money come from?"

"It's yours Barbara, twenty thousand. The Feds pay well for information. Hell! They recovered a million dollars in cash and the cocaine they got is worth ten million on the street. I thought it should have been more but at least you don't have to pay taxes on it."

Barbara screamed gleefully.

James parked and they went to Barbara's apartment.

"Stay with me tonight, Bill."

"I thought you'd never ask. I'm beat. A good shower is just what I need."

Lt. Joe "Bill" Bradley

"You're going to get more than a good shower. Go in the bathroom and get started. I'll get you some towels."

James undressed and stepped into the shower. The hot water felt relaxing. The shower door opened and in stepped Barbara. Her naked body was trim and firm. The flesh around her breasts and waist was pure white. The rest of her body was golden tan from Houston's hot sun.

"You need a back scrub, Copper?"

James turned his back to Barbara and felt a pleasure he had not felt in a long time.

After the shower, Barbara dried him off. He did the same for her. As they went into the bedroom, Barbara pulled him onto the bed and reached for the light switch. It had been a good party but the best was yet to come.

CHAPTER 11

THE DUNKING STOOL

    Through the years, every cop acquired friends and information spots which are called "watering holes." These watering holes are where policemen can go to drink, let his hair down, and try to be a citizen instead of a cop.

    Detectives Hancock and Edwards had such a spot. It was a Greek restaurant and bar located on the waterfront adjacent to the Houston Ship Channel. This restaurant was generally full of Greek sailors. It was also popular with the citizens of Houston because of the authentic Greek food. They also enjoyed watching the sailors dance. Greek bands were brought from overseas to entertain. When the bands visas would run out, another band from Greece was brought over.

    Harry was the owner of this nightclub/restaurant and was a friend of the detectives, even to the extent of joining in on their side when a brawl broke out. It was a close relationship.

One night, Edwards and Hancock were sitting at the bar drinking Greek Cokes, a strong native wine. Harry came over to join the men.

"Hi, boys! You must have the night off. Can I get you some more food?"

"No, we've stuffed ourselves all ready with your butterfly shrimp. It was great!" Edwards said as he rubbed his full stomach.

"Hancock, glance over to the table at the end of the bar. Do you know those two men sitting there?" asked Harry.

Both Hancock and Edwards looked at the two men.

"I know one of the guys and so do you, Harry. You buy wine from him. Isn't his name Fincher?" answered Hancock.

Troy Fincher handled all the liquor and wine smuggled off ships at the docks. The liquor and wine were not stolen, but no tax was paid to the State or Federal governments. It was sold for a good price at every club on the waterfront, as well as to other clubs in the city. Detectives Hancock and Edwards tolerated this, however, because the liquor and wine was not stolen, and also this was their "watering hole" for obtaining information. They also believed that collecting taxes was not their problem; it was the Feds.

"I overheard the guy with Fincher say he was wanted in California by the F.B.I.," Harry said. "He didn't say what for. Fincher introduced him as Peter Knowles. Fincher asked me to put Peter on as a bartender. He said Knowles needed a cooling off spot.

Fincher told me that Knowles was going to put an end to some of his problems. It seems that Fincher is losing cases of liquor and wine when ships are unloaded at the docks. Fincher made it clear that Knowles needed to work for me so that he had a legit cover. Knowles is going to be Fincher's strong arm and put a stop to the wine being stolen. What can I do; I need the goods that Fincher sells me? You know the amount of wine I run through my place."

Edwards broke in, "Put him to work Harry. We'll find out who the bastard is. Let me see his employee application."

"He refused to make one out."

"Harry, we have to go now but we'll be back tomorrow night. When we come in tomorrow night introduce us to Knowles as cops. Everyone here knows us, including Fincher, so I'm sure he'll find out anyway."

The next day Hancock checked Peter Knowles name through the city and state computers. He found nothing.

The F.B.I. was called and nothing was found on Peter Knowles.

Hancock and Edwards returned to the Greek club the next night as promised. Peter Knowles was attending bar.

When the two detectives sat down at the bar, Peter Knowles confidently said, "You two look like cops. What'd you want, a soft drink or milk?"

Peter Knowles gave a false laugh.

Hancock reached across the bar and grabbed Knowles by the shirt collar and lifted him off the floor. "Make it a Lone Star, and it better be cold!"

Lt. Joe "Bill" Bradley

Hancock then eased his hold on Knowles.

Knowles brought two Lone Star beers. He sat a beer in front of each detective. Edwards looked at his beer and complained, "This isn't Miller Lite. I ordered a Miller Lite!"

Without even a comment, Knowles hurried to bring Edwards a Miller Lite beer.

Harry was watching the detectives' encounter with Knowles. He walked behind the bar and put his arm around Knowles.

"Don't pay any attention to these two guys. They're pretty harmless. Let me introduce you to them."

Harry motioned to Edwards and Hancock.

"Peter Knowles, this is Detective Hancock and Detective Edwards, they're Houston Police."

Hancock extended his hand and said, "Glad to know you Pete. I was just funning."

Peter Knowles gave the two detectives a go to hell look and walked to the other end of the bar.

"Harry, we didn't find out a thing about your new bartender. Edwards and I worked out a plan. Let's talk."

Harry and the two detectives moved to a table out of earshot of the other customers.

"Harry, the next time Peter Knowles goes to supervise the unloading of liquor and wine from a ship, call us. I have a good friend in U.S. Customs who'll arrest Peter Knowles. He won't be charged with anything, but we'll make him spend the night in jail and run a fingerprint check on him. I'll fix it where Customs won't seize the liquor or wine, so things will be cool for you. What do you think?"

THE TWELVE JUDGES

Harry got up from the table. "Hey, that's dangerous for me. You can't let him or Fincher know that I'm in on this. Let me go check some customers out, I'll be right back."

After checking the customers out, Harry went over to the bar and talked to Peter Knowles. He then returned to the table where Hancock and Edwards were sitting.

"Knowles is having trouble with the cash register. Do you know what he said about you? He said he thought cops here in Texas wore boots and hats and were dumb ass country hicks. He really doesn't care for you two."

Edwards said, "Go tell the son-of-a-bitch, I'm going home and put my boots on and come back and kick his ass!"

Harry quickly changed the subject back to their plan when he saw how angry Edwards was becoming. He didn't want the detective to start a fight in his restaurant and destroy half the place.

"If arresting Knowles won't screw up my liquor and wine buying, and you keep me out of it, I'm for it. Knowles gives me orders like he is trying to take over my place; Knowles already thinks he's the boss. I want to get rid of him!"

Hancock was angry enough to bust Knowles now but he knew the plan was a better way to get the job done, "Harry, the next time Knowles goes to the docks to handle an unloading job, give us a call. You have my pager number."

Both detectives said their good-byes to Harry and left for the night.

Lt. Joe "Bill" Bradley

Two nights later, Hancock's pager went off. Looking at the number Hancock recognized it as Harry's number. Hancock called Harry.

"Hancock, Knowles just left the bar. I overheard him say on the telephone that he was going to dock 15."

"That's great Harry, I'll call my friend at Customs. They'll put him in jail tonight. When we get his fingerprints, we'll know who the bastard is and if he's really wanted by the F.B.I. I'll call you later and let you know something."

Hancock then called his friend Carl with U.S. Customs. He gave Carl a description of Peter Knowles and where the liquor and wine was to be unloaded and what needed to be done.

Later that night, Peter Knowles was arrested by customs and placed in jail. He was finger-printed and held for three hours.

Knowles was told by Customs that he was going to be released with no charges because they found out the captain of the ship was the person who committed the liquor violations.

After Peter Knowles was released from jail, Hancock met the customs agent at the Police Department Identification Section.

A fingerprint expert classified Peter Knowles fingerprints and then searched the files. The expert, after searching local files, said, "Sorry Hancock, Peter Knowles is not in our files. He must be from out of state. Do you want me to mail them to the F.B.I. Fingerprint Lab in Washington, D.C.? Our reproduction machine is broke and doesn't send good

THE TWELVE JUDGES

copies anyway. There's no telling how long it will take the F.B.I. lab to search the prints."

"Hell no! Don't mail them, it'll take too long!"

"Hancock," Carl said, "I can take the fingerprints to the airport and put them on the next flight to Washington. I could fax the prints, but the lab bitches every time we do saying they need originals. I'll call ahead have a custom agent waiting at the airport. He can take the fingerprints to the F.B.I. Lab and have them classified. I'll be in my office in the morning making a report on Peter Knowles arrest and the liquor violations. You know how us Feds are. Do a lot of paperwork and you keep your job."

"Sounds good to me, Carl. I've got a meeting in the morning with my boss. I guess waiting a few more hours won't make a difference. Knowles will be around. Thanks a lot, Carl. I owe you one."

The next morning Hancock arrived at the factory to find everyone complaining. Word had leaked out of the next assignment.

Lieutenant James came out of his office, "Guess what we've been assigned to do? Chief Ladd has had numerous complaints from the downtown businessmen. It seems that the winos, muggers, prostitutes and some of the street people have taken over the downtown area. Judge Gates at the criminal courthouse has even complained to the Chief that he can't get his regular fill of chicken fried nuggets from McDonalds on Main Street because of the punks hanging out there. Chief Ladd wants downtown cleaned up so guess who'll clean it up? You! Most of you know the regular street people who don't create any problems. They are even complaining that punks

Lt. Joe "Bill" Bradley

are harassing them. Don't arrest the regulars. I don't want this project to last but about three days, so get to it! Dress in street clothes."

Bill Johnson spoke up, "Lu, I've done this before. Let me dress the guys."

All the detectives started booing Johnson and Lieutenant James tried not to smile.

"O.K. Johnson. You're in charge of the uniforms for the day for this group. Watson, borrow a paddy wagon from Uniform Patrol. All of you can take turns transporting and booking prisoners. Kramer, I need you in the office. Have fun boys. And by the way, Hancock, don't arrest Reverend Jim Hicks, the fire and brimstone black preacher on the corner of Texas and Main. You might need to listen to him. He makes a lot of sense."

Washington slapped Hancock on the back saying, "There goes your one arrest."

Hancock stood up turning to Washington and said, "You might as well ride with me so I can teach you something."

Kramer stood and said, "Wait a minute. You know I'm going to have to do the paperwork on this bunch and the chief is going to want a report every day. What do I title this assignment?"

There were a few suggestions, Downtown Cleanup, Wino Roundup, Here Come The Judge With Chicken Fried Balls, and a few others that Kathy refused to write down.

Washington stood and said, "Boss, nearly every lawman you run into now is a member of some kind of squad that indicates how important he is, which is bullshit. There's the Swat Squad, Pawn Shop Squad, High

THE TWELVE JUDGES

Profile Criminal Squad and God knows what names the Feds use. I think we should be named the Search, Hide, Identify, Tactical Squad."

Some in the group agreed that the name sounded professional.

A few minutes passed with the men discussing the name. Kathy couldn't hold back any longer. She burst into laughter, tears running down her cheeks. She was laughing so hard that she had to sit down.

Edwards asked, "What's so funny. It's a great name."

James walked over to the blackboard and wrote, "Search, Hide, Identify, Tactical Squad." He then wrote just the first letter under each word, "SHITS".

James broke out in laughter, as did all the men. It took a few minutes for them to settle down.

James wiping his eyes with his handkerchief said, "That's the downtown groups official name. Boy, I hope I'm present when the chief reads the first report."

The laughter started all over again.

As soon as the meeting broke up, all the detectives threw folders, papers, and anything they could grab at Detective Johnson.

Several minutes later, Kathy came into the lieutenant's office, "You have to come and see this for yourself. It's unbelievable."

Lieutenant James walked with Kathy into the large room where the detectives had gathered. He started to laugh.

Lt. Joe "Bill" Bradley

"You're the scroungiest bunch of street people I have ever seen! I hope none of you get busted by the uniform cops."

Kathy said, "Bill get in the group. I want a picture of you and these guys." Detective Washington kept everyone laughing as Kathy took their picture.

That afternoon, Kramer and Kathy had compiled arrest records on seventy offenders from the downtown area. The arrests ranged from possession of marijuana, to thefts, to urinating on the sidewalk. There had been only one complaint. Edwards had poured a new bottle of 'Mad Dog 20' wine in the street gutter in front of two winos. They had complained of civil rights violations when they were being booked for P.I.

They wanted an officer from Internal Affairs to talk with them.

Despite their initial feelings about the assignment, the detectives enjoyed the masquerade posing as street people.

On the way home that afternoon, Hancock and Edwards stopped at the Rotary Table for a few beers.

"Edwards, I can't understand why we haven't heard from Agent Carl. I think I'll call him."

Hancock called Carl's pager. In a few minutes a waitress came to the bar where Hancock and Edwards were sitting.

"Hancock, you have a telephone call," she told him.

Hancock went to the phone. It was Carl.

"Hancock, I started to the airport this morning but was called to Federal Court. You know Federal Judges won't excuse you for anything. I didn't get the fingerprints on the airplane until about an hour ago. I called Washington, D.C. and we should have an answer sometime in the morning. Sorry."

"That's all right Carl. Call me as soon as you hear something."

Hancock went back to the bar and told Edwards about the fingerprints. Both detectives continued to drink.

After a couple of hours, Juan came over, "Now don't get mad at me, but do you two need a ride home? Both of you have had eight beers."

Edwards slurring his words said, "Juan, Hancock drives better when he's drunk. Anyway, what in the hell gives you the right to count our beers?"

Juan knew better than to say anything else. Later he sent a waitress to tell Hancock that he had a phone call. The waitress walked over to the two detectives.

"Hancock, there's a phone call for you. You can take it in Juan's office."

Hancock slid off the barstool and staggered to Juan's office. "This is Hancock. Whatta you want?"

"Detective Hancock, this is Tracy. Do you remember me? I've called five places looking for you. I'm a waitress at Harry's Greek restaurant. Harry's not here right now but I thought I'd better warn you. Peter Knowles told us that he was put in jail. He's raving mad. He said he was going to get even with you and that other country hick detective. He blames you for setting him up for a bust. Hancock, he's carrying a pistol. I saw it. Be careful when you come out here again. He said he was going to throw you out the next time you came in."

"Why that bastard! Thanks, Tracy."

Hancock went back to the bar and told Edwards what Tracy had said. Edwards was feeling no pain from the beers he had consumed.

Edwards stood up and suggested, "Mr. Hancock, I think we need to go and have a talk with Mr. Peter Knowles. Sounds like he has no respect for Texas cops."

"I think you're right, Mr. Edwards. Let's go get a couple of fifths of whiskey and go see if Peter Knowles wants to drink with us."

Juan was glad to see the two detectives leaving. The last time the two of them got drunk in his place it cost him a lot of money to replace broken chairs and tables. They had also whipped four guys who had been rude to a waitress.

Hancock and Edwards drove to the waterfront club. On the way they stopped and bought two bottles of Old Crow whiskey.

When they reached the club, both staggered to the door. Once inside they walked shoulder to shoulder up to the bar.

Without any hesitation Hancock reached over the bar and grabbed Peter Knowles pulling him over the bar and slamming him on the floor. Edwards took Knowles' pistol from his belt and placed it on the bar.

Harry had just returned to the club. He ran out of his office just in time to see Hancock lift Knowles and throw him over his shoulder.

He then heard Edwards say, "Mr. Knowles, these two country hick cops would like to have a drink with you."

Harry knew better than to intervene at this point. He had seen Hancock and Edwards before when they were drunk and angry.

Hancock carried Knowles out the door of the club and threw him into the back seat of their car. Edwards saw Harry watching them. He waved to Harry and threw him a kiss as they drove off.

The detectives were singing the "Eyes of Texas" as they drove pass the guard shack at the entrance to the Port of Houston.

Hancock had flashed his badge as he drove pass the guard. Trying to put his badge back into his shirt pocket he dropped it on the floor of the car by the brake pedal. Hancock was still looking for his badge as his car rolled down to the water edge of the dock. The only thing that stopped the car from going into the ship channel was a cable support that ran down to the ground from a light pole. The car hit the cable and bounced back like a bumper car at a carnival.

There was a Greek ship moored at this location. Hancock and Edwards pulled Peter Knowles from the car and dragged him up the walkway of the ship. A Greek sailor on the ship, who spoke no English, tried to stop them.

Edwards shoved his 45-caliber pistol into the sailor's ribs. The sailor felt the gun in his stomach and took off running. Edwards laughed and stuck his pistol back into his belt.

It was about 2 a.m. when the telephone rang at Lieutenant James' apartment.

Lt. Joe "Bill" Bradley

"Lieutenant, this is Harry. I've got a pretty sticky problem down here. Hancock and Edwards have been drinking heavy and they're plenty pissed at Knowles, my bartender. I don't want 'em to get in trouble but I know I can't handle them. Please don't tell them I called you."

Harry then told James the entire story about Peter Knowles saying he was wanted in California by the F.B.I. and of Customs putting him in jail.

"Lieutenant, I just received a call from a Greek sea captain and he doesn't know what to do. Hancock and Edwards are on his ship. They chased the captain back into his own quarters shooting at him. He's scared as hell. The Port of Houston guards won't intervene, they know Hancock and Edwards are cops and they are scared too! I don't know what to do. That's why I'm calling you. The captain said he was sound asleep when he heard screams of a man. When he went to investigate Hancock and Edwards shot their pistols over his head. The ship is docked at wharf 10."

"Harry, I'll meet you at the ship! I'm putting my pants on now and I'll be there as soon as I can!"

"Thank you, Lieutenant. But please don't tell Hancock and Edwards I called you."

James dressed and headed for the waterfront. It was a twenty-minute drive. James reasoned, "I've got to get there before someone calls a uniform cop supervisor. There will be hell to pay if they're drunk and get caught by a harness bull."

James sped through the Baytown tunnel on route to the docks. He arrived at the docks in record time. As James drove past the guard at the gate at wharf 10, the guard recognized his car as a police vehicle and pointed towards the ship that was moored there.

James noticed a group of longshoremen gathered along the pier. Some were pointing out over the water while others were laughing. Lieutenant James spotted Harry in the group.

As James got out of his car, Harry ran to meet him.

"Lieutenant, come quick. You have to see this. Those two guys have gone nuts! You gotta do something!"

Lieutenant James rushed with Harry to the edge of the pier.

James looked up and saw a man swinging from the ship's boom. Hancock and Edwards had tied Peter Knowles' ankles to the end of the boom's cable. The boom was used to load and unload cargo, but now was being used as a fishing pole.

Hancock was running the wench motor of the boom. James could hear Hancock singing as he raised Knowles about fifty feet in the air over the ship channel. Hancock then unlocked the brake on the wench and Knowles fell straight as an arrow, head first, into the filthy ship channel water. Anyone who has ever been to a large seaport like Houston knows that a ship channel has two inches of scum on it. The channel is filled with trash, oil, garbage, and on occasions a dead body. If the filth didn't kill Knowles the stench could.

James climbed the catwalk onto the ship.

He could see Detective Edwards was leaning over the ship's rail with a bottle of whiskey in his hand. Edwards was giving orders to Hancock.

Lt. Joe "Bill" Bradley

James could hear Edwards as he barked commands to Hancock, "Up, up, up! Damn you, Hancock, I said up! That's better. You're getting the hang of it now."

Edwards started to sing, "Up, up and away in my beautiful flying machine."

Edwards hollered to Knowles, "Hey, Peter! Do you still think we're country hick cops? You asshole! On the next trip under, catch me a fish."

Lieutenant James walked over to where Hancock was running the wench. Hancock saw the Lieutenant and held out a fifth of whiskey.

"Hi, Lieutenant! Want a drink of Old Crow?"

"Hancock, you crazy son-of-a-bitch. Bring that man back onto the ship!" ordered James.

Hancock in his drunken state grabbed a lever and pulled it. Knowles shot straight down again into the waters of the ship channel.

"Shit, wrong lever, Lu. I'll get it right this time. Do you know how to run this damn thing."

Hancock pulled another lever and Knowles came out of the water all the way to the top of the boom. James looked up and heard a weak "Help" coming from Knowles.

James thought, "At least he's alive."

Hancock pulled another lever and it swung the boom out over the dock above some parked cars.

"Hancock, I said put him on the ship!"

"Hell! Can't you see I'm trying, Lu! I think the gears in this damn motor are drunk."

Edwards turned around from the ship's rail when Hancock was swinging Knowles on the boom out over the dock. He spotted Lieutenant James.

THE TWELVE JUDGES

"Oh shit! Hey, Lu! Isn't Hancock one hell of a fisherman!"

Pointing up in the air, Edwards proudly said, "Look up there what he caught. But crap, he only caught an asshole."

Edwards then looked closely at Lieutenant James' face and thought he had better not say anything else.

"Hancock, bring Knowles down now!" Lieutenant James commanded.

Hancock started working the levers on the wench again. At one point, Hancock had Peter Knowles swinging back and forth high over the ship.

Edwards started to sing, "Rock-a-by-Baby."

Finally, when the boom was over the deck of the ship, Hancock released the brake. Down came Peter Knowles hitting the deck hard.

James walked over to Peter Knowles who was wet and covered with oil and slime and barely conscious, but he was breathing.

"I'm Lieutenant James. Can you talk? If you can't, just listen. I think I can get these two detectives to leave you alone, but you'll still have a problem."

Spitting oil and slime from his mouth Knowles said, "What problem? I don't have a problem, except those two crazy bastards. They're trying to kill me."

"I wouldn't cuss them if I were you. You better listen and listen close," said James.

"Just help me, Lieutenant. I'll do anything you say, if you'll just get me away from those two crazies."

"Your problem is transportation and your mouth. I can hold these two off for awhile. You better find yourself a hole to hide in."

Lt. Joe "Bill" Bradley

"Lieutenant, if you'll help me get away from these two crazy cops, I'll be out of here. I've never seen such crazy cops in all my days!"

James went to the rail of the ship and shouted, "Harry! Come up here."

When Harry arrived on the ship, Lieutenant James was untying Peter Knowles.

"Harry, take this guy with you. I believe he wants to get lost somewhere and he's sorry about what he said about Houston cops. Drive Hancock's car and leave it at your place. Hancock can pick it up later."

When Harry and Peter Knowles left, Lieutenant James turned to Hancock and Edwards, "Stop grinning at me like two shit eatin' opossums. I'm gonna' check with the captain of this ship. Maybe he'll hire you as deck hands and leave you in a foreign port."

Hancock and Edwards followed the Lieutenant to his car. Edwards started singing again, "Bad, Bad, Big Bad John."

James stopped and looked at Edwards. Edwards stopped singing and said, "I'm just a country hick cop. We just wanted to be friendly."

The car was quiet as James drove the two detectives to the factory. He put on a pot of coffee. When the coffee had made, James discovered Hancock and Edwards asleep in the back room of the factory. Lieutenant James went home leaving them to sleep off their whiskey.

The next morning Hancock and Edwards were gone when Lieutenant James arrived at his office. They didn't show until late afternoon. Neither one felt or looked too good.

THE TWELVE JUDGES

They were telling the other detectives about last night when Kathy told Hancock he was wanted on the telephone. Hancock picked up the telephone.

"What! You're kidding me! The reason you couldn't get me last night because I was on a secret assignment with Lieutenant James. Come on by, we'll go find that bastard!"

Lieutenant James and the other detectives had overheard Hancock on the telephone.

James asked, "What's going on Hancock?"

"Agent Carl of Customs said the F.B.I. Fingerprint Lab identified Peter Knowles. His name is Tony Neivers. Lieutenant, the bastard is wanted in California for murder. It seems he's not a Mafia member but one of their hit men. Carl is coming over. They claim Neivers has killed eleven men, mostly connected with union business. Carl said there are three murder warrants on him at this time. No wonder the F.B.I. wanted him."

"Hancock, you and Edwards better take some of the other detectives and see if Peter Knowles or whatever his name is, is still in town. Wait, I'll call Harry. Maybe he knows where to find Knowles."

Agent Carl walked into the office, "Hancock, you really picked a good one and screwed things up. My bosses and the F.B.I. are on my ass! They all want to know where I got Neivers fingerprints. I had to tell them about arresting Neivers and he was using the name of Knowles. I gave them Knowles' Houston address. Fifteen F.B.I. agents went to Knowles apartment but he was gone. They really are pissed at me. They are making me write a report on all of this.

Lt. Joe "Bill" Bradley

I wanted to but I didn't mention your name; so, you son-of-a-bitch, you really owe me!"

"Carl, the Lieutenant is calling Harry now. Maybe Knowles is still in town. You should have been with us last night. You missed all the fun."

Lieutenant James walked out of his office, "Harry said that Knowles didn't even pack his clothes at his apartment. He took Knowles to his car and the last thing he heard from Knowles was, `I am leaving the State of Texas, with those two crazy cops running around, no one is safe'."

Edwards told Agent Carl about last night and Carl said, "Peter Knowles is right, you two are crazy! Come on, I'll buy you a beer."

Both Hancock and Edwards shook their heads without saying a word. They both looked sick.

James and the detectives learned from Agent Carl a month later that a Sheriff Department in Arizona had arrested Tony Neivers, alias, Peter Knowles.

At Tony Neivers' extradition hearing to be returned to California, he told the Judge, "I'll waive extradition to any state except Texas, especially Houston, Texas.

CHAPTER 12

FAIR PLAY AT THE ASTRODOME

Lieutenant James' secretary, Kathy, walked into his office and said, "Chief Ladd is on the phone. I think he wants you to come to his office."

James picked up his telephone and answered, "Chief, I thought you would be playing golf. It's much too pretty of a day to be doing police work."

"James! Get your butt over to my office now! Captain Runnels of the Homicide Division is in my office. The captain has more killings than he can handle. Houston's going to set a record this year for murders and that looks bad for the mayor and me. You've been sitting on your ass too long! I haven't been on T.V. in a month," screamed Chief Ladd.

Chief Ladd continued to holler, "I'm not in the mood for any bull-shit, so get your ass over here."

The Chief slammed the phone down.

Lt. Joe "Bill" Bradley

Lieutenant Bill James slowly hung up the phone and wondered, "Who put a bee under the Chief's saddle?"

James saw Detective Joe Kramer as he went out, "Kramer, take charge of things. I've got to go see our fat chief."

James drove from the factory to the main police department. He parked in one of the Chief's aid's parking spot and went into the main police station. He started for the elevators but saw a crowd waiting and one of the two elevators was again out of service. "Damn elevators" he said out loud. "There is always one elevator out. I wish that I had the service contract on these elevators for the past 20 years. I would have been a millionaire."

James climbed the three flights of stairs to the Chief's office.

Walking up to the receptionist, James said, "Hi, Ms. May. Is my fat chief in?"

"You know he's in, Bill. He has Captain Runnels of Homicide with him. They're expecting you."

"Don't buzz him, Ms. May. Let me surprise him."

Ms. May giggled as James opened the Chief's door. Captain Runnels got up from his chair and shook James hand.

"Hi, Bill. Glad to see ya."

The Chief did not move from his chair.

"Damn Chief, you could get up when I enter the room. After all, I got you through the police academy and you should show me some respect."

THE TWELVE JUDGES

"Sit down, Bill and don't be a smart-ass. I've got more problems that I can handle. As usual the biggest problem is that I don't have enough policemen. Captain Runnels will fill you in on one particular problem."

Captain Runnels spoke up, "Lieutenant, you remember the creep, Matthew Oliver. He's the sorry bastard that a Judge turned loose who was killing and raping young girls."

"Yeah, I remember him. Luna, who used to work for you and now works for me, spoke of him. Also, some of your detectives told me about him. They were really upset when he walked free. Wasn't he the one that murdered young girls by choking them to death, then he raped them and cut off their breasts and mutilated their vaginas."

"That's the one. The S.O.B. is at it again. In the past year, we have received inquiries from other police departments about him. Girls have been murdered in St. Petersburg, Florida, Selma, Alabama and we believe a murder in Lafayette, Louisiana is his work. All of the murders fit Oliver's M.O. There was no evidence at the scene of any of the murders to connect Matthew Oliver. I've talked with the police in those cities and they feel the same as I do. None of the departments have seen him or know where he is at this time. I believe that Matthew Oliver's at it again and I believe he's headed for Houston. This is his hometown."

"What can I do for you, Captain? You have some of the best Homicide Detectives in the world."

Chief Ladd broke in, "Just shut up, Bill and listen to Runnels. He doesn't need flattery."

Lt. Joe "Bill" Bradley

"Sorry, Chief."

"Bill, I need your help for a number of reasons. My detectives are snowed under on who-done-it cases and drive-by murders. They have to work overtime nearly every day. I can't spare the manpower to put Oliver under surveillance. Also, you've got a detective working for you that knows Matthew Oliver inside and out. He knows his habits, his hangouts and where he takes a crap."

"You're talking about Robert Luna."

"Yes! Luna worked the murder cases involving Oliver and knows him like a book. Bill, I know you and your reputation. You can do things my detectives can't do. I know you don't follow the letter of the law but I also know you get results. You can concentrate on one case at a time. We can't."

Chief Ladd stood up but then slowly sat back down in his chair saying, "I didn't hear that."

Captain Runnels laughed and continued, "I want you to take on Matthew Oliver as a project, if you will. I know you can make a case on the bastard if he comes to Houston. Just make any kind of case that will put the bastard away where he belongs. I'll have copies of all the cases sent to your office for review if you decide to take the case."

Chief Ladd stood up again looking straight at James, "What do you mean, 'If!' I'm the Chief of Police and James is a piss-ant lieutenant. He will take the case!"

"Damn right, Captain. I'll take the case! It'll be a personal pleasure to put the bastard away. Besides, Luna will transfer back to Homicide if he finds out Oliver is in town and he can't work on him."

THE TWELVE JUDGES

Chief Ladd rose from his chair the third time, "Putting him away doesn't mean six foot under, Bill. I've faded enough heat from the D.A.'s office already on you and your squad."

Toying with the Chief, James said, "In front of Captain Runnels, are you ordering me to take this case?"

Chief Ladd's face grew red, "It's a direct order for you to take the case. But! But, but I know how you work! I'm ordering you to take the case but not to kill Oliver. All I need is an investigation by that squirrel Assistant D. A. Jamie Owens."

Lieutenant James promised Chief Ladd that he would go by the book and keep him and Captain Runnels informed.

As James was leaving the chief's office he heard the Chief say, "Bill gets results, but since he's started with that bunch of detectives, I've lost ten pounds, my golf game is terrible, and I'm being treated for an ulcer. He's going to get me fired one of these days."

When James returned to his office, he told Kathy to call all the detectives in for a meeting.

It took nearly an hour for Kathy to locate the men and have them report. When they had gathered, Lieutenant James asked Detective Luna to sit up front.

Detective Roosevelt Washington started a chant, which the others took up when Luna walked to the front.

"Teachers pet, teachers pet."

"I'll be brief for now," James began. "I want all of you to give Detective Luna your attention."

Lt. Joe "Bill" Bradley

Turning to Luna, James began, "Luna, Matthew Oliver has started up again. Three girls were murdered in three different states over the past year. The M.O. used indicates Oliver was the killer. The police in the other states have not been able to locate him."

James could see Luna's face grow tense when he mentioned Matthew Oliver's name.

Detective Luna asked, "Am I being transferred back to the Homicide Division to handle the investigation on him?"

"Hell no, Luna! We're going to drop all the cases we're working on and this group is going after that sorry son-of-a-bitch."

Detective Luna's face lit up, "That's great! I know we can get him with this group. We'll take care of his sorry ass!"

James continued, "Captain Runnels of Homicide is sending us all the cases involving Matthew Oliver. Luna will coordinate all information and give you a run down on Oliver's habits. You have the floor, Luna."

Robert Luna stood before the group. His face showed the seriousness of his thinking regarding Matthew Oliver. He began, "Don't think for a minute that Matthew Oliver is just another narcotic using rapist killer. He's very educated, cunning, and plans each encounter. He is a brutal killer.

"He loves sporting events. Not the sport itself, but the crowd of young girls the sporting event attracts. This is where he picks his victim. He always poses as a schoolteacher and dresses the part. Before he approaches a victim, he learns all about the school, even the principal's name.

"He doesn't use narcotics but does drink. He goes to the better bars. He is a smooth talker and picks up dates at the bars. He is a sharp dresser. He has never killed a woman that he's picked up in a bar. He likes his girls young and innocent. His pleasure is that of killing the girls and then raping them after they are dead. All are young high school girls. Oliver always seeks employment at a lady's shoe store. Again, he has never killed or raped a customer. I'll get the list of alias names he has used in the past. He probably will use one of them. If he's headed back to Houston, we'll find him working in a shoe store. We could start our surveillance at his job if we find where he is working."

Luna continued, "The son-of-a-bitch has to be stopped! He's the type that will never stop killing and raping until he's behind bars or dead. I'll have a picture and a rap sheet on Oliver at our next meeting. Lu, do you have anything else to add?"

James rose quickly from his chair, "Yes. You might as well get started making a list from the yellow pages on every woman's shoe store. Also, every day, check the newspaper want ads for shoe salesmen. All of you read every case Homicide brings over. After you've read the cases, we'll get together and Luna will lead a discussion on your ideas concerning Matthew Oliver."

The detectives spent the days studying files on Matthew Oliver. Detective Joe Kramer had computerized every woman's shoe store in the greater Houston area.

Luna got the photo lab to blow up a life-size picture of Matthew Oliver. He taped it on a wall in the factory.

Lt. Joe "Bill" Bradley

Washington bought some steel pointed darts and Matthew Oliver's photo became a game of who would buy lunch. The X drawn on Oliver's crouch had become the winning target.

A week had passed since the last group discussion of Matthew Oliver. Detectives were getting tired of going to shoe stores. James had called a meeting and everyone was present except Detectives Joe Kramer and Robert Luna.

James asked, "Has anyone seen Kramer or Luna this morning?"

Detective King spoke up, "Lu, I think they're probably at the county tax office. They go there every day."

"What are they doing at the tax office?"

"Luna told me that Oliver is a nut when it comes to doing little things right. He believes that if Oliver comes to Houston, he'll change the license plates on his car from out-of-state to Texas. You know, when a person moves into Texas he has 10 days to register his car but it takes the tax office months to put the records on the computer. They're at the tax office going through all of the recent license registrations by hand. It's one hell of a job."

Detective Murphy asked, "What if Oliver buys a car here in Houston?"

"They are going through those records too," King said.

As the discussion continued some of the detectives complained that they were avoiding good information from their informers on thieves because they had to inspect women's shoe stores. They all

THE TWELVE JUDGES

understood that Oliver needed to be caught but were becoming bored with looking at women shoe stores.

Lieutenant James was just about to end the meeting when Detectives Kramer and Luna came in the door. Luna was waving a piece of paper.

"Look what we found? The bastard did come back to Houston!"

Luna handed Lieutenant James the paper. It was a copy of a Texas vehicle registration. James read the information aloud to the men, "1984 Volkswagen Bus, Texas license number 935KWL, registered to Matthew Oliver, P.O. Box 2311, Houston, Texas."

Luna added, "The bastard bought the car in Alabama."

"I can't believe he put the car in his name," remarked Detective Washington.

Luna broke in, "I told you how confident he is in himself. He'll put his car in his name because he owns the car. When we find where he's living, the apartment will be in a fictitious name."

"Why would he get a post office box?" King asked.

Luna replied, "The post office box will also be fictitious. That way no one will be able to trace him if he kidnaps a girl. We're going to have to locate him where he gets a job."

"I'll have a bulletin issued to the uniform Radio Patrol," said James. "If an officer spots Oliver in his Volkswagen, they're not to stop him, but to notify this office as soon as possible."

"That's great idea, Lu," Detective Park said.

"That's why he's a lieutenant, stupid, and you're not," added Detective Murphy.

Lt. Joe "Bill" Bradley

"Lieutenant!"

"Go ahead, Luna, what were you going to say?"

"In the past, Oliver has liked the southwest part of Houston. He has always rented an apartment in that area. I think we should divide the area and all of us start checking apartment parking lots for his Volkswagen."

"O.K., Luna, you and Kramer divide up the area among the men and let's get started. There're a lot of apartments in the southwest and it's going to take some time. We better check the apartments in the evening hours also. King, call your friend that's a postal inspector. We need to make sure the post office box that he listed on his car registration is fictitious and if in the application he listed a good address. If any of you spot Oliver's car, set up a surveillance and contact me."

As Kramer and Luna laid out a map of the city of Houston, James called his secretary into his office and dictated a bulletin to the Radio Patrol Division.

After the detectives received their assignments they left the factory for the southwest part of Houston.

Detective King had confirmed that all the information listed by Oliver on the application for his post office box was fictitious.

James called Captain Runnels in the Homicide Division and informed him of Matthew Oliver's return to Houston.

"Bill, I hope you find the bastard soon. If he sticks to his pattern, he's overdue to kill. If I can be of any help, don't hesitate to call. My detectives are pissed 'cause they can't work the case. I'll pass on

THE TWELVE JUDGES

Oliver's car license number to them. I'll have to order them to stay out of your way. They really want the bastard too!"

"Thanks, Captain. This group of rouges that works for me, will get Oliver one way or the other."

"I know the reputation of your group. I hope it's the other, Bill. That son-of-a-bitch doesn't deserve a trial."

The day seemed long to James as he waited for word that one of his detectives had spotted Oliver's car. Before he left for the day, James contacted each detective by radio. All wanted to work overtime and continue the search. Oliver's car had not been found. Lieutenant James and his secretary closed the factory and left for the day.

James had just finished reading an article in a fishing magazine and was headed for the shower when his telephone rang.

James answered the telephone on the second ring.

The caller asked, "Is this Lieutenant James?"

"Yes. This is Lieutenant James."

"Lieutenant, this is Officer Bates in the police dispatcher office. Unit 10 B 40 has spotted the Volkswagen wanted in the bulletin that you issued. Unit 10 B 40 wants to know what to do. There was no answer at your office."

"That's great! Tell Unit 10 B 40 to back off from the area and name a location where my detectives can meet him. Where is the Volkswagen?"

"It's parked at the Cherry Hills Apartments on Old Spanish Trail by the Astrodome."

Lt. Joe "Bill" Bradley

"Ask Unit 10 B 40 where my detectives can meet him."

James heard the dispatcher ask 10 B 40 to pick a location away from the apartments to meet the detectives.

"Lieutenant, he'll meet your detectives at the Shell Service Station a block away. I'll hold him out of service until then."

"Thanks Bates and thank 10 B 40. He did a great job. My detectives will be on their way as soon as I can get in touch with them."

James called Detective Luna first. James could feel Detective Luna's adrenaline flowing through the telephone. James didn't have to tell Luna but one time that the Volkswagen had been found. Luna quickly said see ya and hung up. James knew that Luna was on his way.

James then called Detective Thomas Murphy and told him the location. James asked, "Can you get your equipment without any trouble tonight and get started? This is one case where you and Park are really needed to be telephone men again."

"No problem. I'll call Park. We'll go by the factory and pick up the van. An apartment is really easy to bug."

James continued, "In the morning, check with the apartment leasing office. They might have an apartment close by Oliver's apartment that we can rent."

James continued calling his detectives. His last call was to Detective Jack Hancock.

"Hancock, you coordinate the surveillance. Take no chances. I don't want Oliver to spot any of

THE TWELVE JUDGES

the men. If you have too, call the Helicopter Division. Have them get a chopper in the air to follow Oliver in his Volkswagen."

"O.K., Lu. I'm on my way, but calling for a helicopter is useless. There's never one around when you need one."

"Hancock! That's what citizen's say about cops. If needed you will call for the helicopter."

James didn't call Detective Kramer. He wanted Kramer in the office to help coordinate things from there.

When James walked into the factory the next morning, Kramer was on the police radio, "Here he is now, I'll tell him."

"Tell me what?"

"Hancock has located the apartment Oliver is in. The Volkswagen is still there. He contacted a helicopter unit by radio but they said they were on another assignment."

James saw Kathy bringing him a cup of coffee.

"Kathy, get me Captain Betts of the Helicopter Division on the phone."

She sat the cup of coffee on his desk and placed the call.

"He's on the phone, Bill."

"Captain Betts? This is Lieutenant Bill James. I need one of your Fox units in the air as soon as possible. Have them head for the Astrodome and contact unit 101."

"Can't help you Bill. I only have one Fox unit flying today and he's doing morning traffic reports for a couple of radio stations."

Lt. Joe "Bill" Bradley

"Screw the traffic! A damn helicopter's not going to help the traffic mess in Houston. Is that all the shit you do, damn public relations? I'm making this call for Chief Ladd. The Chief said to get your Fox unit to the Astrodome area now!"

"O.K., Lieutenant. If the Chief wants to fade the heat with the radio stations that's fine with me."

"He will! Get your fox unit out there!"

James hoped Captain Betts didn't call the Chief to verify his story or complain the way he had talked to him.

James hollered for Kramer to contact Hancock and tell him a Fox unit was on the way.

James heard Hancock over the police radio say, "I don't believe it!"

It was after nine when the Fox unit contacted Hancock.

"Fox 1F10 to 101."

"Go ahead Fox."

"What do you need 101?"

"101 to Fox. There's a blue Volkswagen, Texas license number 935 K-King, W-William, L-Lincoln parked in the Cherry Hills Apartments on O.S.T. There are exits from the apartments onto Fannin and O.S.T. Streets. We need you to follow the Volkswagen when it leaves."

"Clear, 101. We'll spot the VW and then sit down on the Astrodome parking lot until it leaves. Call us when it moves."

At nine forty a white male wearing a black business suit approached the blue VW.

"101 to all units, we have activity at the VW. Did you copy Fox?"

THE TWELVE JUDGES

"Fox to 101. We copied. Just give us the direction he leaves the apartments. We're going to get high enough so he can't spot us."

"101 to Fox. He's leaving the apartment parking lot and turning south onto O.S.T. Street."

"Fox to 101, we have him. You can drop off of him now. We'll keep you informed."

"101 clear."

"Fox to 101. He's now at the fork where O.S.T. joins South Main. He's headed south on Main."

"101 clear."

"Fox to 101. He's getting on the South 610 Loop headed north."

"101 clear, we're headed that way."

"Fox to 101. He's still on the Loop and just passed South Post Oak Road."

"101 clear. We're on the Loop now."

"Fox to 101. He's taking the Beechnut exit. Standby."

"101 clear."

"Fox to 101. He's turning left under the Loop onto Beechnut headed West."

"101 clear."

"Fox to 101. He's parking in the Meyerland Shopping Center. He's out of his car headed for the Mall. Standby! He has entered the Mall on the northeast corner."

"101 clear. We're turning onto Beechnut. We should be there in a couple of minutes."

"101 to all units. I have his car spotted. Meet us on the Beechnut side of the parking lot. Fox can

Lt. Joe "Bill" Bradley

you hang around in the area to give us time to spot the suspect in the Mall?"

"Fox to 101. Sorry, but we've been in the air all morning doing the traffic reports. We need to get back to Hobby Airport for fuel. You'll have to contact our captain for further assignment."

"101, I figured as much, but thanks anyway."

After all the detectives had gathered at the meeting spot, Hancock said, "I'd better contact the lieutenant."

Detective Luna broke in, "We had better get somebody inside the mall and locate Oliver. I've got a feeling this is where he's working. I can't go in, Oliver knows me by sight."

Hancock agreed. "King, Davis, Watson, Johnson, and Edwards, go inside the Mall and see if you can locate Oliver. If you do, let us know. I want Washington out here in case Oliver comes back to his car. Washington's the only one that can follow him in this Houston traffic."

"I can't believe my ears. Hancock gave me a compliment," remarked Washington.

"It was a slip of the tongue," answered Hancock. He then continued with his instructions, "Murphy and Park, I'm sure you know what Lu wants done to Oliver's car. After I contact Lu, Washington, Luna and I will be your lookouts."

The detectives assigned to the mall left. Detective Hancock called Lieutenant James and informed him of their location and the surveillance plan.

"Sounds good, Hancock. Have Murphy and Park put a bug on the VW."

"They're headed for Oliver's car now."

"I hate to keep all of you on surveillance but we can't lose this bastard now. Keep me informed. I'll join you later."

Hancock casually strolled passed the blue Volkswagen. Murphy was under the car. Park had used a slim jim to gain entrance to the car. He was working under the dashboard cussing.

"Shit! How do they expect me to plant a microphone under the dash without any damn room. This car was built for midgets."

It didn't take Murphy and Park long to finish their work. They walked to where Hancock, Luna, and Washington were standing. As they approached, Hancock could hear the two detectives arguing over what frequency the transmitter under the car's dashboard should have been put on.

The four detectives walked back to the good time surveillance van. Park waked back to the Volkswagen. Murphy opened the side door of the van and turned on one of several police radios that had been installed in the surveillance van. He then instructed Hancock to wave to Park.

Park, still standing by the Volkswagen waved back and then turned facing the VW and hollered at the empty Volkswagen, "Hey you mother! I bet you're hearing me loud and clear."

Murphy stepped from the van and waved at Park.

"The son-of-a-bitch, was right, he's coming in loud and clear."

After Park had joined the group at the van, they saw the other detectives coming, King said, "You were right Luna, but he's not working in a shoe store. He's selling women's shoes all right, but for a clothing store. Man! We would have never found him if that uniform officer hadn't been on the ball. The clothing store doesn't close until nine tonight. Do you think he's working from nine to nine?"

"He probably gets off at 5," Luna offered. "We'll just have to wait him out."

Murphy spoke up, "How are we going to work this? The Lieutenant wanted us to make a visit into Oliver's apartment and plant a transmitter and bug his phone. None of you know how to work the receiver in the Good Time van to pick up the signals from the transmitter on Oliver's car. If we lose him, the boss is going to have our ass. We're also suppose to try rent an apartment."

"I'll call the lieutenant on the mobile phone. Let him make the decision." Hancock called the Lieutenant. He told him they had a problem. "If Oliver comes back to his car when Murphy and Park are at his apartment, we won't be able to tract him if they're not here. No one else knows how to work their electronic gadgets."

After a few minutes, Hancock hung up the phone.

"Well, what did he say?" questioned Murphy.

"He said if Murphy and Park couldn't get to Oliver's apartment and do their thing by 5 p.m., he'd better look elsewhere for some real telephone men."

Murphy gave a shrug and looking at Hancock grumbled, "I told you we shouldn't have called him. We need to take Davis with us. He can get into the apartment faster than we can."

"All right, but the Lu said you'd better be back before five."

Detectives Murphy, Park, and Davis left for Oliver's apartment.

Matthew Oliver's apartment was on the first floor. Detective Murphy stood at one end of the hall while Park stood at the other. They didn't want Detective Davis to be surprised while picking the apartment door lock.

Davis carried a small black bag with his prize lock picking tools. He looked at Murphy and then at Park. Each nodded their okay. Davis picked the lock and opened the door stepping inside.

He was joined quickly by Murphy and Park. Park went directly to the telephone in the bedroom and went to work.

Unscrewing the mouthpiece of the telephone, he placed a drop microphone inside. The mouth speaker that he placed in the telephone looked identical to the part he removed. The only exception was that the part he placed in the telephone had a built in transmitter.

Park then located the phone in the living area and repeated the procedure.

While Murphy was busy placing a transmitter under the coffee table, Park remarked. "Do you need some help little boy? I'm already finished with my assignment."

Murphy looked up from under the coffee table and said, "Asshole! You could speed things up by helping Davis search the place. Just be sure if you move anything, put it back the way you found it."

Lt. Joe "Bill" Bradley

Park walked away laughing. Davis was busy going through the hanging clothes in a closet.

"What area still needs to be searched, Davis?"

"Take the bathroom, I'm almost finished with the rest."

Turning the door knob to the bathroom door, Park felt resistance. He put more pressure on the door. When the door was halfway opened, he saw what was blocking the door. Teen magazines and torn pages were everywhere. He reached down and pushed them out of the way.

Park picked up one of the torn magazines. It was "Teen's Dresswear." Pictures of teenage girls from the magazines had been cut to shreds. Looking around the bathroom Park saw women's panty hose, panties and bras cut into pieces. The undergarments were thrown all over the floor among the shredded pictures.

Park picked up a magazine but dropped it as though it was on fire. He picked the magazine up again and smelled it. It had the smell of a man's semen. An eight-inch deer skinning knife was stuck in the wall beside the toilet.

"Come in here," hollered Park. Murphy and Davis rushed in.

"Look at the floor of the bathroom and at the knife stuck in the wall."

"Holy shit!" exclaimed Davis.

"We're dealing with a real sick nut!" said Park.

"It appears that Oliver arouses himself sexually by stabbing pictures of young girls and underclothes and masturbates on them. I found a magazine with semen on it. I'm going to take it with us in case we need it later for evidence."

Davis said, "You can't use it as evidence. Have you forgotten we're burglars?"

"We can use it for comparison if the bastard commits another rape and murder and we miss him."

Murphy spoke up, "Don't say that. We won't miss this bastard! I'm finished planting the bugs. Put the bathroom back the way it was. Let's get out of here!"

Davis slowly opened the front door of the apartment and cautiously stepped into the hallway.

"It's clear. Come on."

Davis had trouble locking the apartment door as it had a large dead bolt. Just as he locked the door, a young couple came out of an apartment two doors down. They looked at the men and then went on their way.

The three detectives then returned to the shopping center where the others were waiting. The operation had taken just over an hour.

Park told the other detectives what they had found in Oliver's bathroom.

Murphy had turned on the radio receivers in the van before they left for Oliver's apartment.

Murphy asked, "Did you hear us in the apartment?"

Detective Gary Edwards spoke up, "Yeah, we heard you call Park an asshole and which one of you farted. The fart sound rocked the van."

"Well at least we know the transmitters are working," said Hancock. "Also, Lieutenant James called while you were gone. He wants all of us to meet

Lt. Joe "Bill" Bradley

him at the assembly room at the police substation down the street. Washington, you and I will wait here in case Oliver leaves his job. Murphy and Park will stay with us in the surveillance van."

James was waiting for the detectives when they arrived. The lieutenant was told about the trip to Oliver's apartment and the bathroom scene. He was also informed that there were no vacant apartments near Oliver.

"I don't have to tell you that we're dealing with a person who is about to kill again," began Lieutenant James. "He's like a psycho hawk circling over a field looking for his prey. Where he'll strike is unknown. We have to be ready. When you're on surveillance following him and if you get a feeling that he's noticed you, pull off. Let someone else fill in. Don't take a chance of being burned.

"It appears he'll get off work at five. I'm going to place you all along the route to his apartment. Washington and Hancock will follow him when he leaves the shopping center. They'll announce his route every few minutes over the police radio. Stay off the radio unless you don't receive their transmission clearly. Tonight, after we know he has retired, some of you can go home and get a few hours sleep. He has never approached a victim in the morning hours. But we must keep someone on him at all times.

"Murphy and Park will drive the van with the monitors. They will follow Hancock and Washington in case Oliver is lost in traffic. Murphy and Park can then pick up the signal from the transmitter attached to his Volkswagen.

THE TWELVE JUDGES

"Keep one thought in your mind at all times! To make a case on this bastard, we're going to have to catch him at the moment his victim becomes in fear for her life. We're going to have to stay on top of him to make sure he doesn't hurt his victim before we can get to him."

James continued, "All of the M.O.'s of his murders in the past follow the same pattern. He cons a young girl to take a walk with him telling her that he's a teacher. When he gets her alone, he knocks her out and then rips the clothes from her. After he chokes her to death, he rapes her and then he mutilates the body. If it turns out you're the one following him, and he is with a girl, have your pistol in hand. Don't hesitate to shoot the son-of-a-bitch, if in your mind the girl's life is in danger. If anyone makes a mistake and shoots him before he commits an act, make sure he's dead! Then the bastard can't testify against us. Kramer has a list of the locations were you'll be parked on the route to his apartment. Get your assignments and be ready!"

All the detectives were in position as James and Detective Kramer waited at the Cherry Hills Apartments. James had decided to let Matthew Oliver make all the moves.

At 5:15, Hancock's voice boomed in over the police radio.

"101 to number 12. He's moving. The traffic is really heavy. He's taking the 610 South Loop headed south."

"Number 12 to all units. 101 says he's moving. Stay alert!"

Lt. Joe "Bill" Bradley

"101 to number 12. It looks like he's going home. No he's not! Standby. He passed the exit for South Main. He's getting off at Fannin."

Also over the air waves came, "Damn, Washington! You nearly hit that car. Did you see that? She gave you the finger."

"101 to all units, he's two cars in front of us and he's making the U-turn under the freeway. 101, Oh crap! We're blocked off under the freeway."

"105 to 101, we're at the Loop and South Main. He has to come this way. We'll pick him up."

"101 to all units, we're out of traffic now but we don't see him. You think he got back on the freeway?"

"109 to 101, the meter says he's not moving. Maybe he went to eat. Are there any joints there on the feeder road?"

"101 to all units. We see him now. His car is parked at Sally's Restaurant and Bar. He must be inside. Did you copy number 12?"

"Number 12 to 101, I copied. Do any of you man-about-town detectives have a coat and tie with you?"

"I do, Lieutenant."

"Number 12 to I-do."

"Sorry, Lu. Number 110 to number 12. I have a coat and tie with me."

"Number 12 to 110, put it on and go into Sally's. See what our man is up to. 101, find a spot where you can watch his car. 105, stay where you are. He has to come your way when he leaves Sally's."

THE TWELVE JUDGES

Detective Bill Johnson donned the coat and tie that he had hanging in the back of his car. He walked into Sally's.

He spotted Matthew Oliver sitting at the bar talking with a woman in her 40's. There was an open stool next to the woman so Johnson sat down. He ordered a Pearl beer. There was a lot of noise in the place.

It was Happy Hour for the working people. Johnson slipped his hand into his inside coat pocket and turned on his tape recorder. He thought, "I wonder if Murphy and Park can delete the noise the drunks are making from this tape. Knowing those two, they probably can."

Johnson leaned toward the woman talking with Oliver. He was able to overhear a few words. Oliver was talking about some high school football game. Johnson heard Oliver tell the lady he had been with the same school as a teacher for 5 years. He also heard mention of the Astrodome.

Johnson wished he could climb on top of the bar, stand up and shout, "Shut up you sons-of-bitches so I can hear! I'm trying to record a damn killer!"

After Johnson had been at the bar for about 30 minutes, he saw Oliver suddenly stand up. Oliver shouted in the face of the woman he had been talking to, "You bitch. I really didn't want you to go with me to my apartment. You're too old for me anyway. I like young women and I can get any of them I want."

Oliver slammed a ten dollar bill down on the bar and told the bartender, "Buy the lady a drink. She looks too much like my mother for me to buy her a drink."

Lt. Joe "Bill" Bradley

Oliver then headed out of the bar for his car.

Hancock saw Matthew Oliver as he left Sally's.

"101 to all units. Subject is leaving. He's in his car and is on the feeder street headed for South Main."

"105 to all units. We see him. He has turned onto South Main and is headed north. He's coming your way, Lu."

"Number 12, clear. All units if he goes to his apartment, 101 and 109 will stay with him. The rest of you meet me on the Westside of the Astrodome parking lot.

The Volkswagen was followed to the Cherry Hills Apartments. James watched as Oliver parked. Detective Kramer's camera whined as he snapped picture after picture of Oliver walking into the apartment complex.

"Let's go to the Astrodome parking lot, Kramer. Hancock and Washington will keep us advised." They passed Murphy and Park in the surveillance van.

All of the other detectives were already on the dome parking lot when Kramer and James arrived. They were standing in a group. Detective Johnson was telling them about his encounter with Oliver in the bar. Johnson repeated his story for James and Kramer and then played the tape he had recorded. Some of the conservation was audible, but most was not. The crowd noise in the bar was too much.

When Johnson had finished playing the tape, he said, "I did hear Oliver say he was a teacher and something about a football game. Do you think Murphy and Park can take out the background noise?"

THE TWELVE JUDGES

James was halfway through his answer to Johnson's question when he stopped in mid-sentence. Looking up at the Astrodome marquee they were standing under, he said, "I'll be a son-of-a-bitch! Look up there!"

All eyes turned upward.

The marquee read, "High School Football Playoffs, Saturday night, 7:30, Central Vs. Wayne, No Reserve Seats."

Excitedly, Johnson said "Remember on the tape, Lu! Oliver mentioned a high school football game and he mentioned the Astrodome!"

"I heard that too!" exclaimed Lieutenant James. "That's why the marquee got my attention."

Detective Kramer broke in, "The game's tomorrow night. It would be hell to cover the entire Astrodome."

Lieutenant James could feel both the excitement and the distress in his detectives as he continued, "We can't cover the whole damn place! We're going to stick to Oliver like pigeon shit on a car. This has to be the place Oliver was taking about. I'll contact the Astrodome Security; we might need their help.

"Kramer, contact Murphy and Park in the surveillance van. See if they've picked up any conversation in Oliver's apartment."

Kramer walked over to the car and picked up the mike, "111 to 109."

"109, go ahead 111."

"111, number 12 wants to know if there's any activity at your end."

Lt. Joe "Bill" Bradley

"109 to 111. Tell number 12 to call us over the mobile phone."

Kramer rejoined the group, "Lieutenant, Murphy said to call him on the mobile. I don't think he wants to talk over the police radio."

James picked up his mobile telephone and called the surveillance van, "What's going on Murphy?"

"He's made four phone calls Lu, trying to get a date but he's struck out each time. All the women said they'd never go out with him again. They all hung up on him. He sure has a line of bullshit. It sounds like he's just sitting around watching T.V."

James told Murphy about the football game to be played at the Astrodome the following night.

"Damn Lu, sounds like that football game fits his M.O."

"Stay on surveillance, Murphy. I'll get Kramer to make a schedule so you can be relieved. Expect a long day tomorrow. I've got a feeling we're all going to a high school football game."

When James walked back to the group, Kramer whispered in his ear, "Davis helped Murphy and Park at Oliver's apartment. He feels that he did wrong, leaving the deer knife he found in Oliver's apartment."

James walked over to Davis, "You did a fine job, Davis. You had to leave the knife. I would've done the same thing. If you had taken the knife, it might've scared him away or put Oliver on notice that the cops know he is in Houston."

"But, Lu. What if he hurts a young girl with that knife and I had the opportunity to stop him from using that knife?"

"He wouldn't stop, Davis. He would just get another knife. We're going to get that bastard, one way or another! Kramer, have you got a schedule made for tonight?"

"Yes, Sir, and they're to call you if anything happens."

"Great, Kramer! Take me back to the factory so I can pick up my car." On the drive back to the factory, James turned over and over in his mind what would be the thinking of Oliver if he goes to the Astrodome? He knew that Oliver would pose as a teacher, but where in the hell had he planned his attack? The Astrodome is huge. There will be a crowd of people. Where would he take her? He thought of the lower level. No, too many security guards, that's where the teams dress. Then he thought of the upper levels. They'll be broadcasting the game on level three. He couldn't go there. And then, there's the club level. Hell, I'll have to check and see if any of the elevators will be running to the Sky Boxes. There won't be anyone in the Sky Boxes. It would be a perfect place. If his victim screams, she can't be heard. Then James spoke out loud, "Closed circuit T.V."

Kramer asked, "What did you say, Lu?"

"Kramer, the Astrodome has closed circuit T.V. If I can get use of it, we can spot Oliver in the crowd and keep a camera on him all the time. You're going with me to the Astrodome Security office in the morning. I'm going to put you with a walkie-talkie on one side of the field with a T.V. cameraman and Watson on the other side to test this theory."

Lt. Joe "Bill" Bradley

"That's a great idea, Lu. But, who's going to operate the cameras?"

"If I have to pay the cameraman myself, I'll get them. Make sure all the men have walkie-talkies that work. I'm going into my office, Kramer. I don't think I should wait until tomorrow to contact the Astrodome Security. Do you know who heads their security?"

"I believe Captain Jones does. He's head of the Traffic Division. I'll come in with you. Boy, the T.V. cameras are a great idea!"

Both men entered James' office just as his pager went off. Checking the number, James recognized the number being that of the surveillance mobile phone. He called the number.

"Lu, this is Murphy. The bastard hasn't left his apartment but he is sure worked up!"

"Murphy, what do you mean worked up?"

"Oliver went crazy in his apartment. He started talking to himself as if a woman was with him. He cussed and cried. We heard papers being torn. All the time he would holler, 'You bitch! Get up and put your clothes on. I don't want you. You're too old.' Then Lu, you won't believe what we heard. We could hear him masturbating and it sounded like a woman was with him! He acted out both parts. We then heard him shower and it sounds like he's watching T.V. again."

"My God, Murphy. He's a mad dog. He needs to be taken out and shot!"

"Just give me and Park the word, Boss."

"Stay on surveillance until you are relieved. If he leaves his apartment tonight, I want to be called immediately."

"O.K., Lu."

THE TWELVE JUDGES

James told Kramer what Murphy had said.

"Lu, I haven't been able to get the Homicide pictures out of my mind since we started this case. What he did to those young girls, my God it was awful. I'm going to pray tonight that Oliver goes to the Astrodome. He has to go to the Astrodome tomorrow night! We have to catch him and put him away for good!"

"I know, Kramer. I know."

James was able to locate Captain Jones at home. Lieutenant James explained why the T.V. cameras were needed. Captain Jones said he would not even go into his office at the police department tomorrow, but he would meet James at the Astrodome and make sure the cameras were set up and working. They agreed to meet at the Astrodome at 2 p.m.

The next morning, Matthew Oliver was followed by three detective cars to the clothing store in Meyerland Shopping Center. James gave the other detectives until noon to report to the factory.

At noon all were present except Murphy and Park. They had stayed on surveillance.

James began the meeting, "All of you make sure your walkie-talkies are working. Detective Luna believes as I do; Oliver is going to the Astrodome to look for a victim. If he doesn't, we'll still stay with him wherever he goes. If he does go to the ball game, you'll have to cover him like a blanket. There are enough of us where we should be able to keep him in sight at all times. I'm telling you, don't lose the bastard!"

James continued, "We can't let him kill again. When you get to the entrance of the Astrodome,

Lt. Joe "Bill" Bradley

there'll be security guards standing outside. Walk up to one and tell him you're there for Captain Jones. The guard will let you through the gate. One good thing, there's only one entrance open for high school games. Luna and I have picked a spot in the Astrodome already. We'll be in the Sky Boxes, in the end zone with binoculars. Watson and Kramer will be with the T.V. cameramen. Keep them informed as to where Oliver is at all times. Luna and I will monitor the T.V. set in the Sky Box."

"Sounds like we're making a movie, Lu," voiced Washington.

Luna added, "It does, but the star of the movie is going to be a fallen or shooting star! If you get what I mean."

After his meeting with his detectives, James left for the Astrodome with Detectives Kramer, Luna, and Watson.

They met Captain Jones at the security office. The two cameramen, who were to operate the T.V. cameras, were introduced. Detectives Kramer and Watson left with the cameramen to be given a quick lesson on the operation of the cameras.

Captain Jones handed James a cup of coffee, "We have quite a good security set up here. I meant to ask you last night on the phone, do you want a video tape recording of the suspect you will have under surveillance?"

"I don't believe so, Captain. What if something happens? What if an innocent person gets hurt by one of the detectives when they're trying to apprehend the suspect in the crowd? The video film would sure be good evidence for some attorney. You

THE TWELVE JUDGES

know attorneys will sue you this day and time for anything."

"Oh hell! You're right, Bill. I didn't think of that. We had one attorney sue us because his client got drunk during a baseball game and while throwing up in the men's room he fell, knocking a tooth out."

"Did you lose the suit?"

"We ended up paying the dental bills. Our attorney said we were lucky on that one. What time do you want to set up in the Sky Box?"

"It's after three now, Captain. We might as well get set up now. Will our walkie-talkie's work inside the dome?"

"They'll work good inside but you can't talk to anyone outside of the dome."

"There's sure a lot of steel in here."

"You're right, too much steel. I can talk to my units outside of the dome from my office but I have an antenna that runs outside. There are telephones in the Sky Boxes that you can use."

Looking at Luna, James said, "I'll keep an open telephone line to Murphy and Park in the Good Time van. They can keep us informed as to the movements of Oliver."

James and Luna followed Captain Jones out of his office to the main elevators that run from the ground floor of the Astrodome to the Sky Boxes.

In the elevator, James asked, "Is the elevator in service all the time?"

"Yeah, Lieutenant. The Fire Marshall makes us keep it open. Do you want me to put a guard at the entrance of the elevator?"

Lt. Joe "Bill" Bradley

"No. If the elevator is a part of Oliver's plan, we don't want to scare him off."

As the three men rode toward the top of the Astrodome, Luna said, "Wouldn't it be nice if that son-of-a-bitch comes to us."

The Sky Boxes are high above the playing field and make a horseshoe running from end zone to end zone. Each box has its own lounge with a bar, T.V., bathroom and seats. Wealthy corporations rent these boxes for the Houston Oilers and Astros games. The Houston Fat Stock Show and Rodeo was an annual event in the Astrodome and it was always amazing to see the Astro Turf taken up and dirt put down for the rodeo. Each box has also its own telephone. Looking at the football field below, reminds one of looking at a large wide angle T.V. Most of the boxes are rented during sports events by companies to entertain their clients. James decided to use the Sky Box that was nearest the elevator in case he and Luna had to leave quickly. After confirming that the telephone was in proper working order, Captain Jones left James and Luna alone in the Sky Box.

There was a television in the lounge that James would use to monitor Oliver's activities. Detective Luna turned it on. It was closed circuit and the views from the cameras where Kramer and Watson were situated could cover all of the Astrodome. James and Luna watched as the T.V. cameras panned the empty Astrodome.

James picked up his walkie-talkie, "Kramer, can you hear me?"

"Loud and clear, Lieutenant. Tell Luna to go to the rail at the sky box. We'll put him on T.V."

THE TWELVE JUDGES

Luna ran down the steps to the rail. James watched the T.V. monitor as the cameraman swept the empty Sky Boxes and came to Luna. The T.V. monitor showed a picture of Luna very clear.

James asked, "Kramer, can you zoom in on Luna?"

The camera zoomed in and Luna's face filled the T.V. screen.

"That's great, Kramer. We should be able to follow Oliver except when he goes to the bathroom or to a concession stand. As long as he's in the stands, we can follow him otherwise the men will have to leave when he does."

Lieutenant James then called the surveillance van using the telephone in the Sky Box. Detective Murphy answered.

"Murphy, inform the others that they'll not be able to contact us inside the dome by police radio while they're outside. Give everyone the telephone number where I'm located. Inside the Astrodome, the walkie-talkies are okay. Luna and I are in a Sky Box next to the main elevators. Here's the telephone number, 856-4301. Keep your mobile phone open to the dispatcher in case we need more man-power. Oh hell! Just stay on the line with the dispatcher until you get ready to come into the dome."

"Boy, Lu. You're sure going to run up a bill for the city on this mobile telephone."

"Screw the city! They waste tons of money on expensive toys for the Swat Team. I guess we can spend a little money catching a killer. It's nearly five o'clock, so tell the others to be alert."

Lt. Joe "Bill" Bradley

James moved a chair to the door of the lounge so he could see both Detective Luna at the rail and watch the T.V. monitor. He hung the telephone cord over his shoulder as he sat down so that he could easily reach the open line.

James thought to himself, "God, forgive me for saying this, but let us stop this bastard permanently tonight."

A few minutes after five, James heard sounds coming from the telephone receiver. He put the telephone to his ear.

"Lu, are you there? Lu, he's moving!"

"I'm here, Murphy. What's going on?"

"Lu, he's following the usual route from his work to his apartment."

James could hear the police radio over the open telephone line as the detective followed Matthew Oliver.

James heard Hancock holler, "Run the damn red light!" They had lost Oliver on South Main Street. The rush hour traffic was heavy. They had lost him at a red light. Oliver had not gone to his apartment. The detectives were exasperated. Then James heard Murphy tell the other units.

"My meter indicates he went straight on South Main. He didn't turn on O.S.T. toward his apartment."

A few minutes went by and James heard over the telephone the radio transmission from Hancock.

"We found him! He's at a strip shopping center across from the Medical Center. He's picking up some cleaning."

THE TWELVE JUDGES

James didn't have to see the men to know that a sigh of relief crossed the detectives faces because he felt it also.

Matthew Oliver was then followed to his apartment. The electronic bugs inside Oliver's apartment were working. Murphy reported to Lieutenant James that Oliver had gone inside and was now taking a shower.

James said to Luna, "Oliver's going out tonight; he's taking an early shower."

At 6:30, both high school bands were on the field. They were taking turns practicing for their half time performances. The game was to start at 7:30.

Earlier, James traded places with Luna and was watching the bands. One band was dressed in bright red and white uniforms and the other band was dressed in black and gold. They made a beautiful sight on the field.

At 7, Luna ran down the steps where James was standing, "Murphy's on the phone. Oliver has gone to his car. He's dressed in a red blazer with white pants."

Both men looked down at the red and white marching band that was practicing on the field. At the same time, both said, "The son-of-a-bitch is-s-s coming here!"

James climbed two steps at a time and grabbed the telephone.

Murphy was on the other end shouting, "Luna, Luna, where are you, Luna?"

"It's me, Murphy. Where's Oliver headed?"

"Lu, he's going straight to the Astrodome. You and Luna figured him right."

"Murphy, have you contacted all the other detectives."

"Yeah, Lu. Since we know he's headed for the dome, some of the detectives took off so they could park and be ready for him. They will be waiting at the ticket booth before he arrives."

"That's good, Murphy. Just make sure you don't lose him."

"Lu, we won't lose Oliver again. Washington's gonna' stick to him like black licorice on a fly's ass."

James heard Washington tell Murphy, "You mean, like bar-b-q sauce on a honky, don't you?"

James heard Hancock tell Murphy over the police radio that Oliver had just passed through the parking lot gate at the Astrodome. James could feel the adrenaline in his body surge.

"Lu, Oliver's parked and is headed for the ticket booth. We're parking now. We'll be inside shortly."

James hung up the telephone and joined Luna. They peered down onto the playing field waiting for a call over their walkie-talkies.

Detective King's voice broke the silence, "Lu, Oliver rode the escalator to the second level and is walking slowly through the crowd. He's at the thirty yard line on the north side of the field. Hancock and Washington have joined me. They're going to walk and get ahead of Oliver."

"Kramer! Watson! Did you copy?"

"Clear number 12. We have the cameras pointing in that direction. We can't pick him out because of the crowd and the overhang. The cameraman said as soon as the crowd begins to sit

THE TWELVE JUDGES

down and they finally spot him, they won't lose him unless he goes out a door to another level."

"Number 12 to all units. No need to use your radio numbers in here. Just talk and keep him in sight."

"Lu, Oliver's in line for a hot dog or something," announced King. "Edwards is in line right behind him. Oliver really fits in with the Central High crowd with his red blazer. I thought he'd be easy to follow since he was dressed in a red blazer and white pants, but all the fans in this section are wearing red and white. Lu, he's leaving the concession stand now carrying a drink and a hot dog."

Hancock broke in, "He's standing by section 3-4-1-W. He's looking over the crowd in the stands. Hey, there's the kick-off."

"Lu, we got him on camera! Hell! We have Washington on camera too. He's standing right next to Oliver."

James made his way up the stairs of the Sky Box. The picture on the T.V. set was excellent. He watched as Oliver turned and disappeared from the screen. The T.V. camera panned over to the entrance that led down to the seats where Oliver had been standing. Oliver appeared and walked down a few rows and took a seat. The camera zoomed in for a close up.

James gave his detectives further orders, "Don't get too close, but make a complete circle around where Oliver is seated. Use your earplug in your walkie-talkies so no one can hear our transmissions. With all the kids here today, it will look like you have a Walkman."

Lt. Joe "Bill" Bradley

James watched the T.V. monitor as the camera went from a close up of Oliver to a full scene shot. He saw his detectives take seats around Oliver.

The crowd watched the football game while Lieutenant James and his detectives watched Matthew Oliver. James ran down the stairs to where Detective Luna was peering through his binoculars. The time clock showed 34 seconds until the half.

Luna kept his binoculars glued on Oliver as James said, "Go take a look at the T.V. monitor. We really have excellent picture of him."

Luna responded, "This Sky Box would make one hell of a deer stand. If I had a rifle, I could blow the bastard's head off!"

Luna rushed up the flight of stairs to the T.V.

"Lu, this is Kramer. We have him on close up again. He's been talking to two girls seated in the seats below him. He moved down one row and joined them."

"Clear! You guys be on your toes! He might make a move during the half!"

James went back to watch the T.V. set with Luna.

Luna said, "This picture's really clear. I saw him give one of the girls some money. There they go, all three are leaving their seats."

James spoke into his walkie-talkie, "All units. He's moving."

The detectives followed Oliver from where he had been sitting to the concession stands.

They saw Oliver speak to the two girls and then go into the men's restroom. The two girls went into the ladies restroom.

THE TWELVE JUDGES

After a few minutes Oliver came out and walked directly back to his seat in the stands. He was joined later by the two young girls. They were carrying popcorn and cokes for themselves and Oliver. James and Luna watched as one of the girls patted Oliver hand and gave him a kiss on the cheek.

Hancock must have seen the girl kiss Oliver as he said, "Lu, is that kiss enough probable cause to shoot the bastard now? Washington says it is."

Over the walkie-talkies came, "It's enough for me to shoot the s.o.b. Hell yeah, shoot him. That's a sexual assault if I ever seen one."

Luna returned to the rail with his binoculars while James watched the monitor. The start of the fourth quarter had begun.

Midway in the fourth quarter, Kramer still excited by the drama unfolding said over his radio, "James, Lu, are you watching the monitor? Can you read Oliver's lips?"

"I wish I could, Kramer. It seems he's really putting a story on those two girls. What do you think Oliver is telling the girls?"

"Watch him Lu! Every so often he turns to the girls and holds up one finger making circles and then points up. I think he's telling the girls about the Astrodome."

James looked toward the game clock, six minutes to play. Central High was two touchdowns ahead. James turned back to view the T.V., when he saw Oliver and one of the girls stand up.

"Lu, he's moving! One of the girls is leaving with him!" Detective Kramer was excited. "Did you

335

Lt. Joe "Bill" Bradley

receive my transmission, Lieutenant? Did you hear me Lu?"

"Yes, Kramer. Stay cool! I can see the other detectives following him out of the stands. Keep the camera on him. The other men will tell you Oliver's location if he disappears from the T.V. screen. Murphy, Park, if it looks like he's headed to an exit, get to the van fast. They open all the exits right before the game is over. Hancock, Washington, you do the same if he heads for the exit. Don't lose this son-of-a-bitch!"

"He's walking around the inside of the dome, Lu. He passed up the exit where his car's parked. Washington and I are right behind him."

"Clear, Hancock. The rest of you stay close behind. The bastard knows where he's headed, stay with him! The elevator's in the opposite direction so I guess we can count it out."

Detective Luna joined James at the T.V. monitor. "Where do you think he's going? Do you think he might be going to the girl's car?"

"Could be, Luna. If he does, we're in trouble if the girl's car is parked on the opposite side of the Astrodome from the detective's cars. They open all the exits after the game."

James spoke into his walkie-talkie, "All units. If our subject leaves the Astrodome and starts to get into the girl's car we might have to take him down. We can't take a chance by letting the girl drive away with him. We could lose him in the traffic. I have a Fox unit circling outside. Give Fox the description and location of the car if he gets into one."

THE TWELVE JUDGES

Washington broke in, "He's not going outside. Oliver and the girl just went through a door marked 'For Employees Only' next to a closed concession stand."

"Get through that door!" barked James. "There's no telling where that damn door leads."

"Lu, the cameraman says, the door leads to large storage rooms where food and drink supplies are kept and also to a freight elevator."

"A freight elevator! Shit! That damn captain didn't mention a freight elevator. Hancock, you and Washington get in there fast!"

"Lu, we're inside now. Oliver and the girl aren't in here. They have to be on the freight elevator. It's going up! It's passed the second level."

James and Luna looked at each other then both men took off running down the Sky Box level towards the 50 year line area. James hollered as he ran, "That's where the freight elevator must stop to get off at the sky boxes."

As they ran, both men heard Hancock, "The elevator stopped at the Sky Box level. We're coming up as soon as the damn elevator returns!"

Luna was the first to arrive at the door that led to the freight elevator. He slowly opened the door and had his pistol ready. Oliver and the girl were nowhere in sight.

Just as Lieutenant James joined Luna, both heard a piercing scream. The scream came from a room down a hallway.

Luna and James moved quickly. The screams grew louder. Pistols drawn, both men burst into the room.

Lt. Joe "Bill" Bradley

The young girl was lying on the floor looking up with frightened eyes at Oliver. The girl was naked. Her clothes had been torn from her body. Oliver was trying to pull her to a standing position by her long blond hair. Oliver had his knife at her throat. Both men pointed their guns at Oliver.

They couldn't shoot because the girl was in their line of fire.

Oliver looked up and seeing James and Luna shoved the girl toward them. The girl stumbled and she fell into Luna.

Oliver turned and bolted through the door behind him. Holding the girl with one arm. Luna got off a quick shot just as did James. Neither bullet found their mark.

James hollered, "The bastard is ours now! Let's get him!"

James and Luna moved past the screaming girl.

As they opened the door where Oliver had escaped, they saw a door across the room slowly closing.

"He went through there, Lu!"

A sign on the door read, "Danger, Maintenance Men Only." James flung open the door with pistol in hand. The door opened up to a circular stair case that went straight up.

James looked up. He caught a glimpse of Oliver as he disappeared at the top of the stairs. "There he goes, Luna!"

James couldn't remember climbing the stairs, but found himself on the top landing of the stairs with Luna behind him.

THE TWELVE JUDGES

There was no place for Oliver to go except up a catwalk to the center of the Astrodome. The catwalk was used by workmen doing maintenance on the roof and to hang large speakers.

Oliver was running up the catwalk but then stopped and looked back. He then ran a few feet stopping again to look at James and Luna. Oliver hung over the rail, looking down. He was high above the Astrodome playing field; the only place the iron catwalk led was to the center of the Astrodome's roof, which was the highest point of the dome. The only exit Oliver had was back down past James and Luna.

"We've got that bastard now! Watch him, Luna! He's got to come down through us!"

It was 208 feet to the floor of the Astrodome from this point. Both lawmen advanced slowly. Oliver continued up the catwalk stopping at the highest point under the Astrodome roof.

Oliver stopped, turned, looked at James and Luna slowing advancing. Oliver realized there was no place to go but back down.

Matthew Oliver's body turned in circles like a cat chasing its tail and then he stopped, stood straight up to face James and Luna. Oliver still had his deer knife in hand and waved it back and forth in front of his body. His eyes were searching for an escape. There was none.

As the two men approached Oliver, James hollered, "Give it up, Oliver! It's over! Put the knife down!"

Oliver screamed, "Luna, I recognize you, you sorry ass cop! I beat you in court before and I'll beat you and the system again! I have rights, you know!

339

Lt. Joe "Bill" Bradley

Those girls deserved what they got, the way they dressed and teased me. You can't prove a thing. I have rights!"

All of a sudden, Oliver screamed, raised his knife over his head and charged down the catwalk toward James and Luna.

Luna made a grab for Oliver's hand that held the knife. He missed. The knife sunk deep into Luna's shoulder. Luna felt the pain as he dropped to his knees on the walkway. Luna grabbed Oliver's legs even with the knife still protruding from his shoulder.

At the same time, James hit Oliver on his head with his pistol. The blow knocked Oliver partly over the rail. Luna lifted Oliver's legs causing Oliver to lose his balance. Oliver grabbed the rail and hung on. James hit Oliver in the head a second time with his pistol. Blood began to pour from Oliver's head. With one hand James grabbed Oliver by the throat. Blood ran down Oliver's forehead into his eyes and onto James hand.

For a split second James looked down and into the eyes of Luna holding onto Oliver's legs. Both men knew instinctively what they would do next. They couldn't let the lawyers win again at the expense of another young girl.

In one motion as if heaving a sack of grain onto a truck, James and Luna lifted Oliver high over the rail of the catwalk and threw him over the side.

They watched as Oliver's body turned cartwheels as he descended to the playing field below.

Oliver's screams faded as he fell. He hit the Astroturf field below. Both men leaned over the rail looking down at the body of Matthew Oliver.

THE TWELVE JUDGES

Bill James calmly said, "Damn, he hit squarely on the fifty yard line. This is one time the bastard didn't score. Fifty yard line! Damn Luna we are one hell of a team!!"

Luna pulled the knife from his shoulder and leaned against James. James took his handkerchief and placed it over Luna's stab wound to stop the bleeding. Both men smiled at each other not saying a word. They knew what they had done was the only justice Oliver deserved. James put his arm around Luna as they walked back down the catwalk. There would be no trial for Matthew Oliver.

James' detectives, crowded on the stairs, were waiting at the entrance to the catwalk. There were smiles on everyone's face.

"King, you and Edwards take Luna to the hospital. He's going to need some stitches in his shoulder," James ordered. "The rest of you go down on the field and wait. I'll call Homicide. This is one scene I'm sure they'll want to make. How's the girl? Homicide is going to need her for a statement."

Kramer spoke up, "She's with Davis, Lu. He calmed her down and we've found the other girl also. I've called the girls' parents and they are on their way."

James and his detectives silently rode the freight elevator down to the floor of the Astrodome.

They walked out on the playing field to Oliver's broken body. James looked down at Oliver and then looked up at the catwalk.

"208 feet. That's a hell of a fall, even on Astroturf."

Lt. Joe "Bill" Bradley

He was glad that the game had ended and there were just a few people present when Oliver fell.

James saw Captain Runnels with two of his homicide detectives coming at a fast trot across the playing field.

Captain Runnels was out of breath when he said, "Bill, I knew you'd get the bastard!"

Looking at Oliver's dead broken body, Captain Runnels looked up at the roof of the Astrodome and then at James, and said, "Son-of-a-bitch didn't want to be taken alive, I guess he jumped, didn't he Bill?"

"No Captain, he—."

Runnels cut him short, "Lieutenant, listen to me. I don't want to know what happened. I said he jumped! My report and the news media reports will read that he didn't want to be taken alive so he jumped. You understand! Then we won't have any problems."

"O.K. Captain. If you say so, he jumped," answered James.

Captain Runnels turned to his detectives and said, "Can you believe that the bastard didn't want to be arrested." Pointing straight up at the Astrodome roof, he said again. "He jumped. Damn, you say its 208 feet. I guess he thought he would bounce when he hit the Astroturf. He didn't."

James and his detectives gave an accounting to the Homicide detectives of what had taken place up to the time of Oliver's death. They were all then dismissed from the scene so Homicide could finish their investigation.

The next day in the office, Lieutenant James had to tell Kathy to hold his calls. The news media wanted a personal interview but he had decided to call

THE TWELVE JUDGES

Evelyn Mixon of the Houston Post and let her get an exclusive. He owed it to her.

Jamie Owens from the District Attorney's office called a number of times. On his third call, James told Kathy he would talk with him.

"Hi, Jamie. You calling about Matthew Oliver?"

"Yes. I read the homicide report. Jumped? I don't believe that! What if I told you, I had witnesses that saw you and Detective Luna throw Oliver from the catwalk?"

"I would say, Jamie, that your witnesses probably had a brown nose up your ass and couldn't see a damn thing! What are you after, Owens? Oliver killed several young girls. Your system of justice almost allowed him to kill again, so get off my ass!"

Jamie Owens was lost for words, "Just make sure you police by the book. I do congratulate you. Matthew Oliver was a bad one."

"Thanks, Owens." James hung up the telephone. He then dialed Luna's home telephone to check on him.

Luna answered, "Don't call my house again, you understand!"

When Luna realized the call was from James he said, "The news media calls every five minutes. I've been waiting for you to call. I've got your favorite Mexican dish ready for you."

James said, "Break out the scotch, I'll be right over."

When James arrived at Luna's home and rang the doorbell, a beautiful young Hispanic female greeted him. James was dumb-founded as he

Lt. Joe "Bill" Bradley

recognized the girl as being "Angel". She took James by the hand and led him into the dining room where Luna sat.

    Luna spoke, "Lu, I see you have met my wife."

    All James could say was, "great" as he hugged Angel.

CHAPTER 13

ORGANIZED CRIME AND POLITICIANS

    For the next few weeks, routine police work set in. Lieutenant James brought five folders from his home to his office that contained volumes of information. The information spanned years on Louis Monelli, a Mafia member from New Orleans, Louisiana.

    The Mayor of Houston and Houston politicians in the past always claimed to have kept organized crime out of Houston. James knew better. So did other law enforcement agencies. The Mafia were present in Houston with their money and influence.

    From time to time Bill James studied these files during the long afternoons of relative quiet that came after a long day at the office. This was a project or

Lt. Joe "Bill" Bradley

hobby that was always a question in James mind. Why had the Mafia never been touched in Houston?

Rumors were strong that Louis Monelli had been sent to Houston years ago by the New Orleans Mafia organization.

Monelli had been ordered to buy real estate and hotels. Monelli also had orders to try to infiltrate the oil refinery unions. He was slowly but surely making his way into the unions.

Louis Monelli's real estate holdings now consisted of several hotels in the Houston area. He also controlled the businesses that supplied many hotels in Houston with everything from food to light bulbs.

Monelli was also a homebuilder. The homes he built were in the two hundred and fifty to five hundred thousand dollar range in the exclusive Memorial area of Houston.

James read an intelligence report from the Vice Squad that it was thought that Monelli's money came from prostitution and narcotics. Nothing had ever been proved on Louis Monelli.

During the years that Monelli had been in Houston, Monelli became very strong politically. He was a member of many charitable groups that the Houston wealthy supported.

Whenever information involving Louis Monelli surfaced, Lieutenant James put this information in his personal files, which he had been keeping at home. The files even contained social events that Louis Monelli had attended.

In his years of being a policeman, James had never had the opportunity to investigate the Mafia.

This had always been left to the Intelligence Division of the police department and the F.B.I.

The Houston Police, the F.B.I. and the I.R.S. had each investigated Louis Monelli. None had ever been able to obtain any evidence of wrong doings but they knew of his connections in New Orleans.

Law enforcement agencies knew that Monelli received orders from New Orleans on the buying of property and businesses in the Houston area.

Lieutenant James decided to review his files on Monelli during the slow times in his office. After reading some of the material in Monelli's folder one morning, James called Detective Kramer into his office.

"You need me Lu?"

"Sit down Kramer; I want your opinion on something."

Kramer sat down on the couch in Lieutenant James' office.

"Kramer, here's a file. I want you to take it home with you this weekend and study it. Also, go to the Intelligence Division and see Sergeant Will. Get the latest information that they've got on Louis Monelli. Tell Sergeant Will that the information is for me. He'll keep his mouth shut. Don't contact anyone in Intelligence but Sergeant Will. Study the folders over the weekend. Monday morning, tell me where this son-of-a-bitch is vulnerable. I have read this file so many times I think I am missing something. Maybe you can find what I've been missing. I've got a wealth of talent working for me now. No cop has ever been able to touch this bastard because of his political connections and money but I believe we can.

"After you study the file, make me a list of what we'll need to get this investigation started. I've got a few ideas of my own. If we put it all together we might come up with something. A banker called me and said that he heard that Monelli was trying to buy the pro football team here. With his background and New Orleans connections, we don't need his kind running our pro team."

"Sounds like a challenge, Lu."

"It is, Kramer. This man has a license to do anything he damn well pleases in this city. I aim to get into his business!"

James spent the weekend fishing in Galveston with a couple of friends. They caught a number of large bull redfish, which they dropped off at a local rest home for the elderly. James and his friends had done this for years and the home really appreciated the fresh fish.

Monday morning, Kramer walked into James office, "What a file! I read it five times. Lieutenant, you asked me to make a list. Here it is."

James started reading the list. Halfway through, he said, "What do you need with the plans for the water, electrical, gas and telephone systems at Monelli's home?"

"I need it for research. Besides the plans of his home, I need the same for his yacht in Galveston and the blueprints of his home. I need every fact and rumor about Monelli."

"Kramer, this is a damn long list! But, we'll get it. I'm sure that if I can't get it then one of the other guys should have a contact that can get some of this."

THE TWELVE JUDGES

"The investigation on Monelli will start now," James continued, "by doing detailed surveillance on Monelli's home and office. He lives behind the area of the Shamrock Hotel, on a large private estate. I know you read in the files that his telephones are checked often for bugs; so tapping his telephones is out. Daily surveillance reports will be channeled through you. We'll do surveillance for a week and then we'll get together with the other detectives for a discussion. You haven't told me where Monelli is vulnerable."

"I don't know yet, Lu. Let's get all the info we can and I'll be able to find out."

Lieutenant James called a meeting and gave his detectives a run down on Louis Monelli. Surveillance teams were organized.

Louis Monelli's home and office were on round-the-clock surveillance the following week. Pictures were taken of all persons coming and going. Every piece of information was reviewed by James and then given to Kramer. All the detectives were told by James to get all the information they could from their informers about Monelli even if it was rumors.

Murphy and Park were able to supply Kramer with all telephone numbers going into Monelli's home. They were also able to confirm that Monelli had his phones routinely checked for electronic bugs. Park even came up with a diagram of the alarm system.

Charles Watson, with his connections at credit card companies, was able to supply Kramer with purchases made by Monelli and his wife.

Checking with safe and lock companies, Hancock and Davis were able to determine that

Lt. Joe "Bill" Bradley

Monelli had three safes in his home, two floor safes and a walk-in vault.

Rumors of Monelli's business and political activities were strong. It was known that Monelli entertained often on his yacht and at his home, and rumors were that at these events Monelli made audio tapes and videos of all the guests who attended.

The Vice Squad reports showed that Monelli routinely supplied businessmen and politicians with prostitutes and narcotics. It was even suggested that Monelli might have videos and audio tapes of all payoffs to influential individuals. Monelli even picked up the tabs for businessmen and politicians going to Las Vegas.

Lieutenant James compiled and studied all of this information. He knew that if he could acquire Monelli's tapes he could put Monelli out of business for good. It was a dream, he knew, but sometimes dreams are realized if you help them along.

Detective Kramer had mountains of material on his desk that the detectives gathered about Monelli. The stacks of papers were so high, that when a detective approached Kramer's desk, the guys couldn't tell if he was there until Kramer's voice sounded. All of this information pertained to Louis Monelli.

Kramer walked into Lieutenant James office and commented, "I had no idea that the guys could get so much information on one man."

"I guess you don't know where to start?" questioned James.

"Yes I do, Lu. But, you've got to give me a few days off. I need to research this material and put it in some kind of order."

"I thought you were reading everything as it came in," James said.

"I'm trying, Lieutenant, but there's so much information I need to weed out the good from the bad. As soon as I do, I'll call you."

"O.K., Kramer. Just don't let any of this material get lost and keep this project quiet. Jamie Owens, our personal pain-in-the-ass assistant D.A., would like to get involved in this matter."

James walked out of his office with Kramer.

"King, you and some of the guys help Kramer load his car with all this material." Kramer's car trunk and back seat barely held all of the Monelli files.

Four days later, on a Sunday afternoon, Lieutenant James' pager sounded. James looked at the telephone number but he didn't recognize it. He called the number.

"Lu, this is Kramer. Can you meet me?"

"Sure Kramer. Where?"

"I'm on the Rice University campus, in building T."

"What are you doing at Rice, Kramer?"

"When you get here you will see."

Kramer then gave Lieutenant James directions to his location.

James drove into the downtown area on the Gulf Freeway getting off at Fannin. The Sunday traffic was heavy. James drove out Main Street to the Rice University campus. After locating building T, he followed Kramer's directions to a side door. Walking down the outside stairs to the basement, James came to a door which read, PRIVATE-PROFESSOR KRAMER, COMPUTER RESEARCH. James tried

Lt. Joe "Bill" Bradley

the door. It was locked. James knocked on the door and waited.

A bearded man who appeared to be in his fifties with what had to be two-inch thick glasses appeared at the window of the door. James heard the lock in the door turn and then the door opened.

"You must be Lieutenant James. I am Professor Kramer. Come in please."

The Professor spoke with a heavy German accent. James couldn't believe what he was seeing. The Professor was a spitting image of Detective Kramer, just older. The professor studied James over the top of his thick eyeglasses. "I said, come on in. Just don't stand there staring at me!"

James looked around. The room was huge. There were large computers, there were small computers, and there were computers and terminals everywhere. Lights were flashing, tapes were spinning and computer printouts covered the floor. The scene looked like something out of "Star Wars".

Detective Kramer was seated at a computer terminal busy typing and trying to eat peanut butter and crackers at the same time. There were empty Coke cans and empty peanut butter jars covering one table. By the smell and look of things, both men had been in this computer room for several unbroken days.

Kramer looked up smiling when he saw Lieutenant James.

"I guess you've already met my uncle. This old man put me through law school. He's pissed that I'm a cop and not a computer genius like him."

Professor Kramer complained, "I don't understand these young kids. Do you Lieutenant? I

THE TWELVE JUDGES

teach some of the brightest minds in the world. When they graduate they go out and use the knowledge I taught them to make bloody fighting computer games and money. I just don't understand them."

Laughing, James agreed, "No, Professor, I don't either."

Kramer sat back down at the keyboards of a computer and turned to Bill James, "Ask me a question, Lu. Go ahead; ask me a question about Monelli."

James accepted Kramer's challenge. "Okay. Is Monelli's home ever unoccupied?"

Kramer typed on the computer keyboard and in an instant the computer monitor read...

"Once a month-New Orleans meeting
Three body guards-New Orleans
Wife-Stays home
Wife has body guard (1)-Home
Wife shops-Without body guard
Otherwise-Always two body guards at home"

"Lu, Ask me another question?"
"Where is the walk-in vault located?"

Again Kramer typed on the computer keyboard and once again the screen displayed an instant answer to the question that Kramer typed even drawing a diagram to where in the home the vault was located...

"Library-Monelli's home
Diabold Brand, Model 7400
Size-10' X 12'
Manufactured in 1980"
Installed by Zindler & Sons Safe Company"

Lt. Joe "Bill" Bradley

"Lieutenant, I helped my uncle program all the information we collected on Louis Monelli. Uncle programmed this damn computer where it will answer any question about Monelli you ask. His program even gives you its opinion. It even told us what it would take to open the safes and walk-in vault. Sit down here and read these computer printouts."

Lieutenant James moved a jar of peanut butter from a chair and sat down and began to read.

A printed list of names showed that Monelli had wined and dined several very important political and social people.

The Kramers had developed a paper trail on all of Monelli's businesses. It appeared these businesses had been bought with mob money and were being used to laundry money.

Kramer was able to confirm that Monelli had not only written records but also videotapes of all persons who had attended his parties at his home and yacht.

There was a proven list of contracts that had been awarded to Monelli's construction companies from politicians who had attended his parties and had received kick-backs.

The printout gave every land transaction Monelli was involved in and listed his partners' names. The paper trail on Monelli's companies passed through twenty DBA's. Each name listed in the computer printout showed the person's criminal record, if they had one, along with their address, business, and other pertinent personal information.

THE TWELVE JUDGES

The computer printout even paired prostitutes with certain persons at parties. It even listed license plates of police cars that had Monelli under surveillance at different times. It gave the date, time, location of all persons who attended his parties and if the person used any type of narcotics.

There was so much more information that Bill James could not possibly absorb it all. James stopped reading and asked, "Kramer, if we were to search Monelli's home, without him knowing, what time would be best and can it be done. I don't see that in the computer printout."

"You didn't read far enough," Kramer said. "Let me find it for you."

Kramer took the printout and turned several pages, "Start reading here, Lieutenant."

James began to read that Louis Monelli leaves Houston, Texas on the 15th day of each month for New Orleans, Louisiana. He goes there to meet with other members of the New Orleans crime family. A Lear Jet from New Orleans picks him up at Hobby Airport. Monelli takes three bodyguards with him leaving one bodyguard at home. His wife remains at home and she usually shops for clothes by herself while he is away. It gave her favorite shopping places.

James read further. Louis Monelli stays in New Orleans for three to four days on these business meetings with his boss.

Professor Kramer entered the discussion, "I will answer your question on how to get into Monelli's home. You know, Lieutenant, I must go with you when you break into Monelli's home."

Lt. Joe "Bill" Bradley

Lieutenant James looked at Professor Kramer in amazement, "Sir, we are not going to break into Monelli's home."

"Of course you are. That's the only way to get the tapes and videos. With all this information and the best computers in the world, breaking in and stealing his books is the only way! I know all this information on Monelli like I know my hand. I can be of more help than my nephew. He's still young and makes mistakes."

"Uncle, you can't get involved in this," said Kramer.

The Professor looked over his thick glasses said, "Do not tell me what I cannot do. I ask the lieutenant if I can go, not you. If I cannot go, I might do what you cops say, squeal. Besides, I'm already involved and you are going to need my brain after the invasion. I guess you would call it an invasion."

James couldn't help but admire the old professor.

"We'll see professor. We really don't have a plan yet."

James was folding the final computer printout on Monelli when he heard the two Kramers start to argue.

"Uncle, we have to destroy all of the extra printouts."

The professor was shaking his finger at Detective Kramer and saying, "You clean this up. I did most of the work. I need to make some diskettes on all the information. If that lieutenant is anything like you, he will lose his printout."

THE TWELVE JUDGES

James thanked the professor and left. He stopped at a small seafood restaurant on the way home and bought two shrimp "Po Boys". At home James spent most of the night reading and studying the computer printouts on Monelli. The information compiled on Louis Monelli was unbelievable. Lieutenant James laughed, as he thought of how he would use Detective Frank Davis. The next morning James showered, dressed and drove to his office.

James started his meeting with his detectives.

"We are ready to go after Louis Monelli. It's been said that he can't be touched. Remember, we aren't going to try and make a case on him. We're going after his books, all the videos and tapes that he has on businessmen and politicians. He's been paying some of them off for years. We'll make sure this information falls into the hands of the right law enforcement agency. I hate to use the word burglarize, but we're going to enter Monelli's home and acquire his records. I've studied what Kramer and his uncle have put together on Monelli. There's no other way but this way. Are there any objections?"

None of the detectives said a word.

"It'll take awhile to put this operation together. We'll continue surveillance. The first assignment will go to Lover Boy Davis."

Turning to Davis, James said. "Kramer will give you pictures of Mrs. Anita Monelli and a run down of her habits. I want you to get next to her."

Detective Davis turned red as the rest of the detectives started to raze him.

Lt. Joe "Bill" Bradley

"Davis, I want to talk with you and Kramer. The rest of you read the computer printouts on Monelli and continue the surveillance."

Davis and Kramer followed Lieutenant James into his office.

"Davis, here's a printout on all of the locations where Mrs. Monelli shops and a background on her. It appears she is bored to death with her old man. She regularly has lunch at Neiman Marcus in the Galleria Shopping Center. I want you to use all of your charm and meet her. I don't care how you do it. Somehow, we need to look at the contents of her purse. Who knows, she might be carrying the combinations to her old man's walk-in safe. We need a copy of her house key. If you do get your hands on her purse, copy everything in it. Kramer will give you some expense money for clothes so you'll fit in with the Neiman Marcus crowd. You're also going to need an apartment. How much money do you think you'll need?"

Davis thought for a minute and said, "About two thousand."

"Two thousand! Davis, I want you to dress the part, not look like you just stepped out of the Esquire magazine. Kramer, give him a thousand to start with."

Detective Davis left James' office with Kramer. Kramer gave Davis more information on Mrs. Monelli to study.

Detective Washington started a betting pool on the length of time it would take Davis to meet Mrs. Monelli and lay her. Even Lieutenant James gave Washington ten dollars and bet Davis would lay Mrs. Monelli on the third day.

THE TWELVE JUDGES

The next morning when Detective Davis came to work he looked as though he just came from the River Oaks Country Club, the most distinguished club in Houston. His dark blue suit and alligator shoes revealed the money he had spent. There were catcalls from all the detectives.

James walked out of his office. He took one look at Davis and said, "You really do look as if you stepped out of Esquire."

"I'm on my way, Lu. I'm having lunch at Neiman's today."

Davis turned to the other detectives and said, "Eat your hearts out, guys. Too bad you're not a class act like me. Hey, Edwards, you ever seen clothes like this? I bet not."

Detective Davis then strutted out the door.

Davis drove to the Galleria Mall. He was early according to the information about Mrs. Monelli. It was eleven o'clock.

He walked through the elegant shopping mall stopping to watch young ice skaters. The Galleria Mall has a large ice skating rink located in the center of the mall.

Davis remarked to himself, "Ice skating, and its 90 degrees outside, no where but in Texas."

Detective Davis watched the ice skaters until 11:30 a.m. then walked to the restaurant inside the Neiman Marcus store.

Frank Davis spotted Anita Monelli as soon as he walked into the dining room. She was dressed in an expensive summer dress that accentuated her tanned skin. Her hair was a luxurious golden brown, which she wore shoulder length and soft against one side of

Lt. Joe "Bill" Bradley

her face. But for all her beauty she had that unmistakable look of loneliness. She sat at a corner table by herself seemingly lost in her lunch.

There was a table next to her unoccupied. Davis sat down at the table and opened a clothing magazine he had bought.

Frank Davis ordered a cup of coffee and began turning the pages of the magazine. He grumbled out loud so that Anita Monelli could hear.

"I don't know what they mean by color coordinated. It won't matter what I buy; it still won't give the impression I want."

Detective Davis turned to Anita Monelli and said, "Pardon me, Miss. I hope you don't think I'm out of line, but I sure would like to have your opinion on something. I'm in a bind, and I really need some advice. The men's suit department has nothing but male sales associates. You would think they knew men's clothes. They couldn't tell me a thing."

Anita Monelli glanced up from her plate and appeared to be annoyed. She was pleasantly surprised to see what a handsome man had asked a question. He had a lovely smile that seemed so innocent yet worldly. Anita found the mixture intriguing.

"What was your question?" she asked cautiously.

"Tomorrow, I'm scheduled to speak before a women's real estate group. It's important that I appear to be intelligent and knowledgeable. We all know that women know how to dress, men don't. I need to buy a suit, tie and shoes that'll make me a knockout and is certainly in style. I don't know whether wide lapels or thin ones are in. The way you're dressed, I'd bet you're an expert on styles and colors."

Davis causally moved over to Anita Monelli's table and continued speaking, "I even bought a magazine to help me decide what type of suit to buy. Take a look. Oh, please let me apologize; my name is Frank and I didn't even ask if I could sit down."

"That's all right, stay seated. My name's Anita. You're correct. Behind every well dressed man is a woman to tell him how to put it all together."

"Anita, may I tell you something and you won't ask me to leave?"

"Depends!"

"You're taste seems to be impeccable. Could I possibly impose upon you? Would you help me select a suit? It wouldn't take long and I'll even buy your lunch."

Anita Monelli laughed softly and said, "The salesmen here at Neiman's know me very well. What will they say if I'm seen in the men's department with you? They know I'm married to…"

"Tell them that I'm your lover," interrupted Davis. "That'll get their attention."

Anita kept laughing and said, "I can't shop with you here, but I'll meet you some place else. What do you say to Jim's Clothing Store on the second floor of the mall? They also have handsome clothes."

"You've got a deal! But, if you don't show up, I'll find you and create a scene."

"I'll be there. Now, let me finish my lunch."

Detective Davis left Anita Monelli and returned to the mall.

"Damn, I didn't even pay for my coffee!"

Lt. Joe "Bill" Bradley

He walked until he located Jim's. He didn't go in but waited at the balcony rail that over looked the ice rink.

Talking to himself he said, "Well old boy, you haven't lost your touch; here she comes."

Looking as radiant as a school girl skipping class, Anita walked over to Frank Davis and took his arm. "I shouldn't be doing this. But you do seem like a nice person and this shopping lesson is harmless."

Anita and Davis entered the shop together and began to browse through the clothing. Eventually, Anita chose four suits for Frank to try on. On the fourth suit, she turned to the girl waiting on them.

"I think this one is made for him, it shows his pretty tush." Anita and the salesgirl giggled together.

"I thought men were the only ones that admired a good looking tush," Frank responded.

"You don't know very much about women, do you?" Anita replied.

Anita turned on her heels and made her way to the shirts. She chose a shirt, tie and shoes to compliment the suit.

Frank Davis paid the bill, which was over six hundred dollars. He was secretly hoping that the lieutenant would understand how important it was to buy these clothes. After buying the suit, Davis and Anita walked out to the mall.

"Thanks a lot, Anita. I have enjoyed this. Don't take this wrong but I sure would like to see you again. I don't care if you are married. Couldn't we just meet as teacher and student?"

Anita squeezed his hand and smiled.

THE TWELVE JUDGES

"I could use an ice cream cone after such an exhausting afternoon," Davis suggested. "Let's go the ice cream parlor and get a double scoop."

"O.K., Tush Man. Lead the way."

After paying for their ice cream, Anita and Frank sat outside the parlor at a patio table near the ice rink.

"Anita, I'm in the commercial real estate business. I'm not married. I don't live far from the mall and I don't have any pets. That's my life in a nutshell. Tell me about yourself."

"I am married, but I have no children. I love to shop. My husband entertains a lot, but I don't care for the social scene like my husband does. He's very wealthy but also very possessive, but he does let me spend his money. I come to the mall often just to get away and breathe a little. My husband parties a lot with younger women. I found some pictures of him and his girl friends on our yacht." Suddenly Anita Monelli abruptly stopped talking and looked frightened.

Frank Davis gently placed his arm around her shoulders and gave her a soft kiss on the cheek.

"It's our secret," Davis assured her.

"I'm telling you too much, Frank. I don't really know you! You're very easy to talk with."

"There must be a mystic attraction between us, Anita. I'm very at ease with you too."

Anita changed the subject. They talked for awhile about his real estate business.

"Anita, what plans do you have for the remainder of the day?"

"I'm going home. Why do you ask?"

"In my business, I get a lot of free time. I love movies. I go often. How about a movie? It would make my day perfect, a new suit, meeting a beautiful woman and holding hands in a movie."

Anita looked at her watch. "Why not? Sounds good to me, but only if you promise to buy me some buttered popcorn."

"That is a deal. Let's go, Anita."

They walked to the end of the mall where the movie theaters were located. Davis was buying tickets, when he spotted Detectives Washington and Hancock. Davis thought, "The bastards are checking on their bets."

Inside, Davis bought Anita some buttered popcorn and a coke. There weren't many customers in the movie at this time of the day. Davis led Anita to the last row of seats in the theater. He didn't want Washington and Hancock sitting behind him if the bastards followed him into the movie.

Halfway through the movie, Davis put his arm around Anita. She didn't resist. She leaned closer to him; she could feel the rhythm of his breathing and smell his body next to her.

A few minutes had passed when Anita reached and took Davis' hand that was around her shoulders. She pulled his hand down and pressed it against her left breast. Davis felt the excitement take over his body. He placed his right hand under Anita's chin, tilted her head and kissed her long and hard. Anita responded to his kiss with a passion that she thought had long since died.

"Frank, I feel like a high school girl. We'd better stop this before I lose complete control."

"I have an apartment nearby," Davis whispered. "We could both go there and lose control. I would love to kiss every inch of you."

"Frank, I wish I could go with you but I can't."

"You're worth waiting for, Anita. Please promise me that you'll see me again."

"I'm attracted to you, Frank. I can't deny that, but I must be very careful. You don't know my husband. Sometimes he has me followed."

"Damn it! I don't care about your husband; I want you. But, I want you to feel comfortable with the idea of being with me."

"I believe that I want you too, Frank. Maybe I'm too comfortable with you. Maybe I can meet you tomorrow at your apartment. Give me directions. I can't promise anything."

Davis gave Anita directions to his apartment. Davis told Anita that he could meet her at 1:00 in the afternoon after he had given his talk to the real estate women.

Anita kissed Frank and quickly left the movie.

Davis waited for ten minutes and then left the movie. Anita was nowhere in sight but there stood Detectives Washington and Hancock.

"Well, Lover Boy, you didn't fair too well today," Washington teased.

"Kiss it, Washington! I'm meeting her tomorrow."

The three detectives then discussed how they were going to get to Anita Monelli's purse without her knowing it.

Hancock said, "Let's go to a bar to discuss this further; I think better off my feet with an ice cold beer.

Lt. Joe "Bill" Bradley

Davis, you can buy our beer. After all, you're on an expense account."

After a few beers, Frank Davis followed Hancock and Washington back to the factory. When Davis entered he could hear Washington and Hancock already telling the others of his meeting with Mrs. Monelli.

"Can you believe Lover Boy? He picked her up on the first try."

Davis walked into Lieutenant James office and placed his clothing bill on the desk.

"Well, I met her. She's a nice woman, Lu."

"She must be nice considering what you paid for that damn suit. I got a feeling I'm going to have to con the Chief out of some more expense money because of you. When will you see her again?"

"Tomorrow at my apartment. Lu, tell Hancock and Washington to wait a few days before we try for her purse."

"Davis, every time you meet with her, we need to look at her purse. We've got three safes to get into at the Monelli home and she just might have the combinations to one or more of them in her purse. We really must get her house key."

"Hell, Lu! This type of work is hard and I need more time. This is also a very delicate assignment and the pressure is great."

James just shook his head and mumbled, "Get out of here and go to work, Lover Boy. Pressure my ass."

The next day at one o'clock Detective Frank Davis waited in his apartment. Davis had been able to rent a nice furnished apartment after he had flashed his

THE TWELVE JUDGES

badge and told the manager he was F.B.I. and needed the apartment. He was dressed in a white terry cloth robe and had iced down a bottle of wine in the bedroom. A few minutes after one, there was a faint knock on the door. Davis opened the door and there stood Anita looking radiant.

"Hi, beautiful."

"Hi, yourself, beautiful Tush Man."

Davis took her in his arms and kissed her. "I dreamed of you last night and now I want to live my dream."

Anita started to answer. Davis placed a finger across her lips and whispered, "Don't say a word."

Davis took Anita's purse and laid it on a chair in the entrance hall. He then led her next to the couch in the living room. Standing there, Frank began very slowly to undress her. First, he unbuttoned her blouse folding it very neatly and placing it on the couch. He slipped her skirt down to her feet and folded the skirt placing it also on the couch. Anita was wearing only a bra and panties. Davis kissed her as he removed her bra. Frank kissed Anita's flat stomach as he knelt slowly slipping her panties off. Davis could feel the heat of Anita's body. Anita stood before him naked. Davis untied his robe and stood before her naked. Davis picked Anita up in his arms and carried her into the bedroom kicking the door closed behind him.

He gently placed her on the bed kissing her. He then closed the curtains of the bedroom and turned up the music on the radio.

Closing the curtains was a prearranged signal to Hancock and Washington who were watching Davis' apartment.

Lt. Joe "Bill" Bradley

Hancock ran to the apartment door and eased the key in the lock so not to make any noise. He unlocked the door and stepped into the foyer.

He saw a woman's purse in a chair. Hancock quickly took the purse, closed and locked the door, and rushed to the car where Washington was waiting.

Washington drove at break neck speed to a Stop-N-Pick store two blocks away. The store had both a copying machine and key duplicating machine. Every item in the purse was copied.

They then returned to Davis' apartment and placed the purse back on the chair. When Hancock returned to the car and they were driving off, he said, "Must be somebody sick in there Washington. I sure heard a lot of moaning and groaning."

Washington swerved just missing a car; he laughed so hard that tears ran down his cheek.

The next morning at the factory everyone was down on Detective Johnson. He had won the pool bet.

"Us Lover Boys never take over two meetings to get laid," Johnson bragged.

Lieutenant James called Detective Edwards into his office.

"Edwards, have you got a plan for the project I assigned to you."

"Yes, Sir, Lu. You said you wanted a distraction! I'm going to give you a show that will confuse the police and fire departments so much that it'll keep them busy for hours. It'll also knock out all of Monelli's security alarms at his estate. Even if the security system has a battery backup the alarms won't go off. I talked with Murphy and Park. The three of us found the right location and marked everything. All of the alarm systems in Monelli's home are on phone lines. His outside cameras and monitors will be knocked out too. Everything depends on electrical power and Monelli doesn't have a power backup in his home in case of a power failure. All of the phone lines and electric lines are underground in that neighborhood. Lu, when I blow the manhole where Monelli's phone and electric lines are located, it's going to knock out power in all the homes and businesses in that area. It'll take the power company a few days to restore power."

"You're going to blow what?"

"It's the only way, Lu."

"Hell! We can't do that! This isn't a military operation," Lieutenant James shouted.

"Lu, we've got to buy some time. It's gonna take the guys a while to get what we need from that house," argued Edwards. "This way, we won't be noticed. All the cops in the city will be busy."

"Well, I guess you're right. In order for the job to go down, we'll need to confuse the neighborhood. I just don't want anyone hurt! I don't give a damn how many homes lose their electrical power. If we get the evidence we need from Monelli's home then the citizens who lost their power probably won't give a damn about sitting in the dark a few hours."

James was pacing his office as he considered every angle of the project.

"Are you sure about the Medical Center, Edwards? I don't want to cause any problems there," James cautioned. "You know, Monelli's home is just a couple of miles away."

Lt. Joe "Bill" Bradley

"Lu, I double checked on the Medical Center. The explosion won't affect their electrical power. Even if it did, each hospital has their own back-up power units."

"Also," Edwards continued explaining, "I've got three barrels of thick crude oil. When I plant my explosives, the barrels will be in the manhole. It's gonna be one hell of an explosion and fire. You wanted a decoy, well I'm gonna give you one."

"Okay. It sounds good to me, Edwards. Who's going with you?"

"Hell! I'm going by myself. The other guys have shit in their necks. They think I'll blow 'em up. None will go with me and I'm glad. I'll set the explosion off two blocks away with an electronic remote unit. The explosion won't even knock windows out in the neighborhood," Edwards reassured the lieutenant.

Detective Kramer burst into Lieutenant James' office shouting, "Lu! Look what was in Anita Monelli's purse!"

Kramer handed Lieutenant James a sheet of paper. Hundreds of numbers were written on the paper.

"What's this Kramer? Don't tell me the safe's have this many combinations."

"Sorry Lieutenant, that's Uncle Kramer's figures."

He handed the Lieutenant a copy of a card found in Anita Monelli's purse.

It read…"My Jewelry, L-12, R-21, two turns to 1"…

"That's one of the safes, Lu. Now look at this. This was found in Anita's purse also."

A business card read Zindler & Sons Safe Company. The back of the card read 1369, then spin wheel. "Damn it! Kramer, don't keep your lieutenant in the dark. Just tell me what you've got."

"This, Sir, is the combination to the walk-in vault! It has to be. Look what she wrote at the bottom of the card. `Videos of Louis and me'. This must be where the videos are kept."

James handed the card back to Kramer and ordered, "Check with our friend in the safe business and see what he says about these numbers."

"I already checked, Lieutenant. The safe man said the vault will have four numbers. The numbers are 1-3-6-9. He doesn't know if you start with a turn to the left or right or how many spins between numbers but I think I've solved that problem. I called Uncle Kramer and gave him the numbers. He's programming all the possibilities into his computer using information as to the make, model, and serial number of the vault."

"Sounds like we're close to making a move on Monelli's home," announced James.

"Edwards, can you get a couple of burn bars in case we don't come up with the right combination to the walk-in vault."

"Sure, Lieutenant. There're some new types on the market that'll burn through a vault door in minutes. The only draw back is that there's a good possibility of burning some of the contents of the vault."

Lieutenant asked Kramer, "What's the phone number of Davis' apartment?"

Lt. Joe "Bill" Bradley

"It's there on your pad, Lu. I gave it to you yesterday."

"Sorry, Kramer, I forgot. Let me know what your uncle finds on the numbers. Tell the other guys to get all their equipment ready. We could move any night. Tell Luna to make a detailed layout on the chalk board of the Monelli estate and the surrounding neighborhood."

As the two detectives left his office, James called Detective Frank Davis at his apartment.

"Davis, it looks like Anita has access to the walk-in vault. It's getting close to the time when Louis Monelli makes his monthly trip to New Orleans. Do you think you can find out for sure when he's going?"

"I think so, Lu. Anita's coming over tomorrow. Lu, she's really too nice a lady to be married to that son-of-a-bitch. She's a real lady, quiet, refined and understanding. I could really get serious about her."

"Don't let your emotions get in the way, Davis. Remember, it's a job. Do you think you can get her to spend a night with you? I don't want her at home when we go in."

"I'll try," Frank Davis answered. "She told me that once when she was away from home too long; her husband's bodyguards came looking for her. I'll talk to her. Like I said, Lu, she's coming over tomorrow."

"Davis, keep reminding her to check that she isn't followed. You'll be in danger if they suspect she's having an affair."

"I thought of that, Lu. I told her to drive through a shopping center and then through a residential neighborhood to make sure she's not being followed."

"Do you need anything, Davis?"

"Hell yes, Lieutenant! I'm going to miss out on all the fun when you hit Monelli's home. If I get her to spend the night with me, I could use some more cash. I want to cater a dinner for her."

"Davis, this operation isn't the Wheel of Fortune. I'll give you two hundred dollars more just because of the stress you say you are under. Like hell, you're under stress! But, I guess you need to treat her right."

"If you weren't my lieutenant, I'd tell you to kiss my ass."

"But I am your lieutenant; don't forget it! Davis, be careful. We're dealing with some bad actors. Be sure and let me know if she'll be home the night of the raid."

"You and the others be careful, Lieutenant."

The next day, James examined every detail of the operation with his detectives. When they had studied the plan, James made them do it again. It was important that nothing was left to chance. The operation had to run smooth for the safety of everyone and a successful conclusion.

"I want every man to know his job going in. There should be only one person in Monelli's home, the bodyguard. Davis is going to find out if Anita Monelli will be home. If she is at home when we enter, the first one to her, take her upstairs and lock her in a bathroom. Make sure she doesn't get a good look at you and there is no telephone in the bathroom. Damn, I hope she won't be there. The operation will begin as soon as it's dark. When Edwards sets off his explosion, Hancock and Washington will enter

Lt. Joe "Bill" Bradley

Monelli's estate to find and disable the bodyguard. Because electrical power will be off, Hancock and Washington will force open the gates to the estate before they go to the house. Watson, you drive the wrecker and go in first. Back the wrecker to the front door. The front door's made of solid wood but has a glass window with iron bars. King will be riding with you. King, fast as you can, hook the wrecker's wire cable to the door, so Watson can pull the door off. It would take too much time to pick the lock. For some reason, Anita Monelli didn't have a key to her home in her purse. I can only guess that the bodyguards clear everyone who comes in, even her. As soon as we're in the home, Johnson, you'll start working on the walk-in vault. Edwards will join you later in case we have to burn through the vault. Hancock, you and the others find the other two safes. One of the safes, I believe we have the combination to it. Take everything from the safes except money and jewelry. If you can't open the safes, roll it to the front door and Watson can load it on the wrecker. We'll take the damn thing with us and open it later. Remember, time is critical! Luna, you had better stand guard outside. Kramer and I will go through any papers found in the home. As soon as the walk-in vault is opened, I want everyone to start loading the two vans. All we're after is Monelli's account books, papers, tapes and videos.

"Washington, as soon as the first van is loaded, take off for Black's ranch. Cletus Black is going to let us use his hunting lodge for a few days. You'll have to go through four locked gates. There'll be a Mexican ranch hand at each gate to let you through.

THE TWELVE JUDGES

"All of you start spreading a story that we're going on a deep sea fishing trip out of Corpus Christi. I've already told Chief Ladd we're taking some overtime off. Make sure all the vehicles are in good running condition. Everyone wear your Shiner Beer jackets. I don't want anyone shot by mistake. As soon as I hear from Davis when Louis Monelli's leaving for New Orleans, I'll let you know. Any questions?"

Detective King shot his hand in the air and shouted, "Will Cletus Black feed us the big steaks like he did once before?"

"King, you know Cletus, he'll have anything you want and more."

Lieutenant James returned to his office. Kathy followed him in, "Kramer said to give these to you. These are the possibilities for the combination to the walk-in safe. There are sure a lot of them."

James looked over the list. "The combination is somewhere on this damn list. That old uncle of Kramer's knows what he's doing."

Just then the telephone rang and it was Detective Davis.

"Anita just left my apartment, Lu. Her husband's leaving for New Orleans Sunday afternoon. She can't spend the night with me, but she said she could stay until eleven thirty. Will that give you enough time to get in and out of Monelli's home? I sure don't want Anita there when you go in."

"It'll have to be enough time. I don't want her there either. Set your date with her at your apartment for Monday night, that'll give us three days to get ready."

Lt. Joe "Bill" Bradley

"O.K. Lu, I'll call you when I know for certain that Anita's coming Monday night."

Late Sunday night James was in his apartment watching a John Wayne movie on T.V. when his telephone rang.

"Lu, this is Davis. It's set for Monday night. Anita is coming over early. I'll keep her here until eleven. She even bought me a VCR and is bringing some movies over."

"Davis, that's great! I had mixed emotions about hitting Monelli's home with her there. Just make sure you keep her there until eleven."

"I will. Be sure and tell all the guys I wish I could be there. And Lu, be careful."

"We will, Davis."

After talking with Detective Davis, James called each of his detectives advising them about Monday night.

Monday morning when James arrived at the factory everyone was present. He held a meeting to go over the layout of Monelli's home and the detective's assignments once more. Lieutenant James sent out for barbecue sandwiches from Slim's for lunch. The detectives sat and played dominoes to past the time.

James called Cletus Black at his ranch, "Cletus, we're coming in late tonight. Do you think that'll be a problem?"

"Come anytime, Bill. Everything's ready for you and your detectives. Give me a time so I can have some steaks ready for you."

"Cletus, we should all be there around one a.m. Tuesday morning."

THE TWELVE JUDGES

"As soon as I see the first light of your cars, I'll have my cook throw the steaks on."

"Thanks, Cletus. See ya tonight."

Kramer opened the door to James' office and said, "Murphy and Park are on the surveillance on Mrs. Monelli. They reported that Anita Monelli left her home and is now at Davis' apartment. The bodyguard is still at Monelli's home."

Lieutenant James stood up. "It's getting about that time. Tell the guys to get ready."

Lieutenant James walked out of his office to where his detectives were waiting, he could feel their excitement.

"Everyone ready?"

There was a resounding, "Yes, Sir."

"Edwards, you leave first. When the rest of us get in place, I'll let you know. Washington let me know when the bodyguard's been gagged and tied. I then want everyone in Monelli's home fast!"

James and his detectives left the factory in pairs, spaced apart by five minutes. Kramer rode with Lieutenant James.

On the way every few minutes Kramer would say, "Man, what an operation. Do you realize that I could still be re-writing rules and regulations of the department?"

As they turned off Holcombe Boulevard behind the Shamrock Hotel, James heard Detective Murphy's voice over the police radio.

Bill James turned to Kramer and commented, "Ya know, Kramer, that secret frequency on the radios that Murphy installed for all of us sure works well."

"109 to 12."

Lt. Joe "Bill" Bradley

"12 to 109, go ahead."

"109 to 12, the guard's no longer at the house. Just as we got here, he left in a black Ford and drove out South Main. We followed him. He stopped and went into a strip joint."

James wondered why the bodyguard had left the estate. He shrugged it off thinking the guard probably figured his bosses are gone, why not go out?

"12 to 109. Looks like we've got a break. The guards probably gone for the night."

"12 to all units. Get to the entrance of Monelli's estate. As soon as you're ready, 101, tell 104 to GO!"

A few minutes passed when Lieutenant James heard 101 say, "101 to 104. Go, man, go!"

All of a sudden a fireball rose three hundred feet into the air over the trees in the area lighting up the night. The sound and pressure from the blast rocked the Lieutenant's car as James drove to the Monelli estate. Hancock waved him through the entrance at the estate.

Kramer remarked, "My God, how much explosives did Edwards use. I bet it broke out every window in this area."

As James brought his car to a screeching halt, Detective Watson was gunning the motor of the wrecker. King had hooked the cable to the front door of Monelli's home. The wrecker jumped forward pulling off not only the front door but also the facing and several bricks with it.

The night was filled with sirens from fire trucks and police cars. It sounded as if every emergency vehicle in the city was headed for the explosion site.

THE TWELVE JUDGES

As Lieutenant James stepped from his car he could smell the pungent oil burning and see the red glow that filled the night from Edwards' blast.

Inside the Monelli home, Detective Bill Johnson was already at the walk-in vault located in the library. He was spinning the wheel on the vault, trying Professor Kramer's computer combinations.

When James entered the home he noticed a number of his detectives were running up the winding staircase that took up most of the entrance into the home. James walked into the library where he found Detective Kramer trying to open the drawers to a large desk.

"It's locked, Lieutenant. What do I do?"

"Pry the damn thing open! I think Monelli will know someone's been in his home."

Kramer got a crow bar from Johnson's tool box. He pried the desk drawer's open and searched each one. As he came to anything that he thought might be useful, Kramer would set it aside.

Hancock came into the library, "Lu, we found one safe upstairs in the master bedroom. It's full of Mrs. Monelli's jewelry. We can't find the other safe."

"Keep looking, Hancock, it's got to be here somewhere."

Hancock turned on his heels and hurried off in the direction of the game room.

Detective Edwards burst into the library, skipping and hollering like a kid, "Lu, you can't say I didn't cause a distraction. The damn blast even knocked me down. Guess I must've used too much plastic explosive. Man, when it blew, the manhole cover went straight up like a flying saucer. It came

Lt. Joe "Bill" Bradley

down cutting a metal street light pole in two. Man, what a sight. You should have seen it! For a minute, I thought I was back in Nam."

Looking around, Edwards saw Johnson at the walk-in vault. "Johnson, why don't you let me blow the door off the damn thing?"

"Don't touch anything!" Johnson responded, "I want to get inside the vault, not blow the house down. Just keep your mouth shut and hold this flashlight for me. Son-of-a-bitch, I think I hit the right combination."

Johnson turned the wheel on the walk-in safe and slowly the large door swung open.

Johnson's excitement rose. "Lieutenant! Where's the lieutenant?"

"I'm right behind you, Johnson."

Lieutenant James walked into the safe. There were rows and rows of video tapes. On one shelf were envelopes filled with pictures.

Johnson said, "Lu, look at the boxes of tapes. Do you want them too?"

"Hell, yes! Take everything. Edwards, go get the sealed beam lights. It's dark as hell in here. Kramer, get the other guys and start loading. And find Hancock. Tell him the safe he is looking for is inside the vault."

Lieutenant James stepped aside as his detectives started carrying boxes of video tapes and account books out to the vans.

When Hancock appeared at the vault, Lieutenant James pointed to the rear of the vault.

THE TWELVE JUDGES

"There's your other safe. That's why you couldn't find it. Get some help and load the safe on the wrecker."

Hancock returned with Detectives Luna and Washington. The three detectives rolled the floor safe out of the walk-in vault through the library to the front door.

As Hancock stepped out the front door he saw a car, with its lights out, coming across the front lawn straight for the house. It was the bodyguard returning.

Before Hancock could react, the bodyguard jumped from his car. The bodyguard began shooting.

Hancock let out a yell as he fell, wounded, rolling down the steps.

Luna raised his automatic pistol and fired until he saw the bodyguard spin and fall to the ground.

Luna saw a dark figure in the bodyguard's car moving. He aimed his pistol to fire but Detective King had seen the same thing. King fired a full clip of 9mm bullets through the windshield of the car at the person inside. Then there was silence.

James had heard the shooting, but by the time he got outside it was over. Washington was holding Hancock in his arms at the bottom of the steps.

"He's been shot, Lu. He's bleeding pretty bad. I only see one wound. It's in his right hip. I know where to take him, Lu. I know a doctor who will help us. He won't say a thing. Lu, let me take Hancock to him."

James seeing the pain Hancock was in said, "Washington, we better get him to a hospital. He's hurt bad."

Lt. Joe "Bill" Bradley

Hancock, groaning, said, "We're not going to blow this deal by me going to a hospital. I'll go with Washington, but it had better be a white doctor."

James couldn't help but laugh.

As the detectives started to move Hancock, Hancock hollered, "You bastards could stop the bleeding! I don't want to be dead when I arrive at the doctor's office!"

Washington took his pocketknife and cut Hancock's pants. He then tore a piece of the pants off tying it around Hancock's leg. He used the other strips of pants to bandage the wound.

"This should stop the bleeding."

Hancock, showing the pain from the gunshot said, "You son-of-a-bitch! That was a new pair of pants."

Hancock was then helped to one of the pickups. After he was placed in the pickup, Washington jumped in the driver's seat and started the engine. The tires screamed as Washington floored the pickup. It looked as if the pickup was doing fifty miles per hour by the time Washington got to the street.

Lieutenant James walked over to the other detectives gathered around the dead bodyguard who had shot Hancock and said, "Looks like he picked up his buddy at the strip joint."

James stepped over bodyguard's body and looked inside the car. Shot through the head and body was the second bodyguard. He then walked back over to where the first bodyguard lay.

King was kneeling beside the body and said, "It looks like the bodyguard went out for pizza and left the house unguarded. I'm glad the one inside the car didn't get to his machine gun. The pizza he was holding even has bullet holes in it"

James thought a minute and said, "Shit! We didn't need this. Let's move fast. All of you should've been wearing the surgical gloves I gave you. Kramer! Check with each man and make sure they didn't take their gloves off. Get the jewelry out of the safe upstairs and any money you can find. We'll make this look like a burglary and a robbery. Finish cleaning out the walk-in vault. Let's get the hell out of here! King and Luna give Kramer the two guns used in the shooting. Everyone check and make sure we don't leave anything that can tie us to this scene. King, find all of Luna's and your empty shells and give them to Kramer. Let's get moving and get the hell out of here."

Ten minutes later Lieutenant James was the last to drive out of the Monelli estate. There were still sirens in the distance but the red glow now was dim in the night sky from the burning oil drums.

James drove to the South Loop not saying a word until they were on I-10 headed west to his friend's ranch.

James took an exit off of I-10 on some back roads so he could cross the Brazos River. He knew a bridge where the water was really deep. When James came to the river bridge he stopped the car and walked to the rail of the bridge.

"Kramer, it's about fifty feet of water here. Bring me those two pistols and empty shells."

Kramer got the pistols from the back seat of the car and handed them to the lieutenant. James field stripped each pistol and then threw each part into the swirling waters below. He and Kramer got back into the car and headed for the ranch in Brookshire, Texas.

Meanwhile back in the city, Washington was weaving in and out of traffic at a high rate of speed. He cussed the other drivers on the road as he passed them.

"I think Houston's got the worst drivers in the world. Get the shit out of the way, you bastards! Get your ass out of the way, stupid!"

Hancock said weakly, "Slow down, Washington. You're going to kill us both before we get there."

That was the last word spoken by Hancock. He passed out.

Washington braked hard as the pickup came to a sliding halt at the doctor's office. He put Hancock on his shoulder and carried him to the door, leaving a trail of dripping blood. Washington kicked the door hard and kept kicking it until a light came on inside.

Doctor Simmons lived above his clinic. When he finally opened the door, Washington rushed by him and laid Detective Hancock on an examining table.

"He's been shot, Doc. Fix him up. He's my best friend."

Doctor Simmons unbuckled Hancock's belt. He took a sharp knife and cut the remaining pants and shorts away from the gunshot wound. The wound was still bleeding.

Doctor Simmons' wife came in.

"Susan, hold the pressure point on the inside of his leg. It looks like the bullet entered there and came out at the hip area."

"Damn, Doc! I didn't see that wound. I thought the bullet stayed inside."

Handing Washington a bottle Doctor Simmons said, "Washington, wash your hands and then wash his wound with this. I'll set up the x-ray machine and see what damage's been done by the bullet. He's lost a lot of blood. His pulse is weak and he's going to need some blood. Hand my wife that I-V bottle so she can get it started."

Three quick x-rays were taken by Doctor Simmons. When he examined them, Doctor Simmons pointed out the path of the bullet to Washington.

"The bullet slightly clipped the main artery in the leg and glanced off the hip joint. He's lucky he didn't bleed to death."

The doctor's wife had clamped off the flow of the blood to the leg and the bleeding had stopped. Doctor Simmons removed a vial of blood from Hancock and started the process to get his blood type. Every few minutes, the doctor would check Hancock's eyes and pulse.

"He's got O-Positive blood, Washington. What type are you?"

"I'm O-Positive, Doc."

"Pull that examining table over next to your friend. He needs some of your blood."

"Doc, I can't give him my blood. He'll kill me when he finds out he's got black blood inside him!"

Doctor Simmons laughed, "I guess I'll also be in trouble when he learns that a black doctor patched him up. Oh well, your black blood will mix with his white blood and he'll never know the difference."

"He won't be happy, Doc. He's the biggest redneck you've ever seen."

"I thought he was your best friend?"

"He is, Doc. I love him, but this best friend is liable to shoot my black ass! Pardon me, Mrs. Simmons."

Doctor Simmons gave Hancock a shot to keep him out.

"Washington, do what I tell you. I bet this friend would do the same for you."

"Yeah, you're right Doc."

Washington pulled the table over next to Hancock again saying, "You're right Doc, he would but he would never let me forget it."

Doctor Simmons turned to his wife, "Susan, hook up Mr. Washington while I repair this artery."

Doctor Simmons went to work while Susan prepared the two men for the transfusion.

"I hope Hancock doesn't wake up while I'm giving him blood."

The doctor and his wife took great care during the next hour giving Hancock all of their attention and skill.

"How'd he do, Doc?"

"The procedure went well. He'll sleep for several more hours. His hip is really going to be sore when he wakes up. We better put him to bed."

"I can't leave him here, Doc. Can he be moved?"

"No! Washington, you can't move this man."

"I've got to move him, Doc. I can't leave him here. You don't know how bad it will be if he wakes up here. I have to get him somewhere, Doc. Give me some clothes to dress him and help me put him in the truck."

"O.K. Washington, but drive on smooth roads. Don't tear his wound open."

Doctor Simmons handed Washington two bottles of pills.

"Here are some antibiotics. Have him start taking them the minute he wakes and then three a day. These other pills are for the pain. Tell him to take them as he needs them and believe me he'll need them! He's gonna be sore as hell."

Washington and the doctor struggled to get Hancock to the truck even with the help of his wife.

"Thank you, Mrs. Simmons. I owe you, Doc."

Shaking his head Doctor Simmons watched as Detective Washington drove off into the night.

It was ten-thirty when Detective Frank Davis opened his eyes. He was lying naked beside Anita Monelli. She was on one elbow staring at him.

"What are you doing, Anita?"

Anita leaned over and kissed him, "I've been watching you sleep for an hour. You know, it would be very easy to fall in love with you."

Frank reached and pulled her over to him.

Anita softly pushed away and said, "I've got to go, Frank. If I'm late, my husband will question me for two days."

Frank would not let her go. He continued to kiss and caress her. They made love again. Afterwards, Anita took a shower. As she dressed, she could not take her eyes off Frank.

Frank walked her to the door. "When can I see you again?"

Lt. Joe "Bill" Bradley

"It'll be soon, but I'm worried, Frank. I think I'm falling in love with you."

Frank kissed Anita and watched her as she walked down the hall.

Anita Monelli looked at her watch as she was driving into the driveway of her home. It was eleven-thirty.

She noticed that the gates were open which was unusual. She saw a car parked on the lawn in front of her home. The house was dark. There were no lights on anywhere.

Anita parked and got out of her car. She left her headlights on. She saw someone lying on the driveway. It looked like her bodyguard. Anita didn't know what to do.

She walked very slowly to where the body lay. It was her bodyguard. Anita bent over to get a closer look in the dark, and suddenly realized that half his face was missing and blood was everywhere. Anita screamed and fell as she turned to run. Getting back up she continued to scream while running to her car. She fumbled with her car keys trying to get them into the ignition. She got the car started throwing the car into reverse. She pushed the gas petal to the floorboard and the tires squealed as she backed down the driveway into the street.

Just as her car backed into the street an oncoming car hit her car broadside. The crash knocked her unconscious.

The next thing Anita knew, there were policemen everywhere and she was being placed into an ambulance.

THE TWELVE JUDGES

A policeman kept asking her, "Do you know what happened at your home? Who are the two dead men? Where is Mr. Monelli?"

Anita Monelli started to cry and her only thoughts were of Frank as the ambulance sped off with its siren blaring.

Lieutenant James waited, as the last gate into Cletus Black's ranch was unlocked. As he drove toward the hunting lodge he thought, "What have I done to my men and their families? I only pray that the information we got justifies what I did."

As James parked, a man with a shotgun opened James' car door. His boss, Mr. Black had sent the armed guard, to make sure the lieutenant and his men were not disturbed.

Cletus Black greeted James and Kramer at the door of the hunting lodge, "Hi, Bill. Some of your men are already on their second steaks. You sure have a worried look on your face. How about a shot of scotch?"

"Cletus, Hancock, one of my detectives, was shot tonight."

"I know Bill, your detectives told me. Come on in."

All of the detectives stood as James entered. They were concerned about Hancock.

James spoke to his men. "I don't know anything about Hancock. I do know that Washington will take care of him. You men did a hell of a job tonight. If we got what I think we got, we're going to put a lot of sorry bastards out of business. I also want to thank Professor Kramer."

Lt. Joe "Bill" Bradley

Professor Kramer had not been allowed to go to Monelli's home but he had been brought to the hunting lodge by Cletus Black. Professor Kramer had even brought a table top computer and printer with him. The detectives applauded Professor Kramer as he proudly stood up.

James continued, "Tonight, we're going to have a nice, quiet meal, thanks to Cletus Black. Then in the morning, we're going to document every video and every piece of information. Detective Kramer will organize the information and make three copies of everything. Wear your gloves when you handle any of the evidence we got tonight. For now, enjoy yourself and say a prayer for Hancock."

Lieutenant James sat down with Cletus Black and told him of the night's events. Brown was a great supporter of law enforcement, especially the Texas Rangers. He had given many historical items to the Texas Ranger museum in Waco.

"Bill, I know you'll have to hide the fact that your detective was shot. I'd like to pay the doctor who treated him and any other expenses."

"Thanks, Cletus. I'll tell him. The men will want to help also."

After everyone had eaten, the detectives started their domino games. A few hours had passed when the lodge telephone rang. Black answered it.

"Bill, it's for you. It's Detective Washington."

James went to the telephone. The room got very quiet.

"Everything all right Washington? Great! Come on, we're waiting on you."

THE TWELVE JUDGES

James turned to his detectives and said, "Washington said Hancock is hurt pretty bad, but he'll be all right. They'll be here soon."

There was a loud cheer from all the detectives.

"Some of you get a room ready. King, get a couple of blankets so we can carry that big lug inside. It seems that Hancock is still out."

Cletus Black said, "I'd better inform my boys on the gate that they're coming." Black picked up a walkie-talkie and spoke with his men at the gates in Spanish.

Forty-five minutes later, Washington arrived with Hancock. He was taken into the hunting lodge and put to bed. Everyone went to bed except four detectives who were still playing dominoes.

The next morning, Lieutenant James woke to the smell of frying bacon. He knew Cletus Black had his cook at work.

James walked into the huge dining room. Off the dining room was the room that had been set aside for Hancock. The detectives were crowded either at the bedroom door or in the room with Hancock. The invalid was being served breakfast in bed. James made his way into Hancock's room.

"Hi, Lu. Sorry I didn't get out of the way fast enough. The guys told me what happened. We pulled off a good one, didn't we?"

"You did great, Hancock. You just get well. Oh, by the way, after breakfast Cletus Black wants you to help him round up some of his stray cows."

Hancock tried to throw a biscuit at the lieutenant but he was so sore he couldn't raise his arm.

Lt. Joe "Bill" Bradley

After breakfast, Detective Kramer had everyone organized. He set up video VCRs with TVs and a copy machine. Detectives were assigned to view every video and make copies. Notes were taken, typed and put in a folder. Professor Kramer had his head down pecking away at his computer.

Kramer walked over to the table where James and Black were sitting.

"Lieutenant, we've got videos of politicians, attorneys, businessmen, and crooks at sex and cocaine parties on Monelli's yacht and at his home. Some of Monelli's books even show the amount of payoffs. We got what we went after!"

As Kramer was finishing his last statement there was a loud explosion that shook the hunting lodge. Dishes on the tables crashed to the floor. Some of the detectives turned over in their chairs falling to the floor.

Cletus Black and Lieutenant James, along with the other detectives, rushed to the door. Some of the detectives grabbed for their pistols on the way out.

Outside it was snowing paper money. There was money on the cars, in the grass and the wind that was blowing causing clumps of money to stack up on the fences. Money even covered most of the limbs of a large oak tree. Some money was still floating in the air.

Detective Edwards was standing there with a large opossum smile on his face. The palms of his hands were turned up and his head bowed in a gesture that indicated, "What happened!"

THE TWELVE JUDGES

Detectives Murphy, Johnson, and Park slowly appeared from behind the Good Time van where they had been hiding.

"Hope I didn't ruin your breakfast, Lu," remarked Edwards.

"Ruin my breakfast! You scared the hell out of me and everyone else. We thought the Feds were here!"

Pointing at Murphy, Park, and Johnson, Edwards began to blame them. "They couldn't open Monelli's safe. What pussies they are. I even gave them a whole hour to open the safe. They couldn't. So, I blew the damn door off the safe. I guess I used too much explosives."

James broke into laughter as a hundred-dollar bill fell out of a tree and floated down at his feet. "I guess you did, Edwards. I guess you did. You four clowns pick up all of the money and count it. Murphy and Park, since you are so good at climbing telephone poles, climb that tree and get all that money down."

Edwards stomped his feet like a small upset child. "Come on, Lu. Let Parks and Murphy gather and count the money. I opened the damn safe. It's not fair."

James, still laughing, shook his head and walked back into the hunting lodge.

The three detectives were bitching all the time they were picking up and counting the money that had been in Louis Monelli's safe. It amounted to one million, five hundred thousand dollars.

James and the detectives heard another commotion outside. A car had driven up and Detective

Lt. Joe "Bill" Bradley

Davis was taking a lot of kidding from Edwards, Park, and Murphy.

Detective Frank Davis came into the lodge. He walked in wearing a large smile, dressed in expensive hunting clothes, the clothes being the latest fashion for bird hunting. The whistling and teasing began.

Lieutenant James got a chair for Davis at his table.

"Glad to see you, Davis. I hope your assignment didn't dull your police work or stress you out."

Looking at James, Davis said, "It's good to be back with the common people. My assignment was really rough and I'm real stressed out."

Davis leaned over to James and whispered, "Did you hear? Anita Monelli is in the hospital."

He then told James about Anita finding the dead bodyguard when she went home and how she had been injured in a car accident.

Davis continued, "The story is all over TV and radio."

James said, "Yeah, we've seen the news reports. I'm real sorry about the two who were killed and Anita being hurt. Damn, I didn't want this to happen."

Davis continued, "I went to the hospital. Monelli's bodyguards were there so I didn't take a chance to try and see her. I did send her some roses with a pink butterfly. That will tell her they're from me. Lu, I know you'll think that I'm screwed up, but I think I'm in love with her. I know she's in love with me. I've got to see her someway!"

James could see that Davis was serious.

THE TWELVE JUDGES

"Davis, if it's meant to be, everything will work out, but for right now, you stay away from her. No phone calls, no letters! You will not try and see her! We'll talk about this later."

"You're right, Boss. Tell me what you found at the Monelli estate."

James told Davis the details of the seizure and also of Hancock being shot. He also told Davis about Edwards blowing up the manhole and safe.

Davis bent over laughing and said, "See, we told you about Edwards. That's why no one will ride with him in his car."

James finished the story and Davis got up from his chair and walked over to Hancock whose bed had been brought out into the main room of the lodge. Davis gave Hancock a kiss on the forehead.

Hancock turned red in the face and said, "Pretty Boy, I don't need sex from you to make me well, but you could sneak me a shot of Bourbon."

For the next four days Lieutenant James and his detectives compiled records taken from Louis Monelli's home. Boxes of video tapes, voice tapes and record books of Louis Monelli were packed and addressed.

Detective Kramer wouldn't let anyone touch the items after he had inspected them and wiped them clean of fingerprints. He wore surgical gloves and even did the addressing labels himself.

Two different law enforcement officers would receive copies of everything that had been seized. Chief Gene Lyles of the Los Angeles Police Department had just been appointed Director of the F.B.I. by the President of the United States. He would receive one copy. Lieutenant James met Chief Lyles at a seminar and knew his reputation. Being a city cop first and now a federal cop, Chief Lyles would know how to use this information.

The second copy would go to an Internal Revenue Service Intelligence Agent that Lieutenant James had worked with for many years. He was now on duty in Washington, D.C. There's an old saying that Lieutenant James knew to be true, "If there's a regular audit by the I.R.S. you stand a good chance of coming out all right, but if an I.R.S. Intelligence Agent gets on your case, kiss your ass good-bye, because you're going to jail and he'll take every penny you have."

Cletus Black would keep the third copy of Louis Monelli's records and videos in case James ever needed them.

James got everyone's attention. He wanted to speak to all of the men before they headed back to Houston. Hancock was getting around fairly well now since Black brought him some crutches.

"I want to thank each and every one of you for the job you did. Tomorrow, we're going back to work."

There were a lot of damns, hells and groans from the detectives.

James continued, "I don't have to tell you to keep quiet about this case. I've been keeping up with the investigation in regards to what we did at the Louis Monelli home. Our police department, the Sheriff Department, the F.B.I., and the District Attorney is involved in the investigation. When we return to the factory, I want each of you to go through your desk. Make sure you don't have anything that can connect us to Louis Monelli. About the million dollars in cash. I've spoken with each of you separately and everyone agrees. Cletus Black will keep the money for safekeeping. From time to time, when one of you finds a good cause, either a church, family or an organization that needs help, that's where some of the money will go.

"Before we eat tonight, I want all of you to sign Cletus Black's yacht guest book. His yacht has been in the Gulf of Mexico since we started this operation. If they ever check our story about fishing in Corpus Christi, the book will back us up. I'll see you back at the factory at one tomorrow afternoon. I couldn't have picked a better group than you."

Turning to the rancher James said, "We all thank you Cletus for your hospitality." Then James dismissed his detectives saying, "I'll see you all in Houston."

CHAPTER 14

THE MAKING OF A NEW DISTRICT ATTORNEY

Lieutenant James and his detectives returned to their routine work after returning from the ranch in Brookshire, Texas.

They were again instructed by James to double check their desks for any papers that would connect Louis Monelli to their group.

Everyone had several days of telephone messages to answer. Lieutenant James had six messages from Assistant District Attorney Jamie Owens.

Kathy had been busy answering telephones while the Lieutenant and his group had been gone.

Everyone was present except Hancock who was at home and was being carried on sick time. James had filed a report that Hancock had injured his hip while working at home on his roof. James was in the process of returning telephone messages when Detective Albert King entered his office. James could see King was upset.

"Settle down, King. What's the matter?"

"It's that phony playboy assistant district attorney at the D.A.'s office. He's got two of my best informers up tight on some trumped up charges involving fraud charges on some boats. He's making them snitch and work for him. I'm going to whip Owen's ass! The investigators at the D.A.'s office knew those informers worked for me. My informers are so scared of the D.A. that they begged me to stay away from them. I told them, I'm going to whip Jamie Owens' ass! Both of my snitches are ex-cons and they don't want to go back to prison."

James asked, "Why would Owens use your informers? Do you think he is trying to use them against you or this group?"

James continued. "I know damn well something's going on. Jamie Owens is assigned to the Louis Monelli case. Will your informers tell you what Jamie Owens is up to?"

King kept pacing back and forth in front of James desk. "They said they wouldn't, but you can bet they will when I get my hands on those two snitches."

"Sit down, King. Settle down!" ordered Lieutenant James. "Why don't we let your informers work for Jamie Owens. Then we'll know what the bastard's up to."

"I guess you're right, Lu. But I'd still like to whip the bastard's ass."

THE TWELVE JUDGES

"King, convince your informers to stay in touch with you. Will they tell Jamie Owens that you talked with them?"

"Hell no, Lieutenant! They might be scared Jamie Owens will put them in jail, but they're more scared I'll kick their ass and then bury the pieces and they know I will!"

"Good. Let's leave things the way they are for right now."

After Detective King left, James placed a call to Jamie Owens.

"I'm returning your call, Jamie. What can I do for you?"

"Where've you been, Lieutenant?" asked Owens. "I tried to contact you in Corpus Christi when Chief Ladd told me you were fishing. I doubt that you were fishing but it makes no difference now. I want to know what you know about the Monelli case."

"All I know, Jamie, is what I've heard on T.V. and read in the newspapers. It's your investigation. I took some time off with my detectives and we went fishing."

"Don't lie to me, James! I know you have contacts everywhere. You either know who hit Monelli's home or you have heard rumors. Don't hold out on me! It's in your best interest to level with me. Did you know Louis Monelli brought in some heavy guns from up North? Let me give you some advice. If you have any information about the Monelli case, you had better call me. I'm in charge, remember that!"

James could tell by Jamie Owens' voice that he was ready to explode.

Lt. Joe "Bill" Bradley

"Jamie, you'll be the first to know if I get any information on the Monelli case. I'll spread the word and see what I can find out for you. Can I come over and read your files on the Monelli investigation?"

Jamie Owens screamed, "Hell no! All the information I have is confidential. Besides, I'm working with the F.B.I. on the case and they keep everything confidential. You are to give me any information that you find on the Monelli case. Do you hear me?"

"Jamie, I'll give you any information that I or my men find out about the Monelli case. I doubt if we will learn anything about the case. It's too big of a case for us."

Jamie said, "Well thanks anyway. It is a big case and I know I can handle it."

A week went by. Work was normal. The detectives had arrested a Savings and Loan hold-up man. He was turned over to the Robbery Division and they cleared twenty-three holdups.

James called Hancock or Hancock's wife each day to check on his progress. Hancock's bullet wounds were healing just fine and he wanted to come back to work.

Detective Kramer walked into the office. "Lieutenant, I just came back from talking to King. He sure sounded as if something was really wrong. He had me leave the office and go to a pay telephone and call him. Said he didn't trust any city phones. He's got a room at the Allen Park Inn and said he needed to see you as soon as possible. He sounded real excited. He's in room 102."

"If he calls back, tell him I'm on my way."

THE TWELVE JUDGES

James drove to the other side of the downtown area to Allen Parkway where the Allen Park Inn was located. Making a turn off Montrose Street, James drove into the motel parking lot and parked. James walked through the lobby of the motel and outside to the area where the swimming pool and rose and flower gardens were located. In the heat of the summer, this area always had beautiful flower gardens kept immaculate by the owners of the motel. James thought of the many times he had sat on this patio in the cool of the evening having a scotch and water. Room 102 was near the swimming pool.

Lieutenant James slipped his pistol into his waistband when he got out of his car. He didn't put his coat on because of the heat. James placed his large hand over the pistol to hide it. He came to room 102 and knocked. The door opened.

"Anybody with you, Lu?"

"No King, is something wrong?"

"I want you to hear a tape recording I made of my informer; you know the one that Jamie Owens' investigators arrested and is now working for Owens."

James sat down at a table in the room. Detective King pushed the play button on his pocket tape recorder. The recorder started. It was Detective King's voice.

> "I told you, damn it, that you were going to tell me the truth! Now start talking! It had better be the truth! Don't let me catch you in a lie!"
> There was a crashing noise as if someone fell over a table or chair.

403

Lt. Joe "Bill" Bradley

"I will Mr. King, please let me get up."

"Get up and go wash the blood off your face and then sit down in this chair and tell me the whole story. You had better not lie to me."

King quickly turned the recorder off. He looked at James and said, "Sorry, Lu. I thought I had run the tape forward enough. You weren't supposed to hear that."

King started the tape again. The sound of running water was heard being turned on and then off.

"I'm ready Mr. King."

"Well get to talking, I don't have all day."

"Yes Sir, Mr. King. You know I'm in the boat business."

"Hell yes, I know you are in the boat and used car business."

"Mr. King, I have an acquaintance that was busted with a small amount of cocaine. I'm not going to lie to you, Mr. King. I was making some money also on this deal. Not on the cocaine Mr. King but I was going to make some money helping my friend who was charged with possession of cocaine get his case to go away."

King said, "Go ahead with your story."

"I know a Sheriff Deputy that works in a District Court as a Bailiff. I've used him before to help me fix cases. I have paid him good. I met him through an attorney. He can do what he says, but boy he charges an arm and a leg. I contacted him. He wanted $10,000.00 to get the cocaine case transferred to his court so he could get his connection to handle it. I told the guy with the cocaine case that it would cost him fifteen thousand to get the case to go away. He agreed to pay. I had everything set up and was going to make five thousand when I got busted."

"Who busted you?"

"Oh you know, those two suck ass investigators assigned to Jamie Owens from your police department."

"Yeah, I know them. Why did they bust you?"

"Mr. King, I went to the Texas Parks and Wild Life Department and got certified copies of titles on two boats I owned. I then sold the two boats using the certified copies. I kept the original titles to the two boats. I then took the original titles on the two boats to a bank and put the original titles up as collateral and got loans. I needed the money to pay off a gambling debt. The bank found that the original titles were no good and that I had already sold the boats on certified copies of the titles. The bank called the District Attorney's office. I was arrested by the D.A.'s investigators. At first they just wanted the bank's money. When I told them I couldn't pay, they said I was going back to the joint. I didn't know what to do. I couldn't call you. They wouldn't let me use a phone. Can I smoke, Mr. King?"

"Sure. Go on with your story."

"I made a big mistake. I told the two investigators I could give them something bigger than me, if they wouldn't file charges on me. They said it would have to be really something good. I then told them about the District Court Deputy who was going to fix a case for $10,000.00. Mr. King, I even told them of the rumor about the District Attorney."

"Why did the District Attorney's name come up in such a small dope case."

"You'll see, Mr. King let me finish my story."

King continued, "What was the rumor about the District Attorney? You are talking about the head man, right?"

"Yes Sir, Mr. King."

The informer continued his story, "The deputy collects cash money on cases to be fixed and then splits the money on those cases with the D.A. The

D.A. is the one who has the power to get any case transferred to any court in the system. The D.A. transfers certain cases into the court where the deputy works and makes a recommendation to the Assistant D.A. assigned to that court to have that case dismissed. He usually tells the Assistant D.A. who handles the case that the person charged in the case has given him information or that he is a political friend."

Detective King's voice becomes excited at the informer's statement about the District Attorney.

"Son-of-a-bitch, you're kidding me aren't you?"

"No, Mr. King. Check the records of cases that have been transferred into that court. You'll find that a lot of cases transferred into that court have been dismissed. The assistant district attorneys in that court are just out of law school so the District Attorney tells them what to do on each case."

"What did the investigators do after you told them about the D.A. and deputy?" asked King.

"At first they didn't believe me. Then the two detectives left me in a room for a long time. Then they returned, Jamie Owens, an attorney from the D.A.'s office, was with them.

I had to tell him the story all over again. Then the three of them left, leaving me alone for over an hour. When they returned, Jamie Owens pointed a finger at me and told me that I was going to work for him or go back to the joint for a long time. He scared the shit out of me, Mr. King. I can't go back to the joint Mr. King. I'm dead if I do. There are some in the joint that I helped you send there and they know it. I'm a dead man if I go back."

King said, "Go on with your story."

The informer continued, "Owens told me that he was really the man who ran the District Attorney's office. He's an arrogant bastard, but he sure scared the shit out of me!"

King said, "You've already said that he scared you. Sounds like Owens really had your ass up tight."

"He did, Mr. King. They left me alone again. I could hear them talking in the next room but they talked in whispers. When they came back, one of the detectives had a tape recorder with a suction cup for a telephone on it that could record a telephone conversation. Jamie Owens told me to call the District Court Deputy. He even told me what to say and the questions to ask. They even wrote it out for me. I called the deputy. I told him I had the ten thousand dollars. I arranged to meet with him the next day. When I finished the telephone conversation with the deputy, Jamie Owens took the tape recorder. They listened to the tape of the deputy and me. Owens then left. The two investigators told me I could leave but I'd better be in their office at 8:00 a.m. the next morning."

"Did you show up at their office?"

"Hell yes, Mr. King! I cut a deal with them. I didn't want to go back to the joint. Owens told me he could get me 20 years if I didn't cooperate."

"What took place the next morning?"

"The detectives brought a man in from the Sheriff's Communications Department. He put a tape recorder under my shirt. He told me the recorder would last for two hours. Look, you can see where he taped it on me. The hair on my chest was pulled out when they removed the tape player later."

"I don't want to look at your skinny chest, asshole, keep talking."

"The communications man put a microphone under my tie. Jamie Owens told me what to say to the deputy and gave me ten thousand dollars in cash to pay him. I was to come straight back to the investigator's office as soon as I met with the deputy."

"Did you meet with the deputy?"

"Yeah, I met with him in the basement cafeteria of the courthouse. I gave the deputy the money. I discussed with the deputy how he was going to fix the case and about him having to pay the D.A. The stupid deputy talked his head off."

King said, "I guess they let you go and busted the deputy."

"Hell no, Mr. King! But I did get what they wanted on the tape recorder. The deputy even told me that he had to take the District Attorney his part of the money today because the D.A. was going on a trip. That's on the tape too. I got everything on the tape recorder Jamie Owens wanted, I thought, and still think I did."

"What do you mean, you thought?"

"When I got back to the investigator's office, Jamie Owens went nuts. He jerked the recorder off me and went into the next room with his investigators. I could hear them but couldn't understand them so I put my ear on the wall. You know how those offices are. The walls are just thin partitions that don't go to the ceilings. I could hear them playing the tape recorder. The tape of me and the deputy talking was clear as a bell. The two detectives and Jamie Owens were shouting and acting like a bunch of kids. After they listened to the recording a second time, they came back to the room where I was. Jamie Owens walked over to me and told me that I had screwed up. He really gave me a bad time cussing me and all. Owens said the tape recording of the deputy and me was blank and was of no use to him and couldn't be used as evidence. Owens tried to act like he was really disappointed but I knew he wasn't. I knew the tape recording was good, but I kept my mouth shut. Jamie Owens told me that I could leave. I asked Owens if he was going to charge me. He said he wasn't as long as I kept my mouth shut about the deputy and the D.A. fixing cases. The two investigators threatened me telling me that I could disappear very easy if I told anyone about the D.A. and deputy. I promised I would keep my mouth shut but I'm still looking over my shoulder and will for a long time. That's all, Mr. King. Please believe me."

King said, "I believe you. I'm sorry you fell and hurt yourself. You'd better stay in touch. If Owens or the investigators call you again, you contact me. I may want to put a recorder on you."

"Mr. King, are you trying to get me killed?"

"Do you really want to make me mad again?" asked King.

"No, Mr. King! I'll call you, Mr. King. Thank you Mr. King."

King said to his informer, "I can't believe that the District Attorney would team up with a low-life asshole deputy. Are you telling me the truth?"

"Mr. King, I'm telling you the truth. I said I wouldn't lie to you. There is something else."

"What do you mean there's something else?"

There was a pause on the tape.

"Mr. King, the deputy has been procuring young fifteen year old girls for the D.A. to screw."

"You're saying the D.A. is screwing fifteen year old girls."

"It's the truth Mr. King. It's on the tape I made for Owens. A secretary who works in the courts has a daughter who is only fourteen. The D.A. is screwing her and the mother. That's why I believe that nothing will come of the case they have against me because I know that too. The deputy told me that he had got other young girls for the D.A."

King couldn't believe his ears. He paused and then told his informer, "You had better have told me the truth. You can go now, but your ass better stay in touch with me. I better not have to come looking for you."

"I will, Mr. King. See ya."

Detective King stopped the recorder.
"Can you believe that, Lu?"

"Boy if this is true King; I think Jamie Owens has the District Attorney by the balls. I wonder how he'll handle this."

"Here, Lu. You keep the tape. Let's go to the bar and have a drink. Bob, the owner of the hotel knows you are coming by. He said he would buy the drinks."

"Sounds good King, since he's buying."

The next two weeks produced a number of small cases for James and his men.

Several of the detectives had tried to bust Ivory, the con man, who ran the numbers racket in the black community. The detectives, led by Washington, were discussing the last encounter with Ivory. Detective Washington told the others how Ivory beat them again.

"We had him good this time, I thought. Four cars were following Ivory. At every location where Ivory picked up money and betting slips, we switched and had a different car follow him. Ivory pulled into a funeral home. We figured he was going to pay his respects to a dead friend because there was a funeral

Lt. Joe "Bill" Bradley

going on at the time. Ivory and his helper carried flower wreaths and boxes of flowers from his pickup truck into the funeral home. We stayed outside watching his pickup. We watched as a casket was loaded into a hearse. Everyone at the funeral came out to their cars and the funeral procession left. We waited for awhile and then decided to go in the funeral home and bust Ivory. We thought his money and betting slips were still in his truck. When we went into the funeral home, Ivory was no where to be found. His pickup truck was empty. I questioned the funeral owner's wife. She said that Ivory had requested the use of a hearse so her husband put another one in the funeral procession. She said Ivory loaded the hearse with boxes of flowers. I knew right then that Ivory had carried off the betting slips and money in the hearse. We rushed to the cemetery but Ivory and the hearse were gone. The bastard beat us again!"

Everyone was teasing Washington that Ivory used a dead man to beat him. Washington kept repeating, "You wait, I'll get the bastard yet!"

A month passed. An investigation team made up of the District Attorney's Office, the Houston Police Department, the Sheriff Department and the F.B.I., led by Jamie Owens, was still investigating the Monelli burglary and killings. The newly elected Governor of the State of Texas was even demanding a solution to the Monelli case.

One morning when Lieutenant James was asleep at his home, his telephone rang. Looking at his clock he saw it was an hour before his alarm was to sound. Reaching for the telephone, he let it ring a few more times before answering it.

THE TWELVE JUDGES

"Lieutenant, are you awake?"

Recognizing Detective King's voice James said, "I am now."

"Have you seen the morning paper?"

"No, King. What's in it?"

"You've got to get up and read it. I hope your heart is in good shape. I've got some more information to add to the headlines. I'm on my way to your place. I'll buy you breakfast if you can eat after reading the headlines."

King hung up. James put on his robe, went outside and picked up his morning paper.

The headlines read:

"DISTRICT ATTORNEY RESIGNS AND TAKES JUDGESHIP

GOVERNOR APPOINTS JAMIE OWENS AS NEW D.A."

Lieutenant James went back into his home turning on his coffeepot to perk all the while reading the lead story in the newspaper. The lead article read:

> **"The Texas State Legislature created a new District Court for Houston. The present District Attorney of Houston resigned and has been appointed by the Governor of the State of Texas to be the Judge for the new District Court.**

Lt. Joe "Bill" Bradley

The article went on to say that the governor had appointed Jamie Ownes as the District Attorney for Harris County.

James threw the newspaper aside and thought, "Now I know how Jamie Owens used the information on the informer's tape! He used it to blackmail the present D.A. into resigning and taking a judgeship so he could become district attorney."

There was a knock on the door. Detective King came in. He had stopped by a Mexican restaurant and brought breakfast tacos.

Spreading the breakfast out on the kitchen table King said, "Boy, Jamie Owens moved fast didn't he?"

King in a playful voice said, "You want to hear the details of how the Governor came to appoint Jamie Owens or do you want to eat?"

"Let's do both."

As the two men sat down at the table, King began.

"Jamie Owens called my informer back to his office. My informer didn't want to, but I made him take my pocket recorder with him. They put him in the same room as before. He listened through the partition again. The District Attorney and the court deputy, who my informer had paid off, joined Owens and his investigators. Jamie Owens told the District Attorney about the tape and then played it for him. The District Attorney at first denied everything.

"My informer was then brought into the room. My informer said that when the deputy saw him he nearly fainted. Jamie Owens then told the D.A. that they had pictures of him accepting money from the deputy and they knew about his sexual preference for young girls. Owens told the D.A. that he could trace all the serial numbers of the money given to him. The District Attorney turned white and fell back into a chair. The deputy was easy. He confessed to everything. Then they put my informer back into the room where he had been. He listened through the wall again. He heard Jamie Owens tell the District Attorney and deputy that he had a solution for their problem.

"Jamie Owens told the District Attorney that he wasn't going to release the tape or the information about him screwing young girls to the news media if he would sign the resignation papers he had drawn up. Owens told the D.A. that it had already been arranged that he would be appointed by the Governor to a judgeship. The District Attorney signed the resignation."

Lieutenant James leaned back in his chair and said, "I knew Jamie Owens would do anything to become District Attorney. We're really going to have to be careful now, he'll go after a cop every chance he gets."

"Lu, you haven't heard the whole story yet. Guess how the governor came to appoint Jamie Owens as District Attorney?"

"Money, I guess."

"You hit it right on the head, Lu."

"You know Jamie Owens is from a wealthy Houston family. He's never worked a day in his life. His father-in-law is even wealthier than the Owens family. The father-in-law has tons of money. After the District Attorney and the deputy left, my informer

Lt. Joe "Bill" Bradley

heard one of the investigators ask Jamie Owens how much money his father-in-law had to give to the Governor's campaign to get Jamie appointed as the new D.A. The informer said Jamie Owens laughed and said it cost the old coot $300,000.00 but now he has a son-in-law that is the District Attorney of the largest county in Texas."

Lieutenant James and Detective King finished their breakfast. Detective King gave the tape to James.

King said, "I'm headed for the factory. You going by and congratulate the new D.A., Lu?"

James reply was, "Get your smart ass out of my house." King left for the factory.

As James started his shower his telephone rang. It was Chief Ladd.

"You read the paper or see the T.V. news?"

"Yeah, Chief. I guess you're happy since Jamie's your asshole buddy."

"Damn you, he's not my buddy! I have to get along with him and work with the bastard. Bill, I don't have to tell you that Jamie Owens doesn't like you and you better keep a watch over your shoulder."

"Thanks Chief. I appreciate your calling."

"Just be careful, Bill. Owens is going to be dangerous with all that power."

"You're right, Chief. Thanks."

James finished his shower and headed for the factory. As he drove the streets of Houston to his office, Lieutenant James thought, "I hate to admit it but Jamie Owens will do a good job as D.A. but the powerful money click that he is in will still run Houston. Will there ever be a time when a District

Attorney can't be influenced by money or political pressure?"

CHAPTER 15

THE HEAT IS ON

Since Assistant District Attorney Jamie Owens had been appointed by the Governor of Texas as Harris County District Attorney, the investigation into the Monelli case was in full swing. Jamie Owens was making statements to the news media that he was getting close to solving the Monelli case. Owens stated that it appeared to have been orchestrated by local thugs.

Lieutenant James had received telephone calls from his friends in the Texas Rangers and U.S. Customs. It seems that the Jamie Owens' investigators had paid each of them a visit.

The investigators were inquiring about the cases they had worked with Lieutenant James and his detectives.

Lt. Joe "Bill" Bradley

As James was completing his monthly performance reports, Kathy came into his office, "Chief Ladd is on the phone."

"Hi Chief. What can I do for ya?"

"Bill, I'm getting a lot of rumors about our new D.A. I know he's after your ass! I told you not to piss him off. You and your men best cool it for the time being, go fishing or something. Jamie Owens is feeling the power of his office. He really likes publicity; believe it or not, more than I do. That little shit sent two detectives over to my office this morning. The bastards are on loan to him from my department but they wouldn't tell me a damn thing! They wanted my okay to pull every case from the computer system that you and your men have worked. I told them hell no, so they called Owens. Those two investigators have forgotten who their real boss is; just wait. I'll transfer them back under my control and have them walking a beat on the waterfront. Can you believe that sorry Owens threatened me with a court order to get your records? I can't fade the heat with the media right now with the city mayor's election coming up. I let 'em have copies of all your cases. I'm sorry. Bill, tell me the truth, is there anything in those cases that could hurt me? Are you involved in the Monelli case? I plan to be chief a long time. Don't let me lose my job just because I didn't know what was going on."

"Chief, there's nothing in those cases. They're all good, clean, legal cases. You know I wouldn't do anything to hurt you. You're a great Chief. I know that little bastard is trying to connect me to the Monelli case but he can't. My men and I were fishing and I can back that up. Owens thinks I know who pulled the

THE TWELVE JUDGES

Monelli job and thinks I have information that I am keeping from him. Chief, all I know is what I have read in the newspaper and rumors. By the way, I also learned that Owens' investigators are talking to a lot of people about me and my group. I think he is just jealous about some of the big cases we've cleared and he wasn't involved."

"Bill, that's not all; Louis Monelli has put up a sizable reward for information. You know how he works. He buys a lot of people. The only good thing is, Jamie Owens would like to convict Louis Monelli. Bill, are you telling me the truth about the Monelli case?"

James answered slowly, "No."

"Shit, I knew it! Damn it! What do you know?"

"I know that whoever got the Monelli tapes, videos and books will make it hot for a lot of crooked politicians and businessmen. Chief, I'll slow my men down. Just let me know if you hear anything else."

"O.K. Bill, but watch yourself with Jamie Owens."

"I will, Chief. Thanks."

After talking with Chief Ladd, James saw Detectives Park and Murphy waiting to talk to him. He waved them in.

"Things are really heating up, Lu. Parks and me just came back from an electrical warehouse where we buy our supplies. Investigators from the D.A.'s office have been there asking around. They wanted to know what we've been buying. It seems that the new D.A. thinks someone in our department is wiretapping. We don't know anyone tapping phones, do you?"

Lt. Joe "Bill" Bradley

"Did the investigators find anything?"

"They found some invoices where we bought some telephone wire and cable. They had a court order to go through the records. The owner wouldn't give 'em the time of day. Shit Lu, I bought those supplies to run a telephone out to my garage."

Lieutenant James had to smile after that statement.

Murphy continued, "There's also an investigation going on at the Houston Phone Company. They're trying to locate any employee that's been helping cops tap phones. Don't worry Lu, about our man; he's too smart for 'em. They don't know who he is and even if they did, he wouldn't tell them anything."

Lieutenant James took a deep breath and leaned back in his chair. He considered what Ladd and the detectives had just told him.

James turned to Murphy and said, "We'd better have a meeting and alert the rest of the guys about what's going on. Tell Kramer to contact everyone and have them here in an hour. Murphy, you and Park had better sweep the telephones in my office and check the factory. Jamie Owens is not above getting a court order to place a bug on either of my phones or any place I might be. He can get any type of court order anytime he wants one!"

All the detectives gathered in the meeting room of the factory.

Murphy and Park assured the Lieutenant that the factory and the telephones were clear of electronic monitors.

"Park, Murphy, I know it'll cause a lot of extra work, but I want the telephones and the factory swept every morning for listening devices and bugs on the telephones."

Lieutenant James began to tell the detectives of the investigation going on by District Attorney Jamie Owens.

"We're going to go by the book until this investigation blows over."

Detective Watson asked, "How did the D.A. get on to us?"

"He doesn't have a thing, Watson. Owens knows that you guys are the best and the only ones capable of successfully making the cases you have. Owens suspects that we know a lot about the Monelli job. He knows what type of cases you have made and he's probably guessing how we obtain some of our evidence. I'm sure he's heard all types of rumors about us. Our group hasn't been a kept secret since the chief brought the news media over here on the John Peters case."

Detective Luna broke in, "I know how the D.A. heard some of the rumors about us. His investigators went to Monty County. They talked with the county commissioner we arrested with the Texas Rangers on the heavy equipment case. I learned that the commissioner told the D.A. investigators that the police had to be wiretapping his telephones, otherwise he would still be in the business of buying stolen heavy equipment."

James said, "I've heard that too, Luna. Owens' investigators are picking up bits and pieces but they will never get the true story. Any informers that you

Lt. Joe "Bill" Bradley

have, you'd better contact them and convince them not to talk with the investigators. Watch what you say and take it for granted that our telephones are bugged. This'll probably blow over in a couple of months. Now get to work but stay alert!"

As Lieutenant James walked back into this office, his private telephone was ringing.

"This is Lieutenant James."

"Boy, that wasn't a nice hello."

"Sorry, Barbara. It hasn't been a good morning."

"Well, let's make it a good afternoon. I'll meet you at the Steak and Ale on Memorial in one hour. I'll have a table in the back with a double shot of scotch ready for you."

"That sounds good. I'll see you in one hour."

James drove through Memorial Park on the way to meet Barbara. There were a lot of people, slim, fat, short and tall running along the jogging trails in the park that parallels the street.

"Damn, I need to get back to exercising. I'm really getting out of shape," James said to himself.

Bill James had noticed a car behind him when he left the factory. It was still behind him. The park road made a loop by the city golf course so James took the loop. He parked at the golf course clubhouse and went inside. He looked around and then returned to his car. The same car that he had seen behind him pulled out just as he did. Out loud James cursed, "That son-of-a-bitch Jamie Owens! He's having me followed."

James let the two investigators follow him to the Steak and Ale Restaurant. He decided not to try and lose them just yet.

THE TWELVE JUDGES

As he was parking, an attendant ran over and wanted to park his car. James told him no but handed him a dollar anyway. Inside he located Barbara. She gave him a warm kiss and they sat down.

"You don't look well, Bill. I bet I can make you perk up."

James looked at Barbara and picked up his drink and downed it in one swallow.

Barbara said, "You are either upset or real thirsty the way you handled your first drink. I'll order you a double. Maybe then, I'll get lucky."

"I'm glad you called, Barbara. I needed to get away before I lose my Irish temper and shoot Jamie Owens right between his spying eyes."

"Bill, let's leave. Come on. We can go to my place."

James drank his second double scotch and said, "I was hoping you'd ask. But, we have a slight problem. There are two of Owens' investigators outside. That idiot D.A. is having me followed. The investigators don't care if I know they are back there. They just want to know where I go and try to get me to lose my temper."

"That's no problem, Bill, I'll drive! They can't keep up with me, my car's fast."

"What do you mean you'll drive? You can't lose 'em."

"Come on, Cop. I'll show you!"

James left some money for the drinks and they walked outside. Barbara even opened the car door for Bill. As he sat there waiting for Barbara to get in behind the steering wheel, he thought, "This should be good."

427

Lt. Joe "Bill" Bradley

Barbara drove onto Memorial Drive. James adjusted the rear view mirror on his side so he could see the detectives' car.

"They're behind you, dear."

"Shut up, Bill, and watch."

Barbara turned into a wooded subdivision of homes. She sped up, making right and left turns. After a few minutes she said, "Bet you don't see them now."

Bill looked back. "You're right, I don't see them but I bet they're nearby."

Barbara drove back to the entrance of the subdivision. There across the street sat the two investigators in their car waiting.

Bill said, "You really lost them!"

"Oh, shut up! I'll think of something."

Barbara came to the 610 Freeway Loop. She entered the Freeway at 60 miles per hour. James glanced back and the investigators were still behind them. In and out of traffic Barbara drove.

"They're still on your pretty tail. Five to one you don't lose them."

"You're on, Smart Ass!"

Barbara exited the Loop and drove down the main street of a black community. At one corner there was a group of young black men standing around. Lieutenant James knew this area. The corner was a hangout for men looking for work. Construction employers came by each day looking for workers.

Barbara pulled up where the group was standing. She jumped from the car and ran to the group of blacks. James noticed that the two detectives following them had stopped a block behind them.

THE TWELVE JUDGES

Barbara started waving her hands and pointing in the direction of the detectives. She then ran back to her car and jumped in. The tires on her cars spun as she drove off James turned and looked back. The group of blacks had walked out in the street. The group stopped the investigators and was attempting to pull them from their car.

"What in the hell did you tell those guys?"

"Remember our bet, it was five to one that I couldn't lose them. Now you owe me five good lays."

"I don't mind losing a bet like that, but what did you say to them?"

"I told them that I worked with the welfare department and was out here helping their poor black brothers and sisters. I also said that the two men in the car behind us were harassing me and were redneck assholes."

Barbara laughed as she drove to her townhouse. James laughed too, but not at the detectives they had lost, he laughed because Barbara was so proud of herself.

Barbara drove into her garage. She got out and pushed a button closing the garage door.

Barbara's townhouse was not far from the downtown area. Her living room picture window outlined the skyline of the tall buildings downtown.

Bill mixed them each a drink. Barbara disappeared and he could hear the bath water running. When she came out, she took him by the hand and led him into the bathroom.

"I've fixed you a good bubble bath, Copper."

She then undressed him and he sat down in the tub. As Barbara began to scrub his back, he grabbed

Lt. Joe "Bill" Bradley

her and pulled her into the tub with him, clothes and all. She lay on top of him kissing him.

Getting undressed, Barbara got back into the tub and they acted like two kids for the next hour. After the bath, they went to bed and made love.

The next morning Lieutenant James was awaken by noise from the kitchen. He got up, showered and dressed. As he walked into the kitchen, he was still patting his face with toilet paper where he had cut himself while shaving.

Barbara smiled at him, and gave him a kiss, "If you would bring your own stuff over here, you wouldn't have to shave with my razor."

"I like using your razor. When I shave I think of where your razor's been."

James walked over to the window and looked outside.

"The two investigators that were following us must have checked your license plate. They're parked down the street."

Finishing breakfast, Bill got ready to leave.

"Do you have to go? Why don't you spend the day with me? I could start collecting my bet."

"I've got a lot to do today, Barbara. I'll call you later."

"Here are the keys to my car. Want to make another bet that you don't lose the investigators parked down the street?"

"I'm not going to use your car. I'll slip out the back so they won't see me. Let the bastards sit there all day in the hot sun."

THE TWELVE JUDGES

James kissed Barbara and slipped out the back door. He walked down the alley to the street and started walking.

"Damn, I should have used Barbara's telephone to have one of my detectives pick me up!"

He kept walking looking for a pay phone. Lieutenant James came to a bus stop. There were four people waiting for the bus.

"Does this bus go downtown?"

A small frail lady with a waitress uniform said, "It sure does, but it makes a lot of stops."

James thought, "It's been years since I rode a bus." He decided to wait with the others.

Shortly, a city bus pulled up to the curb. James waited his turn and stepped onto the bus. He dug into his pockets and pulled out some change. He held out his open hand with the change and asked, "How much is the fare?"

The bus driver looked at him and picked up two quarters from the Lieutenant's out stretched hand and dropped them into the meter.

The bus drove off with James still standing. He made his way to the rear of the bus and sat down.

As the bus made its stops, Lieutenant James looked around. He was enjoying this bus ride. In front of him were two high school boys with their schoolbooks. They were trying to get the attention of a pretty girl next to them.

He noticed that the woman in the waitress uniform was sitting behind the bus driver. She was carrying on a long conversation with the driver.

A gentleman in a business suit had his head down in the morning newspaper trying to solve a

Lt. Joe "Bill" Bradley

crossword puzzle. The woman next to him was leaning over the newspaper assisting him.

Four black high school age boys were snapping their fingers trying to put a rap song together.

James looked at each person on the bus. School kids, businessmen, nurses, waitresses, laborers, all in their own thoughts.

James thought to himself, "Even with all the sorry politicians and the high crime rate, there's a hell of a lot of good people in this old town."

James got off the bus in the downtown area. He found a telephone and called his office. Murphy answered the phone. He told Murphy where to pick him up and that he needed him to take him to his car. When Murphy arrived he told James that the factory was clean this morning of any electronic bugs.

At his office, James checked his phone messages with Kathy.

"Agent Steve Phillips with the F.B.I. has called you several times. He said it was important."

"Thanks, Kathy. I'll call him now."

James had known Agent Phillips for years. Houston had been Phillips second F.B.I. office. He had been an agent in Los Angeles and then he was transferred to Houston. He had been in Houston since then. James and Phillips had worked several cases together. The first large case they worked involved a stolen car theft ring where the autos were being shipped out of the Port of Houston to South America. Phillips had been a Sheriff Deputy in Florida before joining the F.B.I. He was street wise and had a lot of common sense. It took new F.B. I. agents five years or more to gain knowledge of the street. Most agents were college graduates and all they knew was paperwork when they came out of the academy. City cops had street sense after their first year on patrol. Phillips fit in very well with local law enforcement.

James dialed Agent Steve Phillips number.

"Steve, this is Lieutenant James."

"Lieutenant, can you meet me? I need to see you now! We need to meet. Can you meet me now?"

"Sure, Steve. Name the spot."

"I've got to catch a plane to D. C. I'm leaving the office in a few minutes. Meet me at the Hobby Airport, across from the Delta Airline ticket counter there's a small bar where we can talk. See you in about thirty minutes."

"I guess there's no need to ask you what you want."

"You're right Bill. I don't want to talk over the telephone."

Lieutenant James left for Hobby Airport wondering what Agent Phillips had on his mind. When he arrived, James parked in the public parking area instead of where police cars usually parked. James figured that since Agent Phillips didn't want to talk over the telephone, he better not park where the police usually do so no one will know he had been at this location.

Phillips was sitting at the bar when James arrived. Both men shook hands.

"Bill, what I'm about to tell you stays with us, O.K.?"

Bill answered, "As long as you don't warn me of my rights and there's not a tape recorder in your brief case, you have my word."

Lt. Joe "Bill" Bradley

"That's good enough for me, Bill. We've gone through too much together for us to part ways. I'm on my way to D.C. You know a new Director of the F.B.I. was just appointed by the President; his name's Lyles. He's a close personal friend of mine. He was the Chief of Police in L.A. when I was assigned there with the bureau."

"I remember, you've talked about him before and I met him once at a seminar."

"He's a great guy, Bill. He believes in getting results like we do. He knows your reputation."

"Cut out the honey, Steve, he doesn't know me, get to the point!"

"The point is, Lieutenant, The District Attorney, Jamie Owens, is after your ass. At this time all he has is a bunch of circumstantial evidence against you. I hate to admit it, but that's all the F.B.I. has too. Both the bureau and Owens believe that you either did the Monelli job or helped someone do it and something went haywire. Director Lyles of the F.B.I. has ordered me to bring our investigation on the Monelli case to him personally. He wants to review it. The Director told me an odd thing happened in the Monelli case. It seems the Director has received an anonymous gift; a number of boxes filled with all kinds of information on Louis Monelli. The boxes had video tapes, account books and pictures. The Director said the information was dynamite."

James said, "I hope he can use the information."

"Don't admit to me that you are involved," cautioned Phillips.

THE TWELVE JUDGES

"I only said, I hope he can use the information. I didn't admit to a damn thing!"

Steve Phillips leaned across the table and spoke directly at James, "I don't want you to tell me a damn thing, just listen. Jamie Owens hasn't been given any part of the information from our investigation. The U.S. Attorney's Office in Houston doesn't even have access to it. Director Lyles ordered it that way when he received the boxes. The Director called me at home and asked what I thought. I told him about you and your detectives. After hearing what I had to say, Lyles ordered me to Washington. I don't know if the Director wants our information to go to Jamie Owens or if he wants to fry your ass or what. I do know he's very excited about all that he received through the mail."

Phillips continued, "Bill, I hope I'm not ordered to investigate you. If I am, I'll tell you. I owe you that for being a friend. If you did pull the Monelli job, my hat's off to you. I'll call you when I get back from Washington. When I do call you, hang up and go to a safe phone. I don't have to tell you how Jamie Owens works; he's probably tapping your telephones. It's time for my plane, Bill. I have to go."

"Come on Phillips, I'll walk you to the gate."

At the boarding gate, the two men shook hands. "Thanks, Steve, a cop can't have too many friends. Have a nice trip."

All the way back to the factory, James went over his conversation with Agent Phillips. James considered Phillips a very close friend but he also knew Phillips was a Fed and that's where his loyalty was.

435

Lt. Joe "Bill" Bradley

Detective Kramer saw Lieutenant James as he entered his office. "Chief Ladd called. He was going to play golf today so he told me to pass on a message to you."

"What's the message?"

"The Chief said that the District Attorney wanted Internal Affairs to investigate you and our group for taking too much time off. The D.A. wanted them to check and see if we really went deep-sea fishing out of Corpus Christi. Chief Ladd said to tell you that he told Owens to stick it!"

"Sounds like the Chief has finally traded his golf balls for some real balls. Tell Johnson, Watson, and Murphy that I would like to see them."

Detectives Johnson, Watson, and Murphy walked into the Lieutenant's office. James looked up and said, "Who in the hell is this guy? Where did you find him, under a bridge?"

Johnson looked like a hippie from the sixties. He had a wig on that was tied in a ponytail. Long round gold earrings dangled from his ears. A three day beard covered his face. His clothes looked like something Goodwill had thrown out.

"Don't tell me. Let me guess. You're going to be in the Gay Parade next week," James remarked.

"Hell no, Lu! But don't you really dig my outfit? All I need now are some peace beads and a weed pipe."

"Well don't keep me in suspense," laughed James, "What in the hell are you up to?"

"I'm going to bust Ivory, the numbers man. Washington and Hancock can't, so I told 'em to stand aside, I would. I'm going to hang around one of his

THE TWELVE JUDGES

betting places and watch the bets and the money pickups. Lu, you know where I can get a grocery cart?"

James said, "Damn, Johnson, you even smell the part. You three sit down and listen. I've been thinking long and hard about the ongoing investigation involving us. We need to know what the other side is doing. I'm not too worried abut the District Attorney's office, but I'm worried about the F.B.I. I have a close acquaintance working for the F.B.I., but you know the Federal cops, they let the chips fall no matter what. And also, they have the money to buy information. What I'm about to suggest is dangerous. If we get away with what I think you three can pull off, I won't be as worried. If you were to get caught, I'll take the heat but you might be looking at some criminal charges and possible jail time. I think we're presently in a position where we have no other choice. I don't know what the F.B.I. is up to and I need to know."

Detective Johnson looked at the other two detectives and said, "Who do we kill?"

James turned to Detective Watson, "Watson, I've a book that the F.B.I. uses for public relations. It has a colored picture of their credentials. Do you think that you could duplicate two F.B.I. identification credentials? They would have to be good enough that the F.B.I. couldn't spot them as forgeries."

Watson got up from his chair, "I'll be back in a minute, Lu."

Watson went outside to his car and returned to the office. He handed James an identification folder. The identification folder contained the credentials of an F.B.I. agent.

Lt. Joe "Bill" Bradley

James asked, "You made this, Watson?"

"Sure did," Charles Watson bragged. "I've used it for a year or more. I copied it from the real McCoy. An agent had his home burglarized and I recovered his identification from a crook. I made me an F.B.I. identification before I returned it to the agent. It sure comes in handy at times."

"Damn, it's good!" Handing the folder back, James said, "Do you think you can make two more?"

"Damn right I can, Lu!"

Lieutenant James asked, "Johnson, do any of the present F.B.I. agents in Houston know you or Murphy?"

Murphy said, "I don't know any of the agents and none know me. In fact I don't want to know them."

"Here's what I think will work," James said. "You know how F.B.I. agents dress. They wear conservative business suits, conservative ties, conservative shoes and very neat hair cuts. They really get uptight and shook up when F.B.I. Inspection Teams come unannounced out of Washington to review their cases. In the past, I've even hidden material for some of the agents on cases they were working on when an inspection team came to their office. Their desks have to be in a certain order. Every paper clip has to be in a certain place in their desks. Murphy, those new transmitters you built, about the size of a quarter, how long will they last?'

"About three months, Lu, with the batteries that are on the market now."

"Murphy, you and Johnson are now F.B.I. agents. I heard a rumor the F.B.I. is having unannounced security checks on their offices and communications. Of course the rumor will be from me. I think you need to check their offices. Do you think you can con your way into the Houston office posing as F.B.I. agents checking their security and at the same time plant a couple of bugs?"

Both Murphy and Johnson said, "You bet we can!"

Johnson said, "I'll dress Murphy to look like he's a Washington, D.C. super sleuth."

James asked, "You know what'll happen if you get caught? Do you still want to do it? This plan is so far out in left field that it might work. The F.B.I. would never believe that someone would put transmitter bugs in their office."

"Do we get F.B.I. pay?" Johnson asked. "They sure make damn good money. A lot more than we do."

"Johnson, if you pull this off, I'll make the guys give you one hell of a party."

"Consider it done, Lieutenant," Murphy said.

Leaving the office, Detective Johnson asked Detective Watson, "You think the F.B.I. would snap if I used the name John Wayne."

Detective Watson spent the next two days at the photo lab in his home making the counterfeit F.B.I. credentials. When he finished them, Watson presented them to Lieutenant James.

"Joseph Hall and Donald Blake. Sounds like F.B.I. agents to me. You really did a nice job, Watson."

Dressed in their conservative business suits, Detectives Johnson and Murphy looked every bit the part of F.B.I. agents.

Lt. Joe "Bill" Bradley

Johnson had a girl friend that worked for an airline. She made false airline tickets showing a flight from Washington, D.C. to Houston and back again. Murphy wanted the tickets to flash to the F.B.I. when the detectives were ready to get their ass out of the Federal Building. It was a good idea.

The next morning, Detective Park and Watson parked the good time van across the street from the Federal Building.

From this parking lot, they were to monitor the transmitters that Murphy was planning to plant in the F.B.I. office to see if they worked.

Detectives Johnson and Murphy got out of the van to go into the Federal Building. A block away from the Federal Building Murphy remarked, "Have you ever seen a building like Houston's Federal Building? The architect must have been a bird watcher. The building looks just like a pigeon coop."

As they entered the building Johnson showed his counterfeit F.B.I. credentials to the guard on duty so they didn't have to go through the metal detector that had been set up for the public. Federal Judges were always scared of being shot.

They rode the elevator in silence to the sixth floor. As they entered the reception area of the F.B.I. office, a young girl greeted them.

"May I help you?"

Johnson answered, "Yes. Please inform the Special Agent-In-Charge that Agent John Hall and Agent Donald Blake are here from Washington, D.C."

The authority of Johnson's voice caused the young girl to hurry.

THE TWELVE JUDGES

The receptionist dialed the intercom. "Mr. Smith, there are two F.B.I. agents from Washington to see you. Yes, Sir, I'll tell them."

Turning to Murphy and Johnson, she said, "An agent will be right out to escort you to Mr. Smith."

Murphy smiled and said, "Thank you, Miss."

It was a long two minutes until a door opened and an F.B.I. Agent greeted them. Murphy noticed the agent was wearing the same color, brand and type of suit as Johnson. He had to turn his head to keep from laughing.

"Sorry to keep you waiting. I'm Agent George Leach. What brings you to Houston?"

Trying to sound very official Johnson abruptly responded, "We'll tell the SAC."

The agent looked disappointed and said, "Follow me, please."

Murphy and Johnson followed the agent down a long hall. At the end of the hall, Agent Leach knocked on the door.

Before entering, Johnson noticed in the squad room, other agents were going through their desks and straightening things. The Houston agents thought they were about to be invaded by an inspection team.

Murphy and Park were introduced to the SAC.

"This is our SAC, Darrell Smith."

Johnson, who had been carrying a white shoebox, started to shake Agent Smith's hand. Instead, he put the white shoebox on the agent's desk.

"Open it, Sir!" commanded Johnson.

The Agent-In-Charge did not know how to react. He reached for the white shoe box and opened it. Two sticks of fake dynamite were in the box with a note attached.

The Agent-In-Charge read the note out loud. "You have just been blown up by terrorists, have a good day."

Agent Smith sat down in his chair and gave a false laugh, "Who are you guys?"

Turning to Agent Leach, Smith asked, "Did you check these gentleman's credentials?"

Trying to resume his composure, Agent Leach said, "No, Sir. I'm sorry, Sir."

The SAC glared at Agent Leach as Murphy and Johnson handed the Agent-In-Charge their counterfeit F.B.I. credentials.

Agent Smith looked at the credentials and handed them back to Murphy and Johnson.

"Agent Hall and Agent Blake, what can I do for you? It looks like we got off on the wrong foot."

Detective Johnson began to speak, "Sir, we're traveling the country unannounced. You know what's going on in the Middle East? Washington ordered us to every F.B.I. home office. You're not to tell any other office we've been here. We're not an inspection team. We are not here to question your security. We're here to impress upon you and your agents the necessity of being security conscious. The world has a lot of nuts in it today. Sir, we'll not be here long or take up much of your time."

Turning to Murphy, Johnson said, "Agent Blake, what time is our plane back to Washington?"

Murphy pulled an airline ticket from his breast pocket and said, "It's at 1 p.m., Agent Hall."

Johnson turned to the SAC to reassure him, "Don't feel bad sir, we've blown up the last three home offices we've been in."

Once again, Smith managed another false laugh.

"Agent Leach, show these gentlemen around. I'll be in my office if needed."

Agent Leach took Detectives Murphy and Johnson into the communications room. They were introduced to the agent that ran the radio system. Word had spread quickly that Murphy and Johnson were not an inspection team. Johnson noticed that everyone was putting materials back on their desks.

Agent Leach and the communications agent gave Murphy and Johnson a tour of the Houston home office of the F.B.I. Johnson took notes all during the tour. Everyone then sat in the conference room while the two impostors, Blake and Hall, questioned them on security.

After an hour, Murphy said, "I'm satisfied you run a good ship here in Houston. This is just a short trip so stay alert. You never know when the Director will send an inspection team. We'd better go. We've a plane to catch. Our trip around the country is really just to make offices aware of security."

The four men walked back to Smith's office. Johnson extended his hand and said, "Sir, it was a pleasure meeting you. You have one of the better home offices we've been in."

"Thank you, Agent Blake. Can one of my men drive you to the airport?"

Lt. Joe "Bill" Bradley

"No, Sir, we have a rent car. I would like my dynamite returned. Might need to blow up another office."

The Agent-In-Charge handed Murphy the shoebox.

"Have a good trip. Sorry you couldn't stay longer."

Agent Leach walked Murphy and Johnson to the elevator door. They shook hands with the agent and left.

On the way down, Johnson jumped up and down in the elevator trying to hurry its descent.

"Move you son-of-a-bitch! We need to get our ass out of here!"

Outside the two detectives walked quickly away from the building.

As they got into their car and were driving off, Johnson remarked, "Let's get out of these clothes. I feel I need to go and preach somewhere."

Then he asked, "Murphy, did you plant the bugs? I didn't see you if you did."

"You're not supposed to see me. They're planted. I just hope they're working."

Detectives Park and Watson, in the Good Time van, could hear nothing but the sounds of cloth rubbing on the transmitter bugs when Murphy and Johnson had entered the F.B.I. office.

When Murphy planted the first bug, the voice of the Special-Agent-In-Charge came over their receiver loud and clear. "Agent Leach, show these gentlemen around."

Detectives Park and Watson got even more excited when they heard over the monitor the questions

THE TWELVE JUDGES

asked by Murphy and Johnson in the conference room. He knew both bugs had been planted.

They drove the van to a parking lot three blocks away.

All they heard the remainder of the day from the transmitters was talk of cases being investigated by the F.B.I. There was no conversation about the Monelli case or the Houston Police. They did hear one agent say how chicken-shit the Washington office was on their inspections.

The next day, Kramer made up a schedule for the Good Time van. Detectives Luna and King had today's duty. They were to report any information discussed about the Monelli case.

Detectives Murphy and Johnson were in the Lieutenant's office telling him about the inspection of the F.B.I. office.

"Lieutenant, you should've seen the communications they have. Park and I would go wild if we had their stuff. Boy, they must really have the money to spend judging by the equipment they have."

James said, "Murphy, you and Park are wild enough for me with what you have now. I would hate to see what you would do if you had the F.B.I. communications equipment. You two need to start growing a beard so you can't be identified. You will probably have to wear the beard for over a year until things cool down."

The phone rang. Lieutenant James answered the telephone.

"He's right here." James handed the phone to Murphy. "Park wants to talk to you."

Lt. Joe "Bill" Bradley

Murphy took the phone. He listened for a few minutes and then said, "Are you nuts! Get your ass over here now! What do you mean, don't tell the Lieutenant! I'm in his damn office, you idiot! Listen to me. Don't do a thing."

Park hung up on Murphy.

Murphy turned to James, "Lu, you're not going to like this. Park wanted me to go with him. He's at the Criminal Courthouse. He said he's going to bug the District Attorney's office."

James jumped to his feet shouting, "What! Can you get him back on his mobile telephone? Owens has his telephones and office checked ever so often for electronic bugs. How does Park expect to do it? The investigators and the D.A. know Park. You'd better get over there as fast as you can!"

"Come on Johnson," Murphy said. "You can drop me off at the Courthouse. I'll call you, Lu."

As Detectives Johnson and Murphy sped across Main Street headed for the courthouse, all of a sudden, traffic came to a stop. Sirens wailed in the distance and became louder with each second that passed. Detective Murphy got out of the car and started running toward the courthouse. Two fire trucks rounded the corner nearly throwing one fireman off the back as they headed to the courthouse. Murphy began to run faster. When he got to the front of the building, firemen were going in and people were running out. Murphy could see smoke coming from a third floor window. The firemen were opening all the windows on that floor.

A fireman shouted, "Go ahead, there's nothing up there but smoke. Some bastard who probably got a raw deal from a judge, exploded a smoke bomb."

Murphy rode to the third floor with a couple of firemen to where the D.A.'s office was located. The smoke was still pretty thick in the halls. Firemen were setting up fans to clear the smoke.

Murphy looked around but couldn't see anything but firemen in every direction. They were all wearing oxygen masks. He wished he had one. The smoke was beginning to get to him so he started back to the elevator. Suddenly a fireman grabbed his arm.

"Come with me, young man. I'll lead you to safety. I'm the Super Duper Fireman!"

Murphy recognized the voice under the mask. It was Larry Park.

Park pulled Murphy into the next elevator going down and pushed the basement button.

Park's car was parked in a zone in the basement which read. "For D.A. Investigators Only."

Park handed Murphy the car keys and said, "You drive. Super Duper Fireman has to change clothes and there's no phone booth nearby."

Park got into the back seat and started taking off the firemen's gear.

Murphy drove out of the basement onto the street heading for the factory. On the way, Park revealed what he had done.

"A city fireman let me use this gear. I went to the District Attorney's floor carrying the gear in a sack. I found a closet in the hall that had an electrical breaker box. I started a small fire and set off a smoke bomb. I put the fireman's gear over my clothes. The oxygen mask hid my face. When the first fireman arrived, I joined them. Boy! Edward sure makes a great smoke bomb! People bailed out of the D.A.'s office! You should've seen Jamie Owens run, he bolted down the stairs. I always thought that a gentleman would allow the ladies out first. Jamie Owens is no gentleman."

"What made you think Owens was a gentleman?" interrupted Murphy.

"When they had all cleared out, I planted a couple of transmitters. That makes me as good as you, even though you did your planting in the Federal Building."

"Park, the lieutenant is really pissed at you. You know you gotta clear things with him."

"I know, I guess I felt left out when I didn't get to go with you to the F.B.I. office."

Murphy wheeled the car around the last curve before the factory and came to a screeching halt.

"Park, I don't know if I want to go in with you or not. Lu is really pissed. He's gonna have your ass."

As Murphy and Park walked toward Lieutenant James' office, Park stopped just before he entered. He turned around backwards and backed in. He knew he was in for an ass chewing. Park didn't say a word as Murphy closed the door. Park just stood there not turning around to face Lieutenant James. Park stood very quiet while Murphy told the lieutenant of Park's escapade.

When Murphy had finished the story Lieutenant James got up from his chair and walked around to face Park. He put his face right next to

Park's ear and hollered at the top of his voice for all to hear, "Park, you're fired!"

Park stood there in amazement. He started to move and Lieutenant James hollered again.

"Stand still. Don't you dare move."

James put his face again close to Park's and hollered for all to hear, "You're hired back!"

James walked back to his desk, sat down and said, "Turn around Park."

He turned to face Lieutenant James.

"You are plumb crazy! We got heat on us now and you pull a stunt like that. I have to admit it worked. You did a hell-of-a-job but you went against my orders. Since I've hired you back, do you think you can follow orders?"

Parked answered with a loud, "Yes, Sir!"

"Well then, get your ass out of my office and go to work! If Owens finds those bugs he's gonna blow his top. Boy, I would like to see his face if he finds them."

As Murphy and Park walked out they heard the Lieutenant say, "No one, but these men, could've pulled that stunt off!"

In the following days the detective's time was spent listening to bugs in the offices of the F.B.I. and District Attorney. The electronic bugs were working fine.

At the F.B.I. there was not much discussion of the Monelli case except what was already known.

Lieutenant James guessed the investigation was put on hold until Agent Steve Phillips returned from Washington D.C.

Lt. Joe "Bill" Bradley

At the District Attorney's office, the Monelli case was the only case being discussed. They were hitting dead ends on every move. Owens was working his investigators day and night.

On the day that F.B.I. Agent Steve Phillips returned from Washington D.C. he walked into the Agent-In-Charge office and closed the door.

Detectives Park and Murphy, who were in the Good Time van, listening to the F.B.I. when they heard the Agent-In-Charge, Darrell Smith, ask, "Did you have a good trip? I'm real anxious to hear what the Director said. Why didn't he call me?"

Agent Phillips answered, "The Director wanted me to tell you in person. He doesn't like telephones when discussing cases involving organized crime."

The SAC kept asking the same questions, "What did he say about the Monelli case? Did he say anything about me?"

Agent Phillips thought as he started to answer, "Boy this SAC is in for a shock."

Agent Phillips continued, "The Director said he wanted you to drop the investigation on the Monelli case but you were to go along with the D.A. as if you were still investigating."

"What! What! We've got a lot of hours invested in the Monelli case. You told me yourself that you thought Lieutenant James and his bunch of crazy rouge detectives pulled the Monelli job."

Agent Phillips was getting a little irritated with his SAC. He finally said very slowly, "Just listen, will you? The Director wants you to call him when we're finished talking. He'll confirm what I've told you. If you don't believe me call him now."

THE TWELVE JUDGES

"I believe you. I just don't understand. Okay. Go on, Phillips."

"Sir, he wants you to be in Washington on Monday morning with ten of your best agents. I'm to go also. The Director has received, through the mail, boxes of video tapes and account books on Louis Monelli's activities. The boxes and information are from an anonymous source. You know and I know who the source was. The Director's exact words were, 'This is one time the F.B.I. is going to stay out of an investigation involving local cops and local politics.'"

"How good is the information, Phillips?"

"The information is unbelievable! It's what we have been after for years. It's going to keep us busy for the next two years."

Phillips continued, "This is the first time we've gotten a clear look into organized crime in the Houston area. It's going to blow your mind when you see what politicians have been bought by Louis Monelli. The Director will give you the additional manpower needed. He hinted to me that you were to head the investigation on Louis Monelli."

"Great, that's a feather in my hat! Should we call the director now?"

"Yes, sir, but first, about Lieutenant James and his men. The Director has already made contact with the United States Attorney General. The Attorney General is going to contact the U.S. Attorney here in Houston. The U.S. Attorney will contact the District Attorney, Jamie Owens. Jamie Owens will be told that the F.B.I. doesn't have enough evidence to prosecute anyone in the Monelli case. Truthfully, Sir, we don't have the evidence at this time. The U.S. Attorney will

Lt. Joe "Bill" Bradley

tell Owens that the F.B.I. will continue to investigate the Monelli case but that the District Attorney's office will handle the prosecution if there is any. Here's the Director's private telephone number."

Agent-In-Charge Smith called the number. The phone only rang once.

"Sir, this is Special Agent-In-Charge Smith in the Houston office. Yes, Sir. Agent Phillips is with me now. Yes, Sir, I'll be there Monday. Thank you, Sir. And Sir, it's an excellent idea that you have started having agents from Washington inspecting each F.B.I. home office security. You're not! Oh! But I thought. You're not. Oh nothing, Sir. I had heard that you were thinking about inspecting home offices security. Thank you, Sir. I'll see you Monday."

Agent-In-Charge Smith hung up the phone.

"Steve, the Director sure gets to the point fast. I'm going to be in charge of a task force on Louis Monelli. But I don't understand the Director not knowing about the agents he sent here from Washington to check our security."

Agent Phillips asked, "What security check?"

Smith told of the visit of the two F.B.I. agents from Washington, D.C. He told Phillips about the fake sticks of dynamite brought by the agents in a shoe box.

"What were these agents' names?" demanded Phillips.

"I have their names written here."

Looking at a pad on his desk, the SAC said, "Agents Joseph Hall and Donald Blake. They're from the office in Washington."

"Were they checked out, Sir?"

THE TWELVE JUDGES

Smith started to show fear in his eyes. "Yes. I looked at their credentials myself."

"Sir, I think we had better call Washington and check on the two agents," suggested Phillips.

"My God, Phillips, do you know what it would do to my career if they weren't agents?"

Phillips said, "I'll call Washington, Sir. I have a friend in the Inspection Division."

"Call now! Call now! You have me worried."

Agent Phillips called his friend with the F.B.I. inspection team in Washington. After talking with the agent, Phillips hung up the telephone.

Agent Phillips, shook his head saying, "Oh, shit! The Bureau isn't checking security anywhere and there are no agents by the names of Hall and Blake."

Phillips picked up the phone and called the communications room.

"Barowski, come to the SAC's office, ASAP!"

Barowski was the electronic expert for the Houston F.B.I. When Agent Barowski arrived, he took one look at the SAC's face and knew something was wrong. Smith's face was very pale.

Phillips was telling the SAC, "Sir, only you, Barowski, and I will know about what I think we will find."

Barowski noticed that Phillips was trying to be serious and all the time trying not to break into laughter. Phillips couldn't hold back. He started laughing. Tears ran down his cheeks. Still laughing, Phillips had trouble writing on a pad. He handed the pad to Barowski. The note read, "Check all the offices for bugs. If you find one, don't tell anyone. Tell the other agents that you're doing a routine check."

453

Lt. Joe "Bill" Bradley

Phillips was still laughing as Barowski left the office to get his electronic equipment so he could sweep the offices.

The SAC's face was still pale. He sat in his chair not saying anything.

Barowski returned to the SAC's office and set up his equipment.

As soon as the equipment was turned on, Barowski looked at Phillips and said, "I have a strong reading on a transmitter somewhere in the room."

Barowski took another instrument and walked over the room. It reminded Phillips of someone looking for buried treasure. Barowski got down on his knees and pulled a small item from under the front lip of the SAC's desk.

"Here it is, Sir. Boy, this is a good one. I bet it'll transmit ten miles or more."

The SAC's face turned from pale to a greenish color. He then threw up in his waste paper basket.

Phillips followed Barowski throughout the office. Another electronic bug was found in the conference room.

Barowski handed the two bugs to Phillips and asked, "What's going on, Steve. Is the SAC testing my abilities?"

"No, but keep quiet about the bugs. I guess we should have left them there and set the bastards up that planted them"

"You're talking about the two Security Inspection Agents, aren't you?"

"Yes, and Barowski, you had better keep your mouth shut. The SAC's a good man and this would hurt him in Washington."

THE TWELVE JUDGES

As Barowski walked away, Agent Phillips put the two electronic bugs on the table. He bent over and hollered into the small transmitters.

"You really owe me now you son-of-a-bitch!"

Phillips knew that only a certain group could have planted these bugs. He hoped Lieutenant James was listening.

Detectives Murphy and Park had heard all the conversations in the SAC's office and the conference room.

"Murphy, sounds a little like they're pissed. We better get our ass and this van away from the federal building as fast as we can."

"Call the lieutenant on the mobile phone. Tell him what happened and that we're taking the van to the Houston House parking garage. I know the security there and besides, we'll get better reception from the District Attorney's office."

Murphy called Lieutenant James' private number.

"Lu, your friend is back in town. You know the one I mean?"

"Yes, go on."

"He found some roaches in his office."

"I know what you mean. Damn! You learn anything else?"

"Sure did, Lu. You'll like what we heard. Have Kramer drive you to where we are. Tell Kramer that we're up high in Houston. He will know what I mean."

James hung up the phone receiver and called Detective Kramer into his office.

Lt. Joe "Bill" Bradley

"Murphy said to tell you they're up high in Houston. What does that mean?"

"They are at the Houston House Apartments downtown. There's a retired cop who has security there. I've been there with Murphy and Park before on surveillance. You really get good reception from the top floor of the parking garage."

"Let's go, Kramer. You drive."

Detective Kramer drove into the parking garage of the Houston House. A white haired gentleman at the guard gate walked out to the car.

"Hi, Kramer. Hi, Lieutenant. Murphy and Park are on the top floor of the garage. Lu, if you need anything just let me know."

"Thanks, Roger. How's the wife and family?"

"Everyone's fine, Lieutenant."

Kramer drove up the ramp to the top floor. Murphy and Park got out of the van to meet them.

They told Lieutenant James about the conversation they had heard from the F.B.I. office.

"I really do owe Phillips. Now we don't have to worry about the F.B.I. being on our ass. You two keep monitoring the D.A.'s office. Keep me informed as to what Jamie Owens is up to."

James and Kramer left the Houston House and headed back to the factory. On the way, the police radio sounded.

"Base 12 to number 12."

"Go ahead Base twelve."

"Call your office, Lu."

"Number 12 clear."

James picked up his mobile telephone and called his office. Kathy answered.

"Bill, Agent Phillips wants you to call him."

"I bet he does. Thanks, Kathy."

James dialed Agent Phillips number.

"Steve, you're back from Washington!"

"You know damn well I'm back. I have a sick Agent-In-Charge because of you. He can't even keep water down. Let's meet somewhere you asshole."

James couldn't resist an answer to that statement, "Your SAC catch the flu bug or something?"

Phillips shot back, "Damn you, James. Think what would have happened if you would have been caught. It's a good thing I was in Washington, D.C."

"Sorry, Phillips. Don't know what you are talking about. I'll head for the Rotary Table right now. You know where it is. I'll even buy you a drink."

Phillips hung up talking to himself.

"Let's go Kramer. When Phillips arrives at the Rotary Table, let me talk to him by myself. He is really upset."

Juan was not present when they arrived at the Rotary Table.

James took a table in the rear of the restaurant and Kramer went to the bar. It wasn't long before Agent Steve Phillips came in.

"Hi, Steve. You have a good trip?"

"Bill, you are just as crazy as your detectives. What got into you? You need to name your group the eleven crazy screws led by a one crazy nut. What were you thinking? You took a hell of a chance. You better be thankful the Director is an ex-cop and still thinks like a city cop. You bet your sweet ass that I'm a friend of yours. The bugging of my SAC's office is

Lt. Joe "Bill" Bradley

going to be kept quiet. You better not brag about it either."

"Don't know what you are talking about Steve. Did one of my men screw up and violate some criminal's rights?"

Agent Phillips said, "Still can't trust a federal man can you? Don't try to blow smoke up my ass. I know what you did."

Phillips reached across the table and dropped two small items on the table in front of James. The items were the quarter size transmitter bugs.

"What are these, Steve?"

"Just take the damn things, Bill! Don't act like an ass hole with me!"

"I don't know what I would do with these but thanks anyway, Steve. I hear these type of bugs are expensive."

Phillips then leaned over the table and said, "Bill, you've got something I want."

"What would you want from me?" asked Bill.

"You know damn well what I am talking about. The credentials for Agents Hall and Blake. I sure would like to meet those two agents."

"Once again Steve, I don't know what you are talking about. Credentials. Don't tell me two agents had their's stolen."

Phillips was growing angry, "Bill, I should get up and tell you to kiss my ass and walk out but I know the old saying cops have. Never trust a federal man with your ass. You're wrong about me, Bill, and someday you'll see how wrong you are. Bill, the Director of the F.B.I. knows the Monelli information mailed to him came from you."

THE TWELVE JUDGES

"How does he know that, Steve? Are you trying to bait me?"

"Because, you bastard, I know you! He's my boss and I told him it was you."

James smiled and asked. "He's not going to come down on us, is he? He has no reason too!"

"Hell no, Bill. He's leaving that up to the District Attorney. He said that any cop who would stick his ass out as far as you did deserves a break. He's really pumped up about the information you sent. Understand this Bill; you're on your own with Owens. We can't get involved."

"I understand, Steve. You wouldn't have made a case on us anyway if it was us that pulled the Monelli job."

"Bill, you're forgetting the Federal Laws on Conspiracy. They're so broad that we can make a case on anyone."

"I guess you're right, Steve. Thank the Director for me and tell him that he'll be the first to know if we break the Monelli case."

Agent Phillips didn't react to that statement. He finished his drink and ordered another one.

Steve Phillips then told Bill about finding the electronic bug in the SAC's office. He could hardly finish the story because of his laughter. When Steve got up to leave he said. "Bill, I still would like to have those two fake F.B.I. credentials. They would sure make good displays in the F.B.I. museum."

James answered, "After this thing blows over, you will probably receive a package in the mail, but not until then."

Lt. Joe "Bill" Bradley

Agent Steve Phillips left the Rotary Table and James joined Detective Kramer at the bar.

He told Kramer, "Agent Phillips is a good cop. Too bad he's a federal man."

The bartender asked James if he wanted a drink. James said, "It's too early for another drink. Hell! Let's have a drink anyway and toast the F.B.I."

After the drink, Lieutenant James and Detective Kramer drove back to the factory.

James placed a phone call to Attorney Bob Thornton.

"Bob, things are heating up pretty fast. Jamie Owens has all his investigators working overtime on us. I think it's time for us to meet."

"I think you're right, Bill. Rumors are floating all over the courthouse. Let's have dinner tonight. Why don't you bring a date, if you can get a date? My wife said she was going to find you a woman if you can't."

"Tell Susan I'll bring a date. Is Arthur's Seafood all right with you?"

"Sounds good, Bill. I'll see you at seven."

James called Barbara and told her about the dinner date. She said she would be ready at six.

James didn't have to go to the door of the townhouse as Barbara came out as soon as he pulled into her drive.

She looked great! The unrestrained black dress she was wearing gave her an appearance of a model.

Barbara and James drove to Arthur's Seafood restaurant.

Bob Thornton and his wife were already seated. Susan was delighted that Bill had brought a date.

THE TWELVE JUDGES

James had warned Barbara that Susan would play twenty questions with her. Barbara handled herself very well.

After dinner, Susan said, "Come on Barbara, I know these men want to talk. Let's go to the gift shop and spend some of their money."

When they had gone, Bob Thornton ordered another drink.

"Boy, Barbara is sure a looker, Bill. She must be hard up to be with you."

"She's a fine woman, Bob. She really takes care of me."

"Bill, Jamie Owens is coming after you even if he has to manufacture evidence himself. The rumor is that everything he's got is only circumstantial and it's not even good circumstantial evidence. He'll probably arrest you and your men. He wants the publicity. Owens doesn't believe you pulled the Monelli job but he thinks you have a lot of information on the Monelli case that you are not giving to him. He has a couple of ex-cons who are still in prison that he is going to use to try and prove you wire tapped them to get evidence. I need to meet with you and all your men. We need to plan some strategy. I'm going to bring in another attorney to assist me and I also want Detective Kramer on my team. Kramer's a sharp attorney and will know the police side. When and where can we get together?"

"Bob, you remember my friend who owns the ranch outside of Houston?"

"Yeah. It's in Brookshire, isn't it? I've been there to a barbecue once with you."

Lt. Joe "Bill" Bradley

James continued, "We can meet anytime at his hunting lodge. It's secluded and has all the comforts of home. No one will know we're there."

"Sounds good. Call me so we can set a date. It had better be soon."

Susan and Barbara returned from the gift shop. Barbara was carrying a Teddy Bear.

"Since you won't sleep with me, I bought you something to sleep with."

Bob Thornton leaned toward Bill and whispered, "You won't sleep with her? You are working too hard! You better go to a head doctor."

James and Thornton flipped a coin to see who paid for dinner and James lost. They said their good-byes outside and James drove Barbara to her townhouse.

"Want a nightcap or something?"

"I would rather have the something," answered Bill.

The next day at the office, Lieutenant James called Cletus Black and told him he needed his hunting lodge again.

"Bill, it's ready anytime you are. You want guards on the gates?"

"Just one on the last gate. We'll need to be there about two days."

"Come when you're ready. You have a key."

James then called Bob Thornton and informed him that the hunting lodge would be ready the next day. He decided to leave Detectives Luna and Watson in the Good Time van listening to the District Attorney's office.

THE TWELVE JUDGES

Detective Kramer notified the other detectives of the meeting at the hunting lodge.

The next day, Lieutenant James drove to Brookshire, Texas and to the hunting lodge. Only the last gate was locked. A Mexican on horseback rode up, jumped off his horse and unlocked the gate.

James was the first to arrive. He unlocked the door to the lodge and went in to wait for the others. As he was putting a pot of coffee on to brew, the others started to arrive.

Bob Thornton came in with his associate attorney.

"Bill James, this is Ruben Steinberg, one of the sharpest minds in our business."

Since all the detectives knew Bob Thornton, Lieutenant James introduced Ruben Steinberg.

When introductions were complete, Lieutenant James said, "Now all of you give Bob and Ruben a dollar. That'll seal the attorney client privilege so what you tell them they can't repeat."

Hancock blurted out, "They better not repeat anything we tell them. They want to live don't they."

Ruben Steinberg really got a kick out of each detective handing him a dollar bill.

Lieutenant James continued, "We're going to discuss the Monelli case and our actions in other cases as a group. Then Bob and Ruben will talk with each of you individually. Bob the floor is yours."

Bob Thornton stood before the group. "All of you know I helped Bill form this group. I don't condone some of the methods that Bill uses to make cases. But maybe in our society today, seeing how criminals get off, maybe you believe that you need to

Lt. Joe "Bill" Bradley

stretch the law a little to beat the professional criminal. You're going to have to trust me and Ruben Steinberg completely. I know how the D.A., Jamie Owens, works. He cannot stand bad publicity and if the pressure gets too much, he moves too fast. We're going to put pressure on Jamie Owens. Starting out with the Monelli case, I need to know what part each of you played and what physical evidence the D.A. might have."

Starting with Detective Murphy, each detective truthfully told of his part in the Monelli case. It was late afternoon before the detectives finished.

"What about you, Lieutenant James?" Bob Thornton asked.

Lieutenant James added to the detective's stories. James also revealed that the guns used in the shooting of the bodyguard and prostitutes were in a river. James didn't say which river. The electronic bugging of the F.B.I. and District Attorney's office were not mentioned.

Everyone was really hungry when Black brought in his cook to start frying steaks.

After dinner, Bill James, Bob Thornton, Ruben Steinberg, and Joe Kramer went into one of the bedrooms. They wanted to have a conference. The four talked until midnight.

Most of the detectives either watched T.V. or played dominoes.

James came out of the meeting and joined his friend, Black. They sat talking of their past fishing and hunting trips to Louisiana and Mexico.

Bob Thornton, Ruben Steinberg and Kramer joined the rancher and James. All three looked tired.

THE TWELVE JUDGES

"I sure would like a drink before I turn in. We covered a lot of ground tonight."

James got up from his chair. "Bob, I'll fix you a drink, sit down."

Eventually everyone left James and Thornton alone. The others had gone to bed for the night.

"Bill, Joe Kramer is wasting his time with you. The boy would make one hell of an attorney. I've offered him a job in my firm if he ever leaves police work."

"He's good, Bob. Kramer's been my right arm. What do you think after talking with my detectives?"

"I know that you've got one hell of a group put together. I wouldn't want this group after me. If it wasn't for that conceited Jamie Owens, I think we would be in good shape. As I told you, Jamie Owens wants to make a name for himself. You can bet that he's going to arrest you with T.V. cameras rolling."

"Bob, I can fade the heat, but I can't sit back and see my detectives ruined. Just think what their families will go through. Do you think you could cut some kind of deal with Jamie Owens and get him to leave my detectives out?"

"You're pissing me off, Bill. Have confidence in your attorneys. There's no way in hell Jamie Owens can get a conviction on you and your men. He doesn't have shit! Now let's go to bed."

The next morning, as usual, Cletus Black had a delicious breakfast ready. After eating, the three attorneys went into conference again.

At mid-morning the telephone in the hunting lodge rang. Lieutenant James answered the telephone, it was Detective Luna.

Lt. Joe "Bill" Bradley

"Lu, the D.A.'s investigators have turned Houston upside down looking for you. That's not all. They bugged your telephone and our offices at the factory. They did it last night. We're still listening to them discuss how they did it. Jamie Owens got a court order from Judge Pugh for the wiretaps. The court order is good for six months. We heard one investigator say that they needed the tapes to convict your ass, cause they had nothing else."

James said, "Well, we knew the D.A. didn't have the balls to wiretap us on his own. The judge that gave him the court order worked for Owens at one time. Stay with it. I'll send you some relief later today."

James walked into the room where Bob Thornton was having his morning conference and announced. "Jamie Owens bugged the factory and my phone last night. Detective Luna heard the investigators say they didn't have any good evidence against us."

Ruben Steinberg asked, "How did your detective hear that Lieutenant?"

James looked at Ruben and then at Bob Thornton. Bob Thornton threw up his hands.

"Ruben doesn't know about your team planting bugs in the D.A.'s office. You know bugging of the District Attorney's office is a crime. An attorney cannot be part of a crime."

Ruben fell back onto the bed staring at the ceiling and said, "You didn't bug the D.A.'s office did you? God help us all!"

Bob Thornton reached over and pulled Ruben Steinberg to a sitting position.

THE TWELVE JUDGES

"Ruben, the bugging of the D.A. is to stop today. The bugging of the F.B.I. office has all ready stopped."

Ruben Steinberg fell back onto the bed again.

"They bugged the F.B.I. too! God help me! I'm too young to be disbarred."

Thornton turned to James and Kramer and said, "Bill, you and Kramer go outside for awhile. Let me talk with Ruben."

James closed the door as he and Kramer left the room.

Kramer asked, "Do you think Ruben will continue to work with us?"

"I don't know. I wonder why Bob didn't tell him about the bugging of the D.A.? Ruben knows about the other cases where we used electronic surveillance."

Thirty minutes later, Bob Thornton came out of the bedroom.

"Everything is all right. I was going to tell Ruben today about the bugging of the D.A.'s office. I figured the bugging would be over. He wants to talk with Park and Murphy. He said he needed to know more about electronic monitoring. Bill, Ruben is a brilliant civil rights attorney. He's on our team and if an out can be found, he will find it."

James answered, "Your word is good enough for me, Bob."

Ruben Steinberg talked with Detectives Murphy and Park until lunch time. When he finished, he came out where lunch was being served.

"Eat fast, Lieutenant. I want to talk to you, Bob, and Kramer."

Lt. Joe "Bill" Bradley

As Ruben Steinberg ate lunch, ever so often, he would pick up his food with a fork and inspect it and say, "I'm just looking for a bug." Then he would nearly choke on his food laughing.

After lunch, the four men returned to discuss the inevitable arrest of James and his men.

Ruben Steinberg had four legal size pads of notes he had taken while talking with all of the detectives.

Steinberg began, "Gentlemen, I'm going to suggest, no I am going to insist that we follow my guidelines to a successful failure of District Attorney Jamie Owens. I'm in too deep to back out of this case now. Besides, I'm learning new areas of the law. Lieutenant, you sure put a lot of crooks away that needed to be put away. I've been up against Jamie Owens in court many times and I know how he thinks and acts. He jumps to conclusions and moves too fast. That's why I've beat him in court a number of times. Here's what we are going to do."

Attorney Ruben Steinberg shared his plan with Attorney Bob Thornton, Lieutenant Bill James, and Detective Joe Kramer.

When he finished Bob Thornton said, "This is why I wanted Ruben on our team. I think his plan is so far fetched it will work."

James called his detectives together. Ruben Steinberg told the group his plan. The detectives laughed and carried on as if the case had already been won. Each detective shook Bob Thornton's and Ruben Steinberg's hand as they left for the factory.

James sent Murphy and Park to relieve Luna and Watson in the Good Time van.

THE TWELVE JUDGES

Murphy and Park had also made arrangements with a member of the cleaning crew at the courthouse to let them in after closing hours so they could recover their bugs from the D.A.'s office when they were no longer needed.

It cost James a couple of hundred dollars but it would be one hell of a problem if Owens found them. Tomorrow would be an eventful day.

Lieutenant James arrived back at his office and called Chief Ladd. "Chief, did you get the message that the guys and I went fishing?"

Chief Ladd snapped back, "You go fishing too much, Bill. Don't you realize that Jamie Owens is investigating you?"

Knowing that the D.A.'s investigators were listening to his telephone conversation, James said, "Yeah Chief, and I'm worried. I haven't been able to sleep at night. I'm going to have a meeting with my detectives tomorrow. Do you want to be there?"

"No! And remember, I'm not involved in the Monelli case or any of your cases. Bill, I can't find out anything that the District Attorney is up to."

"Chief, I know you're not involved in the Monelli case or anything we have done. I'll call you after the meeting tomorrow. We have to get rid of a lot of evidence before you know who gets a hold of it."

"I've got to go now, Bill. I'm talking to the Republican Women of Houston today and then playing golf."

Lieutenant James then went out to his car and used the mobile telephone.

He called Murphy and Park in the Good Time van.

Lt. Joe "Bill" Bradley

"Did the D.A. investigators hear my phone conversation with the Chief?"

"Yes, Sir, and we did too. They had you on a speaker phone. They're excited about the meeting tomorrow. They played the tape of your phone call with the Chief three times for Jamie Owens. Owens said he had you by the nuts and he's going to squeeze them."

"Jamie Owens probably could use one of my balls, he doesn't have any. Shut the operation down when the D.A. Investigators quit work for the day. In the morning, I want you two in the van early. After our meeting, you can meet us."

"O.K., Lu."

James got up early the next morning. He dressed and left for his office. On the way he stopped and brought four dozen donuts for his detectives.

Detective Kramer was already at the factory. Knowing that the D.A. Investigators were still listening to the bugs they had planted in the factory, Kramer said, "I couldn't sleep, Lieutenant. I went through a lot of stuff we need to get rid of. I have boxed everything up. We can take them with us today and burn them in the pit at the Rotary Table."

All of the detectives except Murphy and Park, who were in the Good Time van, arrived within the next hour.

James got everyone together. He stood next to one of the electronic transmitters the D.A. investigators had planted. He wanted the District Attorney to hear him loud and clear.

THE TWELVE JUDGES

"We better get our meeting started. Washington, do you have the boxes of material that will make a good fire?"

"Yes, Sir and I have two empty boxes for the other guys to put their papers in."

"King were you able to find all of the boxes I had hid in my freezer?"

"Got 'em right here, Lu. Boy, this is valuable stuff. I bet the District Attorney would like to have this."

Detective Hancock spoke up, "You didn't invite the D.A. did you, Lieutenant?" Everyone laughed.

"No, Hancock. I don't think we want Jamie Owens at this get together. We better get started. The sooner we get rid of all of this evidence the better my stomach will feel."

Detectives carried the boxes out to their cars and left for the Rotary Table.

Detectives Hancock and Kramer rode with James. As Lieutenant James drove out of the drive of the factory, he heard Murphy on the police radio.

"109 to number 12."

"Number 12 to 109, go ahead."

"109 to 12, call me on the mobile phone."

James picked up his mobile phone and called.

"Lu, the D.A.'s office is going wild. They've already sent investigators to the Rotary Table to set up surveillance. Jamie Owens is giving orders left and right. He's screaming at his investigators to call the T.V. and newspaper reporters so they'll be there when your arrest is made. He plans to make the arrest of you

Lt. Joe "Bill" Bradley

when his surveillance investigators tell him the boxes of material have been unloaded and taken inside."

James said, "Steinberg was right! Jamie Owens is moving fast. The hook's been set. What a mullet! Meet us at the Rotary Table as fast as you can. I want everyone there when the fireworks start."

"We're on our way Lu."

In the rear of the Rotary Table Restaurant, an eight-foot fence surrounded a large Mexican style patio. There were tables, chairs and a large barbecue pit. The area was used for private parties.

When Lieutenant James arrived at the Rotary table, his detectives were unloading boxes from the van and cars.

On the gate entrance into the patio, Detective Watson nailed a sign that read, "Private Party Today, Entrance By Invitation Only."

Hancock and Washington were stacking papers on the fire pit. They told the others that they wanted the pleasure of sending a signal to the District Attorney that the party had began.

Evelyn Mixon, no longer a cub reporter but a seasoned investigative reporter, was sitting at a table with pen in hand. Evelyn had received a special invitation directly from Lieutenant James. She hadn't been told anything but she knew something was going to happen. She was about to get that exclusive story that James had promised her.

Kathy had made place cards and was putting them on the tables for Father Gomez's baseball team.

Detectives Murphy and Park arrived. They locked the fence gate as they entered the patio.

THE TWELVE JUDGES

Detective Washington and Hancock jumped on top of a table and raised a can of beer over their heads.

"Here's to our Lieutenant, to our attorneys and to us."

Everyone raised their beer cans in salute.

James glanced at a window in the restaurant. Bob Thornton and Ruben Steinberg had a camera set up to film the events.

Another camera had been hidden outside to film the on-coming rush of the D.A. and his investigators.

Lieutenant James sat down at a table with Detective Kramer, "You can light your fire, Hancock," ordered James.

Hancock and Washington poured two cans of charcoal lighter fluid over the papers in the pit. When they lit the papers there was a loud whoosh. Fire jumped ten feet from the pit. Black smoke billowed over the top of the restaurant.

Seconds later there was a loud crash at the gate to the patio. The lock on the gate gave way. District Attorney Investigators poured in. One investigator ran for the pit where papers were burning. Detective King stuck out his foot and tripped the investigator. The investigator fell and two other investigators fell over him. All three ended up in a pile.

One investigator was able to retrieve some of the burning papers and threw them on the patio floor to stomp out the fire. It was quite a scene.

District Attorney Jamie Owens entered the patio followed by reporters and T.V. cameraman.

Jamie Owens walked to Lieutenant James making sure his face was toward the cameras. Owens spoke loud. "Lieutenant Bill James, you and your detectives are under arrest for Conspiracy To Violate The Rights of An Individual By Wiretapping."

Lieutenant James stood up. T.V. microphones were shoved in his face. The reporters started asking questions.

"Tell us, Lieutenant James, are you and your detectives involved in the Louis Monelli killings?"

James looked straight into the eyes of the D.A. and said, "Yes, we are."

The District Attorney's mouth dropped at Lieutenant James' answer.

Jamie Owens smiled at the T.V. cameras and said, "See, I told you he was involved."

One T.V. reporter, whom Lieutenant James knew, asked, "Bill, I mean, Lieutenant James, tell us how you are involved."

The commotion silenced as Lieutenant James spoke. "We are involved just like the F.B.I., the Sheriff Department, and the District Attorney. We are seeking information on the criminals who did the Louis Monelli burglary and shooting."

Jamie Owens didn't like that answer.

The T.V. reporter continued to ask questions. "The District Attorney says you and your detectives have been wiretapping criminals to get evidence. Is this true?"

James said, "Of course not. I don't know where the District Attorney got his information? You know a criminal will say anything to help cut his time in prison. Once criminals get to prison they all say they are not guilty."

THE TWELVE JUDGES

Jamie Owens became red faced. He stepped in front of Lieutenant James and, looking at the T.V. cameras said, "I want to show you what Lieutenant James and his men are doing at this location. They are destroying evidence."

Hollering at his investigators the D.A. went on. "Bring those boxes over here and let the reporters see the evidence that Lieutenant James was attempting to destroy."

One investigator tried to get the District Attorney's attention. "But, Sir, those boxes..."

Owens moved to where the boxes were stacked. The T.V. cameras followed, filming the District Attorney placing a box on a table. Jamie Owens turned toward the cameras as he opened the box. The T.V. cameras filmed a beautiful box of beef ribs. The District Attorney closed the box quickly and raced across the patio opening the other boxes. Pecan firewood was in two boxes and the others had beef ribs and beef brisket.

The T.V. cameras filmed it all. The reporters turned back to Lieutenant James.

James said, "I guess we should've invited the D.A. to our cookout. We're cooking for a church baseball team. They won the championship. My detectives and I are their sponsors."

Meanwhile, the District Attorney grabbed the papers that had been salvaged from the fire by his investigators. The papers were blank. He threw them down on the patio. He then began to give orders to his investigators.

"Search each man. I want everything searched, even their cars."

Lt. Joe "Bill" Bradley

Each detective stood and was searched by an investigator. The D.A.'s prize investigator walked over to where the District Attorney was standing.

"Sir, there is nothing on the detectives that involves the Monelli case or anything."

Sweat was pouring from Owens brow. His face was one of amazement.

"Did you find the Monelli file? It must be here somewhere. I heard them say over the wiretap they were bringing it."

Lieutenant James was waiting for such a statement. Looking into the T.V. camera Lieutenant James said, "Jamie Owens, how did you know we were here? Did you wiretap my office?"

The District Attorney was lost for words. The T.V. reporters re-directed their questions to the D.A.

"Mr. Owens, did you wiretap Lieutenant James' office and if you did, why?"

"Yes. Yes, damn it! But, I had a court order."

The reporters kept asking. "Why did you wiretap Lieutenant James' office?"

"I was told he was wiretapping criminals to get evidence. I've nothing more to say at this time. I'll give you a press release later," stammered Owens. "All reporters will have to leave for now."

The District Attorney wanted no more questions. He knew he had been set up. As the last reporter went through the broken patio gate, the D.A. turned to question Lieutenant James and found himself staring into the faces of Bob Thornton and Ruben Steinberg.

THE TWELVE JUDGES

Ruben Steinberg was holding the sign from the patio door which read, "Private Party Today, Entrance By Invitation Only."

The D.A. was irritated seeing the two attorneys. "How did you get in here? This is a crime scene."

Attorney Ruben Steinberg spoke, "Mr. D.A., we got in here by invitation. Did you have an invitation, Mr. District Attorney? By the looks of the gate, you didn't have an invitation. Do you have a search warrant?"

"I don't need a search warrant. I'm the District Attorney and a crime is being committed in my presence."

Bob Thornton spoke up, "You mean it's a crime for these police officers, who are off duty, to cook spare ribs and brisket for a church baseball team."

Jamie Owens screamed at the two attorneys, "I'm through talking with you! Get out! You're interfering with a crime scene!"

Ruben Steinberg smiled at Jamie Owens and said, "These men are my clients. Are they under arrest? If not, you get your ass out of here!"

Jamie Owens nearly exploded. "Yes! They are under arrest and I'm going to get their bonds set so high, you'll never be able to get them out of jail! Now get out!"

Ruben then asked, "Mr. District Attorney. May I see your arrest warrant for Lieutenant James?"

Owens screamed, "I don't need an arrest warrant. Now get out of my way."

The T.V. cameras took pictures of Lieutenant James and his men as they were being handcuffed and

Lt. Joe "Bill" Bradley

taken to waiting cars. They were taken to the county jail to be booked and charged.

Chief Ladd and Sheriff Mills of Harris County were waiting at the jail. Ladd pulled Bill James over to the side when he entered the booking area, "Bill, the Sheriff has bonds made for you and your men. The Sheriff has already shown these bonds to the District Attorney. Owens is madder than a golfer missing a one-foot birdie. Bob Thornton had a judge issue bonds on all of you just before you got here. Bill, this is the hardest thing I've ever done in my life. You and your detectives are relieved of duty until this thing is resolved. Don't talk with reporters and keep your nose clean. Call me every day. Do you need anything?"

"No, Sir, and Thank you, Chief. You too, Sheriff Mills, thanks a lot!"

Sheriff Mills handed Lieutenant James a stack of papers that were bonds for James and his men. James took them over to his detectives who were starting to be processed. He gave them to Detective Kramer. Kramer thumbed through the papers handing each detective his bond to sign. Kramer stopped giving out bonds and began to laugh.

"Lieutenant, did you see that our bonds are Personal Recognizance bonds."

After each detective and Lieutenant James had signed their bonds, Sheriff Mills had some of his deputies drive them back to the Rotary Table Restaurant.

Bob Thornton and Ruben Steinberg were waiting on them.

Bob asked, "How did you like the high bond Judge Peters set on you and your detectives."

THE TWELVE JUDGES

"How did you pull that off, Bob?" asked James.

"I didn't. Chief Ladd and Sheriff Mills did. Bill, you've got a lot of friends that respect you."

Lieutenant James turned to his detectives, "Hancock, start the fire and lets cook some barbecue. All of you call your wives or girlfriends and have them join us. I know they're worried. Bob, you and Ruben have your wives join us. I'm going to call Barbara. Also, I've invited some businessmen and their wives to join us."

Much later that day after the barbecue had cooked, Father Gomez arrived with his champion baseball team.

Lieutenant James was presented with a trophy. Father Gomez then introduced the team giving each player a trophy. As Father Gomez presented each boy with a trophy he told their position on the team and a little about each. The smiles on their faces, if all of them were put together, would light a ballpark.

After the presentations the detectives served their guest a fine meal.

Each young ballplayer was also presented an identification folder and a detective badge from Detective Watson.

The visiting and social hour began.

Father Gomez, seizing the opportunity of the moment removed his large sombrero from his head. He turned to Lieutenant James with a smile on his face and said, "What a good group you have here. I bet they all want to donate to my kids."

He began working the crowd, shaking hands. In a short time his hat was full of money.

Lt. Joe "Bill" Bradley

Watching Father Gomez work the crowd, James thought of the Monelli money in the safe at Cletus Black's ranch. He knew that soon Father Gomez was really going to get one hell of a donation.

CHAPTER 16

THE TRIAL

The next few months belonged to Attorneys Bob Thornton and Ruben Steinberg. The Preliminary Hearing of Lieutenant James and his detectives and the Grand Jury hearings were waived.

Attorneys Steinberg and Thornton filed a motion with the court for a speedy trial.

The case had been assigned to Judge Pugh's District Court, a close associate of the District Attorney. Judge Pugh had been the judge who had issued a wiretap order for Lieutenant James' telephone and the electronic bugging of the factory. Judge Pugh was known in defense attorney circles as a "Yes Man" for the District Attorney.

Attorneys Thornton and Steinberg received a break in the case. They filed a motion in Judge Pugh's Court alleging Judge Pugh was prejudiced against

Lt. Joe "Bill" Bradley

Lieutenant James and his detectives because of his close ties with the District Attorney.

The motion asked that Judge Pugh disqualify himself and send the case to another court.

Before his election as a District Judge, Judge Pugh had been an Assistant District Attorney under Jamie Owens.

Pressure was put on Judge Pugh by a number of prominent attorneys and oil executives who were friends of Attorney Bob Thornton and Lieutenant James.

When Judge Pugh realized that these were the citizens who put him in office and paid his election expenses, he had no other choice but to grant the motion and have the case moved to another court.

Owens was fighting mad when Judge Pugh granted the motion and excused himself as the trial judge.

The case against James and his detectives was then assigned to Judge Ruth Elder. Judge Elder had years of experience on the bench. She was a fair and impartial judge. She was known for putting the best of attorneys in their place, and these also included attorneys from the District Attorney's office.

Judge Elder's first orders were, "There will be no interviews by either side with the news media. The trial will begin in two weeks."

Jamie Owens was pissed about the lost of Judge Pugh but having no news interviews just added fuel to his anger.

Judge Elder had also granted a motion filed by Attorney Thornton that Lieutenant James and his eleven detectives could be tried as one. This caused

THE TWELVE JUDGES

Owens to break his silence and be interviewed by local T.V. stations.

Judge Elder called Owens to her office. It was said he left red faced and angry as hell.

Attorney Thornton called James and told him that this was a good sign for their side.

Lieutenant James was to meet with Attorneys Thornton and Steinberg in their offices two days before the start of the trial.

James walked into the Shell Oil building located in midtown Houston and rode the elevator to the thirty-ninth floor. Thornton and Steinberg were finishing a deposition on an injury case in the conference room so James was ushered into Thornton's office to wait.

James walked over to the large window in the office and looked out over the North area of Houston. James could see the main police station that sat on Buffalo Bayou next to the spaghetti bowl of freeways. He thought of the years he had spent with the police department and how this city had grown. Those had been good years. He thought of how great this city was and the people who had made it great.

James thoughts turned to his detectives. What a loyal hard working group. He knew that his group had done their job. One only had to look at their record.

James thought, "I can't let these men go to trial. Eleven careers are on the line."

Bob Thornton came into the office and greeted James with, "How are you James? You really look concerned. I guess you are, but don't worry. Things are shaping up."

Lt. Joe "Bill" Bradley

James spoke, "Bob, I've been thinking it over. I've spoken to you before about this. You've told me that Jamie Owens doesn't have a case against me or my men but I don't know if I want to take the chance in court. Believe me, it's O.K. with me if you think you can cut a deal with Owens where I plead out if he drops all charges against my detectives."

Bob Thornton stood up and walked over to where James was sitting, placed his hand on Bill's shoulder and said, "Bill, trust me and Ruben. Ruben has put a lot of research and work into this case. If it develops along the way that it's starting to look bad for you and your detectives, I'll consider your suggestion. For right now, let's go with Ruben and his brain."

"O.K. Bob, it's your call. I guess it's just hard for me to accept that I've been charged with a crime after being a cop for so many years."

James, Thornton, and Steinberg spent the next hour and a half going over what evidence they believed the D.A. had against James and his detectives.

As James was leaving the attorney's office, Bob Thornton said, "Keep your chin up and by the way, I've hired a public relations firm that will see that you don't get any bad press. That will be important when you return to the police department, and you will return."

James handed Thornton a large envelope as he was leaving.

"What's this?"

"It's yours and Steinberg's fee. If we owe you more, let me know."

"Bill, you don't owe us anything. You know that."

THE TWELVE JUDGES

"Bob, a lot of policemen gave a few dollars and so did some businessmen. We didn't ask for it. You know how policemen stick together, so take it."

"Yeah, I heard that the captain in Homicide wanted to give a fund raising barbecue but you turned it down."

Taking the envelope Thornton said, "Stay in touch Bill, and don't worry."

On the day of the trial the courtroom was packed. T.V. and newspaper reporters crowded the halls and the courtroom.

Also seated in the courtroom was Cletus Black and Barbara and next to her sat Father Gomez.

James thought, "Father Gomez knows more than I give him credit for knowing."

Attorneys Thornton and Steinberg led Lieutenant James and his detectives through the crowd of reporters into the courtroom. Everyone took their seats.

Eleven chairs were placed behind the defense attorney's table for the detectives. Lieutenant James sat between Bob Thornton and Ruben Steinberg at the defense table.

James looked down the row at his detectives. They looked like a different breed, all dressed in suits and ties. James had to smile. Edwards even shaved his beard and looked almost human in a nice pressed suit.

Lieutenant James looked over at the District Attorney going through boxes of papers at his table.

"Bob, what do you think he has in those boxes?"

Lt. Joe "Bill" Bradley

"Bill, I've got a list of everything Owens has. The boxes are full of all the cases you and your detectives have worked. He also has invoices where Murphy and Park bought telephone equipment and supplies. The bastard even has copies of all your time sheets showing the days you worked. He's going to try to use the information to show probable cause for Judge Pugh granting a wiretap on your telephone. Most of the boxes are for show."

The courtroom was noisy with reporters interviewing policemen and attorneys who had come to watch the trial.

The court bailiff banged on the microphone at the witness chair. He said in a loud voice, "All, please rise!"

Everyone in the courtroom stood.

James could feel the tension in his neck as he stood.

"Hear Yea, Hear Yea. The 329th District court of the State of Texas is now in session. Honorable Judge Ruth Elder presiding."

The Deputy of the Court opened the door to the judge's chamber. A stern faced woman in her fifties, dressed in a black robe walked in. She took her seat at the judge's bench. She nodded towards the District Attorney's table and then towards the defense table. Picking up the day's docket, Judge Elder said, "Please be seated."

Judge Elder began, "Cause Number 975487, The State of Texas vs. William B. James, Jack R. Hancock, Robert C. Luna, Frank D. Davis, Gary B. Edwards, Albert C. King, Roosevelt G. Washington, Charles P. Watson, Larry M. Park, Thomas A.

THE TWELVE JUDGES

Murphy, Billy B. Johnson and Joe K. Kramer are charged under Section 182, of the State of Texas Penal Code with Violation of An Individual's Civil Rights By Electronic Means. Gentlemen, how do you plea?"

Still standing with their attorneys, James and his detectives said in one voice, "Not guilty, your Honor!"

Judge Elder continued, "Be seated, please. Before these proceedings begin, I wish to warn the news media and persons in this courtroom. There will be no picture taking or any outburst. Persons not obeying my order will be removed from my courtroom. Is the defense ready to proceed?"

Ruben Steinberg rose from his chair and almost in a bow said, "The defense is ready, your Honor."

Judge Elder turned to the District Attorney, "Is the State of Texas ready to proceed?"

Jamie Owens stood. "Your Honor, I'm not really ready. I have a motion to file. The State of Texas is asking for a postponement of two months."

Attorney Thornton leaned over and whispered in Lieutenant James ear, "That's a dead give-a-way that the bastard doesn't have a case."

James hoped Thornton was right and also hoped that Father Gomez had a straight prayer line to the Man upstairs.

Before the D.A. finished his statement, Attorney Steinberg was on his feet shaking and pointing his finger at District Attorney Owens, saying in a loud voice, "Your honor, the District Attorney agreed to this trial date. He never challenged our motion for a speedy trial. What gives him the right to file a Continuance Motion now? The defense is ready and the State should be too! He's just stalling because he doesn't have a case."

Turning and pointing at each detective, Ruben Steinberg went on. "It would be a grave injustice not to proceed. Think of what these men and their families have gone through. I ask the court to deny the District Attorney's Motion for Continuance. He should have filed the motion long ago."

Judge Elder didn't hesitate. "Mr. Owens, your Motion for continuance is denied. You know you should have filed your motion before now for this court to review!"

Judge Elder continued, "Are there any other matters that need to be brought before the court before we proceed?"

Attorney Steinberg still standing said, "Yes, your honor. I submitted two motions to the court two weeks ago. Your Honor and the District Attorney have copies of these motions. One motion is to dismiss all evidence obtained by a wiretap placed on the defendant's telephone and at their work place. I have submitted Judge Pugh's court order to the court that allowed the District Attorney to wiretap my clients. That order is really flawed. There was no probable cause submitted by the District Attorney for this action. I ask that all evidence obtained by the District Attorney by means of electronic surveillance be suppressed."

Jamie Owens jumped to his feet and said, "Judge, how can that order be flawed? It came from a respected District Judge like yourself."

Judge Elder motioned for Owens to sit down and said, "Continue, Mr. Steinberg."

THE TWELVE JUDGES

Attorney Steinberg, his confidence showing said, "The second motion submitted, begs the court to dismiss all charges against the defendants and suppress all evidence gathered by the D.A. An illegal search and seizure violated the defendant's rights. Their arrest was illegal. The arrest was made by the District Attorney and his investigators at a private party being given for Father Gomez and his church baseball team. None of my clients were warned of their rights or taken before a Magistrate when they were arrested. This, your honor, was a gross violation of the Constitution of the United States. Your honor, I have submitted a tape recording of an illegal wiretap conversation obtained by the District Attorney. This wiretap is a conversation between Lieutenant James and the Chief of Police. The tape will speak for itself. Can you believe that the District Attorney wiretapped the Chief of Police of our city?"

The District Attorney jumped to his feet. "I didn't wiretap Chief Ladd. I wiretapped Lieutenant James."

Judge Elder said, "Sit down, Mr. Owens. You will have your chance."

Steinberg went on. "Your Honor, I am also submitting a VCR film to this court that will prove the District Attorney made an unlawful search and seizure and violated the rights of the defendants. Furthermore, let me state again, these defendants were arrested without warrants. If your Honor would allow me to play the audio tape and the VCR film, your honor, would have no other choice but to rule in favor of the motions submitted."

Lt. Joe "Bill" Bradley

Judge Elder in a quick reply snapped back, "Mr. Steinberg, do not tell this court what choice the court has. This court will hear your tape and see the film as it relates to the defendants and your motions."

Jamie Owens jumped to his feet again. "Judge, you can't do this! Judge Pugh gave me oral consent for the electronic surveillance. I had no time to obtain a warrant. The film of their drunken party has no bearing on this case."

Judge Elder, her anger showing, said, "Mr. Owens, you do not tell this court what it can do and what it can't do. Sit down. Proceed Mr. Steinberg."

A T.V. set and VCR player was brought into the courtroom. Detective Murphy handed Bob Thornton a tape recorder and a tape. Ruben Steinberg had the audio tape and film marked as evidence in the case.

The courtroom became quiet when the tape was played of the conversation between Chief Ladd and Lieutenant James. Judge Elder's expression did not change as she listened to the tape.

When the tape ended, a courtroom spectator, on impulse said out loud, "There's nothing but bull-shit on the tape."

There were low murmurs throughout the courtroom. Judge Elder pounded her gavel for silence.

Attorney Steinberg rose from the defendant's table with the VCR film in his hand. He was also carrying an easel and a sign. He placed the sign on the easel where Judge Elder and the courtroom could see it. The sign was from the Rotary Table fence gate. It read, "Private Party, Entrance By Invitation Only."

THE TWELVE JUDGES

The District Attorney jumped to his feet again. "This has nothing to do with this case. He's trying to prejudice the court."

Attorney Steinberg turned to the District Attorney and in a stern voice said, "Sit down, Jamie."

The District Attorney, looking like a scolded puppy, dropped to his chair.

Judge Elder smiled and didn't say a word.

Attorney Steinberg turned on the T.V. and VCR. The film started by showing the District Attorney investigators breaking through the wooden gate at the Rotary Table. The sign on the gate, "Private Party, Entrance By Invitation Only," was visible in the film. As the film continued to play, there were laughs and remarks from the spectators. The film showed Jamie Owens' confused face as he peered into a box of spare ribs. The courtroom filled with laughter. Judge Elder again demanded quiet. She was intrigued by the film.

The courtroom did not keep quiet and it appeared that Judge Elder didn't care. She leaned closer to hear every word in the film.

When the film finished, Judge Elder remarked, "That was very enlightening Mr. Steinberg. Do you have anything else to offer this court?"

You could see the confidence again in Attorney Steinberg as he rose from his chair.

"Yes, your Honor." Then pointing at Jamie Owens, Steinberg said, "Not only did the District Attorney not have a search warrant or arrest warrants, he wasn't even invited to Father Gomez's barbecue."

Pointing to Father Gomez seated in the courtroom Attorney Steinberg said, "That party was

Lt. Joe "Bill" Bradley

for Father Gomez and his boys, who by the way, won the Little League Championship in Houston this year."

The courtroom again erupted in laughter with applause.

A faint smile showed on Judge Elder's face as she called for order.

Attorney Steinberg, still very confident, said, "Because of the Miranda Decision, the Escobeda Decision, the Gideon Decision and the Mapp Decision, whose cases your honor are very familiar with, these twelve defendant's rights were violated by the District Attorney. I ask this court to grant the two motions submitted and dismiss all charges against these defendants."

Judge Elder leaned back in her chair and stated, "Mr. Steinberg, this court will take your two motions into consideration. I will study your motions tonight and make a ruling tomorrow morning. Mr. Owens, you may submit to this court, briefs, concerning Mr. Steinberg's two motions. I think I have seen and heard enough for today."

Judge Elder stood to leave the courtroom. The bailiff in a loud voice said, "All rise."

James, his attorneys, his detectives, and all in the courtroom stood as Judge Elder started to leave. Judge Elder opened the door to her chambers but did not enter. She quickly turned and returned to her chair and announced, "Everyone please be seated."

After the people in the courtroom again took their seats, the courtroom became very quiet.

Judge Elder said in her stern voice, "I am convinced at this time what my ruling should be on the

THE TWELVE JUDGES

two motions filed by Mr. Steinberg. I will give my ruling now."

Looking at Jamie Owens, Judge Elder continued, "Mr. Owens, you are a new District Attorney and I feel someday you will make a good District Attorney but the State of Texas is wrong in this matter."

Still looking straight at District Attorney Owens, Judge Elder said, "Mr. Steinberg, Mr. Thornton, this court has never received evidence of such portions on the violation of a person's rights. Your two motions are granted. The case against these twelve defendants is dismissed."

The courtroom erupted in loud applause. James glanced back to where Barbara had been sitting. She was hugging Father Gomez.

James moved to where his detectives had gathered. All were shaking hands with the attorneys Thornton and Steinberg. Cletus Black was dancing up and down the aisles with his wife.

Washington and Hancock's wives, who had been sitting together in the courtroom, were two happy women. Washington's wife was hugging Hancock and Hancock's wife was hugging Washington.

James felt the pride in his body swell as the group celebrated. He knew this group would be back to work soon and the criminal element in Houston would again dread their presence.

Barbara and Father Gomez finally were able to push their way through the crowd where James was standing.

Barbara kissed James as Father Gomez said, "My Judge upstairs contacted your judge. My Judge

Lt. Joe "Bill" Bradley

agreed to help in this judge's decision so long as you come to confession soon. O.K."

James smiled as he said, "Let's go find a good steakhouse and relax. Father Gomez, I'll even let you pick the wine.

Attorney Thornton turned and looked at Lieutenant James and his eleven detectives. He knew that the criminals of Houston would be nervous about the outcome of this case. Thornton knew that the Twelve Judges would be heard from again.

ABOUT THE AUTHOR

I spent thirty years as a Lieutenant of Detectives with the Houston Police Department. As a boy, my dream was to become a police officer.

Right after I graduated from high school, I went to the police department in my hometown and told them I wanted to hire on as a detective. They told me, "Hey boy, go grow up and then come back."

So, I accepted a football scholarship to the University of Houston. During my stay at the university, I took some criminology courses from Inspector Larry Fultz of the Houston Police Department. That did it, I had to join the Houston Police Department.

I enjoyed my career and every minute of it except for two major events.

The first was losing my best and very close friend Captain Tollie Humphries.

We were partners in Radio Patrol. We were again partners as detectives in the Auto Theft Division. We also made lieutenant about the same time. Tollie then made captain and was pushing me to become a captain when he died suddenly from a heart attack. Tollie was as strong as a bull and worked out every day in the police gym. His death really shook me.

The death of Captain Humphries also affected Herman Short. He was our police chief at this time. You always knew where you stood with Chief Short. I would not characterize Herman Short as a Chief, he was a General.

After Captain Humphries' death, it took me awhile to take the test for captain and I qualified and was placed on the promotion list. Chief Lynn then became the new Chief of Police of Houston. There were openings for captains on the promotional list but Chief Lynn would not promote two others and me. We sued Chief Lynn and the City of Houston. Chief Lynn later was convicted of bribery and went to the penitentiary. We won the case on appeal but our attorney left out some of the civil service law so the city just paid us captain's pay for a year and we didn't receive the rank.

At this time I was in the Burglary and Theft Division. I had a great Captain, Charles "Chuck" Smith, who let me choose some men and form a "Fence Detail". I was also backed by Inspector Daigle. Inspector Daigle and Captain Smith understood me and the rogues that worked for me. They turned me and my detectives loose.

My detectives made me a hero and set records on the recovery of stolen property, clearing cases and getting convictions on fences that no division or group has ever or will ever come close to duplicating. I even got my picture and story in "Time". What a great run I had with this group. The years passed too fast.

I was now getting close to retirement. I had four kids in college at the same time so I had to work extra jobs. Three hotels had hired me on my off time to consult with them on security. One of the services I performed was to check out the cashiers and bartenders for any criminal conviction records. The Criminal District Clerk at the County Courthouse has these records and they are open and free to the public. I was lazy and didn't go to the district clerk's office. I used the police department computers to get these conviction records and that led to the second major event in my career.

It came about because I had one detective I had not personally chosen. He had been involved in killing four criminal suspects before he came to me and I didn't like his macho attitude. He thought he was a "French Connection" detective. He later went to work for the D.E.A. full-time and has added one more notch to his gun for shooting a suspect.

It turned out that this detective wasn't loyal to the squad or to me. He worked undercover with the Special Crimes Division of the D.A.'s office on a certain investigation. They were after a well-known ex-con fence. This detective made several trips to the fence trying to set him up for a bust.

I received a telephone call from a detective who had retired. He was laughing and said that the undercover detective had been recognized on his first visit to the fence as being a cop. The detective said he busted this fence several times and the fence could smell a cop when he walked into his business. The retired detective also said that this fence would even drive to the police station and record license plate numbers of the un-marked police vehicles.

I called the detective into my office and told him what the experienced detective had said.

The detective got all bent out of shape and stated that the retired detective must be crooked if he knew about him working undercover. I tried to explain to the detective about the retired detective but he was too stupid to understand.

Then I learned that this detective ran to Special Crimes of the District Attorney's office and told them that I must be crooked too because I got a telephone call from a retired detective about his undercover work.

An assistant district attorney in Special Crimes listened to this sorry detective and ordered a tap on my office telephone. The stupid bastards put the tap on the wrong telephone. They put the tap on the telephone of a lieutenant who loved to gamble. He loved betting football. He nearly crapped in his pants when I told him about the tap on his telephone.

Of course, I knew about the tap as soon as they placed it. A good friend in the telephone company called me when telephone security got the order from the D.A.'s office to tap my telephone.

The detective got with two former Internal Affairs officers and the three of them told the Special Crimes Division of the District Attorney's office about my checking names in the criminal files for hotels using a police computer. I was relieved of duty and charged with a misdemeanor for checking names of employees of hotels using the city computers.

I have always believed that Internal Affairs should investigate serious corruption of police officers and leave the other violations to the officer's immediate supervisors.

At this time we had a new police chief, Chief Lee Brown. Chief Brown was brought in from another large city where the officers there said he screwed up their police department. In my opinion it only took a short while for Lee Brown to screw the Houston Police Department up. Once, I went one on one with this new chief and a city councilman whose son we arrested for auto theft. I felt like Einstein during the meeting with the two of them.

Silly rules and regulations started to pop up everywhere under the new chief and a new Intelligence Division captain. An order came down that all C. I.'s, informers, snitches or whatever you wanted to call them had to be registered with the Intelligence Division.

This really upset some of my detectives, as they didn't want anyone messing with their informers. I solved the problem. Each month, the Texas Department of Corrections sent a list to the police departments in Texas when felons were going to be released on parole. We copied some of the names from this list and sent it to the Intelligence Divison naming them as our informers. You can't get anything done if you go by all the rules.

The second major happening in my career was when I stood before a judge and pled nolo contendere to a misdemeanor for using city computers and checking names.

After being with the police department for thirty years and being a good clean cop, this was hard and it effected me a lot. I retired and paid a $1000 fine. I would have fought the D.A.'s office but they indicated that they might go after some of my detectives because some worked at the hotels for me. I guess I was ready to retire anyway because of the new Chief of Police who was now running the department.

Some businessmen, led by my good friend, Cletus Brown, heard about the D.A.'s office and Internal Affairs' investigation on me. They arranged for me to go to Austin, Texas where the Governor of Texas signed a pardon for the misdemeanor that I pled to. It's great to have friends.

After I retired, I took some courses in novel writing at Rice University. I learned that I was a storyteller not a writer.

I can't end this without telling of our fishing trips.

Detectives, whose names I can't remember, had the telephone numbers for the large catfish in the Trinity River just out of Huntsville, Texas. They would go out in the boat and in an hour's time, they would come back with three or four large catfish that weighed in the fifty-pound range.

Once, when two detectives went out to call catfish, they returned in about thirty minutes. When they pulled up to the dock, they had two large catfish and a twelve point buck. It seems the buck swam the river at the wrong place. Catfish and venison went well with the beer that day.

We had one F.B.I. agent, Pat Carr, that we all trusted and could work with. He was really a city cop in federal clothing.

There is no other work like police work. Cops are of a special breed. Of course, there are men that are cops that never should have been permitted to wear the badge but the majority are good decent dedicated men.

I found that the best formula for living my life was to put God first, my family second and my job third. When I did this, everything else would eventually fall in place.

I hope you enjoyed this book. I really had fun writing it.

Printed in the United States
19964LVS00001B/14